PRAISE FOR ZH

"I am in awe of Zhang Ling's literary talent. Truly extraordinary. In her stories, readers have the chance to explore and gain a great understanding of not only the Chinese mind-set but also the heart and soul."

—Anchee Min, bestselling author of *Red Azalea*

"Few writers could bring a story about China and other nations together as seamlessly as Zhang Ling. I would suggest it is her merit as an author, and it is the value of her novels."

—Mo Yan, winner of the Nobel Prize in Literature

"[Zhang Ling] tackles a work of fiction as if it were fact . . . With a profound respect for historical truth as it impacts the real world, she successfully creates characters and stories that are both vivid and moving."

—*Shenzhen and Hong Kong Book Review*

"Zhang Ling's concern for war and disaster has remained constant throughout the years as she delves deeply into human strength and tenacity in the face of extremely adverse situations."

—*Beijing News Book Review Weekly*

"[In this novel] we see not only the cruelty of war but also humans wrestling with fate . . . The novel blends the harsh reality of war seamlessly into the daily lives of the common people, weaving human destiny into the course of the war . . . *A Single Swallow* puts the novelist's ability and talent on full display."

—*Shanghai Wenhui Daily*

A

SINGLE

SWALLOW

OTHER TITLES BY
ZHANG LING

Gold Mountain Blues

A SINGLE SWALLOW

ZHANG LING

Translated by Shelly Bryant

 AMAZON **CROSSING**

Previously published as *Laoyan* by People's Literature Publishing House in China in 2017. Translated from Mandarin by Shelly Bryant. First published in English by Amazon Crossing in 2020.

Published by Amazon Crossing, Seattle

www.apub.com

Amazon, the Amazon logo, and Amazon Crossing are trademarks of Amazon.com, Inc., or its affiliates.

ISBN-13: 9780761456957 (hardcover)
ISBN-10: 0761456953 (hardcover)
ISBN-13: 9781542041508 (paperback)
ISBN-10: 1542041503 (paperback)

Cover design by David Drummond

Printed in the United States of America

First edition

To all the names that remain unrecorded on monuments

William E. Macmillan, or Mai Weili, or Billy, or Whatever

I have many names. Almost every time I meet someone, I get a new one.

According to the birth certificate from the Good Samaritan Hospital in Cincinnati, my name is William Edward Sebastian de Royer-Macmillan. As far as I recall, my full name was used only three times during my life. First, on my birth certificate, then on my application to the Boston University School of Medicine, and finally on my marriage certificate. No one ever actually called me by such an oversized, regal name. Even when I was eight and stole a box of candy canes from the convenience store and the shopkeeper informed my father, he summoned me to his desk by calling me just William de Royer-Macmillan. That was the ultimate expression of his anger. Sometimes I tried to say my full name when I was alone, and if I could even manage to get the whole thing out, it took at least two breaths. My family and American classmates called me Billy, except my mother, who just called me B. I often felt my mother—a housewife who cared for a sick husband and five children—possessed the skills of a great mathematician and was thus always able to reduce life's complex details to their simplest, most uncomplicated form, getting to the root of things in just one shot.

When I was twenty-five and about to leave for China as a missionary, my parents gave me a Chinese name, Mai Weili, a transliteration of the first part of my surname and my given name. In my church, I was called Pastor Mai. The residents of nearby villages were much less respectful. The people who came every Wednesday for a free bowl of porridge called me Lao Zhou, a play on the Chinese word *zhou*, meaning "porridge," and a common Chinese surname. It made me sound like an old man, even though I was only in my twenties. The people who came for medical care called me Mr. Mai to my face, but behind my back, they called me Doctor Foreigner. Those who came for porridge or medicine far outnumbered those who came for prayer, but I wasn't discouraged. I believed that after they had partaken of the goodness of God, they would eventually consider the way of the Lord. I learned early on that spreading the Gospel in China would depend on a good pair of legs, not just words. The legs upon which the Gospel traveled were porridge and medicine. Of course, the school was important too, but compared to porridge and medicine, the school was at most a crutch. That's why I needed six porters when I disembarked in Shanghai. Clothes and books only accounted for half of what was in my trunks. The rest was all medical equipment and medicine I had acquired with funds raised in America.

My parents were missionaries sent to China by the Methodist Church. Their tracks covered almost the whole of Zhejiang province from north to south and east to west. For them, living in one place for six months was an eternity. Because of their itinerant lifestyle, none of the four children born to my mother before me survived. Then, when she turned thirty, she was suddenly overcome with panic. My parents had endured beds infested with bedbugs, porridge crusted with insects, leaky roofs made of scraps of tarp nailed together, and outhouses consisting of only bamboo poles, but the fear of being childless forever was beyond bearing. That year, after struggling painfully with their consciences, they applied to the parent church for permission to return home.

The year after they returned to the US, they had me. Over the next seven years, my mother gave birth to two more boys and twin girls. Out of gratitude, or perhaps guilt, they dedicated me, their eldest son, to the church, just as Abraham had offered Isaac. My missionary destiny was fixed before I was born— I heard God's call while still in the womb.

Even so, I did not act rashly. I waited until I graduated from medical school and finished my residency before I left for China. What followed proved the wisdom of this decision—and perhaps its cruelty.

My parents had lived in China for twelve years. After returning to America, they talked endlessly about their time there. My siblings and I listened over and over to stories about how farmers in the Jiangnan countryside grew tea with waterlogged compost from grass and wood ash, or how families on the water trained herons to catch fish, or what the women ate during their confinement period after giving birth, or how, when times were tough, the housewives would add wild herbs to their porridge to assuage hunger. And so, twenty-six years after they left China, following their path to Zhejiang, when I saw the stone steps in the water, sampans crossing the river, children riding buffaloes, and the white camellias in full bloom on the slopes and heard the angry-sounding Jiangnan dialect, I was not surprised. It seemed, rather, infinitely familiar, like a dream I'd had again and again for many years. It seemed not like my future life, but like my past life.

And now, looking at you, Gunner's Mate Ian Ferguson, and you, Special Operations Soldier Liu Zhaohu, I am indeed face-to-face with my past life. Today is August 15, 2015. It's been a full seventy years since we three made our agreement. What is seventy years? For a worker bee producing honey, it's more than 560 lifetimes. For a buffalo plowing a field, it's perhaps three—if it is not slaughtered prematurely. For a person, it's almost an entire life. In a history book, it's probably just a few paragraphs.

But in God's plan, it's an instant, the blink of an eye.

I still remember every detail from that day seventy years ago. The news was first transmitted at your camp. The operator who sent hydrology reports to Chongqing was the first to hear the Japanese emperor's "Jewel Voice Broadcast" on the radio. The emperor's voice was hoarse and choked, and his words as formal as his tone, his speech pedantic and meandering.

"After pondering deeply the general trends of the world and the actual conditions obtaining to our empire today, we have decided to effect a settlement of the present situation by resorting to an extraordinary measure . . . However, it is according to the dictate of time and fate that we have resolved to pave the way for a grand peace for all the generations to come by enduring the unendurable and suffering what is insufferable."

At first, no one understood what was being said. After listening to the news commentary, you learned the speech was called the "Imperial Rescript on the Termination of the Greater East Asia War." In fact, there's a name for the event that is easy to understand. It's called surrender, even though that word was not in the emperor's speech.

The madness that began in your camp spread like the flu to every household in Yuehu, which translates to "Moon Lake" in English. You cut quilts and winter

3

clothes into strips and wrapped them around sticks, dipped them in tung oil, and set them on fire. The torches burning across the hillside made it seem as if the forest slopes had caught fire. God had mercy on you, arranging this day of madness in midsummer so you didn't have to worry about needing warm bedding on a cold autumn night. Then the villagers crowded into the clearing where your unit held the daily drills. Normally, it was heavily guarded and civilians were not allowed to enter, but the sentry didn't stop anyone. Indeed, there were no civilians that day, since everyone was an interested party. You set off firecrackers, drank toasts, yelled and danced like crazy, carried children aloft on your shoulders, and handed each man an American-made cigarette. Even more, you were all eager to kiss a woman—it had probably been a long time since you'd smelled the hair or touched the skin of a woman—but the commander at headquarters in Chongqing, Miles, had given strict orders, and though you didn't obey completely, you didn't dare go too far either. The next day when the sun had risen, the people of Yuehu found that their dogs and chickens had failed to sound the usual wake-up call, having all sounded themselves hoarse the previous day.

That day seventy years ago, the celebrations continued until midnight. After the crowds dispersed, you two—Ian Ferguson, gunner's mate first class of Naval Group China, and Liu Zhaohu (the last character in your name, *hu*, meaning "tiger," in many ways the perfect name for you), a Chinese officer in training at the camp of the Sino-American Cooperative Organization—weren't done celebrating. You came to my quarters. Ian brought two bottles of whisky, which he'd gotten a few days earlier while at the commissariat to get the mail. In the shabby kitchen of my house, the three of us drank ourselves into a stupor. That day, there was no military discipline. Even God closed one eye. Any mistake made then could be forgiven. You, Liu Zhaohu, said whisky was the worst drink under the sun, with a stench like cockroaches floating in urine. Even so, it didn't stop you. You raised your cup for round after round. Later, when we were all half drunk, you suggested the scheme.

You said no matter which of us three died first, after death, we would return to Yuehu each year on this day. When we were together, we would drink again.

We felt your proposal was absurd. You said "after death," not "in the future." No one knows when another's final day will be or the day of his own death. The realm after death is something the living have no way of understanding. Now

4

we see that you were the sage among us. You had already foreseen that with the emperor's "Jewel Voice Broadcast," we were to go our separate ways and that our paths might never cross again. The living can't control their own days, but the dead are not thus bound. After death, the soul is no longer limited by time, space, or unexpected events. The soul's world has no boundaries. To the soul, the entire universe and all eternity are just a thought away.

As we drank that night, we slapped each other's backs and shook hands and, amid our laughter, accepted Liu Zhaohu's proposal. That day seemed far away, so we weren't completely serious. The war had ended. Peace pushed death to its proper place, many steps away from us. I was the oldest of us, and I was only thirty-nine.

I thought I might be the first to make it to our rendezvous at Yuehu Village. I just didn't expect it to come so fast. I had no idea I would die just three months after we had made our appointment.

When I first met the two of you, I had been living in China for over ten years. Like any local, I could easily pick up a peanut with chopsticks, skillfully tie or untie the intricate cloth buttons on my tunic, or, with a bouncing gait, carry a pair of half-filled water buckets on a shoulder pole up a mountain trail. I could speak the local dialect almost flawlessly and even explain most of the content of a government notice to villagers. I had prayed with dying cholera patients and had myself been infected with typhus passed through the fleas on rats. I had been trapped in a burning house and nearly suffocated. I had experienced a three-day grain shortage. When the air raids came, I was in Hangzhou and only barely managed to get to the raid shelter in time. One of the most terrifying experiences was when I encountered bandits while walking one night. Although my wife, Jenny, and I were dressed in local style, as soon as they passed us, they saw we were foreigners. They assumed our wallets would be fuller than a local person's. Brandishing knives, they searched us thoroughly, only to find we had nothing. I believe it was the terror of that event that caused poor Jenny to die during her miscarriage shortly thereafter.

But in every danger, God provided a narrow path by which I might escape. I did not die of war, famine, or epidemic disease. I died by my own hand. The medical knowledge I had received at Boston University helped me save the lives of many others—though my wife was not among them. Only later did I realize that the lives I'd saved had a price, and that was my own life. It was my own medical skills that ultimately undid me.

After our drunken celebration, you two made your way through several cities in Jiangsu and Shanghai to assist the Nationalist government in maintaining order and accepting the Japanese surrender. I, on the other hand, took the *Jefferson* back to America. My mother had written that my father was seriously ill and hoped to see his eldest son—the Isaac he had placed on the altar, whom he had not seen for many years—one more time before he died. As a civilian, I didn't have to wait under the point system to earn a spot on a ship home the way a demobilized soldier like Ian did. So without much fuss, I was able to buy a spot on the ocean liner. In the end, I didn't see my father—not because he died before we were reunited, but because I did.

In Shanghai, waiting for the ship, I stayed in the home of a Methodist missionary. His cook had developed a boil on his back, which was festering seriously and was quite painful. I could have done nothing. This was, after all, the huge city of Shanghai, not remote Yuehu, and as long as one was willing to pay a little bit, there were plenty of hospitals where one could be treated. But my scalpel became impatient. It protested loudly from my medical supply box, so I had no choice but to perform a resection for the cook. My lancet was not on its best behavior that day. It was the first and the last time there was any conflict between us. In a fit of anger, it bit through my rubber glove and made a small cut on my index finger. The operation was a great success, and the cook's pain was immediately relieved. My own wound was very small, with almost no bleeding. It seemed harmless. I disinfected it, and the next day I boarded the *Jefferson*.

By that evening, the wound had become infected, and my finger swelled to the size of a radish. I took the sulfonamide I had with me, but to no effect. I wasn't aware that I was allergic to this drug or that newer antibiotics had been developed in Europe and America. After all, my own medical knowledge hadn't been updated for many years. I went from bad to worse. There was so much pus in my wound, it filled a teacup. The ship, sailing on open sea, was several days away from the nearest port. The doctor aboard suggested removing the finger surgically at once. Not realizing the urgency of the situation, I hesitated. The reason for my hesitation was quite simply that I couldn't live without this finger in the future. Before I had left on my voyage to America, I had given some thought to my plans once I returned to China. I would set up a clinic with a simple operating table and a ward in another village so that the people from neighboring towns would not have to travel hundreds of *li* over mountain paths to the county seat for things like traumatic infection or childbirth. What prompted me to devise this plan was not merely the plight of local people. Within these otherwise noble principles was, in fact, hidden a bit of selfishness. It was for another person—a young Chinese woman who held an important place in my heart.

My hesitation ultimately proved fatal. Thirty-five hours later, I died of sepsis. My death was only documented in two places. The first was the log of the *Jefferson*, and the other was a brief line in the history of the Methodist mission. Before my death, Canadian doctor Norman Bethune had likewise died of a finger infection after an operation, but our deaths were treated entirely differently. He died at an appropriate time and under suitable circumstances and has thus been an example of one who "died in the line of duty," documented in Chinese textbooks from one generation to the next. My death, by contrast, was buried among the news of the Nuremberg trials, the Tokyo Trials, the Chinese Civil War, and so forth and became an insignificant matter, no larger than a speck of dust.

I went from being a missionary with a beautiful vision of a life at peace to being a ghost drifting between two continents. But I didn't forget the agreement I made with you, so every year on August 15, I come to Yuehu and wait patiently for your arrival.

Today is my seventieth visit.

Over the years, Yuehu Village has changed names and been passed between administrative regions several times. Its boundaries were as volatile as the borders of some European countries in wartime. However, for a dead person, time becomes fixed, so later changes are irrelevant. For me, Yuehu is already eternal.

But in the world of the living, it's challenging to find traces of the Yuehu we knew. The church that I built with my own hands was later used as a brigade office, grain warehouse, and primary school. With each change, a new fresco was painted on the outer wall, and the door was given a new coat of paint. The basketball court and drill practice field you leveled are now a densely populated residential area. The American instructors' dorms have been demolished, and the buildings replacing them have been dismantled twice over. Now, it's a dry goods market and a row of small shops. The only building left is the Chinese trainees' dorm, where, in the yard in front of the door, Liu Zhaohu had a fight that would go down in history. In fact, the door is probably the only thing truly intact about the building; it has long since ceased to look like the space of our time. The area inside has been divided into small rooms, like tiny dove cages. Fortunately, those interested in old things have not yet completely vanished. In the past few years, a commemorative stone tablet was erected in the front yard. The stone tablet has been used for many things, including drying cloth diapers in the sun, stacking newly harvested bamboo shoots, and posting notices about treatment for gonorrhea and syphilis. Even so, I'm grateful for that stone tablet. Without it, I might get lost in this cluster of mosaic-tiled buildings.

Year after year, I had been here by my lonely self, waiting for you. If you didn't appear, it meant you were still alive in some corner of the world. I never doubted you would honor our agreement, because you are soldiers, and soldiers know what it means to keep one's word.

After waiting seventeen years, when I made my eighteenth journey to Yuehu, you arrived, Liu Zhaohu. If memory serves, you would have been thirty-eight. I am forever thirty-nine. The world of the dead subverts the rules of the living. In the world of the living, I was nineteen years older than you. In the world of the dead, you are just one year younger than me. Death has brought us closer.

You recognized me at once, because I had been fixed in death just as I was when we parted. I didn't recognize you until you said my name. You were shorter and very thin. Of course, you were already quite thin when you arrived at training camp, but without exception, every Chinese student looked emaciated. Your American instructors whispered among themselves, doubting if such pupils could march and carry guns. They quickly discovered their mistake, but that story would come later. At the time, you were no thinner than the others.

But when I saw you again, using the word "thin" to describe you would be an understatement. You were truly scrawny, almost without any flesh at all. Your skin clung to your bones so tightly, I could virtually see the color and texture of your bones. You had lost most of your hair, leaving only sparse, scattered wisps across your scalp. Your face had a ghastly pallor, but you looked very clean, indicating that someone had carefully washed you before sending you on your way. Actually, the biggest change in you was not your height, your weight, or even your hair. It was your eyes. The fire that had flashed in your eyes when I first met you had disappeared, leaving only two dark pits, devoid of substance.

I still vividly recall what you looked like when you signed up for training. The Sino-American Cooperative Organization training camp had just been completed in Yuehu Village. This so-called completion consisted of requisitioning some relatively solid brick and wood buildings with courtyards from the locals. These buildings served as dorms for the instructors and students, while some farmland was cleared to use for marching, target practice, and sports. Yuehu was chosen as the site for the training camp because of its strategic location. It was surrounded by mountains, making it less likely to be attacked, but was still just about a hundred miles from the area of Japanese occupation and the sea, putting it within marching distance. If necessary, the Chinese troops could set out from Yuehu and put a few thorns into the backs of the Japanese that would never be pulled out, then safely withdraw. The American instructors soon discovered that the legs of the Chinese recruits were very strong, belying their thin bodies. The Americans learned the real meaning of the word "walking" not from dictionaries, but from their marches in China. Anyway, the main task of the training camp was not standard warfare. Rather, it was to gather information and harass the army, putting the Japanese in a state of fear at all times.

The training camp was equipped with Chinese translators. Miles, in distant Chongqing, still didn't understand that, though the national language in China was a single form of Mandarin, there remained countless dialects. This was especially true in the south, where even folks from neighboring villages might feel like a duck trying to talk to a chicken, each speaking their own dialect. The camp recruitment was limited to nearby areas in order to overcome the language barrier. The translator dispatched from Chongqing was a Cantonese fellow, and when he spoke Mandarin, he was the only person in camp who understood it. Out of sheer desperation, the American instructor asked me to help—I was well known as the best old China hand in a several hundred li radius. And that was how the three of us met.

Liu Zhaohu, you had probably traveled a great distance. The back of your clothing was stained with sweat, and drop after drop rolled down your brow. You were panting, and you held a recruitment flyer in your hand. Your Chinese examiner said that the notice was for everyone and asked why you took it down. You looked like you wanted to smile, but your face was tense, and no smile could penetrate such a heavy armor. Instead, you just cleared your throat and said, "I was in a hurry." You didn't talk much that day, and you never had much to say later either. Your mouth was a gate, and it was kept closed more than it was open.

The examiner asked you to write your name on the registration form. You wrote *Yao*, but immediately crossed it out. Then you wrote *Liu Zhaohu*. At the time, I thought the name sounded vaguely familiar, but I couldn't recall where I had seen it before. The examiner asked about your family. You hesitated, as if making a difficult mental calculation, then finally said only your mother was left. The examiner asked if you could read. You said you were just one semester short of graduating from high school. He asked you to write a few words for him. You filled an ink brush and leaned over the table. On cheap rice paper, you wrote the entirety of Sun Yat-sen's final will from memory, all at once.

There wasn't much doubt regarding your admission at that point, though you still needed a simple physical exam. A quick glance indicated with near certainty that you were in good basic health. With a few meals under your belt, you would have no problem with the training.

However, recruiting was in strict accordance with the procedures developed by the headquarters in Chongqing. They still had questions to ask.

"What special skills do you have?" he asked you.

You closed your eyes, thought, and then said, "I can speak English."

When I translated this sentence, Ian Ferguson immediately took an interest in you. Having English speakers among the students would make teaching much easier. He asked you to say something in English for him.

You quickly summoned some of the English words you knew and blurted them out all in a row. Your accent was heavy that day, and several times, you dropped the verb or got the subject and object mixed up. I guessed that your English teacher might have been of Swahili origin. You probably meant to say "I'm very glad to meet you," but what came out was "You very glad meet me." Ian couldn't help but laugh, so I tried to ease the situation for you. I said to Ian, "It's better than nothing."

In the following days, your English had real practical value. It seems you were just nervous that first day.

You blushed in embarrassment when Ian laughed. In hopes of gaining some ground, you reached for the slingshot hanging at your waist. Raising it, you looked up, searching for a speck in the sky. After a moment, you took aim and fired a small stone. A bird fell to the ground. It was a sparrow in flight. You not only aimed well but also understood the principle of lead time.

At that moment, you were granted admission in the minds of all, even though they still had to ask the rest of their questions.

"Why are you here?"

You didn't answer. You just stared at the examiner. I saw the fire in your eyes.

Actually, I had seen fire in others' eyes before. Everyone who signed up for the training camp possessed fire. But your fire was different than the others'. It wasn't the type that would warm others. It's an understatement to say your fire wasn't warm. In fact, it was icy cold, cold as a blade. You said nothing. The only response you offered the examiner was that fire.

Ian told me to add your name to the list for the Army Corps of Engineers. I pulled on his sleeve and whispered that it would be a pity to put someone like you in level one. The students granted admission at that time were divided into two levels. The first was the army corps class. Its graduates would be well-trained soldiers. Students from the other level, an officer's class, would become the grassroots cadres of a special force upon graduation. Ian hesitated, saying you lacked military experience. I replied that experience could be gained, but talent was hard to come by. Ian didn't say anything else. He just wrote your name in the other column. Later, I realized how bold I'd been. I wasn't an official member of the training camp, but I didn't regard myself as an outsider. Fortunately, no one minded my interference.

You passed the medical exam and became a member of the advanced class. They gave you a plain cloth uniform and a pair of cloth shoes. On your chest patch was "Soaring Dragon." That was your unit designation. Below it was the number 635. That was your code name. From that day on, you were not Liu Zhaohu; you were 635. The Americans' training program was top secret, so students couldn't use their real names, and they couldn't communicate with friends or relatives. This was to prevent the leak of classified information and also the possibility of implicating family members. Your true identity was only noted on the registration form, and that was locked in the desk of an American instructor. It's a shame that in the chaotic withdrawal from Yuehu, the Americans forgot to take these forms with them. A long time later, I learned that it was this piece of paper that brought such unspeakable horrors to your life.

At that time, though, none of us ever imagined the direction the future would take.

Nearly twenty years after you applied for training camp, I met you again in Yuehu. It was August 15, 1963. After I realized who you were, surprised, I clasped your hand, which was as thin as a blade. I asked, "Liu Zhaohu, what happened to you? Why have you grown so thin?"

You sighed and said, "It's a long story. It would take another lifetime to tell it. I'll wait for Ian, then I'll tell you both. I don't have the energy to go through it twice."

I didn't press. I just took your hand and led you along the path that had changed so much and that would continue to change even more. We walked softly, slowly. Our steps were best measured not in feet, but in inches. We feared crushing the tender pieces of old memories buried beneath the changes.

We saw a slogan painted in whitewash on the outer wall of the former student dormitory. I determined that it was relatively new, since I hadn't seen it the previous year. It was neat, with artistic characters imitating the Song style, each stroke balanced and sharp. It read "Learn from Comrade Lei Feng!" A soldier in the People's Liberation Army, Lei Feng had been the subject of a propaganda campaign after his death in 1962, depicting him as a model citizen and encouraging people to emulate his selflessness and devotion to Mao.

But you only told me that much later. On the day we saw the slogan, I asked you who Lei Feng was. You thought for a while, then said, "He was a good man." I asked you how that was so. Was he a doctor, helping the needy and dying? Did he give away all he had to the poor? You couldn't help laughing and shook your head. You said, "Pastor Billy, you really are out of touch."

I reminded you I'd been gathering dust in the ghost world for eighteen years. You thought for a moment, then agreed. "You're right. You know more about that world than me."

This wasn't the first slogan I'd seen. Beneath it, there were layers of slogans. This was the longest wall in Yuehu and could be considered the face of the entire village. Slogans appeared there every few years. A few years earlier, it read "The people's commune is good!" Before that, it said, "Let a hundred flowers blossom, and a hundred schools of thought contend." Further down, it reads, "We must liberate Taiwan!" The layer below that was your training camp's rules.

Or . . . no, wait. I missed a layer. Between Taiwan and the rules was "Oppose America and aid Red Korea. Protect and defend the nation!"

"Remember that?" I asked. "Camp rules?"

"Every word," you said.

We stood in the afterglow of the setting sun, reciting the camp rules. You didn't hesitate or pause, and you didn't miss a single word. Neither did I. We were perfectly in sync.

It made sense that you still had every word at hand. Before and after class every day, you stood in front of the Chinese captain, saluting, and recited them. My own ability to recite without error should have been a stranger thing, since I was just a missionary. I was not enlisted, and I was not an instructor or a student. I was only in close connection with my American compatriots at that time, doing something for them that perhaps a pastor should not have done. But going between my church and your camp many times every day, I memorized your rules.

What the captain can't see, think, hear, or do, we must see, think, hear, and do for him.

Then we looked at each other, and, at exactly the same moment, we started laughing. Time is a strange thing. It washes away the outer skin of solemnity and reveals the absurd nature of things. At that time, you thought this was the golden rule. You all only knew that the bound duty of a soldier was to obey. However, there was a limit to your endurance. The rubber band in your mind was elastic, but there was a time it broke. So even many years later, I still recalled that silent but earth-shattering rebellion of yours, outside your courtyard.

You ran your fingers along the wall of the dormitory where you had lived, muttering, "Why is it shorter?"

I said, "It's the weight of the slogans. All those years, all those layers."

We fell silent and continued along the path that skirted the courtyard wall.

We walked to my old church. It had proved to be the strongest building in the village, the best insulated and best lit, so no one wanted to tear it down. The words "Gospel Hall" that had been carved on the stone over the main gate had long ago been chiseled away. In front of the stone hung a piece of wood coated in tung oil, with a five-point star painted in red lacquer at its center and the words "Red Star Primary School" beneath it. The school was on summer break, so the building was empty and quiet. The older children were probably helping in the fields. A few girls age six or seven were jumping a rope made of rubber bands in the front yard, chanting.

> *One, two, three, four, five, six, seven*
> *Twenty-one melon flowers bloom in heaven*
> *Two, two, five, six*
> *Two, two, five, seven*
> *Two. eight. two. nine makes it even*

This was the most popular chant among Chinese girls. I had never worked out the mathematical logic of it, but I liked their voices. These girls had yet to go through life's kneading, so their voices didn't carry any wrinkles or blemishes. They were as crisp as wind chimes. The girls chanted the rhyme over and over, and with each round, their hands raised the rubber-band rope higher. From knee to waist to shoulder to the tops of their heads, each new height tested the limits of their flexibility. One girl, shorter than the rest, finally stumbled. When the rope was held higher than the top of her head, she couldn't clear it. She lost her balance, staggered, and fell flat on her behind. Her companions didn't help her up, but stood amid a roar of laughter. Lips twitching in embarrassment, the girl was on the verge of tears.

Just then, her sister, a girl of about thirteen, came by. She seemed to be on her way to the river to wash laundry. The bamboo basket across her back was full of dirty clothes, and she had a wooden club tied to the side of the basket with a strand of straw. She pulled her younger sister up and wiped the dirt from her pants.

"Is this silly little thing worth crying over? You'll have plenty of things worth crying over in the future," the older sister said.

Her tone of voice didn't sound like that of an older sister. It was more suited to a mother. No, in fact, more like a grandmother.

You, Zhaohu, stopped suddenly in your tracks. Your eyes turned to the girl carrying the laundry basket. For a long time, you stood motionless.

I knew who you were thinking of, but I could not speak that name. That name would make the sky weep and the earth groan.

From then on, I had a companion for my annual trip to Yuehu. All these years since, Liu Zhaohu and I have been waiting for you, Ian Ferguson.

14

I didn't expect such longevity from you. Before we knew it, you had kept us waiting fifty-two years.

For the first three decades, Zhaohu and I remained patient. We suspected you were working, paying off your home. Perhaps you retired and were taking your wife on a cruise to places you had heard about but never seen. You wanted to make up to her all you owed her in this life. Perhaps your grandchildren were still small, and you wanted to make an impression in their childhood from which they could remember their grandpa. In short, we speculated and wove together various narratives to explain your absence.

By the time the fortieth year came around, our patience had worn thin. A man in his eighties would no longer have a mortgage to pay, and his children would no longer need him. If a man of eighty died, his wife—if she were even still around—wouldn't have anything to regret. That is the season when nature's leaves are dying and its fruits fall. It's a good time for a person to die. Were you so reluctant to leave the world of the living that you had forgotten our agreement?

And yet, you didn't appear.

By the time we were in the fiftieth year, we had not only lost our patience, but there was anger creeping in as well.

We too had gone through the war, but we had received none of life's favors. We were young when we departed, and you were leisurely wandering around, outside nature's laws, still not returning even at this late date. Why? What gave you the right? You were in your nineties, a rancid old man whose breath exuded decadence. Shouldn't you relinquish the ground beneath your feet to younger people who couldn't find a footing? You could die. You could have done so long ago.

You must have heard our wrath, mine and Liu Zhaohu's. After waiting fifty-two years, today you finally made your way here.

Ian Ferguson: Comrades, Khakis, an Uninvited Guest, and All Sorts of Things

Here I am, almost without delay. If you went to that cemetery on the outskirts of Detroit, you'd find the flowers on my grave have barely faded.

You probably noticed I'm wearing the plain khakis we wore in camp. In fact, I still have the navy uniform I had tailor-made for me in Shanghai, packed in my suitcase and still in good condition. It was the only uniform I had in China. The tailors in Shanghai probably never imagined victory would bring them such lasting success. From the day we got to China, we stopped wearing our military uniforms. Miles ordered that we only wear plain khakis, with no military hat and no insignia to identify service or rank. It made it easier to avoid formalities when we ran into our commanding officers. But more importantly, if we fell into Japanese hands, they wouldn't be able to learn anything about us from our clothing.

In the fall of 1945, when we finally left the remote village of Yuehu for Shanghai, everyone was full of anticipation. We had a saying: "Shanghai is Shanghai. Shanghai is not China." Shanghai had visible influences from around the world. It hardly seemed like part of China anymore. In a city like that, no one could afford to look disheveled. We needed sharp new suits, and we had to stay on our toes. The first thing we did when we got there was ask the hotel concierge about a well-respected tailor, then we had him rustle up some blue sailor uniforms, each with a neck scarf, white cuffs, flared legs, and on the sleeve, a golden eagle with crossed gun barrels and three bright-red chevrons under its claws, the emblem of a gunner's mate first class. It was finally time for us to take the stage and make sure the attention of those fashionable women in rickshaws along the Bund would not forever belong exclusively to the army and air force.

That navy uniform made in Shanghai has always accompanied me on my travels. Though its color faded, the blue was still pure, and the weave remained as strong as a copper plate. After seventy years, its quality did credit to the workmanship of the tailor.

But I left the world in my plain khakis, according to the detailed instructions I'd left in my will for the funeral home. Alive, a person might wear hundreds or thousands of outfits, but dead he can only wear one. I picked this unremarkable tan as my shroud because it reminded me of equality and dignity.

I know I've kept you waiting, but I'm here now, and I lost no time coming. Please don't greet me with those looks, friends—no, comrades.

I was ninety-four when I died. I lived too long, and inevitably made some new friends. Some were classmates, some were colleagues, and some I knew because we shared interests. We've attended each other's weddings, children's christenings, anniversary celebrations, and funerals. We've been godparents to one another's children. We've trusted our life secrets and our ups and downs to one another, but never our actual lives. So they are only my friends, not my comrades.

I guard this word "comrade" like an Asian girl guards her chastity, not giving it easily to others.

We were strangers before the war, and after the war, I barely contacted you. I once sent a letter to the US address Pastor Billy left me, but it was returned after a few months. I didn't understand why until today. Five years later, at an annual meeting of the American instructors, we remembered old times in Yuehu, talking of Buffalo, Snot, and Liu Zhaohu. When I got back to the hotel that night, I was a little emotional. I couldn't help writing a letter to Liu Zhaohu. I thought it would probably just sink into the sea, because the country was going through a major transformation. After that, I didn't try to contact either of you, and I didn't get news about either of you for the rest of my life.

Although our time together was short, I still call you my comrades.

I was an instructor back then. Liu Zhaohu, you were a student in my class. According to your culture's tradition of giving teachers great respect, there was a clear hierarchy that separated us. Even so, out on assignment, all hierarchies were meaningless, because our lives hung on the same fragile rope. You held one end of it, and I held the other. Your loss was my loss, and mine, yours. We could live together, or we could die together at any moment. So we always had to look out for each other.

I remember that night march. We walked on a mountain road so dark, we couldn't see our hands in front of our faces. Fearing an ambush, we couldn't smoke, and we had to be silent. When you tapped me lightly on the shoulder, I knew I was standing on the edge of danger. This was your native land, your mountain road, and you knew secrets about the terrain that I didn't. One coded signal from you saved my life. Had I taken another step, I would've fallen into the abyss and shattered every bone in my body. I put my life in your hands, an unparalleled trust. That's why you are my comrades, and they aren't.

Another time, we got reliable intel on a convoy of Japanese transporting military supplies. According to the source, it would cross the train tracks two nights later, just a little over fifty-five miles from our position. We marched hard to reach it in time and set up an ambush. The Japanese transport had seen plenty of ambushes and knew how to deal with them. They put an empty car at the front, in case of attack, while the cars at the rear contained the actual cargo. They'd stretched their front lines too far, and the supply lines couldn't keep up.

In fact, our luck wasn't much better than theirs. After several attempts, we still hadn't managed to hit the target. We even lost a few Chinese trainees. Instead of sending men to ambush them, we decided to use a new explosive. The first time we tested this new weapon, it was you who controlled it, Liu Zhaohu. You held the detonator, waiting for me to calculate the timing and distance of the detonation. My eye was crucial, not just in figuring whether the target could be hit but also whether the person detonating the device could withdraw safely. It was a special skill of mine, as a first-class American armorer.

When I first became your instructor, no one was interested in remote or timed explosives. You all preferred close-range weapons, like grenades. You wanted to see the immediate effects of bodies blown to pieces. A victory that you hadn't seen with your own eyes couldn't be a real victory, just as a life that didn't dare to risk everything couldn't be called a life. I was like a chisel, patiently chipping away, an inch at a time, at your stubborn way of thinking. I told you that if a specially trained soldier was sacrificed, it was a huge waste of manpower and material resources. Only by staying alive could you destroy the enemy, so any action plan that didn't include safe evacuation wasn't worth trying. You dismissed my advice and made me out to be a coward, afraid to die. My view was eventually accepted, but that was later, after you'd tasted the sweetness of large-scale lethality that such special technology held.

That day we tested it, Liu Zhaohu, you squatted beside me, waiting on my eye. You put your life in my hands without reservation, because I was your comrade.

And Pastor Billy, even though you didn't wear our tan uniform, and though you didn't see action with us, I still call you comrade. We called you Basketball Billy and Pastor Billy, but you didn't know we had another nickname for you: Crazy Billy. Because you weren't the sort of pastor we were used to, the kind who was all fire and brimstone and the wrath of God at the drop of a hat. You wore a tunic like the locals and rode a dilapidated old bicycle, sweeping back and forth between your church and camp. Afraid the hem would catch in the bike's wheel, you pulled up the end and tucked it into your waistband while you rode. Your hair, which had already begun to thin, looked like a dandelion in full bloom, blown by the wind. Your bike didn't have hand brakes, so you had to pedal backward to stop. That was how you traveled the mountain road, switching between pedaling forward and backward. You were a pastor and also practiced medicine, so all day all sorts of people came in and out of your church, including teachers, butchers, tea farmers, weavers, and even tramps. In your circle of acquaintants, there could've been someone whose wife's brother was a cook at a big restaurant in the county town frequented by members of various secret societies and who knows how many other gangsters and tobacco dealers. Maybe there was also somebody's aunt, a cook for a certain Japanese defense officer, who might inadvertently overhear a few words of a conversation while carrying in a bowl of soup or a cup of tea. And maybe there was someone whose son studied at a school in the city, and his roommate was the son of an officer in the puppet government who bragged incessantly. Your nose was as sharp as a dog's and your tongue as sleek as a snake's. You put both to use in picking up all sorts of information from these people, then pedaling forward and backward to bring it to our intelligence officers. This often got our timed explosives in the right place at the right time.

Old Miles (though he was only in his forties then) said over and over that our safety depended on our relationship with the locals. "If he has the trust and protection of the Chinese people, a person can move through the place as he pleases." This was the experience he summed up for us. As an American who'd lived here more than ten years, you warned us that Americans must not only avoid offending locals but also learn to blend in with them. You taught us to wear Chinese tunics, strap our trouser legs, and put sandals on over our socks (we weren't used to going around barefoot). You said that, on average, we were much taller than the Chinese people, so if we wanted to be unobtrusive, we had to learn to walk with an appropriate posture. What most gave us away was our gait and the way we sat. You repeatedly told us that we should keep the center of gravity low and our legs always bent. You told us to carry baskets on poles, like the locals did, and not use rice, sweet potatoes, or mung beans to hide what we carried, since these were too heavy and the weight of a full basket would be too much while a half-empty basket would raise suspicion. The best thing for us to carry were cowpeas. Once they were dried, cowpeas were light and could fill a whole basket, leaving plenty of room. This made them ideal for hiding small weapons, and it was easy to get the weapons out of them. You even gave us Atabrine to take, which cured malaria and would turn our skin a bit yellow, closer to that of the local people. Your suggestion annoyed our resident medical officer, but a few cups of rice wine calmed him down, and you finally got him to support your idea.

You knew we were homesick. One day, you heard us cursing the pork and luffa rice made by the kitchen without variation, so you taught our cook to turn his wood plane to the other side and shave potatoes with it. With a little vegetable oil, he made fried potato chips that almost tasted like our mothers' home cooking. There was always a wooden box slung over your bike's handlebars. We called it the treasure chest, because crazy objects popped out of it all the time. A thick prayer book was probably the only item a pastor should possess, but you also produced things like emergency medication, a pack of Camels, a tattered copy of *Time* magazine, a tin of chocolate toffee, a bottle of Korbel brandy, and a bag of Colombian instant coffee. To thank you for your free diagnosis and treatment, your variety of friends managed to get rare American items on the black market, things we could only get with great difficulty and danger through the Hump. You had it all, but you never hoarded it. As soon as you took it with your left hand, your right hand was passing it along to us. In your treasure chest, you sometimes hid a few packs of condoms, since you'd occasionally seen women coming in and out of our dorm. You worried we couldn't stand the isolation and loneliness of Yuehu and would defy orders and head into town on our own, looking for some fun. If we got into trouble there, it could cost us our lives. The Japanese offered a reward for any American soldier participating in covert missions. Instead of losing our lives that way, you figured you might as well let us stay in our little nest, committing minor sins that God could forgive later. Every Sunday, when you saw us dressed up and sitting in church to pray, you smiled like a child. If someone missed a Sunday, you just shook your head and clicked your tongue.

You troubled yourself over our lives and souls every day, so even though you never saw the battlefield with us, you're my comrade, and they aren't.

I know you've been waiting for me for fifty-two years. No—for Pastor Billy, it's been seventy. I understand your impatience, even anger. But life and death aren't in our control. Just as you prayed to God to give you a few more years, Pastor Billy, I repeatedly prayed he would give me a quick death. When I turned seventy-two, and my wife left this world, she took with her my passion for life. At eighty-four, I fell in the bathroom and was taken to the veterans hospital in Detroit. I had a brain hemorrhage, paralysis, and aphasia, but no memory loss. I never again left the hospital. From my bed, I asked God again and again, "Why keep my body imprisoned here on death row, but let my brain stay alert?" But fate's detonator wasn't in my hands, and I couldn't determine when it would go off. Just as fate punished you with an early death, it taunted me with mere survival, leaving me bedridden for another ten years.

Actually, I could have lived even longer. As my muscles no longer listened to my brain, my body's energy consumption was compressed into the smallest possible space, like an oil lamp with its wick turned very low, which, though it is nearly dark, burns on for a long time.

That is, I could have gone on living—if it weren't for that uninvited guest.

One day, when I'd been at the veterans hospital for ten years, the nurse told me there was a woman named Catherine Yao there who wanted to see me. I scoured the list of relatives and friends I could still remember. Her name wasn't there. Both my sons had passed on before me, and my daughter had moved to Rio de Janeiro in Brazil with her husband fifteen years earlier. When you live to be nearly a century old, your greatest blessing is that you've attended the funeral of nearly everyone you know. Your greatest sorrow is that they can't repay the respect you've shown them. They won't, or rather can't, come to your funeral.

They not only won't be at your funeral but also won't visit you. I had almost no visitors in my ward during those years, aside from my social worker. After a long time in speech therapy, my ability to speak had been partially restored, but I had few people to talk to. Oh, I wished to exchange the regained freedom from my tongue for my body. A ninety-four-year-old man has far fewer opportunities to use his tongue than his hands or his feet. So on that particular day, I didn't hesitate to agree to see this woman named Catherine. I was lonely, and I wanted to talk to someone from the outside world, even if she was a stranger.

It was a damp day near the end of July and unseasonably cold. Raindrops drew line after line of tears on my windowpane, making the dahlias outside as blurred as a Monet. She walked in and stood next to my bed, silently looking at my thin face collapsed against my pillow. She wore an exquisite cloth hat and an equally exquisite windbreaker. I couldn't tell her age from her features, but the gray curly hair slipping out from under the brim of her hat and her slightly stooped shoulders in the windbreaker made me think she stood somewhere in the hazy zone between middle and old age.

No matter how much she'd changed, I recognized her immediately, even though it was a full twenty-three years since the winter I'd chased her down the street in front of my house. At that time, she wasn't called Catherine. Maybe Catherine was the name she'd taken to adapt to the environment. During those twenty-three years, there wasn't a single day that I didn't regret my actions that day. I felt my wife's death and my illness were God's enduring punishment. During those twenty-three years, I'd never stopped looking for her. I sent a notice to the missing persons column in the newspaper and broadcasted requests for information about her on the radio. I contacted old comrades in Naval Group China and even relevant Chinese government departments inquiring after her whereabouts, but it was all useless. She seemed to have completely vanished from the world.

I hadn't expected to see her again. And then, when I'd given up all hope, she delivered herself, standing right there before my eyes.

"Wende. You look like Wende," I mumbled.

I was equally stunned to find that after a decade of paralysis, a finger on my right hand suddenly began to twitch.

She understood me. I saw moisture gathering in her eyes. She didn't reach for her handkerchief or a tissue, wanting to ignore the tears. She simply pretended to tidy her hat, tilting her head back slightly, forcing the tears to retreat as she did. Then she cleared her throat and, speaking each word deliberately, said, "I don't know . . . any Wende."

She took a beautifully printed business card from the pocket of her delicate coat and placed it on my bed. She said she was a reporter from a well-known Chinese media outlet in Washington, DC. On the occasion of the seventieth anniversary of victory in the anti-Japanese war, they wanted to interview veterans of the US military who'd served in China and compile a commemorative album. She found my name in an old directory of Naval Group China in the Library of Congress.

Her English had improved a good deal in these twenty-three years. If she didn't drag a sentence out, it was nearly flawless, though she did occasionally turn "thank you" into "sank you." Her tone spoke of the capability and experience of a well-trained journalist, solid and stable, with almost no crack of emotion. She pinned me in her sight firmly, and even if she didn't speak, I knew who was in control here.

I suddenly understood the purpose of her visit. She wanted me to know that she knew my whereabouts before I died, and that no matter where I went, she forever held my guilt in her grasp. She wore her full armor and kept the polite distance of a stranger, letting me know she had erased all trace of me from her memory. She hated me, but not with the sort of hate that could be expressed in words. Hate that can find expression is not hate. Hate must come to the end of its own rope before being forgotten.

There was no point explaining or arguing. I reined my emotions in and invited her to sit by my bed. I asked the nurse to translate, since only she understood the odd accent of my speech after the stroke. I told Catherine that I only had energy for one story. My tongue would not fully obey me, so I spoke slowly. Catherine turned on her recorder and began to take careful notes. Occasionally, she interrupted and asked me to repeat a few words that even the nurse couldn't make out. Most of the time, she kept her head lowered so I couldn't see her expression, but from the intensity of her breaths, I could detect the current of her emotions. But that submerged current never flooded its banks, and she remained restrained from beginning to end.

When I finished the story, I was exhausted, like a fish that had been over-salted.

"This girl, Wende—did you find her later?" Catherine asked after a long pause.

I shook my head.

"Memory is a fragile thing," I said.

I was telling the truth.

My first day in Shanghai, in my newly tailored blue military uniform, sitting in the military club and drinking that long-missed first beer in comfort, Yuehu had already become a thing of the past. It didn't take three months for the memory to fade, or even three days.

When I was on the plane from Calcutta back to the States, Wende did come to my mind. But it wasn't really Wende I was thinking of. I was recalling the advice Pastor Billy had given me when I left Yuehu, even though it sounded scathing at the time. Pastor Billy was fifteen years older than I was, and he heard God's voice at a closer range than I did. He knew that human nature was riddled with a thousand gaping wounds. War is one world, and peace another. Each world has its own door, and they are not connected in any way.

In fact, each also forgot the other. After many years, I was still asking myself, Did Wende forget me before I forgot her? Why didn't she respond to my letter? Should I count her silence a regret or my good fortune?

After returning to the US, I still sometimes thought of Wende. For instance, when I was driving alone at night on a highway or perhaps on some sleepless night. In those unimaginably strange moments, Wende broke into my thoughts without warning. But even when I was thinking about her, I didn't really think about her. I was just thinking about a younger version of myself.

The nurse stood up to check my blood pressure.

"Mr. Ferguson hasn't spoken this much in a long time," she said.

It sounded like something was caught in her throat. Her voice was murky and hoarse. That was the scar my story had left on her.

Immediately understanding the nurse's meaning, Catherine stood up to leave.

"Farewell, Mr. Ferguson. Thank you for this . . . unforgettable story," she said.

I noticed her embarrassment as she searched for a suitable adjective. I also noticed that she said "farewell," not "goodbye." She and I both knew that when she went out of the door, it was farewell.

From the bed, I stopped her.

"Can you tell me again what you used to be called? I mean, the name given to you by your mother?" I had the nurse ask on my behalf.

She didn't answer, but she stopped.

"Can you accept an apology from a ninety-four-year-old man? It's probably the last apology I'll offer before I go," I muttered.

My eyes were closed when I said it, because I couldn't bear to see her expression when she turned around. I couldn't bear to see anything in that room, including the half-empty cup on the table, the spider staring with its big eyes in the corner, or the dust collected in the gaps between the blinds.

She kept silent, but I heard the tremble in the air around her.

"Everything that happens in this world happens for reasons suited to its particular time," she said at last.

She left, and all was quiet in the air behind her.

After she'd gone, I could not sleep for two nights. On the third night, I stared wide eyed at the venetian blinds, watching them turn from dark night to a light gray. When I heard a robin utter its first chirp on the branches outside the window, I finally closed my eyes. This time, I closed them forever.

I know we're slowly getting to the heart of the matter. I've already seen from the glint in your eyes that the thing you most want to hear about is the woman I called Wende. No, she was a girl. In fact, she's the reason we're here. If our lives are three separate circles, then she is their intersection. You want to talk about her, but you don't dare, or perhaps I should say, you can't bear to. Now that I've finally broached the subject, let's start with you, Liu Zhaohu. You knew her for years, far longer than Pastor Billy or I did. Her life before she came to the camp was a mystery to me. Please, reveal the mystery to us. Tell us about her past, and maybe about what happened later, if you can.

Liu Zhaohu: Sishiyi Bu, the Village with Forty-One Steps

Ian, to you she's called Wende. To me, she's Yao Ah Yan, "Swallow." When you met Ah Yan, she'd been living at Pastor Billy's house for almost a year, but she wasn't native to that village. She was from Sishiyi Bu, about fifty miles from Yuehu. Today, the villages are practically neighbors, but in those days, people separated by forty-five li might never see each other in their lifetimes. That's why Ah Yan came to Yuehu.

Ah Yan's village was also my village. We knew each other as children. Anyone with a surname other than Yao or Yang had to be an outsider, so you've probably figured out from my name that my family members were outsiders. When Ah Yan was a child, I carried her and fed her rice cereal. Our village was called Sishiyi Bu, meaning "forty-one steps," because of a river. The river sat far below the village, requiring us to walk up and down a long stone staircase. Going down to the river, there were forty-one steps, but ascending, there were only thirty-nine. A third of the way up, there was a groove worn into the hillside, and someone familiar with the path could walk along the groove, jump lightly, and skip two steps. This number was only when the river was in a good mood. With rains or in the typhoon season when summer turns to autumn, the river would lose its reason and swallow a dozen steps in one gulp. Yang Taigong, Great-Grandpa Yang, the oldest villager, told a story that in the autumn of the twenty-first year of the Guangxu reign—that's 1895 on your calendar—it rained for forty-nine days. When the rain finally stopped, he was herding the ducks out the courtyard gate, and looking down, he thought he'd gone the wrong way because all forty-one steps had vanished, leaving only a sliver of stone vaguely visible. But even Yang Taigong didn't know when the stone steps were put in. He guessed that the river and steps existed before the village, since the village was named after the stairway.

Sishiyi Bu was surrounded by mountains on three sides, and the nameless river was the only waterway in or out. It was a narrow river, but rowing a sampan across it required fierce strength. Then, once docked, you had to climb the stone steps. Forty-one steps don't sound like much, but for anyone not used to mountainous terrain, it would be quite difficult. The land was easy to defend and difficult to attack, so even though the Japanese occupied the Chinese coast from the capital to Guangdong, the people of Sishiyi Bu had never seen even a single Japanese person. For the Japanese, it wasn't worth wasting the resources to attack.

Ah Yan didn't know much about any of it. The furthest she'd ever traveled was the county seat. How could she know anything about the capital, Guangdong, or the Japanese? She only heard things from her father's sworn brother, Uncle Ah Quan. Uncle Ah Quan didn't understand those things either, but he heard about them from his son, Huwa, who'd gone to school in the county seat. Huwa returned home every month, bringing a bag full of rice and salted vegetables with him when he left home and news to the village when he came back. This way, news regarding the Japanese found Ah Yan's ears, so she knew there was trouble with Japanese people outside the village.

That boy, Huwa, was me. It was the childish nickname my family gave me and meant "baby tiger." All my speculation about the terrain and the war ultimately proved to be the meaningless talk of a half-scholar. Ah Yan listened, but it didn't make sense. How could the Japanese make trouble? She knew that her father had told her that over thirty years earlier, Sishiyi Bu and the neighboring village, Liupu Ridge, had a fight over a slate plank at the border between them. All the men and boys—even the male dogs—in both villages had gone to the battle, which lasted from sunrise to sunset, until the sky was so dark, one couldn't tell friend from foe. The next morning, teeth covered the ground. The pigs and dogs were covered with red mud for the next several days. The Japanese were fierce, but could they fight like that? After the battle, the two villages were hostile for many years. At some point, the elders of the villages arranged a feast. After sharing food and wine, it had become customary for them to give their children in marriage to the other village so that the two villages could live peacefully together in the future. And so, Ah Yan didn't take the Japanese seriously.

Ah Yan's story is long. I have to skip her childhood and start from when she was fourteen years old, when I was escorted home from school.

The day after I returned one time, in the morning, Ah Yan took a bamboo basket and went to wash clothes. The morning fog still hadn't dissipated. The eaves, the blue paving stones, the branches, and the cats and dogs on the street looking for food were visible, but barely. If you reached out, you could actually grab a handful of water in the air.

"Press it, then press it again. This year's harvest will be secure."

That's what my father—the man she called Uncle Ah Quan—had said once while drinking with her father. Ah Yan had laughed at how my father spoke as if fog really had substance. My father had tapped her head with his bamboo chopsticks, and said, "You don't believe me? Well, people eat dogs, dogs eat shit, and tea leaves eat fog. Look at all the good tea leaves around the world and tell me, which does not come from a misty mountain?"

My father wasn't just her father's sworn brother but was also the supervisor of her family's tea plantation. Her family wasn't the only one who planted tea, and her family's garden wasn't large, not more than a dozen *mu*, but her family's tea was famed far and wide, and not just because their tea was perfect in taste, color, and shape but also because it could stave off hunger, and a cup of their tea was better than a bowl of meat broth.

Though the plantation belonged to her family, my father was the real manager. He'd given the tea grown on her family's plantation a name not easily forgotten: Yunshan tea, or in English, "tea from the cloudy mountain that can fill you up." It wasn't only famous but also reasonably priced, so it was sold as far as the northeastern provinces and Guangxi, in the south. There was always someone asking how my father cultivated "a tea that could fill one up," but my father would just laugh. People asked if it was a family secret, but again, he would just laugh, not saying a word. Everyone was convinced he had some secret formula, and the villagers often wondered whom he'd give it to. My father had two sons, but my older brother had been apprenticed to the village carpenter, Yang, since he was just a kid, and I was in school. Neither of us seemed likely to become tea farmers.

One day, Ah Yan asked her father in private, "Where does Uncle Ah Quan hide his secret formula?"

Her father looked to make sure there was no one else around, then laughed and said that my father's secret formula was nothing but hot air. The rumor about drinking his tea and not getting hungry was started by my father. The talk spread from person to person—first one, then ten, and then a hundred, with each retelling exaggerating the claims. As it spread further, it came to be accepted as true.

Hearing this, Ah Yan came to realize that business could be done in this way.

A few days later, it was time to harvest the Qingming tea. Even the sparrows flying over the tea trees knew it was going to be a good year. My father said it had been many years since he'd seen such ideal weather, with lingering fog and a mix of wind and rain and sunshine each arriving on time, as if they'd arranged everything over dinner and wine, all agreeing to a schedule, nobody quarreling with anyone.

Not even the tip of a single shoot of new tea was visible, and our mothers were already making plans for what was to be done after the harvest. The roof in the front of the house was a little leaky, so they would need a mason to repair the tiles. The tailor would make new cotton jackets for everyone too. Ah Yan's mother's joy that year was not based on the harvest alone. More importantly, she would never need to worry again about adding a new jacket for another woman. After the Spring festival, Ah Yan's father had gotten rid of his second wife. Before her, there had been another he'd sent away. Ah Yan's father had kept other women because he really wanted a son. Two years after he had taken his wife, she'd had Ah Yan, but after that, her belly remained flat. He'd taken a woman, sold to the Yao household by her brother for a few copper coins as they fled the famine in Sichuan. The woman stayed in the Yao household for three years, but her belly too remained empty. Ah Yan's father sent her away and took in another woman. She was a distant relative of the Yao family and a virgin. Because she was so poor, she was willing to become a second wife. Ah Yan's father was of the opinion that if one piece of land didn't bear fruit, it was best to move to another. It hadn't occurred to him that the problem might actually be the seed. At the end of the year, he consulted a famous blind fortune-teller a hundred miles away who told him he could only expect half a son in his life, and the hope finally died within him.

After he sent the second woman away, Ah Yan's father asked his wife if she thought they could find a boy to adopt and make their heir. His wife said that no matter how good an adopted child was, he wouldn't be their own flesh and blood. Why not instead find a suitable young man, and he could become the half a son the fortune-teller had spoken of? The child Ah Yan would have in the future would be their own blood. His wife had her own agenda, but Ah Yan's father didn't reply, and generally, his silence was approval.

This discussion was carried out without Ah Yan's knowledge, and it was my mother who brought it to me. I said, "Shouldn't Ah Yan be the one consulted about her marriage?"

My mother scolded me. "You've studied so much that it's ruined your brain. You're more confused each year."

The "press" my father had spoken of was the sort of fog we had that day. Ah Yan walked to the river with her bamboo basket on her back in the early morning light. Sishiyi Bu was just waking up, each house opening the door to shoo the chickens onto the street, filling the town with cackling and shouts. There was the sound of Ah Yan's mother boiling water to cook rice. Ah Yan was so efficient that she could wash all the clothes in her basket and be back by the time the rice was cooked.

I called to her from the big pagoda tree on the shore. Startled, she rubbed her eyes. As soon as she realized it was me, she laughed, revealing two rows of white teeth.

"Huwa, don't act like a ghost."

In the month since I'd seen her, Ah Yan had changed. I couldn't say exactly what was different about her, but her clothes seemed a little smaller. She was still thin, her shoulders poking against the cloth of her shirt like a pair of machetes.

A child this age is like a weed, growing another inch in the blink of an eye, I thought.

I was four years older than she was. At that point in our lives, even one year could mean two different crops, so she was still a child in my eyes.

"It's so early, and the air is so damp. What are you washing? Wouldn't it be better to wash when the sun is higher?" I said.

I had returned the previous night in the company of a teacher from school. This teacher came to tell my father that I wasn't doing well in school, but instead was leading a group of students every day to protest in the streets against the government's refusal to resist Japan, the soaring cost of living, and China's failing school system. We had grown fiercer, bringing our protest to the door of the county administrator, and as the leader, I was caught and jailed for two days. The old principal had to fight with his life for my release. Fearing I would get into further trouble, the school sent me home.

The story the teacher told was essentially true, but with one major error. I wasn't the real leader. That was our Chinese teacher, but he remained behind the scenes. I was on stage, performing each act, but he was the mastermind.

When my father heard this, he exploded with anger. He closed the door and shouted at me, saying my family had saved money for me to study, not take to the streets.

I retorted, "If the country is gone, what will I study? Might as well just study Japanese!"

My father said, "Do you think you can carry the entire country's burden on your own?"

I replied, "Of course I can't do it on my own, but if everyone works together, we can do it."

We continued to argue with raised voices. I had learned some new strategies at school, and my father could not match my logic. Embarrassed, he became angry and bolted the door, ready to hit me. My mother couldn't bear for me to be beaten, so she put herself between us and bore the brunt of his wrath instead, then sat on the floor, in pain and crying.

Ah Yan's father couldn't help hearing what was going on. At the time, we were living in the residential compound owned by Ah Yan's family. We'd had a separate house about a hundred paces from theirs, but it was very small. My brother had gotten married and had two children, one right after the other, so there were seven of us in one house, making it very crowded. When Ah Yan's father sent the second woman away, leaving empty rooms, he invited my parents to bring me and live there. He said having just a courtyard between the two families would make it easier to discuss the plantation's business. But I knew he just wanted to make it easier to drink with my father.

Ah Yan's father pulled me out and said, "Son, do you think you alone will bear the consequences? Don't you know they implicate everyone related to the guilty party? If you get yourself in trouble, do you want them to drag your parents to jail too? It'll be good to hide from this attention at home for a while."

Then I stopped talking.

When Ah Yan saw me reading that morning under the tree, she asked what book it was. I showed her the cover, and the three characters in the title. Ah Yan recognized the first, 天, and the last, 论, and said that the middle one was vaguely familiar, but she couldn't recall it.

She'd gone to the Jesuit school in the neighboring village for a short time, so she could recognize basic characters for sun, moon, water, fire, mountain, rock, field, and earth. But her mother started having migraines and needed help managing the home, so she had to drop out of school. On the other hand, I went to school in the county seat, where we were encouraged to "bring word to the door," so when I came home, I spent time teaching my two nephews to read. When Ah Yan heard about this, she brought her needlework and sat in on the lessons. She was a quick study and learned more characters in just a few lessons.

"It's *Evolution and Ethics*. It's about ideas like survival and the competition of everything in the world," I said.

Her eyes widened so much they seemed about to swallow her face.

"Yan Fu. Is he a teacher?" she asked, pointing at the name on the cover.

"He was a great scholar. He went to Japan and the West, but he didn't write the book, he just translated it into Chinese," I said.

I asked Ah Yan if she remembered the words I'd taught her before. She said she wrote them in the dirt with the fire tongs twenty times a day. She remembered all of them. I told her I'd bring her a notebook and pencil next time I came home and would make sure it had an eraser on the end.

"Huwa, do you still want to go to school in the county seat? My father said your father would never allow you to leave again."

I snorted. "If I decide to go, who can stop me? But I won't argue with him for now."

Ah Yan didn't say anything. She wanted to, and I knew what it was. She wanted to say, "True, no one can stop you, but who will support you? Who will give you money to buy rice, or pickles, or books, or paper and pen?"

But she said nothing.

"But I'll tell you, Ah Yan," I said. "I'm not going back to school. I'm going to be a soldier."

She was stunned. Her voice cracked as she asked, "The . . . the village security group head has looked for you?"

I laughed loudly and said those Nationalist government soldiers were nothing, scared to death before they ever touched a gun. I'd already made arrangements with some of my classmates. We were going to Xi'an. It wasn't the whole truth. We were planning to go to Xi'an, but Xi'an wasn't our final destination. We were going even farther than Xi'an, to Yan'an, the seat of Communist China, to join the Communist army.

Ah Yan didn't know where Xi'an was, but she could tell it was far away, someplace the sampan couldn't reach. She couldn't manage to say anything before tears started to fall on the back of her hand. She was ashamed. She knew the tears were shameful, but she couldn't hold them back.

"Why are you crying, silly girl? We're going to join a field propaganda team. We don't have to carry weapons. We won't die. The devils are taking over China's territory. If you were a man, you would step up and be a soldier too."

"But isn't Sishiyi Bu at peace?" she asked, confused.

"One, maybe two hundred miles to the east, it's already under Japanese control. The Japanese flag flies over the city, and people must remove their hats in deference. Otherwise, they'll be shot. Tell me, is that the Chinese people at peace?" I said.

"One or two hundred miles is far away. How long does it take to row a sampan there? Aren't there men there? Why can't they protect themselves?" she asked.

I wanted to say that the whole country had to come together in hard times, but after thinking for a moment, I didn't say that either. To a fourteen-year-old girl from the village, this was all alien.

"You'll understand one day," I said.

"Do your parents know you're going?" she asked.

"I'll send them a letter once I'm gone," I said.

"Must you go?" she asked.

I nodded.

"Yao Guiyan, I'm going to ask you for something," I said, looking at her and saying each word very carefully.

She was surprised. Yao Guiyan was her full name, but no one ever used it, except when she had registered for school. The name had a literary quality to it, as if chosen by old Yang Deshun, the village scribe, but in fact, her mother had chosen the name. During the pregnancy, her father had constantly hoped for a son, burning incense and praying to his ancestors, consulting his ancestral scrolls for a suitable name. When he saw she was a girl, her father ceased to care, not bothering to name her at all. Her father only began to care when he realized he would never have a son. After giving birth, her mother looked up and saw the swallows from the previous year returning to build nests under the eaves. So she gave her the name Guiyan, meaning "swallows that have come home." Everyone in the village, old or young, just called her Ah Yan. She had almost forgotten her full name. When I spoke it, she thought I was addressing someone else. Then she realized I had something really important to say.

"You're the only one I've told. Please look after my parents while I'm away," I said.

Ah Yan tried to nod, but couldn't. She knew the tears would return if she nodded. Those tears had already humiliated her once, she didn't want to let them do so again. She choked back a sob.

I said, "OK, OK. Let me go away happily. If I come back alive, I'll teach you to read and turn you into a teacher."

Ah Yan sniffled and started down toward the river. Removing her shoes, she tied their laces together and hung them on a branch, then went barefoot down the stone steps. The slate was wet and slippery with dew. From the top of those forty-one steps, the river seemed like an abyss steaming with white smoke, and in a daze, she nearly lost her footing. Normally, Ah Yan could walk that path with her eyes closed. She'd been going there since she was a month old, carried on her mother's back. Once she could walk, she followed her mother, and later began to go on her own. She washed rice, vegetables, and clothes and rinsed the chamber pot there—there was no telling how many times she had traveled this path. Her feet knew every stone. She'd even named the stones. The third from the top, with the winding crack, was Crooked Mouth, and the twelfth, uneven and full of pits, was Pock-Marked Face. As she descended, she saw a sickly stalk of grass growing from the third rock from the river, so she called that step Yellow Hair.

She knew not only the stones but also the water. Each season when the tea was ready, our fathers would row a sampan to the county seat to sell the leaves, and they sometimes brought her along. When their arms grew weary, she took over rowing. She knew where the river turned, at which bend the sampan would meet the first whirlpool, and where the water seemed calm but had dangerous rocks hiding beneath. But today, she seemed flustered by the stones and water.

She had only gone a few steps when there was a whooshing sound, and the basket on her back shook. Turning, she saw a ball of blue cloth had been added to the pile of clothes in her basket. She shook it loose to discover a short tunic.

"Ah Yan, would you wash that for me while you're at it?"

She must have been amazed that from such a distance I could toss my shirt into the basket. All the boys in the village carried a slingshot, and I was no exception. But while they shot sparrows perched on branches, I shot birds midflight. One stone for one sparrow, and I rarely missed the target. My father had boasted, "If my son entered the ranks, he'd definitely be a sharpshooter."

My father's casual remark was spot on, and I never escaped the life of a soldier.

Ah Yan picked up my shirt and sniffed it. There was a strange touch of shyness in her expression. My heart tugged. I'd never seen Ah Yan like this before. Did she know about our fathers' conversation?

The day before, after they'd seen my teacher off, our fathers went into the house, where their wives were waiting, closed the door, and discussed things. The village security group head had just informed them that the army of the official Nationalist government was drafting men. For families with two sons, one would be taken, and he asked my father to be prepared. My elder brother had two young children, so it was going to be me.

Ah Yan's father said, "Didn't it used to be three sons? When did the rules change?"

My father answered, "Right now, the war is critical. The population can't keep up, so who enforces the rules?"

Ah Yan's father replied, "War isn't opera, and bullets don't have eyes. Why not send Huwa to Ah Yan's uncle's house to hide?"

My father said, "He said if the younger son fled, they would take the older, and if the older son escaped, they would take the father. Every name on the household registration is required. It's etched in stone. He himself has three sons, and one of them must go."

Ah Yan's father said, "Could we pay someone a little money to serve as a replacement?"

My father answered, "It wouldn't be just a little money. It would take at least two hundred silver pieces. Real silver."

Ah Yan's father said nothing. The tea was not yet harvested, so who had that kind of money? They fell silent, except for the tapping of pipes. After a while, Ah Yan's father cleared his throat and said he had an idea. He lowered his voice, indicating he had something important to say. I pressed my ear hard against the crack between the door and its frame.

"Perhaps you could give Huwa to my family and change his household registration . . ."

Ah Yan's father's voice became blurred and indistinct, but my ears had already picked up that kernel wrapped in an echo. In the dark, my brain seemed to shatter inside my head, like a porcelain bowl that had been dropped.

"But it'll be hard for Ah Yan. She's so young . . ." My mother hesitated. Her words dragged like a tail, as if waiting for someone to pick them up.

Ah Yan's mother replied. Her voice was as faint as Ah Yan's father's, and I only caught a few words. "No period . . . yet . . ."

The pipes tapped again. After a long while, I heard Ah Yan's father's voice again.

"Just don't make them consummate the marriage, and it will be fine. Let them live in different houses."

His words were like a knife falling to the ground, and everyone was relieved. I wanted to burst into the room. I wanted to shout, "Ah Yan is just a child. Leave her alone." I wanted to say that war would not accommodate a peaceful marital bed. Please, don't create a child widow. I wanted to say that my father, my grandfather, and my great-grandfather all carried the name Liu, and I could have no other name. But I soon calmed down, remembering my plan. Before their scheme of adopting me as a son-in-law came to fruition, I would have left home, maybe just for a while, and maybe for good. I didn't need to start a new fight.

So I stood outside the door, listening, and did nothing. I got up the next morning, as if nothing had happened, and went to the river to read, just like every morning when I was home. The chaos of these troubled times couldn't reach me. I'd found my own port in the storm. Where I was going . . . oh, as long as I could silently say the name of the place, an ember seemed to burn in my heart. Nothing could stop me. As long as the first step was taken, my feet would know the path ahead. I didn't know a disastrous time in my life was about to begin. It would destroy not only my feet but also my path.

I looked up from my book and saw that Ah Yan had already gone into the river. She soaked the clothes in the water, laid them on the rocks, scrubbed them with saponin, then picked up her wooden club and started to beat them. The mist swirled around her, blurring her figure. Her rhythmic pounding was saturated by it. That mountain, that water, that scene, that figure—they made a soft, quiet ink painting completely oblivious to the terrible war raging outside.

If there were no war, this girl called Yao Guiyan would grow into a beautiful woman. I could see hints of that in her features. She would find a trustworthy, reliable man, hopefully one with a little learning and culture, and she would marry him, then bear a few children who would run around the tea plantation. That person could be me.

Absolutely, it could have been me. I'd known her since she was born. I did not have to go to great lengths to get to know her. I already knew everything about her. I trusted her, and she trusted me. If not, why would I tell her about my plan to run away, when I had kept it from the rest of the world? Why entrust my parents' care to her, rather than to my brother and sister-in-law?

But with just one gesture, the hand of war wiped out the natural path of everything. We had no time. There wasn't time for my love to grow or for her to grow up leisurely. I could only leave as quickly as possible, and she, child that she was, could only assume the burden of caring for two families. *Poor Ah Yan,* I sighed inwardly. She continued to beat the clothes with her club, and the fog began to break up. It seemed as if she drove the fog away. The sun sparkled clearly on the surface of the water. The river awoke, a shimmering pool of gold.

She finished washing the clothes. Wringing them out, she put them back in the basket and slowly ascended the thirty-nine steps. There were a lot of clothes that day, and the basket sagged under their weight. She seemed without strength. Normally, she'd bound up the steps all at once, but today, she stopped twice to catch her breath.

When she finally reached the top, she suddenly heard the wind. It was strange and loud, like long, rumbling thunder. The stones beneath her feet rumbled, but the trees didn't sway. Shading her eyes with her hand, she looked up, trying to see where the wind was coming from. She couldn't see the movements caused by the wind, but she did see a flock of birds. The birds were also strange. They all looked the same, with hard, sharp wings, but the wings didn't flap, as if they were just for show. Ah Yan counted them. There were six. One was the leader, and the rest followed, arranged in a neat triangle.

As she wondered what bird could fly so fast without flapping its wings, they had already reached the river. When they drew nearer, she realized it was the birds that brought the wind. The trees on both banks of the river shook in mindless madness. The grass beside the river bent into the mud. Ah Yan saw that each bird had a round sun on it. Each sun was a horrible red. The six suns crowded together, making a perfectly blue sky suddenly dirty.

"Get down, Ah Yan!" I shouted, jumping up from under the tree and pulling her.

She just said, "Shoes," then found herself pressed beneath me. I held her very tight. I could feel her smothered breathing in the dark space beneath me. She tried to move, but there was a series of loud sounds all around us. It may have been eight or ten, maybe more—it was too fast for me to count. The sound seemed to come from below, cracking the ground with thunder. Another sound emerged from the crack. A wail. It was very sharp. Sharper than the awl Ah Yan used to stitch the soles of her cloth shoes. It made hole after hole in my ears. I had never known that my ears could hurt and that the pain could sprout legs that kicked my heart so fiercely that it curled into a tight ball.

I didn't know how long it lasted, but the ground finally exhausted its trembling and stopped moving. I released Ah Yan, and we both sat up. She looked at me, then cried, "Your face!"

Running my sleeve along my face, I found it was covered in sticky blood. I shook my hands and kicked my feet. I could move. I felt relieved, then said, "I was just hit by a rock. It's nothing. Those evil dogs. An unarmed little village like this . . ."

But my words caught in my throat. Behind Ah Yan, I saw a column of smoke rising. At first, it was faint and thin, almost like mist, but it turned thick and black. Then it exploded into flames. The flames grew as they reached the wind, reaching taller and taller, and quickly they licked the tops of the trees. The trees softened and made a crackling sound.

"The plantation!" I shouted.

We thought of it at the same time. That day, our fathers had gone to the garden together, saying they had to loosen the soil for a final time before harvest so that it could absorb the mist.

Ah Yan jumped up and ran toward the tea garden as if she'd gone crazy. She just ignored the stones and thorns on the path, though they pricked her feet like needles, drawing blood. She didn't care about herself. Or anything else. All she cared about was finding them. I followed and quickly caught her. At the bend in the road, we suddenly stopped, because our feet no longer knew the way. It had been a path, but now was just a huge pit, big enough to contain two or three houses. It was ten feet deep and full of debris. I stood in a daze for what felt like a long time before I gradually realized that the debris was the remains of trees, bamboo hats, bricks, livestock, and people. Shattered like this, they didn't look like themselves. I only felt the strangeness of it all.

In the fork of a broken tree branch, Ah Yan saw a leg, a lonely human leg separated from its body. It looked like it was in a hurry to free itself from its body and get on its way. The shoe was only half on, and part of a heel, pale from an entire winter's hiding, poked through. Ah Yan didn't recognize the foot, but she knew the shoe. The tip of the shoe had a hole, and the black cloth patch covering it was one Ah Yan had sewn with her own hand.

Her eyes went dark, and she fell flat onto her back.

~

Regarding the events of that day, a county record written several decades later reports:

> At about 7:20 a.m. on March 31, 1943, six Japanese bombers attacked Sishiyi Bu, dropping eleven bombs. One fell into the water, one on the mountains, and the other nine hit residential areas and the tea plantation. Nine houses were destroyed, killing eight people and injuring twenty-nine others. There were countless casualties among the livestock.

Among the eight people killed that day were both my father and Ah Yan's father.

The remains found among the ruins were all fragments—a head, half a torso, a leg, a few fingers, a piece of a lung. We couldn't tell who each part belonged to, and it was impossible to piece a whole body back together. Yang Taigong looked on through wise tears, telling us to give up. The remains couldn't be identified, so they were buried together. He said that in the future, no matter which household visited the grave, they would burn incense for all the dead. That night, my brother's master, the carpenter Yang, made a big coffin to put all the remains in. If the bodies had been whole, there would have been eight coffins, but they were all placed in just one. It was heartbreaking.

On the day of the funeral procession, the villagers pooled their money to pay a man from the Yang family to mourn for us. This fellow, the son of the villager Yang Bashu, was adopted from a She woman, who lived in the mountains. Yang Bashu asked the village scribe, Yang Deshun, to give his son a name, and he named him Yang Baojiu, meaning "preserved through the ages." Yang Bashu didn't imagine that the respectable name he'd paid a silver coin for would actually be undermined, but Yang Baojiu had scabies on his head that left several bald spots the size of a coin, and so everyone in the village called him Scabby. Scabby was with Yang Bashu for seven years or so, but before Scabby was even old enough to marry, for no reason at all Yang Bashu suddenly died one night, leaving Scabby all alone.

Yang Bashu had loved his son dearly. He had personally managed every aspect of his household and land, not allowing his son to lift a finger. As a result, when the young fellow was orphaned, he couldn't do anything. In fact, he wasn't even able to carry baskets, he was so weak. He couldn't plant tea because the trees were too high, and he couldn't work on the farm because he'd have to wake up too early. At first, he survived by selling off plots of the family land and a tile-roofed house that had belonged to Yang Bashu. But without work, he quickly spent all the money and before long was living in someone's firewood room. The wind blew through the room from all sides. Summer and winter, he lay on a broken mat on cotton batting with holes in it, living in poverty and misery. He was by then thirty-two years old and still hadn't married.

Though Scabby's life wasn't easy, he didn't starve to death. He had a unique skill. His own mother was She, and all the She women could sing. He inherited a good voice from her, and he had learned a few folk songs. While others relied on their sweat to put food in their mouths, he relied on his voice. Whenever someone in the village died, the family paid him to wail at the funeral.

Scabby had several different ways of mourning. If someone offered a few rolls of dried noodles and eggs, he would cry piteously. It wasn't a half-hearted sort of mourning, but had a tune to the wail, his voice rising and falling, pausing and transitioning in rhythm—more mournful and louder than the weeping of any group of women. If someone added a few copper coins to the noodles and eggs, he would not only add music to the wailing, but words too. The words were simple, but always well suited to the situation. If someone gave a white envelope of copper coins, he'd know the amount just by running his finger over it, and then he'd sing a lengthy song appropriate for the occasion. This long song was not random, but was based on the deceased's life. As the funeral procession passed a mountain, he sang of mountains, and when they saw water, he sang of water, and passing a tree, he sang of trees, all the way from the house to the burial site. The performance was always dramatic.

So Scabby lived off the villagers' misfortune. If things were good, people staying safe and healthy, Scabby's eyes would gleam with hunger. And even the dogs knew that when Scabby wandered the village, he was trying to sniff out some unfortunate death in the streets.

Bitter, oh bitter, your life is more bitter than bitter herbs . . .

On the day of the funeral, after the earthen jar had been shattered as the coffin was lifted, Scabby made his first sound. It was too high, ripping a hole in the sky. The mountain seemed to be under a spell, standing motionless, but the trees quivered. When our mothers heard that sound, they cried so bitterly, they nearly fainted. The rest of the journey, Ah Yan and a neighbor held the widows up as they walked. Ah Yan wanted to cry, but when her tears reached her eyes, they refused to go farther, and her eyes became dry.

> *Qingming Festival, when the fog is thick*
> *the earthen jar is shattered*
> *I escort you through the tea forest*
> *these tea trees are yours*
> *you cultivated them*
> *with your own hand*
> *Now I only see the tea trees*
> *you are not there*
> *Oh, Tea Mountain weeps . . .*

The funeral procession passed through the tea forest. The bombing had ruined half of Ah Yan's family plantation, but the living half was unaware of the dead half—it was thriving, a luscious green, without remorse. It didn't know the chaotic world we lived in. The days were like water, always flowing forward, not looking back, and waiting for no one. Not even these troubled days could stop it.

> *The golden bridge is crossed*
> *and the silver bridge beckons*
> *We cross each bridge in its turn*
> *All the bridges lead us to*
> *the western paradise*
> *On the path to the nether world*
> *you slowly make your way*

There were no golden bridges in Sishiyi Bu, no silver bridges, not even wooden bridges. The bridge Scabby sang of was the sampan. The burial grounds were on the opposite bank, and the procession would escort the remains across the river. Eight strong young men lifted the coffin and placed it on the widest sampan. It swayed and trembled for a moment, then grew steady. The rest of the entourage took the other sampans, weeping as they crossed the river in turn. The river was higher that day, filled with our tears.

> *Twelve hundred pieces*
> *of gold are given*
> *I will send you on your way to heaven*
> *so you can search for*
> *your beloved mother*
> *delighted to see you, your dear mother*
> *while I remain on this side, as a mourner*

On the other bank, we had to leave our fathers, and they would never return. It was then that Ah Yan's tears found an opening, coming in a flood.

After Ah Yan's father was buried, her mother didn't eat or drink. She just lay in bed for three days. My mother, though she was also in deep mourning, went to comfort her. She could hold it together. Yes, of course she could. My mother had sons and grandchildren, and she had to be strong for them. Ah Yan's mother could have borne it too, but she didn't want to. She had no son for whom to bear the load.

My mother said to Ah Yan's mother, "Those dead are gone, but the living are still here. Ah Yan is young. She needs you. You've got to eat, at least a little."

My mother brought a spoonful of rice porridge to Ah Yan's mother's lips. Ah Yan's mother closed her eyes and her mouth. She neither moved nor spoke, letting the rice spill all over her chin.

My mother's words were as effective as trying to scratch lice through a cotton-padded jacket, not relieving the itch or pain. Ah Yan was a fragile young girl. She was too light to keep her mother from despair.

In this whole house, I was the only person whose words could have helped. *Don't worry. I'm your son too.*

But I never said it. My face was taut, my jaw clenched. What I could say would be of no use, and the words that would help were those I couldn't speak.

Ah Yan knew she couldn't count on me. My heart was set on something else, something she had no part of.

Ah Yan grabbed the bowl from my mother's hand and threw it to the ground. It smashed into pieces, the sharp fragments poking holes in the floor. We were shocked. Ah Yan had always been a gentle girl, and no one had ever seen her commit such an act.

"Ma, I know you wish I were a boy, but I can grow tea, raise pigs, cut wood, and embroider, and I'll earn enough to take care of you, all the way to the end."

She reached for a pair of scissors from her sewing box on the windowsill. Unsure what she meant to do, I rushed to her and grabbed her wrist.

"Ah Yan, don't be foolish. I won't go right away. I'll help you harvest the tea before I leave," I whispered in her ear. These words rushed out without a thought, as if I'd had too much to drink. I didn't even consider my classmates waiting for me in the county seat for the long journey to Yan'an.

Ah Yan pushed me away with all her might. Unprepared, I nearly fell to the ground. I was surprised by her strength. She took the scissors, cut her braid, then tossed it on her mother's bed. The braid spread out loosely, like a black snake lying stunned on the ground.

Ah Yan fell to her knees. "Ma, look at me. I'm your boy. From today on, I'll be your son," she shouted.

Still saying nothing, her mother slowly opened her eyes.

~

I had already been preparing for my journey. I'd arranged to meet some class-mates at a teahouse outside the county seat. We would travel together to Zhuji, and from there find a boat to Hangzhou. The railway line north of Hangzhou was held by the Japanese, so we could only plan that far. The rest would have to be decided as we went. The journey to Hangzhou had been arranged by our Chinese teacher. He gave us the addresses of hostels along the way. We were to meet in three days, but I had promised Ah Yan I'd help finish the tea harvest before going. All I could do was write to ask my companions to wait for me in Zhuji, where I would join them.

I'd never seen a Japanese person before. All I knew about them came from newspapers, the radio, and the reports of various refugees on the street. I had planned to leave because of patriotism, the passion of youth, and my teacher's urging. Patriotism is born in the mind, a few steps from the heart, but was not yet a heart-wrenching pain. When my father was killed, the Japanese people I'd heard about became real to me, and my sense of nationalistic enmity became a blood feud. This desire for revenge was born from the depths of my heart, and it pulled at my whole body. If I didn't go, this burden would make me fall to my death. I had no choice.

I would be traveling a great distance, so I couldn't leave without prepara-tions. The first thing I had to prepare, of course, was money. Naturally after what had just happened, I couldn't ask my mother for money. Fortunately, I'd carefully saved the pocket money my father had given me. If I watched every penny, it might be enough for me to get to Hangzhou. The next issue was clothing. My clothes were all in the dorm at school, but I couldn't go back to get them for fear of being seen. But there were my father's clothes. He was only slightly taller than me, so I could wear the clothes he had left.

The hardest part was finding a weapon. It was a long road. There would be mountains and rivers to traverse. Even if we didn't encounter the Japanese on our journey, there were bandits on the seas and in the mountains. I needed to have something for self-defense. There was no shortage of kitchen knives and scis-sors at home, and my mother also had a few awls, but they were all too clumsy or flimsy. The previous morning, I'd passed Yao Er's butcher shop and saw his knives and cleavers on the wall there. I noticed one knife right away. It was probably used for removing bones. Its tip was still stained with blood. Though it was sharp, it wasn't big—just right for slipping into a waistband.

I wanted the knife, and I was sure it wanted me too. It gave off a trembling, trilling sound on the wall as I stared. It was calling to me. This was the knife I was meant to have, but I didn't know how to get it. I stood in a daze at the door of the shop for a long time, but didn't know what to do. Yao Er looked up and, noticing the linen wrapped around my arm as a sign of mourning, he said, "Would you like a cut of marbled pork for your mother?" I knew his words were meant to be sympathetic, but I wasn't used to pity. My face turned red. I shook my head and turned, practically flying away.

That afternoon, my mind was restless. My thoughts were full of the knife. I couldn't stand it. Pretending to need soy sauce, I took an empty bottle and loitered in the streets. I strolled past the door of the butcher shop. Yao Er wasn't there. He was probably relieving himself in the backyard. My ears buzzed. Before I could think, my hand moved of its own accord, plucked the knife from the wall, and hid it inside my shirt. I turned and fled, my heart hammering so hard inside me I was sure that the whole street could hear it.

When I got home, I hid the knife inside my pillow. I went to bed right after dinner. I slept with the knife in my pillow all night. I felt the pillow thumping. I wasn't sure if it was my head or the knife, but I tossed and turned all night, unable to close my eyes. When I got up, I worried my mother would come make the bed or that Yao Er would show up at our house looking for his knife. I found a piece of tarpaulin and wrapped the knife in it, then buried it beneath a stone slab outside the house, where I could retrieve it before I left. After I buried the knife, my hands were still shaking. I'd never stolen anything before, and I'd never handled a weapon. That day, I did both. I knew what the knife was for and that it would again be stained with blood one day—not the blood of an animal, but a human. Maybe even by my own blood. From the moment I decided to go, I did not expect to come back alive.

I took off my clothes and put on my father's tunic. It smelled of him and the river, and saponin couldn't get rid of that smell completely. It was strange, but I calmed down after I changed. Putting on my father's clothes was like putting on his courage. I had my father's and my own courage, so I no longer panicked. At that point, I realized that what I most needed for my journey wasn't money, clothing, or a weapon. It was courage.

The money in my pocket wouldn't get me far. I needed enough to get me to northern Shaanxi, but wasn't sure how to get it. I could be a coolie, carrying goods for people, and might even have to beg for food. I had to be prepared for hardship unlike anything I'd ever faced at home and humiliations I'd never known before. I had to learn not just to walk but also to kneel and even to crawl. I had to prepare to have my pride ripped away and be trampled in the dust. Facing death is a form of bravery, but so is facing life. I had to live to see the day when my knife would be of use.

After changing my clothes, I went out to work in the tearoom. I cleaned the corridors with a long broom, moved away piles of debris, and took down the salted fish hanging beneath the eaves. This was where the fresh tea leaves would be spread. The tea leaves were delicate, so if there were any other smells in the room, they would become contaminated.

After clearing the space, I set a large wok on the stove for stir fixation, the process of drying the leaves at a high temperature to stop the enzymes and bacteria from changing the flavor and color of the leaves. I asked my mother to prepare a roll of noodles and five eggs and carried them in a basket to the stir fixation master in the village. Usually my father and the stir fixation master worked side by side, but not this year. When the Japanese planes came, he had also been in the tea garden, just ten steps away from my father, but he'd escaped with his life. Though he escaped the shrapnel, he was injured when a tree fell on him. I went to his house to check on his condition, though I also intended to ask him to come and instruct me on the process of fixation. He was bedridden, unable to walk. If he agreed to come over, he would have to be carried—which would be showing us immense deference.

Ever since I was a child, I'd observed my father's preparation of the tea leaves. Even when I was away at school, I returned for a few days to help during the harvest season. But I'd always been an assistant, never the main actor. The fire, the wok, and the tea leaves all conspired against a green hand. This season's tea could be destroyed. After a year of good weather, in the end, we might only make a batch of rotten tea.

When I'd seen Ah Yan cut her braid the previous day, my heart melted. I almost wavered. It wouldn't be such a bad thing to stay here. The Yao family had always been good to my family. My father wasn't native to this region, coming from southern Anhui. Years earlier, my father's home had been devastated by hail and drought, and not a single grain was harvested. He took the family and fled by foot to Sishiyi Bu. I wasn't even two years old then. My father felt hopeless and considered selling me to save the rest of the family. When the Yao family heard that my father had grown tea before, they took us in. From then on, my father helped the Yaos manage their tea plantation. If it weren't for the Yaos, I might have ended up as a servant in some stranger's house.

Even so, I couldn't stay. The world had fallen apart. Staying would only help them live in degradation for a little longer, just prolonging the process of dying. I didn't want to watch them live like that. The best thing I could do was save them from the emergency they faced at that time. I would start my journey as soon as the tea was harvested.

~

It rained relentlessly. It wasn't a heavy rain, instead persistent and light, but endless. Even so, the tea leaves could not wait—tea left too long ages, rendering it worthless.

Ah Yan and my mother covered themselves with coir raincoats and went out early. I drove a donkey loaded with bamboo baskets. Picking tea was women's work, not suitable for men's hands. Ah Yan's mother didn't go to the tea field, but stayed home to prepare food and tea for everyone. This was how we had always done things. When we reached the field, there were only a few women there, waiting. My mother counted and found that about half were missing.

"Where is everyone?" she asked.

They looked at each other, but said nothing. When she asked again, one of the younger women stammered, "They want to know if they pick the tea this year, will they still . . . still be paid?"

The tea pickers had been recruited from the villages while my father was still alive. Most came from our own village, but there were a few from other villages too. They all knew a big change had occurred in the Yao household.

My mother raised her head and looked at the sky, sighing. She quietly said to Ah Yan, "There's no telling whether those heartless women have gone to another household to look for work. Picking tea goes slow on rainy days, and there aren't enough people now. Why don't you go to a few houses and see how things stand?"

After a moment's thought, Ah Yan said, "No. If I look for them, they'll look down on us."

Ah Yan unloaded the baskets from the donkey's back. She scratched her finger on an exposed bamboo strip in her hurry, then put the finger in her mouth. I handed her my handkerchief and told her to wrap up her finger to stop the bleeding. She shook her head, but didn't look at me. She couldn't look at me. She was afraid she couldn't hide the hurt in her eyes if she did. She'd lost a lot of weight over the previous few days, casting dark rings around her eyes. She'd had too much on her mind, and that prevented her from mourning her father properly. I worried she would tell my mother that I planned to leave. She knew that the only person in the world who could possibly prevent it was my widowed mother. But she didn't say a word. She gave everyone a bamboo basket. She, like my mother, was unsure about things. But she also knew that everyone's eyes were on her at this moment. They were measuring her to see how tough she was—or rather, how soft.

"Whatever you do, don't let them see you're upset. If you're soft today, you'll forever be a child in their eyes," I told her quietly.

She raised her head and looked at everyone.

"Sisters, aunties, though my family has gone through a hard time this year, you won't be shortchanged in your wages. This year, you won't be paid by the day, but by weight. For every twenty *jin* you pick, you'll be paid three copper coins. I'll inspect and weigh your baskets at the end of the day. I'm sure you already know Uncle Ah Quan's rules. Let's get to work. We have a lot to do."

You could almost hear the abacus beads clicking in everyone's mind. If they worked hard, they could earn almost twenty percent more than in previous years. My mother was puzzled. She wanted to ask Ah Yan something, but Ah Yan had already hung her bamboo basket around my mother's neck and was dragging her into the tea field. My mother turned back to look. Seeing even fewer workers now, she became panicked.

Ah Yan said, "Don't worry. They're just going home to get more women to come work."

Sure enough, fifteen minutes later, they all returned with more people. The Yao family's tea was reasonably priced, but it wasn't a precious variety of tea, like those from a single bud and leaf. My father's rule was to look for one bud with two leaves. Over the years, the Yaos' plantation had several regular customers,

48

and the business depended on maintaining its credibility. In the past, if any of the women were careless, mixing in three- or four-leafed buds or even stems, my father would discover it, and he would let that worker go. There were many tea fields in the region, so a tea picker could always find work, but working for the Yaos meant higher pay. And they not only provided enough lunch but also included egg drop soup boiled with lard. Everyone knew the rules, so they didn't say much, but just started to work.

From the time Ah Yan could walk, she was picking tea leaves. Others picked with one hand, but she could pick with both at the same time. She didn't have to look when she picked a leaf. It was like there was another set of eyes in her fingertips. These eyes allowed her fingers to move through the branches like snakes, knowing where to go, where to stop, and where to pick as they slithered along. Between the nimble movements of her thumb and forefinger, buds and leaves seemed to just fall into her bamboo basket. When the eyes in Ah Yan's fingers were busy, it didn't mean the eyes on her face were idle. In the past, as she picked tea, she kept watch around her, seeing what colors the butterflies were wearing this season as they flitted about the forest or what kind of flower was in the hairpin of the She woman coming down from the mountain to wash clothes in the river. But this year, the eyes on her face didn't work. The butterflies were wet, hiding in the branches where she could not see them, and though the wildflowers on the slopes were in bloom, they all seemed gray. To the eyes of a girl who'd lost her father, everything lost its color.

The tea picked on this day was sure to be more than ever before. When she was distributing the baskets, Ah Yan had calculated that if she paid a daily wage, she couldn't control the speed of the workers. Everyone's fingers had a way of being lazy. Of course, they could still be lazy, but it would be taking copper from their own pockets. No matter what, a bamboo basket could only hold about twenty jin. By calculating wages according to yield, each day there would be an increase in wages, but five days' work would be completed in four. The wet leaves would be heavier, so she would lose a bit today. She made a mental note to do an extra round of straining during weighing and calculations.

Not long after the harvest had begun, the rain stopped. The clouds split into a series of tiles, which then broke into fish scales that were blown away in the breeze. Suddenly, the sky was clear and beads of water glistened on the tea trees. The Qingming sunlight, during the third lunar month, seemed to have the brightness of Duan Wu, in the fifth lunar month, as it shone on our bodies. One hour's difference was like a new season. Ah Yan took off her raincoat and hat and reached to roll up her braid, then remembered that she had no braid, and her head was covered with a white mourning cloth.

I sat in the shade under a tea tree—it wasn't yet my turn to be busy. I would do the work after Ah Yan. On such a hot day, the moisture in the tea leaves would be especially dense, so they couldn't be spread out for too long. Tea leaves left out for too long would turn red. They had to be spread, panned, and shaped almost at the same time. I worried it would take all night to do it.

At midday, the women took the first batch of leaves to Ah Yan's house and took a lunch break. Following along, I saw houses that had been bombed by the Japanese planes. Some had only half a wall left, some only a facade. Parts that had been touched by the fire had been burned black, while parts not caught by the flames were now pale and exposed like old bones. Most of these families had already moved away to stay with relatives. One family had nowhere to go, so they stayed inside the damaged walls. The mother had used broken bricks to build a makeshift stove, and several naked children sat around a blackened blanket that had been snatched from the flames, waiting for the sweet potatoes in the woman's pot to finish cooking. Scabby stood near the woman, chatting idly. Seeing that the woman didn't have time for him, he picked up a stick and began to rummage around the ruins to see what he could find.

The women grew warm as they carried the baskets of leaves, taking off their head scarves and fanning themselves. When Scabby saw my mother, he stood up and greeted her. He said, "My dear aunt, I wasn't lazy when I sang for you that day, was I? When I sang about Uncle Ah Quan, I gave it special attention. My throat was sore for days after."

He was asking for a reward. My mother's eyes turned red, and she lifted a corner of her shirt to wipe them.

One of the nearby tea pickers scolded him. "Scabby, don't you have a heart? Do you know how painful such words are?"

Scabby twisted his mouth and said, "I deserve death. I didn't mean it that way."

He took a few steps back and looked askance at Ah Yan, who was standing behind my mother. "Aiyah!" he exclaimed. Then he said, "Ah Yan, did you cut your braid? All the girls in the city are wearing short hair now. It's the new fashion."

A rosy blush came over Ah Yan's face.

One of the women teased, "Scabby, when have you ever been to the city? In your dreams?"

Everyone laughed.

Scabby stomped his foot and said, "Don't look down on others. One day, I really will make it to the city. What do you want to bet?"

My mother sighed and said, "Well, you're young and energetic. The tea harvest is a busy time. Every family could use some help. Why don't you find work to do? Don't just engage in idle chatter."

Scabby said cheekily, "You, my dear woman, have only my best interests in mind. You're right."

A woman sighed and said, "Yang Bashu was such a good man. What evil did he commit in a previous life to make him raise such a heartless fellow?"

Smelling the lard from some distance away, Ah Yan felt her stomach rumble. Every harvest, her mother made rice cooked with oil over a slow fire, saying that oily rice was the best food to guard against hunger. When we got home and unloaded the tea leaves, the women picked up their bowls and started to eat. There weren't enough tables and chairs, so women had to squat in a black mass all over the floor. But Ah Yan had to inspect and weigh the baskets the women had brought in before eating. When she'd finished, she sat, but was too exhausted to even lift the bowl of rice. In truth, every harvest season was tiring, but this one was more exhausting than ever. In the past, she'd only had to put her body to work. This time, she also had to use her brain. The mental work had always been our fathers' responsibility before.

The tea from the Yao family's plantation was cord-shaped. Once the leaves had gone through stir fixation, they couldn't be aired too long, or they'd harden. When they hardened, it was hard to shape them. With so much tea collected all at once, shaping couldn't be done by hand alone, so feet were used too. The rule among tea-growing families was that work done by hand could be done by women, but work done by foot had to be done by men, since women's feet were considered unlucky. This rule had been in place for as long as there had been tea plantations, and no one dared break it. In the past, there had been four men in the Yao family who took turns stir fixing and trampling the leaves. Now all but one were dead, injured, or gone, so it was left to me to do it alone. All the experienced helpers had already been hired by other tea houses by now. There was no way to get additional help on such short notice, and I could only do as much as my own hands and feet could do. I would not be able to do more even if I had superhuman strength.

After the tea picking was over for the day, Ah Yan's mother opened the bellows to get the fire going beneath the wok for fixation. The injured fixation master lay in bandages on a rattan chair, weakly instructing us regarding the duration and degree of heating. Heat control for stir fixation was a great skill. Ah Yan's mother vaguely knew what to do, but she was no master. That didn't matter, though—on that day, everyone had to become a master. Ah Yan's mother's face flickered light and dark with the fire, the corners of her eyes hanging downward like two pieces of lead. Her hair was covered by a thick layer of ash. Ah Yan came to brush away the ash, but she couldn't do anything. On closer inspection, she realized that the hair—her mother's hair—had turned white overnight.

"Ma, don't worry. Let me manage the trampling. I know how to do it," she said suddenly.

The bellows in her mother's hands stopped, and her eyes widened like two bronze bells.

"Ah Yan, are you crazy? If anyone found out, would our family even be able to sell the tea?"

"Ma, I'm not crazy. If you let me, at least we can still sell a few jin of tea. If not, all our tea this season will be ruined," Ah Yan said.

My mother rushed to close the door, saying, "Ah Yan, be quiet. Aren't you afraid of the gods' wrath?"

Ah Yan snorted and said, "The worst disaster has already happened. What's there to fear now?" She didn't realize that her own destruction had just begun. There were still many disasters lined up along the road ahead, all waiting for her.

I too was taken aback. I couldn't have imagined that this girl from the countryside who had seen almost nothing of the world was far braver than all the affectedly sweet girls I'd met at school.

"Rules are set by humans, not gods. When humans encounter obstacles, don't we have to change our ways? Let Ah Yan give it a try," I said.

Everyone was silent.

The fixation master shook his head and sighed. He said, "Take me home. If I don't see anything, I can't say anything. The world has reached this troubled state, so who gives a damn about rules? Do what you want. Just don't ask me to be a part of it."

I took the fixation master home. When I got back, I fastened the bolt on the door and pulled the curtains tight. Then I lit a pine torch in the yard. Ah Yan sat in the glow of the flickering flames, washing her feet. Our mothers kept sighing. I was tired of hearing it, so I told them they could retire to their bedrooms. My mother left, but Ah Yan's mother refused. She kept her head down, not looking at us. Squatting, she started to pick the stems mixed in with the tea leaves.

I started to teach Ah Yan how to trample the leaves. "You can't use too light a force, or the leaves won't be shaped, but if you use too much force, they'll be broken."

I'd always worked in the background with my father, just following his lead, almost mindlessly. I wasn't sure how to teach Ah Yan. After a bit, she still couldn't get the hang of it, and her legs began to cramp. Looking at the pile of leaves in front of me, I could only think about how there was more to come the next day. I was worried, but I couldn't say anything, because I knew Ah Yan and her mother were both even more anxious than I was. Just then, there was a sudden bang. A flame burst from the torch, startling us. Ah Yan's lips began to quiver.

"What happened?" I asked.

She didn't answer, but put her hand over her heart.

After a moment, she got ahold of herself, and stammered, "Pa. I saw Pa."

Her mother turned around, her face pale.

"Where?" she asked. "Where?"

Ah Yan pointed at the shadow behind the torch. "He's gone now," she said. My hair stood on end.

"You're tired. You imagined it," I said.

"No, I saw Pa," she said. "He said that you have to learn how to manipulate force in your toes. You turn with the left foot and roll with the right, moving the toe and only lifting the sole of the foot lightly. He scolded me for lifting my leg too high. He said I wasn't pedaling a waterwheel, and if I kept on like that, I'd die of exhaustion, no matter how strong I was."

Ah Yan's mother buried her head in her knees and wept. Ah Yan massaged the tendon on her leg, then continued to trample. Watching her, I could tell she really had gotten the hang of it. She was much faster after that. Seeing that it was now the middle of the night, I urged Ah Yan to go to bed, since she still had to pick tea the next morning.

"In a few minutes. We'll be done in just a few minutes," she said. She was so tired, her speech was slurred.

Ah Yan's "few minutes" turned into an hour. When we'd finished trampling the leaves into shape, we put them back into the pan to roast. By the time we finished that, it was already the wee hours of the morning. It felt as if our legs were no longer attached to our bodies. We tried to stand, but collapsed like piles of mud to the ground.

Ah Yan's mother went to the stove and scooped a pot of warm water. "You two wash your faces," she said, "then go to bed. You can get up a bit later tomorrow."

Ah Yan didn't reply. She'd already fallen asleep against my knee. Her short, uneven hair peeked out from beneath her head scarf, half covering her face, and a thin bit of saliva flowed from the corner of her mouth. I didn't move, other than to take off my apron and cover her with it. A child. She was still a child. But there wasn't room for children to grow in hard times. This troubled world was like a knife that didn't even recognize its own family and cut childhood short. All the young people who went through it were turned into adults in one swift stroke.

At that moment, the village's most diligent rooster uttered its first crow.

~

I'd been asleep for less than half an hour when I was startled awake by a knock at my door. It was loud, fierce, and impatient, as if announcing a death.

I got up and ran to the door, where I found that everyone else had already awakened in fright, shuffling with their feet half out of their shoes, unkempt and still in bedclothes.

The village security group head stood outside our door.

"The draft officers have already been to Liupu Ridge, picking up able-bodied men according to the household registry. They'll be here in less than half an hour," he said breathlessly. He'd already run to several homes, and his face was covered with sweat.

"Didn't we agree it would be after the harvest?" my mother said, her voice trembling in panic.

"The Japanese are too fierce. We can't withstand them. A regiment will become a battalion, and a battalion will be left with one company, all in the blink of an eye. We can't wait until the tea harvest is finished," he said.

Hearing this, my mother's heart shattered into ten thousand pieces. She couldn't say a word, knowing only how to weep. Ah Yan's mother pulled her sleeve and said we should figure something out quickly, perhaps find a place for me to hide. The security group leader shook his head.

"Don't even think about it. Their men are guarding the way in and out of village. Military boats are stationed at the exit of the river, just to prevent anyone from escaping."

My mother fell to her knees and clasped the security group head's pant leg.

"My other boy, Longwa, isn't here. He's always traveling as a carpenter. Huwa is my life. Please, I beg you."

My mother repeated the word "please" over and over countless times. She knew the word was cheap, not worth anything, but worthless things could accumulate into something of value. That was something my late father had taught her from his own experience.

The security group head said, "I told Ah Quan just before the Qingming Festival, but he couldn't get the money together. Now, even if you have the money, you won't be able to find anyone to take his place. It's fate. People can't change fate."

The security group head's own son had paid someone to take his place. He had changed his fate. Ah Yan's mother knelt and grasped the other leg of the security group head's pants.

"Ah Quan just passed away. If Huwa goes too, how will this family survive?"

The two women clung to the security group head's pants, their tears dirtying his shoes. He couldn't free himself, and he couldn't kick them off, so he just sighed and said, "I wish every young man in the village could be spared, but it won't matter what I say. Since it's come to this, you should prepare some money for Huwa to take with him. I heard that they're setting out for Anhui, and it's colder there. Give him some copper coins. A little bribery may get him an extra set of clothing and rice to keep him from cold and hunger along the way."

The women didn't take any of this in. They simply clutched the security group head's pants and wouldn't let go. It was like those pant legs were a rope tied to the bank, their lifeline as they floundered in the current. I couldn't watch anymore. I bent over and pulled my mother up. She refused to rise from the ground, and her tears turned the dust into a dull gray paste that clung from her eyes down to her neck. I felt the flesh on my cheeks throbbing, and a string of words was about to rush its way from my belly to my mouth. Ah Yan caught it. She knew that these words, having found their way out, would create a reality no human power could undo, so she rushed forward and blocked the way. She walked over to the security group head and bowed with great deference.

"Sir, if you want to take my husband, don't you have to give a reason?" she said.

The security group head was surprised. "Your husband? When did you marry Huwa? Why didn't I hear about it?"

Quickly catching on, my mother stood up. She said, "Last year, our families exchanged betrothal cards. We planned to hold the wedding banquet after the harvest, but we didn't expect such a huge tragedy. During our mourning period, we couldn't openly hold a wedding."

Suspicious, the security group head looked at Ah Yan's mother. Ah Yan's mother's mind cleared too. She stood up and said, "Our families always intended this. The betrothal cards were exchanged last year."

The security group head's eyes shifted to me. I hadn't yet spoken. My lips twitched, but before I could speak, my mother clasped my arm in a death grip. I pulled away. Ah Yan gently whispered something that finally calmed the blood raging through my body.

"You don't want to join *that* army, right? Let's get out of this first."

The security group head sighed again and said, "Well, this is good. In this confusion of war, a girl might as well marry early to be out of harm's way. But you'll still have to supply an able-bodied man."

Ah Yan again bowed and said very courteously, "Sir, isn't it the rule to take one son out of two? Huwa doesn't fit that. We don't want to make things difficult for you, but it's true."

The security group head's eyebrows furrowed. "What do you mean, not make things difficult for me? Explain yourselves."

"Huwa is an adopted son-in-law, becoming the son of the Yao house. Each home, theirs and ours, only has one son, so you can't draft Huwa," my mother said, picking up Ah Yan's thread.

The security group head looked at my mother suspiciously. "You're willing to let your son take a different surname?"

My mother was stunned for a moment, like she was a student who had been studying for an exam all year, but was confused by the first simple question.

Ah Yan's mother coughed softly, bringing back my mother's resolve. My mother said, "Yes. Yes, it's a natural conversion."

The security group head asked, "Do you have documentation? It's one thing to say it, but they'll need to see it in black and white."

My mother was silent again, then said, "We . . . we haven't finished the paperwork. You know what just happened to our family. We haven't managed to complete the paperwork yet."

The security group head stamped his foot. "What use is that? Who would believe you?"

Ah Yan said, "It's just paperwork, right? I'll ask Yang Deshun to come now."

Before she had even finished speaking, she was out the door.

The security group head said to me, "Your wife is more anxious than you are. You're acting like someone without a care in the world."

Within five minutes, Ah Yan returned. She held a stationery case in her hand. Yang Deshun followed behind her. The old man had most likely been dragged out of bed. The buttons on his tunic were not buttoned up properly, his eyes were pasty with sleep, and as he opened his mouth like a fish to catch his breath after running to our house, we could all smell how foul his breath was.

Ah Yan had already explained the situation to him along the way. Yang Deshun didn't say much, but immediately prepared his pen and ink. There was no telling how many documents of this sort Yang Deshun had written in his lifetime. It was nothing more than a matter of who, at a specific time and place, made a contract with whom, on the basis of which, never to regret, and so on. Yang Deshun accomplished it in one try.

When we gave it to the security group head, he just shook his head. He said, "Do it again and change the date. If you put today's date, it'll be too obvious. Put some day last year."

Yang Deshun said, "The men of both households are gone. Whose fingerprints do we use?"

The security group head said, "The women will stand in. No one will look that closely."

Our mothers pressed their thumbs against the paper with all the force of their gratitude. Ah Yan and I put our own thumbprints beneath theirs.

When the security group head finally left, we all breathed a sigh of relief. Thinking of something, Ah Yan's mother pulled my mother aside.

"When her father was still alive, our families had discussed this, but we didn't negotiate in detail. Have you asked Huwa what his intentions are?" I heard her ask quietly.

My mother hesitated a moment, then said, "His father was going to ask him, but didn't have the chance."

Ah Yan's mother glanced at me and said, "I don't know whether Huwa likes our Ah Yan."

My mother said urgently, "Don't worry. Everyone knows he cares more for Ah Yan than anyone else."

At breakfast, we brooded on these matters silently. No one even looked up. We all kept our heads bent over our bowls, hardly tasting the food as we ate. In the urgency of the moment, no one had taken the time to really think about it. Now that the emergency had passed, we realized some things couldn't be rushed, and if they were, the flavor would be changed.

After we'd eaten, Ah Yan said, "Huwa, can you help me get some more bamboo baskets? Some of them were damp after yesterday's rain, and the water will add weight."

I went, and Ah Yan followed.

Checking that no one was around, she whispered, "When the harvest is over, I'll row the sampan and send you part of the way, then you can go catch up with your classmates."

Looking at her blankly, I said, "Ah Yan, do you understand the consequences of us putting our thumbprints on those forms?"

She shook her head.

"No one will want to marry you in the future. Do you understand?" I said.

She looked at me and said, "You don't want to marry me?"

I sighed deeply, and said, "Did you hear what the security group head said? The casualties on the front line are very bad. Eight or nine of every ten people who are sent don't come back."

She twisted her lips. I thought she was going to cry. I didn't expect her to simply grunt in acknowledgment and say, "If you don't come back, then it's fine. I'll just stay with my mother."

After a moment, she added, "And your mother."

My throat tightened. I hadn't imagined it would not be her crying, but me. "OK, OK," she said. "Don't be sad. Let's get to work."

There was a tea stem stuck in her hair from the previous night. Haltingly, I reached and pulled it out.

"Silly girl, you really are something," I mumbled.

~

Ah Yan tied down the sampan and told our mothers to go on ahead. She checked the stern again and found the tea bowl still there, upside down. No one seemed to have moved it. That was how she could tell. The plank below the tea bowl was loose, hiding a hole, and in the hole was hidden a bundle wrapped in tarpaulin. Over the past few days, with the excuse of washing her feet and tea baskets, she had brought everything I needed for my journey, including the knife I'd buried, onto the sampan. My plan had a number of small problems, and she'd managed to smooth them all out, tying up the loose ends in a tidy little knot. This knot was clutched in her palm, waiting for her to untie it. Today was the seventh day after our fathers' deaths. After burning incense, making the offering at their grave, and eating lunch, she would say she needed to go to the river to wash clothes, and I would say I had to go to the tea garden to gather some tools. Then we would meet at the river, and she would take me in the sampan to begin my journey.

The period between Qingming and the Grain Rain was the worst season of the year. The weather was rarely clear, but on this day, not only was it not raining, there wasn't even any wind. The river was so tranquil, we couldn't see a single ripple. In such conditions, it only took an hour or so to reach the market in Wu Village by sampan. Ah Yan could definitely get back before dark, and I could walk from Wu Village to Zhuji, saving myself a lot of time by avoiding the mountain path.

I left my copy of *Evolution and Ethics* with Ah Yan. "While I'm gone, if you get a chance to study, you can learn a few more words. If I come back, I'll help you understand this book. If I don't come back, then keep it in remembrance of me."

She turned away, hiding her face.

"I don't have anything for you," she said.

Later I found out she did have something for me. Her gift was a pair of shoes. She had made them for her father during the first month of the lunar year. They had strong cloth soles and a thick blue twilled satin insole, and they were strong as a copper coin, but unfortunately, her father was gone before he had a chance to wear them. By glancing at a pair of shoes I had taken off, without measuring, she knew I'd be able to wear the pair her father had never gotten to try. She'd spent two nights embroidering them with flowers. They were not ordinary flowers either, but twin lotuses on one stalk, one pink and one white, cheek-to-cheek. She didn't want to embroider these flowers on the outside, for fear they would make me a laughingstock, so she stitched them on the inside. It was more than a decade later that I first saw them. They were well preserved inside the tarpaulin bundle, but ultimately couldn't withstand the passage of time. By the time I got to them, they were covered with mildew. When I saw the two flowers embroidered on them, I understood her intentions when she stitched them. She hadn't had the courage to give me those shoes then, only daring to put them among my belongings so that I would find them along my journey. If I wore these shoes, my feet would touch the flowers. Such solid shoes would carry me very far. No matter how long the journey, the flowers would stay with me all the way. When I finally wore those shoes, I was already in my coffin. But of course, that's later in the story.

After we had settled on a plan for my departure, Ah Yan had changed. With each casual glance or exchange of words, she would blush. Our mothers assumed it was shyness about our changed relationship, but I knew it was more than that. Ah Yan was keeping my secret. She was a part of my plan, and it was exciting. The more time passed, the larger the secret grew, becoming almost too big for her to contain. She felt she would burst into pieces as it swelled inside her. She couldn't wait to tell the birds in the trees, the clouds floating overhead, or the oleanders bursting with buds, but she couldn't say anything. Sometimes when she saw fellow villagers in passing, she couldn't help but wonder what secrets they might be keeping too. I asked her if she was afraid our mothers would be angry with her when they learned that she'd kept this secret. She said, "I'm not worried. If a person goes through life without secrets, what's she living for?"

We climbed the mountain road to the new grave. Someone had been there before us to make their offerings. A wisp of smoke lingered. From a distance, Ah Yan thought that the color of the grave was strange, like a cloud was casting a shadow over it. Looking up, she saw that the sky was like a piece of blue cloth pulled taut. As we grew closer, we noticed something was also strange about the soil: it was black. The soil forming the mound of the grave looked like it had been loosened and was trembling slightly in the wind, but there was no wind. Ah Yan drew her face close, and in an instant, every hair on her body stood up. What had made the ground change colors was ants.

Thousands? Tens of thousands? Tens of millions? Ah Yan wasn't sure if there was a number bigger than ten million. She didn't know the word for billions. She only thought that all the ants in the world had crawled onto the grave. She couldn't see a single bit of bare soil. They were all pressed together, shoulder-to-shoulder, hand-in-hand, completely covering the grave. They formed a great black mass, moving in unison without beginning or end, because they moved in a circle. Round and round, nonstop, as if they would eventually lift the grave and move it to another place.

"Your fathers are not resigned to their deaths," Ah Yan's mother said. Her legs grew weak, and she dropped to the ground.

Ah Yan lit a joss stick and knelt before the grave. "Pa, Uncle, you came to a terrible death, and we know you feel injustice in your hearts."

Ah Yan suddenly straightened up and said to me, "Huwa, tell them you'll get revenge for them. Tell them, now."

Her eyes drilled into mine.

I said, "If I don't get revenge for you, I'm not a man."

"Pa, Uncle, Huwa has made an oath to you. If you believe him, tell the ants to go away," she said.

The ants continued to swarm on the grave. I held a joss stick in hand, closed my eyes, and knelt on the ground. I had lots to say, but I couldn't say it. *Pa, this may be the last incense your son burns for you,* I said in my mind. Ah Yan knelt beside me, her face to the ground. Her shoulders trembled beneath her blouse, as if insects crawled there too. She was also talking, talking to her heaven. I did not know if her heaven and mine were the same, but I knew my name was in her prayers. *Pa, keep your son safe on his journey. Even if I lose an arm or leg, please let me come home. When I come back, I'll visit your grave. And I'll give you grandchildren,* I said silently.

"Pa, if you can hear me, please make the ants go away."

When I opened my eyes, I saw that the grave was still blanketed in black. The sun was shining, the river was there, the trees were there, and the ants were there.

"Pa, do you have a message for me?" I was suddenly startled. A chill climbed my spine, and I shivered.

My mother slapped her forehead and said, "I'm so stupid. I left the wine at home. Your father loves wine. He's blaming me."

She asked me to take her home to get the wine. On the way back, my mother's head suddenly started hurting, and she started babbling. She said, "Someone is pounding my head with a hammer. The hammer's crashing down, and stars are bursting out, and they're blood-red." My mother had always been hardy. She'd never had this sort of pain before, so I assumed she was just exhausted. This was our busiest tea season, and it had taken a lot out of everyone. I told her to rest at home. After I brought Ah Yan and her mother back from the mountain, I would get her a healer. Thinking back on it now, I can see that my father and Ah Yan's father were shouting from the grave, trying to tell us something. Unfortunately, my mother was the only one who understood. That day, she stayed home.

When I had gotten the wine, I rowed back to the grave. The sun had risen above the fork in the trees, and morning was turning to midday. The sun washed everything white, bleaching the sky, water, and trees to almost the same color. Just then, I saw a strange green movement on the slopes. The green seemed to have rolled in dirt and was so dirty, it was almost yellow. It seemed to have emerged from the ground suddenly. It had no legs, and I heard nothing, but saw it shifting back and forth, floating in the bushes. There were sticks standing up among the green. Oh! They weren't sticks. Sticks wouldn't be so sharp or bright. The things that looked like sticks but weren't were shining in the midday sun, emitting flashes of light, hurting my eyes. After a moment, I realized that they were bayonets.

God! They were coming! Here they were, actually coming to our village.

My analysis of the terrain and offensive and defensive strategies wasn't wrong. But I missed two crucial factors. First, there was no garrison defense here, so our door was wide open. Second, my understanding of the terrain matched that of the Japanese. They had sent a detachment to explore the area and see if they could build a secure supply warehouse nearby.

I wanted to duck out of sight, but it was too late. They'd already seen me.

I heard a whizzing sound, and then my shoulder went numb.

After that, I heard vague laughter.

Then I saw the oar in my hand change color. It took some time before I realized it was my blood.

"Ah Yan, run . . ."

That was my last clear thought before I passed out. I drifted some distance on the sampan, fifty or sixty li, maybe even seventy or eighty. Just before dark, a woman washing clothes in the river saw me and pulled me ashore. I was unconscious for a week due to blood loss. When I could finally move, a month had passed.

Pastor Billy should have a clearer idea of what happened next.

Pastor Billy: Okamura Yasuji's Wolf

This story is difficult, both telling it and hearing it. Each word claws its way from the narrator's heart, through the throat, over the tongue, into the listeners' ears, and along the auditory nerve. When it finally reaches the brain, how much flesh will it have torn along the way, and how many bloody wounds will it leave behind? But we can't skip this story. Haven't we waited seventy years for this reunion just so we could recall those years filled with the flames of war? The girl, she's in the foreground, center, and background of this story, so no matter what direction we take, we can't escape her.

This happened seventy-two years ago. Fortunately, I didn't tell this story seventy-two years ago, or fifty-two, or even thirty-two. If I had, it would have brought great rage, sorrow, and compassion. Time is a miraculous thing. It can wear down the thorns of emotion, gradually eroding them to dust, and from this dust, a new sprout grows. That sprout is the power of life. Telling this story now, those old emotions are still present, but they are just paving the way. Now, what rises in my heart and moves me is a silent emotion. Isn't that girl the sprout? The weight of a mountain pressed down upon her, but she could still poke the tip of a living shoot up from under the rocks. Never mind that the sprout is disproportionately small compared to the mountain. You might ask, Did it really take seventy-two years for this tiny sprout to emerge? Then how many centuries will it take to grow into a tree? But let me tell you, this sprout will live for hundreds of thousands of centuries.

Liu Zhaohu, in your story, her name is Yao Guiyan, and she goes by Ah Yan, meaning "swallow." Ian, in your story, she is Wende, which to you meant "wind." In my story, she is Stella. Stella means "star," and it's the name I asked God to give her. *My God, please give her a star, even if it is the smallest one,* I said to God. *And use this star to guide her, so that she will not be lost.* God granted my request. He gave a star, but not to her. I gradually realized he'd given the star to me. She was my star. She lit my path, showing me the way. I was the one who was lost. Ah Yan, Wende, Stella. Swallow, Wind, Star. Those were her three names, or rather, three sides of her person. If you separated them, they were three entirely different parts, and it's hard to imagine that they were all of one body. But together, you could hardly see the seams between them. They blended as naturally as water and milk.

Even if you were given a thousand or ten thousand chances, you could never imagine the first time I met Stella. It transcended the boundaries of human imagination. Such cruel scenes are generally seen only in the animal world.

It was a spring morning seventy-two years ago. The Qingming Festival had just passed, and it was warm. If I remember correctly, that day was the most beautiful day of the year. The color of the sky had never been seen before or ever again. Everything in nature seemed to be singing. The sun sang of its power to nourish all things, the mountains and plains sang of the cleansing verdure brought by the rains, the trees sang their delight in the blossoming of their branches, and the flowers sang of desire stoked by the wings of bees and butterflies. Who would have thought when there were thousands of ordinary days to choose from, brutality would visit on a day of such rare beauty? On that day, I finally grasped something I had read, but never understood. I caught the meaning of T. S. Eliot's incomprehensible poem, "The Waste Land."

> *April is the cruelest month, breeding*
> *Lilacs out of dead land . . .*

That day, I was going to visit an herbalist in another village. I had several such friends in this area. "Herbalist" is something of a formal name. He was more rightly known as a witch doctor. I was not visiting him to preach the Gospel (God forgive me), because people like him had heads of granite, making it hard even for God to find the smallest crack leading in. I was visiting him to ask about the growing environment of a certain type of herb and how it could be distinguished from other similar plants. Herbalists are often reluctant to pass along such advanced knowledge to others, especially their peers, but I had a way in. My stepping-stone was very simple: a few pieces of American candy or a printed handkerchief like those that women in the city loved. Having lived in the area for years, I knew that the people most willing to open the door to me were children and women. I wanted to get to know these people because my own medical supplies were dwindling. The medical supplies that had required six porters to carry when I'd disembarked in Shanghai had been used up over the years. Though my parent organization in America used various channels to transport a new batch of donated medicines to me each year, the friends I had in the area also helped me source medicines that were in short supply on the black market, replenishing my stores. Even so, relative to the massive demand, this supply was merely a drop in the bucket, so I saved the limited Western medicines to use in emergencies. For patients with colds or bumps and bruises, I used herbs and their variants, such as powders, ointments, and so forth. As taught in the book of Matthew, I learned to be "as shrewd as a serpent" over the years.

It was about forty-five li from my place to the village I was visiting. Such distances were not very far but also not close. People had a variety of ways to travel, according to the level of wealth—sedan, by horse or mule, wheelbarrow, walking, and so on. I had a form of transportation that was rare in the area: a bicycle. It had been left to me by a missionary who was returning home. I couldn't accurately discern its age or origin, and the only silent thing about it was the bell. It had no brakes, a few spokes were broken, and the tires had been patched on numerous occasions with a variety of innovative materials. Even so, it was the most efficient and convenient means of transportation on these rural trails. I had tended to many emergencies on that bike.

I had grown tired as I approached my destination, so I stopped the bike, found a rock to sit on, and took a drink of the tea I'd brought from home. A breeze started to blow, gradually drying my sweat so that the fabric no longer clung to my back. The grass on the side of the road bent in the wind. It rose and fell, sounding like the babble of running water. I suddenly noticed that a large patch of grass beside me was flattened. It wasn't a mule's hoofprint or the footprint of a person hurrying by. Neither human nor animal feet could have trampled such a large area. It looked as if a heavy object had been dragged over the ground. As I was trying to understand what could have made it, I heard a rustling noise. Turning, I saw a person stand up in a shallow ditch behind me, crying out. The light was behind her, throwing her face into shadow, but I could see it was a woman. She was stooping over, holding something. She tried to move toward me, stumbled, then stopped, her body swaying. It looked like she was about to fall. I put down the tea and ran toward her. When she saw me, she was stunned. I guessed that in the sunlight, she could tell that my eyes were blue, that I was a foreigner. After a moment's hesitation, her knees buckled, and she knelt involuntarily. As she fell, she leaned forward, and her arms stretched slightly forward, as if showing me the thing she held in her hands. I finally realized what it was. It looked like a loosely coiled snake. Half of it was stuck in her belly, and the other half scattered over her palms. It was red and glistening faintly purple, with uneven lines snaking over it.

God! It was intestines. She was holding her own intestines.

I noticed that she was missing three fingers, and there was a long gash across her belly. The black blouse she wore was stiff with dried blood. Her neck jerked strenuously, as if she were indicating something farther up on the slope, and her lips twitched for a moment. She said, "My . . . daughter . . ." Then she fell like a sack. I slapped her cheeks, hoping to keep her alert, but the blue sky and mountains reflected in her eyes had become murky. I rushed to get the medicine box tied to the back of my bicycle. It was an automatic response, despite the fact that I had nothing in the box that could save her. By the time I got back, she had no pulse. Of course, she'd actually died much earlier. She was just holding on to her final breath until she saw me.

Recalling her final words, I ran in the direction she'd indicated. On the slope only twenty paces away, there was a bundle of white like a rock protruding from the grass. Approaching, I saw that it was a white blouse—or more accurately, it was the tattered remains of a blouse. Beneath it, a body lay in a huddle. I turned it over. It was a young girl, and she was unconscious. She looked about twelve, maybe a little older. She was almost completely naked. There were no visible injuries to her, but there was sticky, wet blood on her thighs. It was still flowing. Pulling her legs apart, I found a thick wooden stick jammed into her, stained purple with blood.

Later, when I recalled that scene, I could never quite conjure the emotions I felt at the time. I could only recall the pain. It stands to reason that the pain started in the eyes, then perhaps moved to the heart and belly. But at the time, my eyes, heart, and belly were all numb. It was only my ears that hurt. It seemed that ten thousand planes flew into my ears all at once. A wild roar hijacked my ability to think, and my mind was nothing but a blank. I just kept repeating a single word: "animals."

If this girl didn't get immediate debridement and treatment, she would die from blood loss or infection. But I didn't have the necessary equipment in my box. I would have to go home right away. The rational doctor inside me overcame the shocked pastor. I calmed down, took off my tunic, and twisted it into a cord. I lifted the girl and tied her across the handlebars of my bicycle with the makeshift rope. As I rode, I leaned forward as much as possible, hiding the girl's naked body. If anyone had seen this foreigner dressed in an unseasonably light undershirt riding wildly against the wind with his back hunched over the handlebars, they would have thought me a madman. But I didn't care. Halfway home, I remembered the dead woman I'd left in the ditch, but there was nothing more I could do for her. I prayed some good Samaritan would come along, like the gentile in the Bible who stopped to help the Jew in trouble. A dead person's dignity was never as important as a living life.

My bike caused me no trouble that day, and I made the journey faster than usual. When I dismounted from the bicycle, I saw blood on the seat. It was my blood. I hadn't even noticed that my thighs had been rubbed raw as I rode. That old bike, whose age and origin I could not determine, performed great military acts in that time of war. If it were a soldier, or even a dog, it would have been given a distinguished medal. But it was just a bike. Still, if I had the right to confer honors, the medal I would give it wouldn't have anything to do with military efforts during war. In all its service, I'm most proud of how it performed in saving Stella's life that day. Of course, she wasn't yet called by that name then.

I took the girl into my house, put her on my bed, and immediately began debridement. I had no anesthetic, so I could only give her a sedative. I tried to be gentle, but she was still woken by pain in the middle of the procedure. She screamed and tried to get up, but with no strength left, she just leaned against the wall. It wasn't horror that came into her eyes when she saw me. That terror came later. It was a look of uncertainty about where she was.

"Don't be afraid. I'm a doctor. American," I said as gently as possible. "You've been injured, and I'm trying to treat you."

My words seemed to remind her of the nightmare she had endured not long before. She was suddenly aware of her nakedness. She wrapped her arms around her chest and tried to curl her body up, but couldn't cover her whole body. Her sense of shame made her start shaking. I put my coat over her, and she calmed down a little, then recalled a matter of urgency.

"My mother. Where's my mother?" she asked with a hoarse whisper.

I hesitated. I couldn't be sure how much she'd seen. Finally, I settled on a vague lie.

"She's home already. Don't worry."

Her mouth twitched, like she was trying to smile but didn't have the strength. She believed me. This was the first and only lie I ever told her. I would tell her the truth, but not then. I wanted to wait until she had recovered enough resilience to bear such grievous news. Though she was calmer, she wouldn't cooperate. She refused to allow me to unwrap the coat covering her body. I couldn't help but be amazed that one so badly injured still had such willpower.

I told her, "Your injury is serious. If we don't deal with it as soon as possible, it will cause an infection."

She looked at me blankly, and I realized she didn't understand the word "infection," so I said, "It will become inflamed." She still didn't understand. I tried "rot and decay," and she finally understood. I watched in her eyes as two things battled in her mind. One was shame, and the other was putrefaction. Finally, shame won out, and her hands clasped the corner of the coat tightly.

"Child, do you understand that if I don't treat it quickly, you could die?" I said.

A trace of horror flashed across her eyes. But it was too small. It was just a spark and was quickly snuffed out by shame. She clutched the coat even tighter.

"If you don't let me treat you, later you might not be able"—I chewed over the end of the sentence in my mind, changing versions several times, then finally settled—"to have little ones."

Saying such a thing to such a young girl felt cruel, but it was the only thing I could try now. In a rural, reclusive village, the threat of barrenness could be worse than death. I saw that the fingers clutching the coat moved a little. I took a handkerchief from my pocket and covered her eyes.

"Imagine we're in a dark forest, too dark for either of us to see. You're not wearing clothes, and neither am I. You can't see me, and I can't see you. We each can't even see ourselves. OK?"

She finally lay back, allowing me to remove the coat. The debridement was very painful, and I knew she wanted to scream, but shame sealed her lips. She clamped her mouth shut tightly. The impression her teeth made in her lips deepened, and her lips turned blue, while her teeth turned red, covered in blood. I put a towel into her mouth so she could bite it. Finally she screamed, allowing the towel to absorb the sharp edges of her voice, leaving only a few blurred chirps. Even though I feared infection, I didn't want to give her antibiotics. Instead, I fed her rice porridge and chicken soup to restore the nutrients she needed. I hoped she carried enough antibodies in her young body to battle the bacteria without assistance. But I lost. Her wound became infected. She came down with a high fever and slept a great deal, muttering a string of words that I couldn't understand. The only word I caught was "Ma," and something about a brother whose name was indistinct. I gave her water and wiped her body with alcohol, using well water to make a cold compress, but none of the cooling methods worked. Finally, I had no choice but to give her the last of my antibiotics. She probably never had any Western medicine before—perhaps no medicine of any kind—so she was especially sensitive to it.

The next morning when I came to check on her, in the guest room I kept for traveling missionaries, she was awake and sitting at the foot of the bed. Her back was toward me, and she was looking out the window at the branches full of oleander blossoms. She had no clothes, so she wore one of my old tunics, with the sleeves rolled up. If she'd stood up, it would've completely covered her feet. I asked my cook, a local Christian woman I'd hired, to see if there were any suitable old clothes for the girl in her house. I told the cook what had happened to the girl because I knew she could keep the secret. Luckily, no one in Yuehu knew her. Not only could she recover quietly, but she could also avoid anyone finding out what happened. I knew from my experience that nothing could cleanse the shame of a girl who met such a disaster, save death.

I felt her forehead, then said, "Child, your fever has subsided. That's very good."

She pulled back and trembled involuntarily. For a long time after that, whenever someone came near her, she would tremble.

"You can call me Pastor Mai or Pastor Billy," I told her.

I spoke carefully, quietly, as if she were made of porcelain and might break at the slightest touch. She didn't speak, but just nodded.

"What about you? I don't know your name," I said.

She hesitated for a long time, as if that were a difficult test question.

"My name is San . . . Sanmei," she said timidly, after a long pause.

A generic name, meaning "third girl." She was probably not used to lying. The way she kept blinking showed her discomfort. I could tell this wasn't her real name. Why didn't she want to tell me her real name? In that name, there must have been a number of relatives and family members or perhaps a matchmaker. She didn't want me to get involved with those relations, because I knew the secret they must never know. It was only then that I really saw her face. She was a pretty girl, though her eyes seemed slightly mismatched to her face. After a while, I realized it was because she had the face of a teenager but the eyes of an adult who'd seen the world. I couldn't look directly at such sad eyes.

In the little wooden box I always had with me, there was a thick book of prayers. It held prayers for weddings, funerals, christenings, baptisms, confirmations, graduations, loss of job, illnesses, loss of loved ones, and even the loss of a pet. But I couldn't find a word in God's whole lexicon to comfort a girl who'd lost her innocence at a time when she did not even know what it meant. I racked my brain, only to see just how impoverished my diction was.

"Your home? Where do you live?" I asked.

There was hesitation on her face, like when I'd asked her name. Then she said, "Wu Ao."

Wu Ao was the village I'd been going to visit that day, where the herbalist lived. I had found her very near it, so I couldn't tell whether she'd told me the truth or not. I wanted to say her name, but I couldn't call her Sanmei. That wasn't really her, and it wasn't really me.

"Stella. Can I call you Stella? While you're here, at least?" I said suddenly.

She looked at me, puzzled.

"Stella means 'star,'" I explained. "When you go out alone in the dark, you can look at the stars, and you won't be afraid. You will always find your way home."

A light flashed across her face, and the teenage girl suddenly rushed back into her eyes. But it was short-lived, disappearing in an instant. Perhaps my words prompted another thought in her. She was silent for a moment, then said, "Pastor Billy, I want to go home."

I sighed and said, "Not now, child. You're too weak. You need to eat and rest. When you have recovered, I'll take you home."

I got the chicken stew my cook had made that morning. She finished it, but didn't put down the bowl. With lowered eyelids, she asked, "Pastor Billy, do you have any rice? Half a bowl will do."

I remembered that she'd only had fluids for the past two days. She must have been famished. I went to the kitchen and found leftover rice, soaked it in boiling water, and added some pickled radishes. She ate very quickly. As soon as her chopsticks touched the bottom of the bowl, she started to feel embarrassed. Her mind was weighed down by an immense mountain, but her stomach was brazen. Her mind now cursed the brazenness of her belly.

Young. She was still so young. A young life flows like a river, and even cut by ten thousand blades, it can always close the cuts over seamlessly.

"There's more in the kitchen." Taking her empty bowl, I got her more rice.

In this way, Stella, that little star, came to live with me. When she could walk on her own, I let her help in the kitchen, washing vegetables and picking beans, or mend some old clothes, mostly because I was afraid she would be bored. Her activities were confined to her room, the kitchen, and the backyard. I kept my eye on her and never allowed her to set foot beyond the garden, because I was afraid she would provoke the villagers' curiosity and they would start asking about her.

She was diligent in her work. The cook was satisfied with her, though she rarely spoke to the cook. Even with me, her conversation was limited to polite daily greetings. When she spoke to me, she hung her head down and rarely looked at me, as if there were something hiding inside the tip of her shoe or her sleeve. I knew there was a fragile secret between us, and that the slightest hint of indifference would shatter that secret, and she would fall into a deep abyss, shattering herself. For this reason, I always observed that invisible boundary and stepped with great care.

One day, Stella saw me copying hymns. She walked in, her first time coming into my room on her own initiative. I was not proficient in Chinese calligraphy and was clumsy with the brush and paper. She stood quietly behind me for a while, then asked shyly, "Pastor Billy, can I copy it for you?"

Surprised, I asked, "You went to school?"

She said, "I went for a little, then my brother taught me."

I asked, "Is your brother named Hu or something like that?"

It was her turn to be surprised. She said, "How do you know?"

I said, "You called for him when you had a fever."

She blushed all the way to her neck. That blush changed her face, as if moisture had suddenly come to a dry land. In that moment, Stella was beautiful. I stared at her blankly and felt a tug inside me. *God, you finally let me see the face she should have.*

"Your brother, where is he now?"

As soon as I asked, I knew I'd been too blunt. I had crossed a dangerous line, yet again ruining the possibility for real conversation. It seemed that every time I should retreat, I took a devastating step forward instead. Sure enough, the blush faded, just as suddenly as it had come. In its place was a film of pale sadness.

"I don't know," she said.

Saying nothing more, I gave her my seat. From her posture, I could see she wasn't used to using a brush, but her wrist was stable and strong. She clearly didn't know all the words, and I could tell which ones were new by her hesitation and how she kept checking the original as she followed the shape of each stroke. As Stella wrote, she seemed to become a different person. She put all her concentration into her brush, so that even her breathing became dignified. In that moment, there was no war, no death, no pain. At that moment, she wasn't even in the world.

My observations were affirmed repeatedly in the following days. Although there were countless places in our conversations that were off limits and I could stumble into an abyss at any time, there was also a place that was always safe, without rifts or barriers. No matter how far I traveled in that region, I would never violate any boundaries. That safe place was her thirst for knowledge.

One day she copied Psalm 23:

> *The Lord is my shepherd; I shall not want.*
> *He maketh me to lie down in green pastures;*
> *he leadeth me beside the still waters.*
> *He restoreth my soul;*
> *he leadeth me in the paths of righteousness for his name's sake.*

Yea, though I walk through the valley of the shadow of death,
I will fear no evil, for thou art with me;
thy rod and thy staff they comfort me.
Thou preparest a table before me in the presence of mine
enemies;
thou anointest my head with oil; my cup runneth over.
Surely goodness and mercy shall follow me all the days of my
life;
and I will dwell in the house of the Lord forever.

When she had copied it, she asked me to read it to her. After I read it, I asked, "Do you understand?"

She thought for a moment, then said, "It says for people to be courageous?"

"You know God?" I asked in surprise.

She nodded and said, "He's the Western bodhisattva."

"God is not a bodhisattva," I said. "There are many bodhisattvas, but only one God."

She replied, "I understand. Your God is bigger than the bodhisattvas, so he controls them."

I didn't know whether to laugh or cry.

"God and the bodhisattvas are useless," she said. "They only control good people, not bad people."

A small dagger pricked my heart. I wanted to tell her, *That's exactly what I thought when I saw you lying in the grass that day.*

"Stella, sometimes I can't understand God either." I sighed. "God doesn't protect you from being harmed, and he doesn't cure all diseases, and he doesn't guarantee you a peaceful life."

Her eyes widened and, confused, she asked, "Then why do you believe in him?"

"He may not bring peace into the entire world, but he can bring peace into your heart, if you believe in him," I said.

For a long time, she sat silently staring at the psalm she had copied.

"Pastor Billy, can I borrow this piece of paper that gives people courage?" she whispered.

"You can have it. When you are afraid, read it, and you'll feel safe," I said.

She blew the paper to dry the still-wet ink, then carefully rolled it up and put it inside her cloak at her bosom. She didn't, neither then nor later, truly convert to Christ, but I always felt she was closer to God than I was. She had heavenly eyes, capable of leaping over the barriers of text and ideas and entering into the heart of faith.

She had finally accepted my role as doctor and no longer resisted my examining her. Her wounds had healed well. By this time, her only complaint was that the wound was itchy, and she had some intermittent pain on the right side of her lower back. The itchiness was a sign of healing, so I wasn't worried about it, but I couldn't find the cause for the pain in her lower back. I asked her to give me a detailed description of the feeling.

"It's like someone is grabbing my flesh with their fingers, and no matter what, they won't let go," she said.

I suddenly remembered the moment Stella's mother had asked me for help. As if struck by lightning, it hit me. She had held on to her daughter with an iron will, so tight she lost three of her fingers. She had imparted some of her own life to her daughter. This was the last memory she had given her daughter. I didn't tell Stella the truth.

"It's nothing. It will be fine in a few days," I said.

She stayed with me for about a month. One morning I saw her standing in the yard. It had rained the night before, darkening the rattan on the stone. It was still early, and the sun had the thick greasiness of oil paint. The jasmine was in bloom, filling the air with its delicate scent. Stella stood on a rock, her hands cupped to catch water dripping from the eaves. When she had collected a handful, she tossed it into the air, filling the sky with golden beads. I noticed she was getting plumper, and the lower portion of her blouse had begun to show the faint contours of her body. Everything would eventually pass. I gave thanks secretly in my heart. She would soon be a young woman, and when she thought back on this time, she would say, "Oh, that was just a nightmare." Perhaps she wouldn't think of this experience at all. She would pluck it out like a weed, completely removing the experience from her memory. At breakfast that morning, I asked if she wanted to go home. She was startled. She had asked several times to go home, but I had refused until she was fully recovered. Now that the time had come, I saw her hesitation.

"I'll go with you and find a good way to explain it to your family," I said after a moment.

In fact, I had no idea what explanation I could come up with. A young girl away from home for a month, then escorted back by a foreigner. Without white-washing or explanation, it was a matter that would require a lifetime to clarify.

Her face suddenly changed, and she shook her head. "No," she said, "what-ever you do, you can't do that."

"All right," I said, "then I'll accompany you to the entrance to your village."

She didn't refuse. She knew that in this time of turbulence, she couldn't go alone, especially now, with what she had been through.

~

Stella was amazed by the bicycle. She sat behind me, and as soon as I started, she screamed and grabbed my waist tightly. I had never heard her so expres-sive, and it brought a faint joy to my heart. I saw the taut nerves gradually relax. Unfortunately, this didn't last long. Stella immediately realized that she was being silly and, embarrassed, restrained herself. I began to feel her weight on the back, and we fell silent, lost in our own thoughts. I could guess what was on her mind, but she didn't know what was in mine. I owed her the truth about her mother. All this time, I'd been wondering how to tell her. The truth was a knife. I couldn't bear to see her suffer a sudden shock the moment she got home, so I had to help her skin grow thicker along the way. Halfway there, I said I was thirsty and stopped the bicycle. As I poured myself some water, she suddenly fell to her knees before me, pressing her head to the ground as she kowtowed three times.

"Pastor Billy, you are my lifesaving bodhisattva. I should not lie to you. I don't live in Wu Ao. My home is separated from Wu Ao by the river. I have to take a sampan across."

I hurried to pull her up, but she refused as strongly as if her life depended on it. "And, my name is not Sanmei. That's my mother's name. My name is Ah Yan—like the swallow that flies in the sky."

I sighed softly.

"No matter what you're called at home, you're Stella with me," I said.

She stood up, as if she had put down a heavy burden. But I knew she had another burden—the one I was about to give her. I drank slowly, weighing the words carefully. The truth was very heavy, and I had to slowly clear a path for it.

"Stella, that day, did you see how the Japanese treated . . . your mother?" I asked, testing the ground.

She shook her head. "She was holding on to me tightly. I didn't see, but I heard her screaming. Then they kicked her into a ditch."

"Do you know what happened after that?"

She raised her head and glanced at me. The corner of her mouth twitched.

"She died," she said evenly.

I was shocked.

"How long have you known?" I asked.

"You told me my mother had been sent home, but later, you asked me where my home was. I knew you had lied to me."

My God. A lie I fabricated couldn't even withstand the casual glance of a young girl.

"You . . . miss her?"

I asked it coldly, even callously. Secretly, I wanted her to cry on my shoulder. Tears wouldn't comfort her, but they would comfort me. But she didn't weep. After the first day, I never saw her shed a single tear.

"When I was small, my mother told me that every star in the sky was once a person on the ground. When a person dies, they are transported from the ground to the sky. You called me Stella and said it meant 'star.' I knew that this was a message from my mother."

I fought my own tears. This girl's bravery broke my heart. Much later, I realized that, besides the fact that it was God's gift to her, there was another reason for Stella's courage. She had a pillar in her heart, and even if the sky fell and crushed the earth to dust, as long as that pillar remained, Stella would survive. That pillar was Liu Zhaohu. Stella's real collapse came when she learned that that pillar had toppled.

I took her little hand in mine. "Stella, let's make an oath before God. From today onward, we will tell each other the truth, OK?"

She nodded.

We continued our journey, the bicycle sending up a trail of flying dust. Neither of us knew, while we were racking our brains to come up with an explanation for her long absence, that news of what had happened had long ago reached Sishiyi Bu. There had been two other women visiting a grave near them when the Japanese arrived that day. They hid behind a large tree, not daring to move, and saw everything. Only after the Japanese left did they dare come down the mountain to get men from the village to come to the women's rescue. When the rescuers arrived, they only found Stella's mother's body, because I had already rescued Stella. The tragedy of that day, with all its details, had become a public secret, known to every household in the village, once the women's whispers had made their rounds.

When we finally arrived at Wu Ao, I helped Stella into a sampan and watched her row to the opposite bank. She made her way up a long stone path. Halfway up, she turned and waved. I've cursed that day for the rest of my life. I wish it could be permanently torn from history. If I'd had a prophet's eyes and foreseen what was going to happen, I never would've let Stella go.

I can't forgive myself, not even now.

~

After Stella left, I went about as usual, preaching, practicing medicine, helping others, and doing things a rural pastor does. But when I was idle, I would think of Stella—of how she wrinkled her nose as she copied the hymnal, how she raised her hands to catch water from the eaves, or how she lowered her head in silence as she picked beans. Several times, I thought of visiting, but knowing the commotion that would arise in the village if a foreigner appeared at her door, I did not. One night I dreamed of her. She looked down at me with wide eyes, filled with unspeakable sadness. I reached out to take hold of her, only to find she had no hands. She had no hands, nor a body, nor even a head. It was just her eyes, floating alone in the air. I woke with a start, soaked in a cold sweat. I decided I would visit her just once, no matter what, even if just to catch a glimpse of her.

The next day, I rode my bicycle to Wu Ao and crossed the river by sampan, reaching the long stone steps. Years on the mountain paths had strengthened my legs so that riding forty or fifty li was no trouble, but that was on flat ground. Carrying the heavy bicycle up those forty-one steps was a completely different matter. When I reached the top, my bike and I were both in poor shape. I leaned it against a tree and sat to catch my breath, thinking of a way to find Stella's home without calling attention to myself. I decided to wait for a child to pass, then give them a few pieces of candy or a copper coin and have them lead me some back way to the house. Perhaps I could even get the child to bring Stella to me and avoid people's eyes altogether.

Just then I saw a group of kids shouting, chasing a child a little older than they were. The pursued child ran like a frightened rabbit, his whole body trembling, his feet barely touching the ground. Unable to catch him, the group of children began to hurl stones at him. He dodged left, then feinted right, but still couldn't escape. His back and shoulders were hit a few times, and the pain made him huddle into himself. His speed was noticeably reduced, but he didn't stop. Covering his head, he continued to stumble along, but his steps were erratic. He tripped over a rock hidden in the grass. Losing a shoe, he fell heavily to the ground. The other children finally caught up. Jeering loudly, they surrounded him and took turns spitting on him. He sat on the ground, arms wrapped over his head, not moving or speaking. The chaos of their voices began to melt together, eventually forming a sort of chorus, shouting, "Pants! Pants! Pants!"

One child started, then they all rushed forward and tore at the child's clothes. I rushed to stop them. As soon as they saw me, they were struck dumb. It was probably because of my height—I was nearly six feet tall, practically a giant here—but also my appearance. Though I dressed like a local, I could only pass from a distance. Up close, my blue eyes betrayed me in an instant. The children in this village had likely never seen a foreigner before.

I knelt down to the child on the ground. Like many boys in this area, his head was shaved, and the stubble formed a faint blue shimmer on his head. His forehead, the corners of his mouth, and the back of his hand were bleeding, and his face and body were covered with dust and saliva. His belt had been undone, and the front of his shirt was torn open, revealing a shoulder and half of a small, underdeveloped breast. God! It was a girl! I took out my handkerchief and wiped blood from her wounds. Seeing a crumpled piece of rice paper in her hand, I took it and unfolded it. It was torn, and the writing had been smeared by mud. I could vaguely make out the words, "The Lord . . . shepherd . . . fear no evil . . ." Shocked, I looked again and realized the girl was Stella. My heart clenched into a knot. I wasn't sure I could control my voice.

"Stella, don't worry. It's Pastor Billy."

She fixed her eyes on me. They were hollow and lost. At that moment, I wasn't even sure she recognized me.

"What do you think you're doing, bullying her like this?" I shouted at the children, enraged.

They were silent. After a long moment, the leader snorted. "The Japanese have all seen it. Why can't we?"

Another child sneered and said, "My mom said she's spoiled goods. She sleeps with anyone. Her own man doesn't want her anymore."

"*Dao ni shi niang!* Get out of here!" I roared.

I knew I'd torn my vocal cords, because I could taste a trace of blood in my throat. The phrase I used was a curse in the local dialect. In Mandarin, the common language, there were some vaguely corresponding phrases, but none carried the same venom as this one. An analysis of each word led to two possible understandings, either of which implied a hope that the worst treatment be visited upon the hearer's mother or possibly all his female ancestors. Taking into account every word I had ever said, I had never used any other language so potent. I'd often begged for God's forgiveness for smaller offenses before, but this time, I wasn't the least bit repentant. The children were defeated by my words. They'd never imagined a foreigner with blue eyes could speak their dialect so easily with such intense anger. With a crash, they scattered like a frightened flock of sparrows.

"Stella, forgive me. I'm too late."

Kneeling before Stella, I wept. I couldn't see myself, but I knew I wept like a woman who'd lost her life savings to a band of thieves. She let me tie the girdle around her waist and put her shoes on her, then wipe the dirt from her clothes. The buttons on the boy's shirt she wore had been torn off, and it couldn't be closed. To cover her half-bared breast, I had to tie my handkerchief around her like a scarf. As I did, she sat motionless, neither cooperating nor resisting, and there was no trace of the strong shame that had once been so apparent in her face. A middle-aged woman ran up the slope toward us. I guessed she had run a long way, since she was panting heavily and holding her chest with one hand, as if her heart would leap into her palm at any moment.

"These evil kids with rotten lungs! Won't they ever die?" the woman cried as she ran. The former phrase she had shouted was one commonly used in the local dialect to refer to a naughty or unruly child.

Looking at me warily, she said, "Who are you?"

I said, "I'm Pastor Billy, Ah Yan's friend."

She sighed in relief, then said, "I know. You're the kind foreigner. Ah Yan said you saved her life."

"Who are you?" I asked the woman.

She hesitated, then said, "I'm Ah Yan's aunt."

"It's only been a month. How did this happen?" I asked.

She sat on the ground, lifted up the hem of her shirt, and wiped her tears.

"Everything was fine when Ah Yan came back. The villagers pointed fingers behind her back a little, but they didn't do it to her face. Fearing she would encounter the Japanese again, I shaved her head and told her to wear men's clothes. Who could have known that the one who would ruin her wouldn't be the Japanese, but Scabby?" she said.

"Who's Scabby?" I asked.

"A local layabout," she said. "When Ah Yan went to chop wood, she ran into Scabby along the way. He dragged her into the forest, and . . . and he . . . he defiled her."

I glanced at Stella and signaled the woman not to say any more. She sighed and said, "Her mind's gone. Whatever you say, she doesn't hear it."

She went on, "When she came home, she didn't tell me, but she didn't dare go out alone again. When Scabby didn't see her, he came to our house looking for her. At night, he climbed the wall, then went through the window to Ah Yan's room. Ah Yan woke me before he could do anything. After that, she didn't dare sleep alone, so she moved into my room.

"But Scabby wouldn't give up. Knowing we didn't have a man in the house, he came knocking on the door in the middle of the night. When I didn't answer, he stood outside, shouting curses, saying that the Japanese had already damaged the goods, so why protect her? I took the kitchen knife and went out to threaten him. Only then did he flee. But to really ruin her, he went to all the women in the village saying Ah Yan had slept with their men, charging a copper coin each time. He was very convincing, and those idiots believed it. So wherever Ah Yan went, they followed her, shouting curses, and told their children to chase her and beat her.

"Her mind couldn't take it. She would alternate between confusion and alertness. I kept the door locked all the time and didn't let her out. But I had an urgent matter to attend to today and forgot to lock the door when I left. She wandered out on her own."

Stella looked at us blankly. Her eyes were on us, but they seemed to pierce through us into some distant place, a delicate smile touching the corners of her mouth. The smile had nothing to do with joy or mockery, but was just a habit of the muscles. I knew her mind was lost. Walking in this world now was just a mindless body. I was torn with grief. I closed my eyes and prayed silently, *God, please give her back her heart. Please.* I felt my prayer was weak and that God was far away from me. At that moment, I did not know where he was or even where I was. *God, I know every request has a price. If it is your will, I willingly shorten my years, give my life for hers. I put my life in your hands. I only ask that you let this poor girl live well,* I prayed.

From the time I learned to speak, my parents had taught me to pray. From the time I was small, I had sought God's blessing countless times, whether it be a serious matter like saving a person's life or as trivial as getting tickets to the circus. If all the prayers in my life were strung together, they would reach the moon. And I didn't know how many God heard, because I rarely got a response. But this time, as I was impulsively praying, he heard me, and he answered. Nearly two and a half years later, when I was aboard the *Jefferson*, when I saw the shadow of Death's wings descend on the cabin wall, I finally heard and understood God's response.

"Where did her man go? Those children said her man abandoned her?" I asked.

The woman was taken aback and turned her head to look at Ah Yan. Shaking her head, she said, "What man? Ah Yan is not married."

"What about her brother? Ah Yan said she had a brother?"

She hesitated, then shook her head again. She said, "Ah Yan is an only child. She has no brother."

In that instant, I made a decision. Usually when I undertake a big decision, I seek God's will first, but I didn't do so on this occasion. I knew God would not refuse me.

"Let me take Ah Yan with me. She can't stay here," I said to the woman.

She was surprised. She hadn't expected such a request from me. She thought for a moment, then knelt and kowtowed to me.

"You are her lifesaving bodhisattva. On behalf of her mother and father, I thank you for your great kindness. If she stays here, there is no way she could survive. I'm just a woman. I can't protect her. When I die, she'll be left without care."

Standing, I extended my hand to Stella.

"Child, come home with me, OK?" I said gently.

Like a marionette whose strings I held, she obediently stood and followed me. When we had gone just a few paces, the woman said, "Wait here for a moment, I'll be right back." Fifteen minutes later, the woman came back carrying an old book.

"This is Ah Yan's favorite book. Please take it with you," she said, giving it to me.

We slowly made our way down the forty-one steps. From above, the water looked different. I couldn't see the stones beneath the water clearly, but I could see the shape of the river's course. It made a gradual bend not far away, and farther, it made a wider bend, until it turned to a place beyond my view. The dandelions on the hillside had blossomed, and their seeds flew in the wind. From a distance, they looked like a cluster of misty clouds. A fishing sampan was tied to the rocks on the shore, and a boatman sat on the bow, smoking a water pipe and listening to the egrets mutter as they went in and out of the water. I carried the bicycle on my shoulder, balancing the medicine box in my other hand. Stella walked silently beside me, head bowed. She wasn't watching the path. She didn't need to. She knew every stone underfoot with her eyes closed. She was looking at the hole that had just appeared in her shoe. As we came to the end of the forty-one stone steps, she hadn't looked back, not even once. She didn't look back once at the place she'd lived for fourteen years, this village called Sishiyi Bu. The woman followed us all the way to the sampan. As the boatman untied the rope, she suddenly clasped Stella's hand.

"Ah Yan, your aunt is sorry. Please don't blame me."

Even after the sampan had traveled a great distance, I could still hear the woman weeping.

~

When we arrived home, I told the cook to boil a pot of water so Stella could have a good bath, and I found a floral scarf to tie over her head and a box of Jenny's old clothes. Soon her hair would grow like grass, and she could braid it again.

When she had bathed and changed, I brought her to Jenny's mirror. She turned away, disgust flashing in her eyes. A hint of secret joy came to my heart seeing this trace of emotion. Her mind wasn't lost, just in a deep sleep. Given enough time and peace, it would eventually wake up. Now that she was here with me, I didn't have to worry about her from a distance anymore. I could set my mind at ease and try to find the crack that would let me in to her feelings.

That night, I felt an excitement I hadn't felt in a long time. Jenny was dead, but I was still alive. I'd been doing all the things we used to do together, but without the sense of purpose that had been behind them. I'd been moving out of inertia, drifting about aimlessly. Now, this girl named Stella was a star God had sent me. With her gravity, she pulled me back to earth, reminding me that I could not only walk but also find a path. I suddenly had a purpose. I couldn't save everyone—that was God's business—but perhaps I could save one person. In God's eyes, a thousand years was like a day, and a day was like a thousand years. In the same way, one person was a universe, and perhaps the universe was a single person.

I didn't keep Stella in the house, as I had before. Instead, I took her through the village, introducing her to everyone I met, saying, "This is an orphan I've taken in. Her name is Stella, which means 'star.' She will live here, helping me around the church." I asked Stella to help me with the small vegetable garden in front of the church. We weeded and harvested, just like any other villagers. I asked the cook to give her tasks, such as boiling water, washing dishes and vegetables, and washing and mending clothes. On Wednesday, when I distributed porridge, we lit a fire, cooked the porridge, and served it together. I asked her to come to Sunday service. She always sat on the aisle of the last row, sometimes sleeping and sometimes awake. I couldn't tell if she listened at all. After service, I asked her to clean the candlestick holders and windows. I watched her as she was doing these tasks and found she wasn't lazy about any chore, but neither did she show any interest in them, no more than she did anything else. When the church closed for the night, I asked her to copy psalms for me or to repair damaged hymnals. This had been her favorite thing to do before, but now it was done only out of obedience. She no longer asked me about new words, nor did she ask me to read to her. After she finished one psalm, if I didn't ask her to copy more, she would just sit silently, sometimes for ten minutes and sometimes for as long as an hour. I carefully moderated my behavior toward her, not showing any concern and never mentioning our previous acquaintance. I knew that both questions and comfort would serve as a reminder of what she most needed to forget.

A few times, I placed the book her aunt had given her within her reach. She didn't even look at it. When she wasn't around, I skimmed through it and found it was the Chinese translation of Huxley's *Evolution and Ethics*. This book had probably traveled a great distance in someone's pocket. The spine and corners were frayed, and there was a name written in fountain pen on the title page: Liu Zhaohu. I surmised that he was the original owner of the book, probably a student attending school in the city, since fountain pens were rare in the countryside. I suddenly understood. Stella wasn't able to read such a difficult book, but she loved it because of the name written on the title page.

Life went on uneventfully, the sun rising and setting again and again. Our conversation consisted of me speaking and her listening or me asking a question and her giving a brief answer. She almost never initiated conversation or expanded on any topic I started. That was all left to me. The only thing that changed was that her hair grew. One day, as she was washing it in the backyard, I noticed her hair had grown into a glistening handful. She was a seedling I had forcefully transplanted. I wasn't sure if the place she'd been broken had healed, and I didn't know if she had planted any roots in the new soil. I couldn't see the roots, so could only guess from the leaf. But this leaf refused to reveal the secrets of its root. I prayed for Stella every day. These prayers, like so many I had prayed before, were taken by the wind before ever reaching God. But one day as I prayed, I suddenly heard a word from God: *My servant, is your leaf yellow?* I wasn't sure if it was a metaphor or a question. After contemplating carefully for a while, I suddenly understood. True, her leaf hadn't sprouted any new green, but it also hadn't turned yellow, which meant the root had not rotted. I couldn't see the change in the seedling because I lacked patience.

I waited, almost hopeless, through this long summer and fall, and into the winter of 1943. That winter was particularly long and cold. My wide circle of friends all brought equally bad news from the outside, news of bombings, cities falling into enemy hands, occupation, and fleeing . . . It was all very strange, as if it had nothing at all to do with Yuehu, as if Yuehu were in the magical Chinese novel *Journey to the West* and contained within a golden circle drawn by a bodhisattva with a golden cudgel. As long as the people in Yuehu were inside this circle, the poison of the world outside couldn't harm it. The war had been going on for several years, but Yuehu's sky had never seen the trail of a plane, and on its ground, there wasn't a single soldier's footprint. On the twenty-sixth day of the twelfth lunar month, it began to snow, and it snowed for three days and three nights. The village elders said they hadn't seen such snow in thirty years. When the snow stopped, I looked out and saw that the trees and houses had all disappeared. The snow erased the edges of everything.

I had sent the cook home for the New Year festival, leaving just Stella and me in the church. In order to save charcoal, we only kept one stove lit. The snow sealed us in, and we warmed ourselves by the stove. I was reading *The Pilgrim's Progress from This World, to That Which Is to Come*, and she was making new shoes for me, stitching together fragments of fabric to form the soles. She spent most of her spare time making shoes for me. The cloth shoes she made would carry me to heaven, even allowing me to take a few turns around paradise. The wind and snow outside had ceased, and the branches no longer scraped the windows. The insects and birds slept, and the loneliness of winter was lengthened many times by silence. When Stella's hand got cold, she stopped and held it to the fire, then continued sewing. The sweet potatoes we'd placed at the edge of the fire grew fragrant. Stella's needle went in and out of the thick fabric, like the scratching of a cat's claws, hurting my ears. When I could stand no more, I tossed the book to the table. I wanted to roar, *Stella, for God's sake, say something! Would it kill you to speak?* But the words stuck in my throat, and I swallowed them. Startled, she put down her work, looking at me with fear and confusion. Then I was glad I hadn't let the careless words slip from my mouth. What if she had responded, *Will it kill you if I don't speak?* I was ashamed. I had spent every day worrying about how to mend Stella's roots, but she was much stronger than I was. Her roots could find their way alone in strange soil, but I always needed to lean on another, to have someone to keep me company.

The long, cruel silence was finally broken two days before the New Year festival, when I was awakened by a sharp knock on the door. Knocking on the door in the middle of the night was never a good thing, especially at a time so close to the New Year. Worried, I got up and opened the door to find two men carrying a stretcher—actually just a quilt draped between two poles. On the quilt lay a patient. The three of them were farmers from the neighboring village. The man had been suffering from abdominal pains for two days, but because of the heavy snow, and because it was the end of the year, they had hoped to wait until after the New Year festival to seek help. But that day, the pain was increasingly intense, and the man had passed out and had to be carried here.

I did an exam and found that the symptoms were consistent with acute appendicitis. The nearest hospital was 112 miles away. In the deep snow, it would take at least three days and three nights to walk there. The only option was to perform an appendectomy on the spot. I had treated various injuries for the villagers who lived nearby, but I had never performed an open surgery in the church. Still, I had no choice. I couldn't just watch him die and do nothing. Fortunately, I had just secured a small amount of narcotics on the black market through friends. I woke Stella and asked her to boil water, sterilize the surgical equipment, prepare the kerosene and alcohol lamps, and move the table to the middle of the room and place a clean sheet on it. Then, I started the surgery.

Though kerosene lamps were hung at each corner of the table, the light wasn't sufficient, so we needed a flashlight as well. I asked one of the men to hold the flashlight for me, but when I made the first incision, he fainted. I asked the other man to take over. He didn't faint, but after a few minutes, he ran outside, retching. I didn't know what to do, until Stella walked over and said, "Pastor Billy, let me do it." This was the second time she'd taken the initiative. The first had been when she copied the psalm. I never imagined that I'd allow a young girl with no medical training to see this gore, but I couldn't worry about that then. The patient could wake from the anesthesia at any moment, so I had no choice but to allow Stella to hold the light for me.

"If you don't want to look, just close your eyes," I said. "I just need you to hold the flashlight steady, without moving your wrist."

But she kept her eyes open the whole time, and the flashlight beam was firm as it followed my scalpel right up until I made the last stitch. She didn't utter the slightest groan of horror. When I finally finished and sat down, covered in sweat, the cock's first crow had already sounded in the yard. Stella wrung out a damp towel for me.

"Will he survive?" she asked me.

This was the first time in a long time that she had initiated a conversation with me.

"There's a strong chance he will. The risk of infection is lower in winter than in summer, and we have some medicine."

A few days earlier, I had received medicine from the parent organization in America and from several other channels too. My medicine cabinet was much fuller than usual. I felt like a wealthy man. The muscles in Stella's face moved oddly. It took me a moment to realize that she was smiling. It had been so long since I'd seen her smile, I couldn't immediately recognize it. All at once, I saw both her fragility and her bravery. She'd been wounded so severely that she couldn't even face the name in a book, but she was braver than any man, even at the sight of blood and blade. I finally found the way to heal Stella. She didn't need comfort, and she didn't need to forget. She needed to save herself by saving others.

My greatest concern was alleviated. The patient only ran a low-grade fever for half a day after the surgery, then his temperature stabilized. After three days of observation, I sent him home to recuperate. On the morning of the fifth day of the first month of the lunar year, a dozen men and women from the patient's village came with drums and gongs, presenting me with half a slaughtered pig, three hens, and a basket of eggs. They also dug a path in the snow to the door of the church, sweeping it clean. For the next month, our contented burps were filled with the pungent taste of preserved meat.

On the day of the Lantern Festival, I called Stella to my room. I wanted to talk to her about an idea I'd been considering since the surgery.

"Last year, we swore to one another before God that we wouldn't lie to each other again. Do you remember that?" I asked.

This was the first time I had mentioned our prior acquaintance. I didn't want to conceal the truth anymore. I wanted to lance it open, and perhaps after the blood and pus had flowed out, healing would be possible.

She nodded.

"You have been devastated in recent months and have endured immense suffering. There are many men who wouldn't be able to endure what you have withstood." It was the first stroke of the knife.

Her mouth twitched. She had reached the edge of an emotional cliff. But an inch away from the edge, she stopped and tightened all the lines in her face.

"You've survived, but have you thought about what you want for the future?"

She lowered her head and stared at the toes of her shoes.

"Do you want a good man to marry you and give you a family? What if that man never comes, but another villain like Scabby comes instead? Will you allow yourself to be mistreated by others, one after another?"

My blade hit its mark with precision. The tightly wrapped boil was lanced, and the emotion that had accumulated for so long finally overflowed the banks, and she began to weep bitterly. Stella's sobs that day can only be described as earth-shattering. They were so dark, they blotted out the sun and so deep they made the mountains tremble. But I was ruthless. My previous error was that I was too softhearted. I had been treating the injury of the heart with medication, forgetting that I was a surgeon. Some injuries had to be healed through surgery, even if there was no anesthesia. I let her finish crying. She took out her handkerchief and wiped her nose.

"I can teach you a skill, and when you have learned it, you won't have to rely on any man ever again. No one will hold your life in their hands anymore. Instead, you will hold their lives in your hand," I said.

"Where could I find such a skill?" she said in a low, muffled voice.

"I can teach you to practice medicine," I said.

She looked at me in amazement, as if I said I were going to teach her to fly over the rooftops, walk on walls, or pluck a star from the sky.

"The closest Western doctor in this region is more than one hundred miles away. You can see patients from the village here, first treating their headaches, fever, and minor wounds. In the future, you can even deliver the women's babies. Once you learn this, who would dare to mistreat you? Their need for you would be far greater than your need for them."

I added, "In the past, you've done things according to my wishes. Now I want you to make your own decision. You don't need to answer right away. Think about it, then tell me your decision."

Silently, Stella turned and haltingly walked away. Immediately, she turned around and came back in. She knelt on the floor, kowtowing three times. I was a little angry.

"Stella, let me tell you something. My God does not allow me to kneel before anyone and doesn't allow me to accept obeisance from others. The first time you did it, you didn't know better, and where there is ignorance, there can be no guilt. But now you know what you're doing."

Stella looked up at me in distress. "If you don't accept my obeisance, how can I declare myself your disciple?"

From then on, I relieved Stella of her housework and began focusing on two things. The first was teaching her English, so she could read general medical texts. The second was imparting some basic medical knowledge to her. I condensed the knowledge I'd acquired at medical school and through my residency at the hospital, putting it in the simplest, most direct language, and taught it to her. That is actually putting it lightly. The truth is that I excluded the deep theoretical principles and the inextricable logic connecting them, and I explained to her only the most superficial, practical parts. I skipped human anatomy and the nervous system, the chemical ingredients of drugs, and the relationship between the internal and external causes of diseases. I taught her how to take body temperatures, how to disinfect, simple methods of cleaning and suturing wounds, and how to treat headaches, fevers, diarrhea, and snakebites. If my professors had seen me imparting medical knowledge through the method of treating the pain wherever the symptom occurred, they would've certainly asked the medical board to expel me. But I had no choice. I needed to train Stella as a rural doctor capable of treating common ailments in the quickest possible way.

Stella's comprehension and memory were beyond what I had hoped, and her hand was steady. She possessed the three basic qualities a doctor needed: compassion, intuition, and calmness under stress. When I came across a patient who wasn't terribly ill, I encouraged her to draw her own intuitive conclusions according to the symptoms. Most of the time, she arrived at the right idea, though occasionally she would be far off the mark. But even if it was one step back for every three steps forward, she was making immense progress. I told everyone in the village that Stella was no longer just a domestic worker taken in by the church, but that she had officially accepted me as her teacher. When I saw patients or went on house visits, I always brought her with me. She was a fixture on the back of my bicycle. Sometimes we took sampans, when the bicycle wouldn't serve. Stella had much greater strength and skill with the sampans than I did, so on the occasions when I was too tired, she rowed by herself.

I dared take Stella out because I possessed something that gave me confidence, a Baby Browning with two magazines for self-defense. It was new, and the barrel gleamed with a blue light. It was said to be from the private collection of an officer in the Japanese army. I got it from a pirate captain. His mother had been suffering from a strange disease. She believed a ferocious ghost kept howling and scratching in her ears. She was unable to sleep, the sound driving her so crazy she wanted to kill herself. The pirate was a dutiful son and had spent a great deal of money on exorcisms performed by Taoist priests and sorceresses, but with no results. He mentioned it to me in passing, and I suggested he bring his mother to see me. I found that the "ghosts" were two cockroaches that had settled into her ear canal. With a few drops of glycerin, I drove them away, the old woman found peace, and I won the gratitude of the son who would have lain down his life for me. Declining all his offers of thanks, I told him that all I needed was a weapon with which to defend myself. A month later, he gave me the pistol. There were only twenty-six bullets for its magazines, but for me, that was enough. If twenty-five bullets couldn't save us, I would save the last one for Stella. I had vowed before God that as long as I lived, I wouldn't let Stella suffer the humiliations she had before, no matter what.

I started saving more than I had before, minding the church's every expense. I was quietly squirreling away my income with a larger, distant goal in mind. After the war was over, I wanted to send Stella to medical school, giving her the formal medical training that would make up for my elementary education, which left out many important facts and put the incidental before the fundamental.

One day a few months later, a boy of six or seven came into the church. He had injured himself chopping wood, and the back of his hand was bleeding profusely. I had instructed Stella many times on how to clean and suture wounds, and on this occasion, I let her do the operation on her own, while I stood by, observing. Stella always got on well with children. She was always able to persuade them to drink even the bitterest medicine or to endure the pain of debridement and suturing. But on that day, she wasn't quite herself. The hand holding the rubbing alcohol was shaking. She fidgeted on the stool and seemed unmoved by the child's cries of pain.

When she finally finished, I asked, "Is something wrong today?"

Uneasily, she stood up and mumbled, "Pastor Billy, I think my wound is infected again."

Looking at the stool where she had been sitting, I saw that it was streaked with blood. I immediately examined her. After the examination, I thought for a moment, unsure how to explain it to her. Her lips trembled, and with fear in her voice, she asked, "Pastor Billy, tell me the truth. Am I going to die?"

I realized my silence had misled her. Smiling, I said, "Stella, I haven't taught you the basic principles of gynecology yet. We can start now. You aren't dying. You've just grown up. You're menstruating."

In that moment, I felt as if every pore in my body wanted to sing. The gloomy days had passed. Though Stella's life had had a rocky start, there were countless opportunities to remedy it. As long as I was willing to work diligently, she would become a happy, useful person, with all options open to her. Looking back now, I can see what a stupid, shallow optimist I was. I knew nothing about the cruelty of fate and the helplessness of the individual.

Not long after that, the training camp of the Sino-American Cooperative Organization came to Yuehu Village, and the trajectories of our lives were derailed and sent in a completely different direction.

US Navy Historical Archives Collection: Three Letters from Personnel in the Field

The First Letter

From:
Ian Lawrence Ferguson
Navy Post Office 86
US Army Postal Service
Postmark Date: June 29, 1944
Passed by Naval Censor

To:
Elizabeth Maria Ferguson
307 Douglas Street
Chicago, Illinois USA

June 25, 1944

Dear Mother,

We're in a new place. I know you're eager to know more, but I trust you'll understand my not being able to tell you much. I can only write about trivial things, according to the military censor. Don't worry, though. I'm safe. You can still use the same military address when you write back, and they'll forward it to me—I'm not sure how long it will take, because the fighting often blocks the mail routes. Your last letter took almost two months to get to me. Hopefully the next won't be as slow.

The first big challenge I faced here was sleep. The Chinese are smaller than us, so I have to curl up and bend my legs to fit in the bed. But the size of the bed is a minor issue compared with the mosquitoes and fleas. In my last letter, I told you all about how we use our courage and wits against the mosquitoes. This time, I'll tell you about the fleas.

I've never seen a flea under a microscope, but I wouldn't be surprised if they had a hundred legs, because they're at least a hundred times stronger than humans. They easily crawl from one room to another and jump from one bed to another. They're the most advanced scouts. No matter how many layers of clothing you wear, they always find their way straight to your skin. They only like the blood of the living—once I saw an old man dying on the side of the road, and the fleas fell right off him. It's better to deal with them in summer, because then you only have to fight with one layer of clothing. Fleas in sweaters can only be killed with boiling water, but then you ruin the sweater too.

Our medical officer, Dr. Lewis, said the fleas have been biting rats and may give us typhoid fever, so we change the straw in our beds every week, the sheets every ten days, and bathe every other day (thankfully it's summer). Even then, we can't keep the fleas from breeding elsewhere and jumping into our beds. Jack, who sleeps on the bunk above mine, woke up last night because he was itching so much. He struggled to decide whether he'd rather have mosquitoes or fleas, but finally settled on mosquitoes. He crawled out from under the mosquito net, woke our poor Chinese servant, Buffalo, and had him boil water. Then he poured a few pots of boiling water over a wooden chair. Then he rubbed flea powder on the legs of the chair and lit some mosquito-repelling wormwood. He tried to sleep sitting in this chair, but he didn't escape either the fleas or the mosquitoes. The next morning, the bite marks on his arms formed two red armies. Buffalo says Americans smell good, and that's why we attract so many bugs. It's strange. Buffalo sleeps shirtless, without a mosquito net, at most burns one moxa stick, and almost never has bites. Maybe the locals have built up their own resistance.

I don't understand how a country where most people don't have enough to eat can feed this endless army of fleas. Fleas can be described without exaggeration as coming from nothing and going from zero to a thousand. But so far no one in our unit has gotten typhoid fever—thank God.

Fleas weren't the only surprise. Today, my encounter with a couple of rats could've been straight out of a movie. On my way to breakfast, as I passed the pantry, I saw two rats stealing eggs. They were the largest rats I'd ever seen, almost like small rabbits. They had a clear division of labor, with one on the table and one on the ground. The one on the table curled its tail around the egg, dragging it along the edge of the table. The one on the ground lay on its back, legs in the air, and caught the egg on its soft belly. Then the other one climbed down and helped the one on the ground turn over. Together, they rolled the stolen item with their paws, like rolling a snowball, into a dark hole in the corner of the room. I could've scared off the pair of daring little thieves, but I didn't. I was too impressed. I didn't know they could communicate well enough to design such a scheme. It was enough to put any professional soldier to shame.

My dear mother, have I told you too many bad things? I hope I haven't given you the impression that there's only poverty here. The countryside is beautiful, and because the population is so large and good land so scarce, the farmers here cherish every inch of soil. In America, hills are usually not farmed, but here the hillsides are terraced for crops to grow. They're well-planned, each terrace growing a different crop—rice, orange, rape, milk vetch, and many others I can't name. In the spring and summer, their flowering seasons, there are yellow, purple, pink, and green flowers, one after another. It's unreal. I've only seen such bright, pure colors in paintings. Most of the low-lying areas are paddy fields, and usually there are water buffaloes there. They're a farm animal, not at all like the buffaloes in Western movies. During farming season, farmers don't usually ride them, trying to save their strength, but when there isn't much work, you'll see the buffalo lounging in the field or kneeling on the roadside, and sometimes children will ride on its back. They seem docile, and they let people drive them easily, but one shouldn't underestimate their temper. I made that mistake once, and I'll never forget it.

One day I was crossing a paddy, and I saw a water buffalo resting there with its eyes closed. It was larger than average, and its back broke the surface of the water like a wrinkled gray rock. Feeling mischievous, I decided to disturb its nap with a pebble. I must have hit a sensitive spot, because the beast screamed, pulling its bulk up from the field and charging me. I was caught off guard, but turned and ran. I don't know how long I ran, but it felt like I'd been running for an hour, but it still chased me. Just as I thought I was going to be gored to death like a Spanish bullfighter, there was a sharp whistle behind me, and the buffalo stopped. Looking back, I saw a boy who seemed to be around eleven. Pointing at my feet, he suddenly burst into laughter. When I looked down, I realized that one of my shoes had been lost in the wet mud, and I'd been running on one bare foot. I couldn't help but laugh too. We looked at each other and laughed until our bellies hurt, and we had to squat on the ground, unable to stand.

The boy helped me find my shoe, and I gave him a bullet casing in return. He was very ugly, with one big eye and one small eye, upturned nostrils, and two protruding front teeth that made it almost impossible for him to close his mouth. Even so, I couldn't stop myself from liking his smile. I asked him if he would like to work for the Americans. Two silver dollars a month, plus food and lodging, an excellent income for the locals. He agreed, and since then, he has been our loyal, hardworking servant. His Chinese name has a difficult inflection that none of us can say clearly, so we call him Buffalo, because of how he and I met.

Mother, I still haven't dared to write directly to Father. I can only imagine how he felt when both of his sons enlisted at the same time. But if he were our age, I think he'd do the same thing. When he's in better spirits, please read my letters to him and tell him I miss him a lot.

Also, would you do me a favor? On the corner of Madison Avenue and Springfield Street, next to the Blue Lake Café, there's a building called the Maria Apartments. A Miss Emily Wilson lives there with her aunt on the third floor, room eight. I met her when I was in that mechanics class at the community college and she was a student in the nursing school. I like her a lot, and she likes me too. We'd gotten somewhat serious before I left. If there were no war, I would've brought her to meet you and Father. Maybe I would've asked her to marry me by now. But now, I have to wait until after the war. After I left, I wrote her some letters, and I got some from her as well, but I haven't heard from her at all in the past three months. If you could find the time to visit and see if there is anything wrong, please let me know. When you ring the doorbell, just say you're my mother, and her aunt will know who you are.

I'm eager for news from home. Has Jacob written? Do you know where in Europe his unit is? Has Father found any relief for the arthritis? Do you still have coffee with Aunt Louise every Wednesday afternoon? Please tell Leah that the cards she and her friends made for her big brother and his fellow soldiers are really cute.

I'll stop here for the time being. I hope you're all healthy and happy.

Love from your son,

Ian

Somewhere in China

P.S. *Please send flea powder and chewing gum in your next package. I break things a lot, and the chewing gum is useful for repairs.*

The Second Letter

From:

Ian Lawrence Ferguson

Navy Post Office 86

US Army Postal Service
Postmark Date: July 31, 1944
Passed by Naval Censor

To:
Elizabeth Maria Ferguson
307 Douglas Street
Chicago, Illinois USA

July 26, 1944

Dear Mother and Father,
Today feels like my birthday, because the postmaster brought me
twelve letters and two packages, all in one heavy bundle. My com-
rades are green with envy. Three of the letters are from you (May
29, June 18, and July 3), two from Leah, three from Jacob, one
from Aunt Louise, one from cousin Daisy, one from my coworker
Andy at the mechanic shop, and one from Leon. You remember
him—my high school classmate, who you thought sounded like a
girl. I was really glad for the letters I got from Father and Jacob.
Jacob had written to me from Belgium and Holland, but I didn't
get his letters until today because the mail routes were blocked.
Father, now I understand that you weren't angry with me for join-
ing the navy, but because I didn't tell you beforehand. I was afraid
to tell either of you, especially Mother, because I was afraid I'd lose
my nerve. I think Jacob felt the same way. I hope you can under-
stand why I did what I did and forgive me.

I was excited all day. I read the letters over and over so many
times, I can practically recite them by heart. You can't imagine how
much letters from home mean to us here. Some American soldiers
farther away haven't gotten mail in nine months. Nine months—
can you imagine? Nine months, completely isolated, without com-
munication. I heard that President Roosevelt personally promised
to make every effort to improve the military's mail service. I hope

he does, and I'll be able to get a steady flow of letters, like one a week, instead of twelve all at once.

Mother, thank you for the precious items in the packages. Of course, coffee powder ranks first. Our supply of coffee is really tight, sometimes even cut off altogether. I only use half a spoonful a day, brewing as much as I can from it. Even stingy Buffalo can't stand it, saying that my last cup is as weak as his mother's foot bath. (His mother has bound feet.) Canned beef is also a rare thing. Our food supply is almost entirely from local products. We don't want for chicken or pork, but we rarely get beef. For vegetables, we usually have green beans, loofa, or rape. When I got here, I wasn't used to all the fried food that the local cooks make, and I often got the runs. Now, my stomach is as strong as a cow's—I could probably digest iron. Still, I can't help but miss Mother's steak. And turkey. I can hardly bear to eat these two cans of beef in just one or two meals. I've been trying to figure out how many bites they contain and how I can make them last until the next package arrives. Of course, once I've opened them, I have to eat them before they go bad.

Father, you asked how we entertain ourselves. Well, however we can, really. We cleared a basic field, where we run or play basketball or volleyball. When we're free, we hunt wild pheasants and turtledoves. If the weather is warm, we swim in the river, even though our medical officers discourage us, fearing we might pick up parasites. We don't have light at night, so we all go to bed early. After dinner, we usually listen to the radio. We don't get American programs, of course, so mostly it's local music like Chinese operas. The opera music is strange, with lots of ups and downs between the high and low notes, and the plot is basically incomprehensible for us, but Buffalo listens enthusiastically, occasionally even swaying and singing along. Sometimes we tease him, putting towels on our heads and pretending to be in the opera, dancing around him like demons. He says we're a bunch of crazy Americans.

In the last few days, there's been news that's caused a great fuss—after the summer harvesting is over in early September, a theater troupe from the city will come here to perform. The locals haven't seen a troupe in years, and our Chinese colleagues are noticeably distracted, discussing this every time they get together. The lead actress is supposed to be very beautiful. No one's actually seen her, but they all talk as if they've known her all their lives—about her voice, her features, her figure. They've already discussed where the stage should be, what sort of lighting they'll use, where the troupe will stay, and what food they'll make. Basically, from now until the performance, I don't expect to hear about anything else.

This is our entertainment, Mother, which is why the Time *magazine you sent is so precious. Even though it's out of date, everything is news to us. I didn't even get the chance to flip through it before it was snatched away from me. When I got it back, the cover was gone and one of the colored inserts was missing. Later, I found the torn page by the head of Jack's bunk: a picture of Vivian Leigh.*

My only regret is that the chocolate had sprouted a layer of green fuzz, probably from the heat. With disappointment, I tossed it to Ghost. Ghost is a dog who followed us here from our last station. He'd never had chocolate before, and after taking a lick, he shook his head vigorously, so I guess he didn't like it either.

I did another silly thing recently. Saying I was going to pick up the mail, I wandered around the small town (which I'm not supposed to do). I couldn't help but stop in for a look in the furniture store. Chinese furniture can be categorized by whether it's a round wooden piece or a square wooden piece. I think this shop specialized in round, and there were some interesting items, like some buckets painted with landscape and flower patterns on them and a wooden basin, probably for laundry, with a handle carved as a goose head. It was really unique. There was also a wooden bucket with a lid, covered in a shiny layer of lacquer and with a delicate pattern carved on the edges. I was taken with it, so I asked how much it was. When I converted it to dollars, I realized it was just over a dollar, so I bought it, planning to put my letters and clothes in it. Since it didn't have a handle, I had some trouble carrying it, so I finally put it on my head and carried it that way. All the way back, I noticed that people were laughing at me. When I got back to camp, Buffalo told me that it's used as a toilet, and it was something mothers usually prepared as part of their daughter's dowry. I was the biggest laughingstock in the platoon all week after that.

Mother, I don't know if you've had the chance to visit Miss Emily Wilson. I haven't gotten a letter from her yet, so I'm getting worried. If you have any news of her, let me know as soon as possible, even if it means sending a simple telegram.

It's late and the light is fading, so I'll stop here. Tomorrow, I'll write to Aunt Louise and Daisy. Daisy said she's singing on the street corner every weekend to raise money for soldiers who've been deployed. I'm really proud of her. I remember how she always used to say that she was born with a good voice, but had nowhere to use it. Now, she's finally found a good use for it. The war has changed everyone so much. The only thing that hasn't changed is my love for all of you.

Yours always,

Ian

Somewhere in China

The Third Letter

From:

Ian Lawrence Ferguson

Navy Post Office 86

US Army Postal Service

Postmark Date: April 21, 1945

Passed by Naval Censor

To:

Mrs. Leah Frasermann

8 Main Street, Room 609

Chicago, Illinois

USA

April 18, 1945

My dear beautiful, naughty sister Leah,
I can't believe you're not Miss Leah Ferguson anymore, but Mrs. Leah Frasermann. You married so fast, without even waiting for your brothers to return home. I almost wanted to get angry, but when I saw your wedding photos, my heart melted. You're enchanting in your wedding dress. How could I be angry with such a beautiful, happy young woman? The young fellow beside you, this Alan Frasermann, doesn't look too bad. Has anyone told him he's the luckiest man in the world? Don't let him forget you have two brothers, both of us combat trained. If he ever hurts you, he'll pay for it in flesh.

Actually, I understand your decision. Since Alan's brother died in the battle at Omaha Beach, I'm sure you're both aware of the fragility and impermanence of life. You no longer trust the damned unreliable thing called tomorrow, so you just want happiness in your hand immediately.

Emily Wilson (now Robinson) thought so too, when she decided to get married. She told me the news herself, though I know everyone was trying to hide it from me. After a few months of silence, she finally wrote last fall to say she was married. She said her best friend's fiancé had died in a plane crash during battle. Her friend was devastated, turning to alcohol and sleeping pills just to get through each day. She didn't want that, so she decided to marry the first man who proposed. Her letter was quite euphemistic—at least she didn't say outright she thought I would die in China. She repeatedly asked me for forgiveness, but really, what is there to forgive? We liked each other a lot, and though we were getting serious and our feelings were strong, we hadn't made any promises. Even if we had been engaged, the war has loosened all promises. I replied to wish her happiness. But I cried when I went to bed that night.

We were all shocked by the death of President Roosevelt. We had a simple memorial yesterday, with our Chinese comrades. Pastor Billy, an American who's been preaching in China for many years, led the service. When the locals heard about it, they all came, and it was so crowded that people had to stand in the aisles and even outside the door. As the pastor read prayers, the people lit incense for the dead. It was a moving scene. On behalf of my comrades, I read Whitman's poem mourning the death of Lincoln, "O Captain! My captain!"

O Captain! my Captain! our fearful trip is done,
The ship has weather'd every rack, the prize we sought is won,
The port is near, the bells I hear, the people all exulting,
While follow eyes the steady keel, the vessel grim and daring;
But O heart! heart! heart!
O the bleeding drops of red,
Where on the deck my Captain lies,
Fallen cold and dead.

By the time I was done, many people were crying. The war is at a critical point. The American warship has lost its captain. What sort of surprises will Mr. Truman—who we don't know yet—bring?

OK, I've said too many sad things. You're still a bride, and here I am dampening your mood. Let me tell you about the gift I found for you and Mother instead.

A few days ago, our servant, Buffalo, and I were walking through the village when we heard a rhythmic hum in a courtyard. Curiously, I peeked through the door of the courtyard, and I saw that it was a young woman weaving. The "loom" was just a few planks nailed together. I'd never seen such a primitive thing. Her foot operated the pedal, and she passed the shuttle back and forth, tossing from one hand and catching it with the other. This required amazing hand-eye (and foot) coordination, and the woman managed it expertly. The cloth she was weaving was green. Of course, calling it green is simplistic. There were so many shades in her green. The lightest was close to white, and the darkest almost black. Combining the countless hues of green this way, the effect it created was a magical, mist-like feeling. I was mesmerized. The woman was engrossed in her weaving and didn't notice us watching from just outside the door. By the time she looked up, we'd already walked into the court-yard. She blushed. In rural China, women—particularly young women—are very shy, not used to talking to strange men, especially foreigners. Buffalo said she was a new bride, judging from the red string wrapped around her bun. I asked him to ask her if she had designed the pattern. She nodded and pointed to two rows of colored thread hanging to dry in the yard, indicating she had designed other patterns too. I was amazed by the artistic instincts of this probably illiterate village girl. In America, she could become a great artist if someone discovered her. I touched the thread hanging from a bamboo pole. They were thick and hard and like colored spaghetti at first glance. Buffalo said the thread was stiffened with sweet potato starch so that the yarn wouldn't break when it was woven, and the seams wouldn't fray. I asked Buffalo to ask the woman if she would sell me some cloth. When she hesitated, Buffalo put on an attitude, saying, "Weren't you weaving in order to sell? You'll sell it at the market, but when this American wants some, you won't?" The woman blushed and gave him a price. I could see from his eyes he thought it was too much. But I didn't counter. The price she named was almost embarrassing by American standards. With such exquisite craftwork, I couldn't bring myself to haggle with such a lovely bride.

I paid for the cloth and had Buffalo collect it the next day. The woman saw us out, bowing low to me. I've already thought about it. Using the cook's wife as a model, I'll have a Chinese-style blouse made for you and one made for Mother. She's a little shorter and thinner than you and Mother, but we can add an inch or two in length. The blouse has a slanting open collar with stitched flower buttons and is good for spring or fall. You'll be the most stylish women in all of Chicago in them.

The whole way back, Buffalo kept mumbling, "Just some handwoven cloth. It's not worth it." He sometimes thinks I'm stupid, sometimes crazy. Most of the time, he just thinks I'm an American, and Americans are both. Since I brought Buffalo to our squad several months ago, my Chinese hasn't improved much, and his English isn't much better, so it's odd that we always seem to understand one another. I've found that when we communicate, we don't speak either English or Chinese, but something between the two, which only we seem to understand. When I get home, I'll have to ask Father's friend John what kind of language phenomenon this is. As a professor of linguistics, he'll know, I think.

It's already dark and almost time for lights out, so I should stop here. Please be patient and wait for my return, and I'll offer you a belated wedding blessing. We'll drink a toast to my dear sister and my brother-in-law, who looks pretty decent. We will ganbei, *which, by the way, was the first Chinese word I learned here. At the time, I only understood the word in the literal sense, which is to drain the glass in one gulp. So every time a Chinese friend invited me to ganbei, I really downed it. The local rice wine is deceptive. At first, it feels harmless on your tongue, but it's like a time bomb, exploding in your stomach after half an hour, then going all the way to your head. Once you realize it, it's too late. But your big brother was knocked out by the sweet wine a few times, then wised up. Now, I've quietly adjusted the definition of the word from "bottoms up" to "scratching the surface."*

Please give my greetings to the Frasermann family. Also, remember to write to me. Letters from home are a lifeline. I live for them.

Love always,
Ian
Somewhere in China

Ian Ferguson: Miles's Dog

I was anxious to come to Yuehu, not just to keep my appointment with you two but also to see Ghost. When we left Yuehu, we left no physical remains. If all the records were lost, there'd be no proof we were ever here. Ghost is a different story. He left his physical body on this land, so his DNA can testify for itself.

I remember burying Ghost and Snot together in the sloping field behind Pastor Billy's church. We put two stone headstones over them, the larger one for Snot. Snot was the nickname your other Chinese students gave him, because he had severe rhinitis, and his sniffing could be heard throughout the classroom, even when he was sitting in the back row. The number on his uniform was 520, and that's how he was known in the training camp, just like you were 635, Liu Zhaohu. But on his tombstone, we engraved his real name: *The grave of the patriotic hero Yang Lianzhong. September 9, 1926–September 5, 1944.* He was actually younger than eighteen when he died. The age he gave on his registration form when he enlisted was false.

The small gravestone next to Snot belongs to Ghost. It's engraved *The grave of the loyal dog Ghost. Died September 5, 1944.* I don't know when Ghost was born, but he was probably about four when he died. His grave only contains a cookie tin with a fistful of his fur in it. In a bit, let's look for those stones, see if they're still there.

The early days in Yuehu were very lonely, especially that first winter. When I returned to the US, I told friends how cold it was in Yuehu in the winter. They would look at the map where I'd shown them and say, "It's subtropical. How come you describe it like it's Siberia?" It's impossible to explain the complex interaction between temperature and humidity in a Jiangnan winter, but you remember. The heavy dampness in Yuehu makes winter feel like a suit of ice permanently stuck to your skin. The stove becomes a stupid toy that only warms a small part of your body. Because of the fuel shortage, the generators were only for communications between our camp and Chongqing, not even enough power to supply us with light. Other than on festival nights, we relied on kerosene lamps, so just like the locals, we went to bed before nine. Before bed every night, Buffalo lit the coal stove, and whether intentionally or not, it was always placed near my bed. But the fire went out in the middle of the night, so in the long hours before dawn, I was often awakened by the cold. My night didn't depend on blowing taps to start, because the exhausting work meant I was asleep as soon as I lay down. Night for me began when the stove went out.

I know complaining about the cold in front of Liu Zhaohu is heartless. War had been raging in your country for many years. Everything was scarce. There were no servants in the Chinese students' dorms and no coal stoves. There was only the stove in the big classroom, and that was reserved for the American instructors. Only the students in the front row could feel a little of its warmth. But I never heard a complaint from any of the Chinese students, not even 520, always in the back row blowing his nose. Forgive me, Liu Zhaohu. We were a bunch of Americans, used to a comfortable life. We were still learning how to endure hardship.

When you can't sleep, your mind flies through countless things you thought you'd forgotten, things that have nothing to do with the present. For example, I suddenly remembered a kitten named Beggar I'd had as a child. One day he disappeared, and my brother and I cried all night. When I got up the next morning, I found him in one of my father's dress shoes, sound asleep. I remembered skipping school when I was twelve and wandering the streets when I happened to look into a window and saw my father having coffee with a strange woman. She glanced at me through the window, and I ran away. When I went home, I was frightened, even though I knew he should be afraid, not me. For the rest of the year, I wondered if my father and mother would divorce and which of them I would live with. But after a few months passed and nothing happened, I stopped worrying. Another time I thought of the Robert Frost poem I'd hung on my wall in Chicago: "The Road Not Taken." It was copied in my own handwriting, and there was a singe on the bottom left corner of the paper from a cigarette butt. I'd wanted to be a poet at the time, and thought that poets were poor and smoked avidly. I learned to smoke, but in the end, I feared poverty, so I gave it up. These memories were like ghosts trapped in a cave during the day. Only when I couldn't sleep was the cave thrown open, and the ghosts burst out, as if released from Pandora's box, waiting for me to acknowledge each one. I lay on my bed, listening to my comrades snoring around me, sometimes afraid that I'd be gradually killed by cold nights like this before the Japanese took my head.

What comforted me then wasn't Pastor Billy or Liu Zhaohu. You were part of the scenery of my daytime world, but at night you disappeared into your own worlds, enduring the torture of your own loneliness. My only comfort at night was Ghost. When I couldn't bear the cold and loneliness, I would reach out from under the covers, because I knew Ghost was sleeping beside my bed. He would lick the back of my hand over and over and touch my arm with his thick, meaty paws, as if to say, *OK, I know. I understand.* Ghost's father was a collie and his mother a greyhound, and he had his father's wits and his mother's legs, combining wisdom and speed. His fur was light gray, making him hard to see as he roamed the countryside. In the military kennel in Chongqing, he'd trained as an outstanding scout dog, capable of leading us on marches. He caught movements that were undetectable to the human ear, seeing traps and trip wires that human eyes couldn't, or finding weapons hidden under branches. When he spotted something, he didn't make a sound, but alerted us to the danger by making his ears stand up.

But because our missions were secret, and dogs like Ghost were too foreign, we hadn't really been able to use him yet. His special skills were gradually deteriorating, and he had become more of a pet to this troop of American boys. When I thought of the effort the trainer had invested in him, I felt a pang of regret. He was an eagle, meant to soar in the open sky, but we'd turned him into a sparrow hopping on and off branches. Still, compared to the joy he brought us, the regret was negligible. Even as a pet, Ghost was unusual. I'd taught him a few tricks that delighted us. For instance, when someone said "Heil Hitler," he'd raise his right foot in a clown-like salute. When someone said "Yamamoto 56," the officer who oversaw the attack on Pearl Harbor, he'd stomp his left foot in a gesture of contempt and anger. When I returned to the dorm after class, he always greeted me eagerly. If I said, "You're so dirty," he'd stop, look guilty, and lick his paw earnestly before handing it to me for inspection. When we played basketball, I only had to ask him, "Who's the best?" and he'd run over and pull the corner of my shirt, whimpering with joy. Before leaving Chongqing, the dog trainer repeatedly told me I couldn't treat a military dog like a pet or he'd become hesitant when performing tasks. But I couldn't help it.

It was in Yuehu that Ghost found the love of his life. We had just been assigned to Yuehu and had to go to the commissariat dozens of miles away once a week to get the mail and post our letters. To a person walking a mountain road, distance on a map is meaningless. Locals determined distance by the time it took to walk from one place to another. From Yuehu, it was a half-day walk to the commissariat, but it was a cushy job because it was the only way to leave camp legally according to military regulations. On top of that, the mountain road passed through a small town. The commander repeatedly emphasized that we were not to linger in town, but anyone who went to collect the mail always returned with a few items that could only be found in the town. It was an open secret that we all understood. Everyone wanted to be the messenger, so the commander decided we'd take turns in alphabetical order by last name. I had the good luck to be the first, because the fellow who was ahead of me had a carbuncle on his foot and couldn't walk. I gave him some of the canned beef my mother had sent, and he agreed to swap with me, even though I wasn't the first to ask.

Pastor Billy suggested I go by water part of the way to reduce the strain on my legs. He had a sampan and offered to row it for me. He'd quickly become an unofficial advisor to our camp, and we sought his advice on all matters, big or small. According to Pastor Billy's instructions, I changed into the kind of clothes local men wore: a long tunic over billowing cloth pants cinched with string at the ankles, a pipe tucked at the waist. Straw sandals and a bamboo hat completed my attire. We also carried a basket of beans, as prescribed in some detail by Pastor Billy. Of course, the beans were just used to hide short guns and grenades, items I hoped we'd never need to use. I sat in the yard waiting for Pastor Billy. Ghost seemed not to recognize me dressed like that. He walked around me warily several times, but didn't come near. When I reached out and let him lick my hand, he smelled something familiar and finally settled down. He'd been sitting for only a moment when he grew agitated. He walked around the yard uneasily, then ran to the gate, stood on the stone steps, and stared intently into the distance. His eyes widened, revealing his pink eyelids, and his ears twitched back and forth. He looked like he'd spotted the enemy. My nerves tensed, and I wondered if our comrades at the commanding elevation point had missed any news. Almost without thinking, I pulled the pistol out of the basket and rushed out the door. Then I saw what had agitated Ghost. There was a furry white bundle on the dirt road nearby. It seemed to have no feet, appearing to roll along the ground. As it drew nearer, I saw that it was a white terrier.

Ghost shot out like an arrow, but when he reached the white bundle, he stopped shyly. The terrier was tiny. Standing next to the eighty-eight-pound Ghost, she barely reached the top of his leg. Ghost was a proud dog. He knew he was special. When we went out, if we encountered a village dog, he wouldn't even grace it with a glance. He walked right past, as if it were a wisp of wind, with no volume or weight. For their part, village dogs all automatically yielded, sometimes whimpering resentfully. But this white terrier wasn't the least bit afraid of Ghost. She looked at Ghost with big, shimmering eyes, and Ghost melted like wax under her gaze.

Ghost leaned over and sniffed the white terrier gingerly. Seeing that she didn't object, he started to lick her. He flicked out half his tongue, licking gently, as if afraid to rip a piece of tissue paper. The white terrier seemed to know from the start that she had wrapped this giant dog around her finger. She sat motionless, like a noble queen, her eyes closed and head raised, allowing Ghost to lick the hard-to-reach spots on her neck. Ghost looked like he had received a reward, and a burst of joyous rumbling emerged from his throat. As I was watching, spellbound, Pastor Billy arrived. Pointing at the white terrier, I told him Ghost's heart had been stolen in less than a second.

Pastor Billy laughed and said, "By my Millie?"

Surprised, I said, "This is your dog? No wonder she doesn't look like the others."

Pastor Billy said, "Actually, she's Stella's. A Swedish missionary left her with me when he returned home, and I gave her to Stella."

Only then did I notice a young Chinese girl standing behind Pastor Billy. She wore a pale bluish-white cloth shirt and had combed her hair into two short braids. Her trousers were rolled up, revealing two thin, but solid, calves. I'd heard Pastor Billy had taken in a Chinese girl as his assistant for treating patients. She must be that girl.

"I've asked Stella to row us," Pastor Billy said.

The girl nodded and said, in English, "Hello, sir."

There was nothing particularly unusual about her, but I vaguely felt that she was different. Later, I realized that it wasn't how she dressed, but her eyes. She looked me directly in the eye. That alone was enough to distinguish her from the other rural women. It was one of the subtle American traces Pastor Billy left on her, a first step away from her birth and upbringing.

I patted Ghost on the head and said goodbye. He wagged his tail half-heartedly. I knew that in his world, there was now only this little white terrier, Millie. There was no room for anything else. Ghost had even lost himself. After that day, Ghost and Millie couldn't stay apart. If he didn't go find her, she came looking for him. Sometimes they met on the path searching for each other, then stayed in some cave or beneath a tree, enjoying half a day of ecstasy. Ghost became just like any country dog of lowly origin, bewildered by love. I reprimanded him a few times, scolding him and reminding him of his origin and mission. He sat obediently, looking up at me, his eyes full of shame, as if to say, *You're absolutely right, but that's the way it is. I can't help myself.* I didn't know that this would have other consequences, but as it turned out, I unexpectedly saw a lot of the girl, since we were both always out looking for our dogs. We went from strangers to acquaintances, all because of those two animals' unintentional lead.

Later, whenever I thought of Ghost's short life as a military dog, I was grateful he'd found true love before leaving this world.

On that day, I picked up the basket of beans and walked toward the river with Pastor Billy. On the way, we came across a group of Chinese trainees running to the drill field to start their routine morning exercises. Their training followed the German tradition of the military academy as they formed a neat array of squares and repeated strict standing at attention, pause, and stabbing motions. Morning exercises were before breakfast and classes, so the students were hungry. They were all skinny, almost none of them filling their uniforms, but they were the healthiest of the men who'd come to register. Our medical officers had eliminated everyone underweight or with an infectious disease such as an abscess or scabies, but what weight index were they using? We'd lowered our already low standard twice. While we American instructors complained about how monotonous the food was, we often forgot that the Chinese students only had two meals a day. Miles had given strict orders that the Americans were limited to teaching special operations technology, and we shouldn't interfere with the management of Chinese students. Even so, our commanding officer couldn't help tactfully bringing up the issue of the Chinese students' food shortage with the Chinese commanding officer.

"The soldiers on the front lines don't have enough to eat" was the response, and it was true.

I saw you, Liu Zhaohu, Number 635, among the jogging students and called you over to ask you to tell the captain that today's military armament class would be temporarily taught by another instructor, Smithson. You were the only one who knew a bit of English, so whenever the translator wasn't there, I asked you to convey simple messages for me. When you saw the girl standing behind us, a slightly stunned expression came over your face. No, not "slightly." It was quite—or no, very, or better yet, *extremely* shocked. Your lips started trembling. You wanted to speak, but didn't know what to say. She didn't wait for you to find your words, but walked quickly past you, almost at a jog. Dust flew up around her feet, and we could hear the scratch of her cloth shoes against the earth.

"You know her?" I asked.

You hadn't recovered from the shock. First you shook your head, then nodded. I dismissed you. At the time, it didn't seem important. As we walked on, I pointed to Stella, who was ahead of us, and whispered to Pastor Billy, "Is it safe? Bringing her, I mean."

"It's OK. She knows the waterways," he said. Then he added, "Besides, I have this." He raised the hem of his tunic to reveal a Browning pistol at his waistband. It was difficult for me to reconcile the image of Billy with that of a pastor. I felt that he must have led an army in a previous life or his eyes wouldn't have such a gleam when he talked about weapons.

Like many riverside villages south of the Yangtze, Yuehu was the name of both a river and a village. Calling that part of the waterway a river isn't quite right, though. It was at most the beginning of a river—or its end. The narrow river at Yuehu was a collection of small waterfalls on the mountain, but one had to paddle farther out to where the river widens to see more spectacular waterscapes. When we reached the edge of the river, we had to take off our shoes and push the sampan out several steps before we reached waters deep enough for us to launch. The stones at the river's edge were pointed, and each step was like treading on a blunt knife. During our training in the outskirts of Washington, in an area designed to imitate China's conditions, why hadn't anyone considered that we'd need to go barefoot? I watched Pastor Billy and Stella. Their steps were steady and firm, since they were used to the ground under their feet. Embarrassed, I swallowed a few yelps of pain. Those few moments on the rocks felt like a year. The beached sampan was heavy, so Stella bent her body, muscles bulging on her arms against the stern, her breath almost sharp and heavy enough to bore a hole into the deck. A heavy cloud of silence floated in the air, like a can of pressurized gas, ready to explode at any moment. It seemed that this cloud had something to do with Liu Zhaohu.

"Is he the one who gave you the book?" Pastor Billy finally asked.

His tone was cautious. He didn't want to set off the explosion. He was just trying to make a tiny pressure-release hole in that can of gas.

"No. That person is dead." Stella's tone was calm, but I saw the blue-purple veins outlining the muscle in her arm.

We spoke no more, but just bent our heads and pushed forward.

We finally pushed the sampan out to where the boat would float. The waterway was still narrow, and there was almost no trace of a ripple on the surface. If not for the wake of the sampan and the occasional drifting duckweed and fallen leaves, the water looked like a patch of luscious green space. Stella rowed alone, while Pastor Billy and I ducked into the bamboo shelter. Though we were dressed as local men from head to toe, our height still made us stand out.

After we were on the sampan for about half an hour, the river gradually widened. We started to see little wharfs where the boat could dock on both banks. Women washed clothes in the river, and the sound of their wooden clubs was wet and muffled. The sampan startled the waterbirds resting in the grass, and they flew up, squawking, wings obscuring almost half the sky. It was still early, and the sun hadn't risen above the treetops, the branches cutting the light into long straight lines. Occasionally we passed islets in the middle of the river. The rocks weren't visible, but clusters of dark weeds emerged from the water. A few times, I feared the sampan would hit the rocks, but Stella quietly gave the oar a light pull, and the bow would glide past the reef. Seeing my surprise, Pastor Billy laughed and said, "It's a piece of cake for Stella. Just wait until we get to the wind tunnel. Then you'll get to see her true skill."

We soon reached the wind tunnel, which was a sharp turn in the river. The wind came upon us almost without warning. I know it didn't come from the sky, because the clouds were perfectly still. It seemed to come instead from the riverbed itself. Where it arose, the river immediately began to stir. The waves became a whirlpool, and the sampan began to sway violently at the edge of the whirlpool, bobbing up and down. The sound of waves splashing against the shelter was almost like sand and stones scattered by an explosion. One couldn't help feeling frightened by the sound. Pastor Billy left the shelter and helped Stella row, holding the upper end of the long oar, while Stella held its center. Though one of Pastor Billy's strides equaled two of Stella's small steps, their feet always landed on the same point. It was like there was a soundless voice regulating their strength and rhythm. They worked together seamlessly.

One of Stella's braids was blown free by the wind, and her hair fanned out like a black palm leaf. Her clothes, soaked by the waves, clung tightly to her body. The wind not only hid in her hair and clothes but also in her eyes. They were filled with the power of the wind, its freedom and its rage. At that moment, it seemed she had mastered the wind and tamed it. No, at that moment, she herself was the wind. Looking at her in a daze, I almost forgot my fear. The way she looked at that moment is seared into my memory, and time cannot blur or erase it. I had a strange thought then. I wanted to give her a new name, one that only I could speak. I didn't want to call her Stella—that was Pastor Billy's version of her, not mine. I wanted to call her Wende, a Chinese transliteration of the English word, "wind." Many years later, when all the dust had settled, I began to see clearly the nature of each of our feelings for this girl. Girl—yes, in my mind she's forever a girl. When I met her, she was fifteen, and when I left her, she was barely seventeen. I didn't have the chance to see her become a woman.

For her, we were three very different men. Liu Zhaohu, you were her past. When I met her, she had already turned that page. And Pastor Billy, though you lived alongside her, you were always concerned about her future. It was only me who ignored both her past and future, capturing her present. I was the only one of us who knew how to sit in the moment, admiring her blooming youth, not allowing either her past or future to destroy her perfection at that moment. Perhaps that's why Wende was drawn to me.

Liu Zhaohu: Death Is Such a Difficult Thing After All

When I saw Ah Yan at Yuehu, I'd been away from home for a year. On the seventh day after our fathers' deaths, I was shot by the Japanese, passed out on the sampan, and was rescued by a kind-hearted soul from another village. I rested in her house for a period of time. The classmates I'd arranged to meet in Zhuji went on without me, then wrote to ask about me when they arrived in Yan'an four months later. Yan'an was the starting point for the rest of their lives. From there, the long, treacherous journey of life stretched before them, leading each to their own fate. One returned to his old hometown after liberation and became an important county official. When I fell into the deepest, darkest pit, on account of our old friendship, he reached out a hand to help me. But that, of course, was much later.

As soon as I could walk again, I returned home. When I arrived, it was dinnertime there, and the road was quiet. At the entrance to the village, I met a neighbor's child, who turned and ran, as if seeing a ghost. I wasn't surprised. I'd been gone about a month, so they must have thought I'd died somewhere. I had only taken a few more steps when the child returned with my mother. She pulled me to a quiet spot, sat down, and said, "Son, where have you been?" She then began to sob. I told her what had happened to me, and she cried nonstop. At first, I thought they were tears of joy, but after a while, I felt something was odd. Even when my mother's tears had stopped, sobs continued to heave in her throat. I suddenly thought of Ah Yan. The Japanese soldiers who shot me that day were only a few paces away from her and her mother. It was impossible to hope that they hadn't seen the two women.

"How's Ah Yan?" I asked with fear.

My mother's sobs stopped for a moment, then new tears began to flow. The new tears overran the trails made by the old ones, forming new paths on her face. Finally, she managed to tell me what happened to Ah Yan and her mother.

I felt strange in that moment, neither sad nor angry. I simply blamed the gods for allowing Ah Yan and me to live. If that shot had killed me, I would have never known. If that knife had killed Ah Yan as well as her mother, she would never have suffered such shame. In troubled times, death was a sort of mercy. But not everyone who asks for death can die. Heaven treats death as a gift, and God gave me no such gift, nor Ah Yan either, so we had to bear the cruelty of living.

"How is she now?" I asked.

"Poor girl," my mother said, "you don't know how cruel the villagers are."

"I want to see her." I stood up, but my mother desperately held me back.

"You can't go. She's clear for a while, then confused. She always says you joined the Communist army to kill the Japanese. If you come back now, you'll give her hope. Don't give her hope."

I was confused. "What hope?" I asked. "What do you mean?"

She sighed and said, "Have you forgotten? If you return now, you have to acknowledge her as your wife."

Only then did I remember that they'd come to draft me into the Nationalist army and that I'd married into the Yao family. It had only taken place about a month earlier, but it felt like a whole lifetime had passed since then.

"If you want to acknowledge her as your wife, I can't stop you. But think about it—will our family have any respect left?" She started weeping again.

I knew I could avenge Ah Yan, walking ten thousand miles, crossing barefoot through a thousand fiery pits, and killing hundreds of Japanese soldiers, all for her. I wouldn't hesitate to give up my own life for hers. But to acknowledge her as my wife for as long as I lived . . . could I do that? My mother saw the hesitation.

"Go to a friend's house. We'll discuss it later. Hurry. Don't let anyone see you here."

My mother shoved all the money in her pocket into my hand, then pushed me away. I walked away from Sishiyi Bu in a daze. It was only then that I realized I had nowhere to go. My classmates were already on the road, and I had no idea where to find them. I couldn't go back to school, because I'd already been expelled for troublemaking and unexcused absence. In desperation, I thought of my Chinese teacher and walked all night to his house. He wrote a letter of introduction for me, then sent me to the Jinhua branch of the Anti-Japanese Student Propaganda Team, where I was to wait for the right time to make arrangements for me to go to Yan'an. That's how I came to join the propaganda troupe in Jinhua. We performed in several cities and villages nearby, sleeping somewhere new almost every day. Most of the time, we slept in the open with half-filled stomachs, but I didn't mind. The difficult travel schedule left me no time to think of the things that had happened at home. But singing and acting had never been my ambition. My ambition was to fight in the war, and my ultimate destination was Yan'an. Everything else was just for expediency.

Later, I received word from my Chinese teacher, asking me to meet him in a cloth shop in a certain market town three days later. When he arrived, he would have two students with him, and we would all travel north to Shaanxi together. The market town wasn't far from Sishiyi Bu, so I decided to go home before I left. I could finally tell Ah Yan confidently, "I'm going to join the army and fight the Japanese, and I won't come back." I would use my life's blood to wash away her shame. And not only that—I would use my death as a way to escape from the dilemma of our marriage.

I went home along the waterway that day. When I'd climbed the thirty-nine steps, as I reached the big tree where I read when I was home from school, I heard rustling in the grass nearby. As I approached, I saw a man holding a woman down on the ground. He was tearing her clothes, and she was desperately fighting, kicking with both legs. Though she seemed strong, in the end, she was no match for a man. I saw her strength gradually give out. Just as the man was about to win, she suddenly mustered a venomous force, freed one of her legs, and kicked it at the man's most vulnerable spot. He howled in pain. Furious, he slapped the woman's face.

"Whore! How many men have already had you? Yet you act like some untouched virgin."

I recognized the voice as the village's professional mourner, Scabby.

"Let her go!" I shouted, surprising them both. It was only then that I realized that the woman Scabby had pressed beneath him was Ah Yan. I hardly recognized her. She'd shaved her head, and her cheeks were sunken, leaving almost nothing to her face but a pair of eyes. Those eyes were dry wells, filled with nothing but terror. They were knives piercing my heart.

I pulled Scabby up and threw him against the tree trunk. Bang! Bang! Bang! One blow after another. His body was like a sack that was full of rice slamming against the tree trunk. Bark broke apart, the pieces scattering over his shirt.

"Pig! Dog! Animal!" I shouted.

My mind was a blank, and my spirit momentarily escaped from my body, floating midair and observing my hand's movements from a distance.

Scabby was stunned by the beating. After a moment, he realized that if he didn't get away, he might be killed. Twisting around, he found an angle that gave him some leverage. He threw a knee up at me violently. Unprepared, I fell to the ground, and he staggered away. When he'd gotten to where he knew I couldn't catch him, he spat out a mouthful of blood and shouted, "Don't sing your moral songs to me. You used the Yao name to escape enlistment, then when you heard she'd been fucked by the Japanese, you disowned her. Everyone in the village knows. You came home but didn't see her, because you knew she was filthy."

He ran off, and I just sat there, gasping. The grass rustled, and Ah Yan moved toward me.

"You're back. Are you leaving again, Huwa?" she asked timidly, sitting beside me.

I could smell her body. I couldn't exactly describe the complex smell—mud, sod, her breath, her body. Or, whose body? A Japanese? Scabby? Or . . . I felt suffocated. I was grateful for the dim light of night. It had fallen just in time to hide what I couldn't in my eyes, my disgust.

"I don't believe what he said. I only believe you," she went on.

I remained quiet. I tried to think of something to say, something that wasn't hurtful, but was still true. But I couldn't think of anything. I knew that whatever came out of my mouth at this moment would wound like a knife.

"Ah Yan, I'm no different from Scabby. I'm no more of a man than he is," I said as calmly as possible. I knew she understood, not from my words, but my actions. I moved away from her.

We didn't speak further. For a long time, we sat, saying nothing, listening to the leaves as they rustled and the sparrows chirping as they returned to their nests. She stood up, shook the dust off, and slowly walked toward home. She was as thin as bamboo, as if she could break in the wind. After a moment's hesitation, I caught up with her and grabbed her sleeve. "Ah Yan, wait. Let me explain."

She brushed my hand away and said gently but resolutely, "Don't ever let me see you again."

She walked into the thick darkness without so much as a glance back. Dejected, I left Sishiyi Bu without even saying goodbye to my mother. The only thing that let me descend the entire forty-one-step stone path was the thought of my upcoming trip. One night. I just needed to get through one more night, then I could start on a path that was completely different from my past. A path lit by torches and stars.

Early the next morning, I rushed to the market town that my Chinese teacher had mentioned, but I waited the whole day with no sign of him. I later learned that he'd been arrested and imprisoned. My plan to go north was dead yet again. I had no choice but to return to the Jinhua Anti-Japanese Student Propaganda Team and continue as a part of the traveling troupe. The desire for the battlefield grew stronger within me each day. I had lost my home and my family, and I now had nothing left in this life. My only wish was to die. I'd wanted to die before, but that was only for the sake of revenge. Now, I wanted to die not just for revenge, but for atonement. With my life I would repay the debt I owed Ah Yan.

One day, in a town where we were performing, I saw a recruitment poster for the training camp. I knew that the moment I'd been waiting for had finally arrived.

～

You both saw the look on my face the day I suddenly saw Ah Yan. I never dreamed I would see her again in this life, and certainly not at Yuehu. Yuehu was supposed to be the first step on my journey toward death. Ah Yan was likewise surprised to see me, but her shock disappeared in a flash. The expression that followed was like someone ready to eat rice, only to find that what her chopsticks picked up was a maggot instead. Or like a person with a brand-new pair of shoes, whose first step landed in a pile of shit.

When I ran back into line that day, I completely forgot to convey Mr. Ferguson's instructions to the captain. During drills, I heard the wrong command, and the captain slapped me in front of everyone. It was a ruthless slap, and my cheek was first burning hot, then numb, like it was covered with a layer of cloth. When the drills were over and we went to breakfast, Snot saw how distracted I was and stole a bite of pickled beans right out of my bowl. There were six Chinese students per table and just enough food to take the edge off our hunger. Anyone too slow wouldn't get any food.

"Damn, look at his notes. Those characters are so crooked, they can't be deciphered. Who is he showing off for?" Snot said to me quietly.

He was talking about the captain. He thought I was upset about the slap, but he had no way of knowing the slap was just a small piece of the humiliation I'd suffered in recent days. He had no idea how many layers were beneath it. The humiliation was so thick, it had formed a crust. Now, no matter how many more layers were added, it would never reach my flesh. Even more, he had no idea that I was thinking about Ah Yan. It seemed that Ah Yan was a different person than she'd been before. She seemed to have grown a new spine, making her walk taller. But more than growing new bones, she seemed to have shed her old skin. She had completely started over. Later, I heard someone in the squad say she was an orphan Pastor Billy had taken in and that he was training her to treat patients. It was several years before I learned how she had actually gotten to Yuehu.

From the way Ah Yan looked at me, I knew I was dead to her. But I couldn't resign myself to it. I wanted to die—not in the way she imagined, but in the way I imagined. I had figured out how I wanted to die and had been planning it for a whole year. But there was a huge difference between a death in which Ah Yan was not present and one in which she was. Without Ah Yan, no matter how tragic or heroic my death was, it would be like walking in the dark wearing fine clothes. But with Ah Yan, my death would have an audience. Now that she was here, I had to consider the mode of my death more carefully. Using my life to take another was something any fool could do. But to use one life to take ten lives, that would be worthy of an audience like Ah Yan. I didn't need to prove anything to the world, but I needed to prove one thing, just to Ah Yan—that I wasn't an ungrateful, cowardly villain.

After breakfast, we went to the classroom. This so-called classroom was just two rooms with the dividing wall knocked down. It had two doors and four cracked windows. When it was cold, the wind seeped in through the cracks, whistling. Three of the walls each held a map, one for the European war zone, one for the Chinese war zone, and one for the Pacific war zone. At the front of the room, behind where the instructor stood, there was a painting on the wall of two strong hands clasped tightly together. A flag with stars and stripes was painted on the left arm, and a flag with a blue sky and white sun was painted on the right. The instructors always stood in front of the hands when they were lecturing, and it looked like the two hands were grasping them.

The first two classes in the morning were Outline of the Three People's Principles for Saving the Nation and Analysis of the Situation of the War in Europe. The instructors were Chinese. I sat straight up, appearing to concentrate. Aside from the fact that I wasn't taking notes, no one could tell that I was actually sleeping. This was a skill I'd learned in the propaganda troupe, where I had gotten used to living without enough food and traveling day and night. I'd learned to sleep while walking, sitting, or squatting. I didn't have to close my eyes at all. I could tell the captain sitting a couple of chairs away was struggling to stay awake too, but he didn't have my skill. When he dozed off, his body slouched down, and he even made a slight snoring sound, which earned him a warning from the lecturer's stick.

Although we were both dozing off, the reasons were very different. The captain struggled because he didn't understand. The admission standard was that we had at least a middle school education, but the captain had only finished elementary school. He'd only been accepted because his brother was an influential figure in this area. The leaders of all the gangs at the wharfs called him Boss. Through our connection to him, we could get goods and people transported by sea more easily. The captain was a few years older than us, and he'd spent two years as a platoon leader in a contingent in the southern army. He was big and tall, with a coarse voice. The commanding officer of the camp had assigned him the job of disciplining the soldiers below him.

I was dozing off because I was saving all my energy for the third lesson of the day. Though my mind slept, my ears were alert. Omaha Beach . . . Juno Beach . . . The Dnieper–Carpathian Offensive . . . Cairo . . . The words were like loose sand, not holding together to form anything. Roosevelt, Churchill, Stalin . . . These people seemed to have nothing to do with me. The ultimate victory in the anti-Japanese war . . . that was something for commanding officers, or maybe the commanders of commanding officers, or maybe even the commanders of commanders of commanding officers, to consider. But I was sure to die far from any ultimate victory. And I was sure I wouldn't die alone. There'd be a lot of people who would die with me.

So I didn't need to know the plans of Hitler or Mussolini, or Tōjō Hideki, or Yasuji Okamura, nor did I need to know what corner of the map the Carpathian Mountains occupied or the specific content of the Cairo Declaration. I only needed to know the operating procedures and the killing characteristics of the carbine, Thompson submachine gun, Colt pistol, and rocket artillery. In these few firearms classes, I acquired the skills to use those weapons with little effort. Standing, crouching, or crawling, I was first in the class in live target shooting, and my score was miles above the second place. When the instructor announced the results of target practice, you came over and shook my hand. "Call me Ian," you said. I think that was the beginning of our personal friendship, the secret brotherhood between two soldiers. You said I had a third eye and that I was a natural sniper. You thought it would've been a waste if I hadn't been born during war.

But I wasn't as strong in every segment of the ordnance classes as I was in shooting. For instance, when we had to disassemble and reassemble our firearms, I nearly failed. You thought I was like most Chinese students, lacking hands-on skills. You'd discovered this weakness in Chinese students early on. You said that by the time any ordinary boy in America went to elementary school, he could repair a bicycle, but many Chinese men had never even used a screwdriver. You said this out of surprise, but when it made its way out of your mouth, it carried a hint of sarcasm and disdain. You didn't know how much you'd hurt our pride. And you were soon to reap the consequences of what you'd said. You also didn't know that even though my ability to fix things wasn't comparable to that of a man my age in America, I wasn't as stupid as you thought. I just didn't apply my mind to it. I didn't spread my energy evenly between tasks, because I didn't want to be a mechanic or a repairman. I just wanted to find the fastest way to become a sharpshooter. I didn't have much time. I'd heard the footsteps of the god of death drawing near.

So I muddled along through the first two lessons, and finally it was time for the third, Armament Knowledge, with Gunner's Mate Ian Ferguson. You'd announced in our previous lesson that in this one you were going to introduce a new type of special explosive with superblasting power. The phrase "superblasting power" had been seared into my mind. In my lexicon, it meant I could exchange one life for many. You walked into the classroom carrying a thick roll of paper under your arm and what looked like a few tubes of toothpaste in your hand. I guessed these held what you had called special explosives. When the captain called us to attention, I noticed that my hands shook slightly with the excitement of a good rider who saw a horse of rare quality. I had just opened my notebook when I heard someone call my number: "Number 635, stand up!" It was the captain.

"Have you done your inspection today?" he asked sharply.

I touched my cap and found that the badge was centered, then touched my collar. My heart tightened. It was awful. My collar was loose. After we'd finished morning exercises, I'd been covered in sweat, so I undid the top button on my collar to cool down. I must have forgotten to fasten it again. I quickly did so, but it was too late.

"You'll stand during this class, so that you can be an example to those who don't observe military discipline," the captain said sternly. Feeling every one of the hundreds of eyes on me, I stood in the corner indicated by the captain. I saw you glance at me, and the corner of your mouth twitched as if you had something to say, but you swallowed it. I felt a naked shame. It was strange. That slap that morning was a much harsher punishment, but I don't remember it having the same sting this did. I thought the shame had formed a crust on my flesh, and I had the spirit of a warrior, immune to all poison. I didn't imagine that, no matter how thick the crust, there would still be cracks. That crack was you, Ian. I cared about my image in front of you. My collar had been loose since breakfast, and the captain must have noticed it in the earlier two classes. He chose to land his punch now, though, because he wanted to hit me where I was weakest.

The captain's hatred of me had started almost at first glance. He didn't like that I stayed in bed, reading, on Sunday afternoon after all the work was done instead of walking to the market, like he and the others did, to go to the noodle shop at the entrance of the market and chat with the newly widowed woman who owned it. And he didn't like that every now and then I sat on a stool to cut my nails, then swept the clippings into the rubbish heap beside the door instead of picking the dirt from the nails of one hand with the other and flicking it onto the walls or the top of someone else's mosquito net, like he did. He didn't like that I carefully wrapped the front cover of each textbook with oilpaper instead of tearing a corner off to wipe snot from his nose or blood from his gums, as he did. There were many things about me that the captain couldn't stand. These were just a few examples that he could give. More than once he stood in front of everyone and cursed me, saying, "Don't pretend to be some fucking Mr. Big Scholar with me."

There were other things about me that the captain hated that he was too proud to admit. For instance, I was always the first to understand the American instructors, while he had to wait for the translators to turn the English into awkward Chinese. I could casually half listen to the class on political situations and still receive a good result on the exams, while he struggled to pass, even though he put in many nights of studying. There can be many reasons for one person's fondness or hatred of another, and sometimes there's no reason at all. Explaining interpersonal relationships is easier in the animal kingdom. When it came down to it, the captain and I were just two dogs with different scents.

This scent I was born with and couldn't change led me to endure a good deal of punishment. There were more punishments lurking on the road ahead, like a sniper ready to strike me anytime, and I couldn't prevent that. I was repeatedly called by the captain to carry his footbath and empty his chamber pot, though he had his own orderly to do those things. I had been given two consecutive weeks of housekeeping duty because the nail I used to hang my notebook on the wall was two millimeters longer than others. I'd once been punched because a corner of my blanket had fallen to the floor. I was made to carry sandbags under the scorching sun when my gunstock had accidentally bumped the student next to me while I was practicing my aim. There are too many instances to mention. Later, I eventually came to realize the truth about such faultfinding. When examined under a microscope, one will see the pores even in the skin of an angel.

I had detected his animosity early on and had avoided him as much as possible, shrinking myself in hopes of disappearing into his blind spot. But I couldn't succeed. I was often involuntarily thrust into view, like when I was asked to translate anytime the interpreter wasn't around or was busy. At target practice, my brain repeatedly warned me not to steal the captain's spotlight, but my hand and gun rebelled. They willfully sought the bright-red bull's-eye. I could only watch as I sank ever deeper into the mire of the captain's disdain. When the captain punished me by making me stand during class, he unwittingly placed me at an advantageous height. I could see the podium more clearly than any of my classmates. Eventually, I was so captivated by the instructor's material, I forgot my own embarrassment. You hung three large photos on the blackboard, one of noodles in a sieve, one of a green onion wheat cake, and one of a long fritter. I heard Snot snicker in the back row. He said, "This American is still asleep. He's in the wrong classroom."

You turned and asked for translation, but the translator said he didn't hear clearly. Snot was confident about the translator. He spoke with a heavy accent, but he was a good old fellow, and he knew what he should translate and what he should not.

"You must be wondering about these photos. Well, these are the special explosives we're going to discuss today."

You whetted everyone's appetite right from the start that day. Squeezing a small amount of the soft substance from one of the plastic tubes, you spread it over your palm and showed it to us.

"This is our newly developed soft explosive. Its blasting power is five to eight times that of ordinary TNT. It can be molded into the shape of a variety of food items. Besides the things in the photos, you can shape it into the sesame balls most common in this area. If you want the effect to be more realistic, you can roll it in sesame seeds and crushed peanuts.

"Besides being a powerful explosive, it can be transported safely, because unlike ordinary explosives, its detonator and fuse do not have to be installed in advance, but can be carried separately, then kneaded into the middle when you're ready to use the explosive."

You grabbed a small piece, put it in your mouth, and swallowed it. Everyone gasped.

"If one encounters an unexpected search or check, you can even take a bite in front of the inspecting party to show it's harmless. Of course, you can't swallow the whole thing."

At this, everyone let out a sigh of relief.

"We've performed precise experiments. The fuse can be anywhere from thirty-one inches to ten yards, according to the specific needs of the situation. Thirty-one inches minimum was calculated based on the height of the average American, but since most Chinese are smaller, a minimum length of one yard is needed, since stride is proportionate to height. If the fuse is too short, the person who sets the explosive won't have enough time to escape safely. If it's too long, the detonation will take too long, giving the enemy time to defuse it."

Only Americans could engineer killing so precisely and cleanly, like a mathematical formula. Thinking of the time I had stolen the knife from the butcher Yao Er's shop, I could only sigh and think I was no more than a frog in a well who'd seen nothing of the world.

Next, you began to introduce another way to detonate soft explosives: timing devices. Once again, Snot couldn't resist saying something that made everyone laugh loudly. You turned to face the interpreter. He stammered and said he didn't hear, but you weren't fooled this time. Your eyes clung to the interpreter's face like a leech, not budging. In the end, he couldn't stand up under a look like that. He laughed nervously and said, "Maybe they feel that if they can't see the effect of the blasting, it's no . . . not so exciting." Of course this wasn't what had been said. What had been said was two things: "If you don't hear the bang, that's a pretty chickenshit explosive" and "At the end of the day, those American motherfuckers are just scared to die." The interpreter softened the edges on the first sentence and completely omitted the second. But the radar in your brain was particularly sensitive that day. You understood the tone in Snot's words, and with that foothold, you intuitively struck on his meaning.

You fell silent. At first, we didn't realize you were angry, because the American instructors rarely flared up at the Chinese trainees. We only saw that your face had grown a little pale, but all the Americans' skin was pale anyway, so we weren't too concerned. Then, the paleness turned steely. Your silence lasted for a long time, beyond the normal span of someone gathering his thoughts. We began to feel confused and uneasy. You finally let out a sigh, then pulled out your wallet and took a folded newspaper clipping from inside. We passed it from row to row. No one but me and the interpreter understood the English text, but the photo above the words was a young, shy-looking American in sportswear.

"That's John Worthington. He lived in my hometown and was engaged to my friend's friend. If there'd been no war, he'd probably be a professional football player," you said. "He entered the military a year before me, joining the air force, and he also served in the Far East. He made sixteen flights on the Hump, landing safely every time. But on the seventeenth mission, his plane crashed. The special explosives he was carrying were like these you're seeing today.

"Do you know how many planes have crashed or been shot down besides his? Do you know how much tax support is required from each family for each instructor and each piece of weaponry to be transported all the way over here? For every one of you sitting in class here, how many people supporting you have had to cut back on food and clothing, even to the point of dying from hunger and cold? You're not ordinary soldiers. You carry the lives of others with you."

You sounded exhausted, so unlike your typical swagger when you played basketball or walked your dog. At that moment, you sounded more like an old man who'd endured a long journey and was physically run-down. Later, I learned it was the death of this young man that prompted your girlfriend to marry someone else.

"If you want to die in your first battle, that's cowardly. Your training is too expensive. You aren't here to learn how to die. The person who rushes to the front and dies in the most tragic manner isn't the winner. If you live to the end, until you've beaten all your enemies, then you're the real hero."

The interpreter stopped stuttering, finishing that entire speech in one breath. As he finished, I heard rawness in his throat. Silence fell. Nobody knew how to respond. The interpreter was the first to applaud. His applause was lonely at first, so lonely it grew awkward. After a moment, there was a smattering of sparse, hesitant responses, which gradually grew a backbone and became more confident. I did not clap. I was in a trance. I felt that the wall that had been guarding my heart had toppled, and a strange light was shining through. I couldn't tell if I had gained freedom or if I was more weighed down than before.

You took a few bills from your wallet and put them in the captain's hand, saying, "After class, go to the store and buy some firecrackers. Get the biggest ones. Doesn't 520 love to hear a bang? Let him hear all he wants." Everyone burst into laughter. Snot wiped his nose with his sleeve and laughed along with them.

That day's class was short, lasting only half an hour. The next subject was field operations. Three simple brick houses had been constructed in an open field, and the fuses were set at lengths of one yard, five yards, and ten yards. The effect of each explosion was similar. A ball of soft explosive shaped like a wheat cake instantly turned a brick house into a pile of rubble. I took off my hat and wiped the dust from my body. I wasn't even aware that you had walked over to stand beside me.

"After seeing the power of these explosives, you still want to die right away?" you asked, winking at me.

I was taken aback.

"You . . . how did you know?"

"I'm always observing. You concentrated when I explained the details of firing and blasting, but not on the aftermath and retreat segment."

I was speechless. Your mind was indeed a radar, and there were almost no blind spots. In all those long years after we parted, whenever I thought of Yuehu, I always felt that the main reason I didn't die on the battlefield was that particular class of yours. But I don't know whether I should thank you for those years or curse you.

"I'll look for you later. I have something to discuss with you," you whispered to me.

That night after dinner, you sent your servant Buffalo to call me.

He didn't come in, but stood outside the door and called, "Six-three-five, the American officer needs you to do some translation."

I followed Buffalo a few steps and noticed we weren't going toward the classroom. I asked where we were going, but Buffalo just ignored me and walked ahead, leading the way. We walked into a clearing in the woods. In the distance, I saw you sitting alone on a rock, smoking, with Ghost lying at your feet. Beside Ghost was the white terrier Millie. Ghost was dozing off, and Millie kept pushing his head lightly with her paw. Ghost wasn't annoyed, but shook his head from time to time, as if shooing away flies.

I put my heels together and stood at attention. Though your khakis had no military insignia indicating rank and the Americans didn't salute when you saw each other, regardless of rank, your practice didn't apply to us. We had to salute every commanding officer of any level and every instructor. You waved and motioned me to sit next to you.

"Where are they?" I asked.

"Who?" you said, not understanding.

"Don't you need me to translate?" I looked at Buffalo in confusion.

Buffalo showed his protruding front teeth and started to laugh.

"If I didn't say that, would they have let you go?" he said.

He wasn't wrong. Chinese students had no free time, aside from four hours on Sunday afternoon. You took your cigarette case out of your pocket and offered me one.

"Smoke?" you asked.

I nodded. Most of our comrades learned to smoke during their first week or two in the camp, and I was no exception. But we only smoked local cigarettes. This was my first American cigarette. American cigarettes were a rare commodity. Aside from the American instructors, I'd only seen our highest local commanding officer have one. I felt the difference immediately. Local cigarettes were made with couch grass, which is spicy and pungent as it travels from tongue to throat to lungs and back out the nose. The American cigarette was also made with couch grass, but its edge was taken off as if covered in a layer of silky cotton, which was soft and had a smell I didn't recognize. I couldn't bear to finish it in one sitting, so I put it out half-smoked, then tucked it behind my ear for the next day. You, on the other hand, smoked your cigarette all the way to a butt. You took your time, as if there were an unreachable island between each drag. I could see that you were looking for an appropriate opening to start a conversation.

"When I was little, my father took me to the zoo. Can you guess which animal I liked best?" you finally began.

I'd never seen a zoo. Having only read about them in books, I had to rely on my imagination to answer your question. I guessed the eagle first, then the lion, since these two animals were the most fascinating to me, but you just shook your head. Then you told me it was the monkey.

I was surprised and asked, "Why?"

You said, "They're very similar to humans. The monkey house at the zoo was like the land of little people in *Gulliver's Travels*."

You said that every time you went to the zoo, you would ignore everything else and just go straight to the monkey house, where you would spend several hours.

"Once, I saw a tourist throw a banana to them. All the monkeys rushed forward. One of the bigger monkeys grabbed it first, but he didn't get to eat it. In the end, the one that ate it was a small monkey. The big fellow was almost twice its size, but the small monkey launched a surprise attack from behind. He jumped on the big monkey's back and snatched the banana over its shoulder. When the big monkey turned around, the little monkey had just the peel left in his hand.

"That was when it dawned on me that even in the animal world, strength doesn't guarantee victory. Strength and dexterity can each be used to restrain the other."

I didn't know what it was you wanted to say, but I was sure you weren't really talking about monkeys or bananas. This was just your lead into another topic. I was vaguely aware that the monkeys and the banana had something to do with me. But you immediately changed the subject.

"Six-three-five, did you study mathematics at school? I've heard that most middle schools in China only teach humanities."

I said, "The school I went to was a local mission school, and it taught both Chinese and European subjects. We had math class and a basic science class."

I didn't tell you why my father would spend money for me to study. Of course, for him, it wasn't so that I could learn to speak a foreign language or master geometry and algebraic formulas. For him, it was enough for me to understand the number of credits and debits in an account. He also didn't care if I could understand the theory of electrical generation. He just didn't want me to inherit his craft and become a tea plantation master. He sent me to the middle school in the county seat so that I could enjoy the gentle life the village scribe Yang Deshun had, helping to write all the documents anyone in our village needed. My father said Yang Deshun hadn't spent a single day behind a plow under the hot sun, yet he had never failed to have wine in his cup and meat in his bowl. He noticed that Yang Deshun was getting old and his hands were starting to tremble as he wrote. When I graduated and came home, I would be just in time to take over the role from him.

You asked, "How were your grades in math?"

I hesitated, then said, "In terms of test results, top three in every subject."

"In fighting, the time it takes to complete a kick or a punch is proportionate to one's height and weight. For someone with a good understanding of math, this is not hard to understand, right?" you asked.

I nodded.

"That is to say, when someone thirty or fifty percent stronger than you in terms of height and weight is throwing punches or kicking, a person of your height and weight may be able to complete three strikes in the same amount of time," you said. Then you asked, "Which part of the upper body do you think you can strike at the shortest distance and with the greatest speed?"

I closed my eyes and considered, then asked, "Is it the elbow?"

"And what about the lower body?"

I followed the same train of thought down several inches and said the knee.

You told me to keep my eyes closed, then said, "Imagine this: Where is the other person's blind spot when fighting?"

I said, "Behind him."

You went on, "And what other spots are close to the blind spot?"

I said, "The sides."

You chuckled and said, "You're a good student."

You told me to open my eyes and stare at you without blinking. You took out your stopwatch and timed me.

"Fifty-eight seconds. That's good. The expression of the eyes is a point often overlooked when fighting. How long the eyes can stay open is limited by the needs of the body, but the expression in one's eyes has nothing to do with height or weight. It comes from the mind. When you fight, your eyes must hold your opponent like an iron vise. Your expression is especially important. A famous military scientist once said that psychology is a secret weapon in modern warfare that does not consume huge expenses. There's some logic to this.

"From today on, I want you to exercise strength in three places: elbows, knees, and eyes."

That day, you trained me to fight in the clearing in the woods until it was dark. We did the same over the next few days as well. I always thought you did this because I was smaller than the other trainees, so you wanted to give me some tips before combat classes began. Later, I realized your true intentions after I won the most spectacular fight in the history of the training camp. That is, of course, had the training camp even been worthy of a note in history.

Ian Ferguson: A Game I Allegedly Fixed

When I announced the groups for combat class that day, I saw a small spark in your eyes, Liu Zhaohu, but it disappeared so fast I wondered if I'd imagined it. I suspected you had fire hidden in you. On the firing range a few days before, when you were aiming the Colt pistol, I saw something close to fire in your furrowed brows and the tightened corners of your mouth. Most of the time you wrapped yourself up, as if in armor, sealing off the exit of your emotions. I didn't know what was putting so much pressure on you, but I guessed that your captain was part of the problem. My grouping method was simple, and no one could take issue with it. I assigned each pair of adjacent desks to one training group. Accordingly, you and your captain were in the same group. The four students who sat at the two desks became partners on a rotating basis, meaning that 33.333333 percent of the time, you would practice with your captain. Considering your good results in math, I kept the decimal to six digits. As for the small strand of selfish reason hidden in this impeccable arrangement, it was known only to you, me, and God.

I'd had an earful from Buffalo about how your captain treated you. He wasn't an eyewitness himself, and by the time the story reached him, it had passed through many hands. The direct source was Number 520, who you called Snot. A reckless boy like him, unable to control either his nose or his mouth, would someday land in deep trouble because of his running tongue and constipated brain. Snot and your cook came from the same village and had been neighbors. The cook always gave his former neighbor an extra half bowl of porridge and a few extra radishes. In return, Snot brought all the salacious happenings to the cook's ears. Of course, he always told the cook not to tell anyone else, since everything in the training camp was classified military information in the strictest sense. But the cook couldn't help but tell his wife, who was Pastor Billy's cook and laundry woman. It's difficult for people sharing a bed to keep secrets from one another, but they never dreamed their pillow talk would one day leak out and rewrite the lives of others. Buffalo was the messenger between the American instructors and Pastor Billy. He ran back and forth between the church and our dorms several times a day. Now, understand, the rumors passed through this circuitous route before reaching me. I knew that each time a story was filtered through a new tongue, it would be tainted with new colors and impurities, resulting in a variety of distortions. Buffalo's ears were always open wide, and they collected all sorts of rumors all day long. I didn't just believe everything he told me, of course, but the way the captain punished you in the soft explosives class that day verified those rumors for me.

From your first day in camp, you were always neat and tidy, with your cap badge and belt buckle directly along your body's central axis. When I trained you to aim and shoot, I noticed your nails were trimmed cleanly. Sorry, but as a munition and weapons technician, I have a near-morbid precision when it comes to details. So I knew that the collar button incident that day was a rare oversight. I could understand that a team like yours needed extremely strict discipline, and even accidental negligence had to be punished. What I didn't understand was the form of punishment. You could've been given extra classroom cleaning duties outside class or extra night guard duty or even lost your free time on Sunday afternoon. But your captain chose to humiliate you in public. It was as if a child had made a small mistake, and his parents could give them a time out but instead chose to slap their face. I understand that in your country honor is sometimes as important as one's life. The way he chose to shame you obviously carried personal feeling behind it. I wanted to say something on your behalf, but I refrained. I couldn't interfere with your internal affairs. Just as you had to obey your commanding officers, I had to obey my superior, Commander Miles of Naval Group China. The regulations were heavy shackles, and I couldn't extend a helping hand to you with them weighing me down. But even if I had helped that time, I couldn't have helped the next. God only knew how many more such occasions there would be. The only person you could rely on was yourself. You had to exert your own strength to save yourself.

At the firing range, you'd proven your strength with your results. But that was only your prowess with weapons. A weapon was nothing but a tool, independent from your body, and results were nothing but a piece of paper with some numbers that proved nothing about your ability to fight when deprived of that tool. The only means of besting your captain completely was to take him on barehanded. So I thought I'd give you some private lessons. In fact, I wasn't entirely biased toward you. The tricks I showed you I also taught in class, but there they were generalized for everyone, but in private, I could tailor them to your physique.

In your country, renowned for martial arts, it was actually a little absurd for a foreigner like me to teach you hand-to-hand combat techniques. In your words, it was like "showing off in the presence of an expert." Our original idea was to add some Western boxing skills to the foundation of Asian martial arts in hope of confusing the Japanese, who had similar martial arts traditions. You weren't a regular army unit, but a band of guerrillas with special weapons and skills. You weren't intended for phalanx battles, but to covertly disrupt operations in enemy-occupied territory and interrupt the supply lines of the Japanese. The fighting skills were to keep you safe and help you escape if you were captured or in a close-combat situation. Their purpose was to defend and escape, not to attack. However, when I trained you in private, individualized sessions, I enhanced the attack part. So, when you later called me the behind-the-scenes mastermind of that sensational fight, it wasn't completely without reason.

Several times during lunch, I saw you sneak into the woods and practice hitting your elbows and knees against a tree trunk. You had to wrap them with thick strips of cloth, which showed your dedication. I also saw you stare at a hole in the tree, the heat in your eyes seeming to burn the hole even deeper, and I knew you were practicing what I taught you. You were smart, but there were plenty of people in the world who were smarter than you, and cleverness is sometimes the biggest obstacle. Fortunately, you were also diligent and persistent. Diligence clips the wings of cleverness, allowing it to stay firmly on the ground. Persistence grinds away the sharp edges of cleverness, not allowing it to take shortcuts through things. Cleverness thus clipped can more fully penetrate the nature of things. With your cleverness, diligence, and persistence, I had some measure of confidence in you, but an almost equal amount of anxiety. Your build was very different from your captain's. If I put you two on a scale, I would've had to add a few stones on your side to make it balance. Your initial performance only increased my worries.

During our initial fighting lessons, you didn't manage to defeat your opponent in any of the sessions. Not just the captain, but the other two members of your group too. Of course, it wasn't an easy victory for them, but no matter how thrilling and intricate the process, what really mattered was the final result. You were defeated so often that I became bored with the fights, because I already knew the outcome before you started. There was no suspense. Your other opponents stopped immediately once they'd won, but the captain didn't. He took a bullfight approach to a cockfight, and knocking you down to the ground was only the first step in a prolonged defeat. Once, when you'd fallen to the ground, he gave you one last fierce kick and you bit off a piece of your lip, making it swell like a huge red grape. Another time he boxed you into a corner. Even after you stopped resisting, he added a punch to your face. The blood that ran from your nose nearly drenched a towel.

I was disappointed in you. If you couldn't win in any of the training fights, how could you win a real one? If every brick had cracks, how could I build a solid wall with them? I began to doubt myself. Were the alertness and keenness you showed when you were alone with me only good for dealing with imaginary enemies? I never imagined that you were using these defeats to fool your opponent into believing that the opening drum was the battle itself. You laid your every loss at the captain's feet, one after the other. By the time the fight truly began, his feet were miles off the ground, and he couldn't find his footing.

The comprehensive evaluation at the end of training was the real beginning of your fight. Each student had to have two freestyle fights against an opponent. Another group of students was having target practice on the activity field, so we held the fights in the open space in front of your dorms. The venue was small, and the students made a circle three rows deep around the arena to observe. The innermost row sat, the next squatted, and the outer row stood. A few shorter students climbed the surrounding trees and sat on branches. Midsummer had passed, but the afternoon sun was still strong, and a thin, shimmering heat rose from the sandy ground. There was the sort of excitement that could only be generated by fighting with bare hands, for which no weapon could substitute. I almost decided to randomly assign opponents, afraid you were going to be badly hurt. But I didn't. I wasn't your parent, bodyguard, or nanny, and I couldn't protect you forever. You were a soldier, after all, and you'd have to face countless unexpected dangers in battle. I couldn't choose your enemy for you. Still, when it was your turn to fight, my chest was tight. You took your shirt off, and I saw your bare torso for the first time. There were bandages on your arms, wrists, and back, and you were very skinny.

It was strange. Your thin body seemed like a blade as you entered the arena, slicing through the air, charged and instantly changing the atmosphere. I couldn't explain the phenomenon. Some decades later, someone finally found a name for it: aura. Of course, your aura that day wasn't from your muscles, since you didn't really have any. Nor did it come from your bones or the bandages. It was your eyes that made the difference that day. Like the eyes of a bitch whose pups have been taken away, your eyes had a faint blue gleam in them. Like a fire, but without heat. Whatever your gaze fell on turned to ice, and whoever saw that light couldn't help but shudder. As you stepped onto the field, you met and held the captain's eyes with this light. He was stunned.

Without missing a beat, you immediately attacked, not giving him a chance to overcome his surprise. You kept your center of gravity very low, half squatting, with most of your mass below the level of his arm. Your radius of movement was very small, making you look like a half-curled ball. Suddenly a blade shot out from that ball. It was your elbow. It was like a hatchet cutting into his side. Not expecting you to attack from this angle, he staggered a bit. But he was no coward, after all. He immediately backhanded and grabbed at your torso. If you'd been wearing a shirt, you might have exchanged several blows with him. But your body was as slippery as a mudfish, and his hands grasped in the air in a useless, almost funny, manner. In the end, he couldn't regain his balance and came crashing to the ground.

The crowd exclaimed. It happened so quickly, they'd hardly had a chance to see what tricks you had used. The captain stood up and waved his hand angrily at me. The interpreter said he was protesting, claiming you hadn't followed the steps taught in class. I shrugged and said, "Sorry. The Japanese won't fight by the rules either." He had no choice but to swallow his anger and prepare for the next round.

This time, he estimated your abilities anew. Like me, he began to see through your earlier tricks. From several paces away, I could see the deep breaths he took to gain control of his strength. The veins in his temples bulged, crawling along his neck down to his chest. His feet were planted wide, the soles of his feet secured like the foundation of a tower. You'd already wounded his pride, and he unconsciously took a defensive stance. You were like a flea flitting around his body, searching for a place to bite, but he closed every pore, his body completely tight, without any trace of a crack. The standoff lasted a long time. You kept attacking, and he kept fending you off. It seemed neither of you would get the advantage. And you were fading, without either the strength or the endurance of your opponent. He was waiting for the fury of your storm to run out of energy. I started to worry again, thinking you were being lured into his trap. As your responses slowed, your moves started to appear sluggish.

But we had misjudged again. This was just a new round of smoke. You were testing the waters with a few shots that didn't take much effort, saving yourself for a massive blow. Suddenly, your legs were off the ground, and you scurried onto his back like a monkey. He'd made a tactical error. He was too defensive, his muscles held too tightly, and it took him too long to turn around. You were counting on this, and your earlier movements were just meant to increase his tension, winding the coil of his body tighter and tighter. Fooled, he couldn't turn in time. You landed your heel like a hammer on the back of his knees, and the tower's foundation began to shake. Though he didn't fall, his center of gravity was off-kilter. You didn't give him a chance to breathe, slamming a punch into his right shoulder. Your fist smashed into him like he was a ripe watermelon, and we heard a dull thud. His balance was destroyed. You dropped from his back as he fell. His right side hit the ground first. On impact, I heard him grunt, then his entire body went as limp as an empty sack. You walked over. I thought you were going to help him up, but you sat down on his back and wiped the sweat off your forehead with the back of your hand.

"Shirt. Shoes," you said to the onlookers.

Someone grabbed the shirt and sandals you'd hung on a branch and tossed them to you. You put on your tan uniform, which already looked old from washing, and fastened each button one at a time. You took your sandals, shook the dust from them, and put them on. Then, you stood up and slowly walked away. The onlookers parted, creating a path for you. No one spoke. As you passed, everyone patted you on the shoulder. When you walked past me, I saw something flash. After a moment, I realized it was your teeth. They were dazzling white, exposed in the wide slit between your lips. I'd never seen you smile like you did in that moment, and it felt unfamiliar. After a while, the captain sat up, and I saw why he'd lain there so long. His right shoulder had been dislocated when he hit the ground, and his right arm hung awkwardly, like a sun-dried loofah. A few soldiers went over to help him, but he pushed them away.

"You little bastards. What're you looking at? Go practice your skills!" he yelled at them. His voice had suddenly grown much thinner.

Pastor Billy: Metamorphosis from Pupa to Butterfly

Stella lived in Yuehu during strange times, when half the world was burning with the fires of war. War condensed a whole life into a few moments, compressing the time between stepping out into the world and saying one's final farewell—the period from birth to death that normally spans several decades.

During those few years, Stella went through a process of growth that would've taken decades in peacetime. Her body grew according to the laws of nature, but her mind couldn't wait for her body, so it forged a path of its own. The biggest lesson she learned in Yuehu was how to deal with shame. Before, she had thought that if she could shrink herself very small and hide, shame would never find her again. But she was wrong. Shame was a shadow, and no matter how far she traveled, it would follow her. Indeed, even if she ran as fast as she could, she would never be rid of it. So she learned to turn around. Learning is a gradual process, but mastering the act came in a moment of lightning and thunder, and the leap from quantitative to qualitative change took only an instant. One day, she simply understood how to face shame directly. She stood upright, turned around, and met it head-on, only to find that the shame that had followed her so persistently was just an empty shell. Once it had been punctured, it completely deflated. It was only when she faced it head-on that the shame lost its power. And that was when she completed her metamorphosis from pupa to butterfly.

Stella's head-on collision with her shame came after Liu Zhaohu won the fight. Those two major events in the sensational history of the camp came about ten days apart. One day the Chinese students were talking around the dining table during breakfast. It was Sunday, so quarters were to be cleaned in the morning, and in the afternoon, everyone planned to go to the market. Since there were no classes, the atmosphere wasn't as serious as usual, the conversation flowing from one topic to another, covering a few things that excited everyone.

The first topic was the graduation ceremony to be held the following week. Though this cohort had only been studying in Yuehu for a few months, it was a high-intensity training program, equivalent to a year in a regular military school. They'd learned elite weaponry at a much more advanced level than regular troops did. They were a group of special soldiers, a cut above the rest. There were many guesses as to who would address the graduating students at the ceremony. Someone said they'd heard it was a general from Zhejiang, one of such a high rank that his whereabouts couldn't be leaked in advance. This rumor inevitably led everyone to think of the names of several high-ranking generals from Zhejiang, like Generalissimo Chiang. Though of course no one dared utter his name—just the thought of it caused trembling in the trainees' hearts.

Second, a large-scale field mission was scheduled to start the next day. The next evening after dark, some of them were to set off for a small town nearly two hundred li away from Yuehu and blow up a Japanese munitions and supply warehouse there. According to reliable intelligence, the Japanese had many tons of supplies there. The names of those soldiers taking part in the operation would be announced after dinner. The skills they had learned over the past few months would finally be tested in that mission.

Also, in four days a theater troupe was to perform at Yuehu. Yuehu was remote, so few people traveled there for entertainment. The play had been a topic of discussion for some time, with new real or imagined details added each day, like a fire, flames growing with each log thrown into it. The new detail that day was that the play would be *The Butterfly Lovers: Liang Shanbo and Zhu Yingtai*, and Zhu Yingtai would be played by the starring actress of the troupe, the renowned Xiao Yanqiu. The people of Yuehu had invited the troupe several years in a row, but with no success. This year, they hadn't invited the troupe, but the troupe decided to come at Xiao Yanqiu's suggestion. Xiao's husband had been captured by the Japanese when he was traveling to buy the troupe's costumes. They forced him to serve them, then worked him to death, leaving him vomiting blood on the road. Xiao hated the Japanese fiercely now, and when she heard there was an anti-Japanese training camp in Yuehu, she offered to bring her troupe to entertain the forces. But the conversation that day concerning Xiao Yanqiu took a wrong turn. The road looked harmless at first, but farther down, it led to an abyss.

That day, a student at Liu Zhaohu's table said he had a relative who was a salt merchant in Yuyao who'd met Xiao Yanqiu in a teahouse there after a performance one night. Xiao's troupe was based in Yuyao. No one could confirm this, but its veracity wasn't really important—the man told his relative's story as if he'd been there himself. He said Xiao was even more beautiful offstage, that after she removed her makeup, her skin was fair and bright and soft, so dewy that the lightest touch produced moisture. He also said she had a mole shaped like a teardrop under her right eye. His words made those seated at the table restless. The idea of a fingertip caressing water from her face had already made their minds stray, but the teardrop mole inspired love and pity within them. These strong young men had been living in isolation in the valley for several months. Just the talk of a woman was enough to make their voices crack. One of the older students, who was married, shook his head and said how lonely it must be for someone as beautiful as her to sleep in an empty bed. They all fell silent, as if experiencing the loneliness of that solitary bed.

Then Number 520, Snot, gave a long sigh. "One night with Xiao Yanqiu, that would be worth dying for," he said dreamily. Snot was the youngest in the group. But his real age was only revealed by the cook after Snot died. His words were like sprinkling a few drops of water onto hot oil. Everyone around the table exploded. Someone said, "Snot, you're barely weaned. What woman have you ever seen, besides your mother?"

Upset, Snot said, "Even so, haven't I seen a dog fuck a bitch? What's the difference?"

Roaring with laughter, everyone joined in. "Listen to this suckling. Let's check to see if his cock is fully grown yet." Embarrassed and furious, Snot threw his bowl down and ran out the door, his face flushed.

It had just been mindless chatter around the table, originating in the crotch and going straight out of the mouth without passing through the brain at all. No one knew then that hormones were explosives. The guys just kept tossing one match after another and then put the matter in the back of their minds afterward. It was only after hearing the explosion at dinner that night that they understood the blaze they'd caused.

Even after Snot ran out, they didn't let him off the hook. Someone chased him and, standing in the doorway, shouted, "Hurry! Find someone to practice with, mama's little boy. You don't want to turn Xiao Yanqiu off, do you?"

Snot ran through the courtyard and out toward the river. His skull was burning as if ten lamps were lit inside it. His face was so hot, he felt his skin would burst. He wanted to put his head underwater and soak it for a while to douse the fiery oil inside him. He didn't realize the devil had already tied a rope around his ankle and was pulling him toward hell's door. Dazed, he went to the river and scooped a handful of water. Just as he was about to splash his face, he suddenly stopped. A few paces away, he saw a young girl squatting on the stones beside the river, rinsing a basket of herbs. The herbs were probably newly picked. She was scraping the roots and leaves with her nails to remove the wet soil. It was hot, and the girl was only wearing a thin blouse. Her head was lowered, revealing a white neck covered in a layer of fine peachy fuzz. Snot felt the oil lamp in his skull overturn. The hot liquid began to flow down his body to his loins, and there it exploded, blowing his body apart, separating his brain from his limbs.

His head was the first part to see the devil. It said to his body, *Go! Hurry! You don't have eyes, so you can't see the devil.*

The body said, *I might be dead tomorrow. What do we need eyes for?*

The head said, *If you don't leave now, it will lead to a big disaster.*

The body said, *I don't care. I'm not going to die without having a taste.*

Snot ran over to the girl and grabbed her waist. He caught her scent, strange and fragrant, not like anything he'd smelled before. Not like flowers, grass, brewer's yeast, or rice. It was light at first, but when he breathed it in again, it was strong, like smoke and fire, as if it could burn three houses at a time or ten haystacks. The girl was shocked. Turning, she saw the number 520 stitched onto the chest of his tunic.

"You . . . What are you doing?" she asked, eyes wide with horror.

Snot panicked. He had thought about what to do, but not what to say. He didn't know he'd need to talk. The girl struggled as if for her life, trying to push his hands away.

"I just want to see . . . take a look," he stammered.

He suddenly hated himself. He felt that the girl's eyes had pierced through him, seeing what a baby he really was, not knowing a thing. His brain had lost control of not only his hands and feet but also his voice. "What haven't I seen? Don't play coy with me," he shouted. His voice sounded very coarse, and when the words left his throat, a few bloody scratches trailed in their tracks. He barely recognized his voice as his own. Trembling, he tried to unbutton the girl's blouse. His hands shook so hard he couldn't do it. He'd never realized the buttons on a girl's blouse were so complicated. Finally, he skipped the buttons and simply tore the fabric.

Her hands and feet weren't strong. All she had was her teeth. She bit his hand hard. With a yelp of pain, Snot released her. A plum blossom bite mark appeared on the back of his hand, first pink, then turning a deep red.

"Your commanding officer! I'll . . . tell your commanding officer!" she panted, pulling away from him.

Snot lifted the front of his shirt and dabbed his bleeding hand. Taking a step forward, he tripped the girl, knocking her to the ground. "You won't dare. You can't afford to lose face like that. You think I don't know who you are? You can hide the awful things about yourself from everyone else, but not from me."

She was stunned. She felt like the sun was trembling in the sky and the ground beneath her was melting, as if it couldn't support her weight. She was falling, deeper and deeper, all the way to the center of the earth.

I've hidden so long and traveled so far, but that damned shadow is still with me. It eventually caught up, she thought.

~

When I finished the second worship service that day, I went straight to the kitchen to see Stella. She was usually in the kitchen by this time, helping the cook prepare dinner, but she wasn't there. When I asked the cook where she was, she pouted and said, "She's been sitting out there alone all afternoon."

Going into the backyard, I saw Stella sitting on a bench beside the oleander. She had her elbows on her knees and her chin in her hands, as if in a trance. Her expression was strange. Her features were still, and a brassy, yellowy tinge had fallen over her face. She looked almost like a statue. She seemed to be pondering profound philosophical questions like the origin of man and the nature of the universe, not tolerating the slightest disturbance.

I stood behind her for a long time. Finally, I cleared my throat.

"Why didn't you come to church today?" I asked. She had never failed to sit through a worship service since coming to Yuehu the second time. She didn't go because of God, but to please me. I said "sit through a worship service" because it was not that she worshipped but because I never knew how much she actually absorbed.

She turned, but didn't answer. After staring for a long time, she finally said, "Pastor Billy, how many cheeks do you think a person should have?"

I looked at her blankly.

She snorted and said, "You forgot the story you told? Turn the other cheek?"

I understood. She meant the verse in the Gospel of Matthew: "Whosoever shall smite thee on thy right cheek, turn to him the other also." I'd taught that in Bible class the previous week.

"What made you think of that?" I asked curiously.

Her lips twitched, and I thought she was going to say something, but she swallowed it.

"I'm just asking," she said.

"Stella, you know Jesus isn't actually talking about your face, right? It's just a metaphor."

She interrupted me before I could finish. "I know. He's talking about how many times someone should forgive others."

It seemed as if she'd thought of something. She stood up and walked out.

"Twice. The right cheek once and the left cheek once. That's enough," she said.

She walked along the road, and the sun had begun to slant. The days were still long in September, and the light had yet to change colors. She could hear hints of autumn in the cries of the geese as they flew overhead. She walked slowly that day, calmly. She even took time to rest under a tree and watch a bird carry a fat worm in its beak to feed its nest of chicks above. She'd already decided what she was going to say, and her heart felt settled. She said to herself, *I've already hit bottom. I can't go lower.*

She later told me that as she walked on the road that day, it felt like there was an operation she'd been waiting to perform, and though she hesitated for a long time, it was finally going to be done. She wasn't operating on others, but on herself. She said that it was like one of her hands festered with pus and blood, infecting whatever it touched. She finally understood that she couldn't save both her hand and her life. The only way to save her life was to amputate the hand. You both know that this was a metaphor. She'd learned to use many such metaphors from the Gospels.

She stopped at the door to the Chinese students' dorm. The door was closed, and an armed guard stood on its steps.

"I'm looking for your commander—the highest-ranking officer," she said to the guard.

He was shocked. Security was tight here, and few outsiders were allowed in. Most of the Chinese students knew me, but only a few had seen Stella, because she never came this way, not wanting to see Liu Zhaohu.

"Who are you?" the guard asked.

"You'll find out later," she said.

"Our commanding officer can't see you."

"Why not?"

"He's in a meeting. If you have something to say, you can tell me."

The guard wasn't lying. The commanding officer really was in a staff meeting, discussing the final details for that night's mission.

"I can't tell you. It's too heavy for you to pass along."

She said it without emotion as she stepped toward the courtyard. The guard stepped in front of her, blocking the way.

"The commanding officer has ordered that no random person be allowed beyond this point."

Stella glared at him and said, "I'm not random. You can't afford to delay my business."

Seeing that he still refused to move, she picked up a stone from the side of the road and smashed it into the door. The Chinese students' dorm was a house that had been loaned to the camp by a well-off family. The two panels of the door were made of black wood, and they were very thick. The stone banged against them like dull thunder, leaving a dent in the door.

The guard came to himself and leveled his gun at Stella. She was stunned. She'd thought through what might happen, but had neglected the gun. It was a surprise. There was no time. The gun was faster than she was. Wherever she went, the gun followed. She had no choice but to risk everything.

She faced the guard and yelled, "If you're not afraid of your commanding officer, then shoot."

Those having dinner inside heard the commotion and ran to see what was happening. Liu Zhaohu was among them. When he saw the guard aiming his gun at a young woman, he came nearer. When he saw who she was, his face blanched in fright. He didn't dare take the gun from the guard, afraid of discharging it. He could only walk carefully to the center of the guard's field of vision.

"Don't shoot," he said.

He noticed his lips were trembling, and his voice was strained.

The guard glanced at him. "Do you know her?"

Liu said, "She's from my village. She's not a spy."

Stella laughed coldly. She said, "From your village? And what else? If you want to tell them, then tell them everything."

Liu didn't answer, but asked, "What's going on?"

Stella pushed him aside and walked into the courtyard, saying, "I want to see your commanding officer."

Hearing this, the crowd quickly called for the captain. When he arrived, he told the guard to put the gun down, then told Stella, "If you have something to say, say it. Why did you smash the door?"

Stella pointed at the guard and said, "You'll have to ask him that. If he'd allowed me in, would I have smashed the door? I have an issue, but I'm not looking for you. I'm looking for the commanding officer."

The captain said, "I'm the commanding officer."

The crowd had gradually formed a circle around the captain and Stella. The atmosphere was tense, and Stella's head was pounding. They were a group, but she was alone. She couldn't deal with a group, only an individual. Their eyes were all over her torso, front and back, and she knew that Liu Zhaohu was nervously pacing back and forth close by, anxious about why she'd come here. She also knew that the man squatting by the big water drum behind her was Snot. His legs must have grown soft when he saw her, just as his face must have turned ashen gray. They were sizing her up, betting she wouldn't dare speak, since she risked losing face if she did. But they had made a mistake. They had pushed her too far. She could handle ten steps, but they had taken eleven, and that final step pushed her to the bottom of the chasm. From the bottom of the chasm, the sky looked different. She had actually found the crack in the darkness. She finally understood that no matter how important face was, it was not more important than life. She understood, but they didn't. They didn't know what sort of earth-shattering things a person was capable of once she had dared to give up her face.

She looked the captain up and down, then said, "I want to speak to the commanding officer. You're not him."

The captain said, "Who says I'm not the commanding officer?"

She pointed to the number on his uniform and said, "The commanding officer doesn't have a number."

A few people snickered. No one suspected that a girl from the village would have such a sharp mind.

The captain's face tightened, and his voice grew thick. "The commanding officer has official duties."

She said, "That's fine. I'll wait here for him to finish his official duties." She took a few steps and sat on the stairs. She guessed the commanding officer was in a meeting upstairs, having noticed the closed windows when she entered the courtyard. No one would close their windows on such a hot day unless they had something important to discuss. Almost as soon as she sat down, the men gathered in the courtyard suddenly scrambled to attention. With a rustle of clothing, they formed a line, stood erect at their full heights, pulled their heels together, and saluted. Stella turned and saw a tall man with a dark face standing on the stairs. He wore a uniform of tan fabric, like everyone else's, and a tan cloth hat, but there was no number on his chest. She knew this was the commanding officer.

"Your nerve is much greater than your years. You're not afraid of being shot?" the man said.

His words were hard, but there was some warmth in his expression. Stella stood up and bowed slightly, suddenly feeling her eyes grow hot. *No matter what, you won't cry in front of these pigs.* She bit her lip, but it was no use. The tears didn't heed her admonition, and two drops inched down her cheeks, stopping at the corners of her mouth, hot and stinging.

"If you have something to say, say it. I really do have important things to do today." The commanding officer took the watch from his pocket and glanced at it.

"Is there anyone who isn't afraid of being shot?" She choked on a sob.

"So you have been wronged?" asked the commanding officer.

On the way there, she'd planned everything she would say at this moment, but with everything that had happened since, it had disappeared. She clenched her fists, digging her nails into her palms, and the sharp pain gradually roused her, bringing the words back to her mind.

"Sir, I have one question. Are your troops here fighting the Japanese?" she asked.

"If we weren't fighting the Japanese, what would we be doing in this hellhole?" said the officer.

"If your family members and neighbors had been harmed by the Japanese, what would you do?"

"Get revenge. If not, what kind of men would we be?" The commanding officer's voice became louder.

Stella turned and looked for someone among the crowd that had gathered in the courtyard. They were in neat rows, and all wearing the same uniform, hat, and belt. They looked like they had been cast from the same mold. But Stella quickly picked Snot out from the group.

"That's good, sir. Can you ask your man, Number 520, how he would get revenge?" Stella said.

Snot was pulled out from the line and put in front of the officer, and he stared down at the toes poking out of his sandals, not saying a word.

"Do you want to tell them, or should I?" Stella asked.

The commanding officer raised Snot's face with one finger. "You can't hide. Tell the truth."

With a bitter expression, Snot hesitated before blurting out, "I . . . I was at the river this morning when . . . I saw her. It was her . . . she started . . ." He stopped.

Hearing what he intended to say, Stella's face turned red. "Pig! Sir, look at his hands and arms!"

The commanding officer pulled up Snot's sleeves and saw bite marks on the back of his hand and scratches on both arms and that they were fresh. The blood hadn't even dried on some of them. A cloud came over the officer's face, and the veins on his temple started to bulge, pulsing as if to the beat of a drum. The only sounds were Snot's sniffing and the grinding of the commanding officer's teeth.

"Captain!" the commander shouted. "He's one of yours. Take him to the gully behind the camp and shoot him. Have everyone watch, and we'll see if anyone dares such a thing again!"

The captain stepped forward, as if he had something to say. The commanding officer cut him off with a wave of his hand.

"Your man has done this horrible thing, and you plead for him? You want me to kill you too?"

The captain choked back the words in his throat. Snot fell to his knees. Everyone could hear his knees scraping the ground through his thin pants.

"Sir, I know I've committed a crime, but I didn't actually do anything. Really, she was too fierce. If you don't believe me, ask her."

Stella felt a thousand caterpillars all over her body—the eyes of the crowd. Everyone knew that the only person who could save Snot at this moment was not the bodhisattva or the Christian God. It was her. On the way to the camp, she'd thought about the possible consequences of her words. She might be treated as a madwoman or a laughingstock or be tossed out like trash. They might give Number 520 a perfunctory reprimand. They might also whip him as a lesson or even lock him up for a few days as a warning to others. But she hadn't expected execution.

"I fought him off before he could . . . ," Stella said softly.

The commanding officer kicked Snot brutally. "You should die for even having that intention. You've destroyed the reputation of your whole unit. Who else dares to plead his case?"

No one dared to say a word.

Suddenly, Stella knelt in front of the commanding officer.

"Sir, please don't have him die like this. It's too easy, too cheap."

The commanding officer was taken aback. He looked at Stella in confusion. "How do you wish him to die?"

"I want him to fight the Japanese devils before he dies," she said.

Snot's mind had already turned to putty, but Stella's words revived him. He bowed before the commanding officer until his head was on the ground. "Mr.

Ferguson said that it cost a lot of money and lives to support us. If I die like this, it's doing the Japanese a favor. Sir, let me die on the battlefield. Let me take a few devils with me."

The commanding officer thought for a while. Sighing heavily, he summoned the captain before him. "After tonight's mission, you turn him over to me. If he escapes, you'll pay the price for him."

The captain saluted the commanding officer, then dismissed Snot back into the line.

"Girl, tell the captain where you live. I'll have them carry water for you for a month in compensation." The commander helped Stella up, then turned to go upstairs.

"Wait, I have something else to say," she called after him. "I come from Sishiyi Bu, a little over forty li from here. Last year on Qingming, my father was killed when we were bombed by Japanese planes. On the seventh day after his death, the Japanese approached my village. My mother had her body slit open, and I was . . . I was . . ."

She closed her eyes. She didn't want to see anyone's face in that moment. She wanted to plug her ears too, but it was no use. Even if her two ears had been cut off, she could have still heard a voice floating above her. It was a voice she didn't recognize, as if it were talking about someone else's life.

"I was taken advantage of by the Japanese."

She knew the tears were on their way again. This time she was prepared. She clenched her teeth, stopping the tears in her throat.

"After I went home, they disowned me. They thought since the Japanese had taken advantage of me, they could too."

She opened her eyes. The hardest part was done. The rest would be easy by comparison.

"After that, I left Sishiyi Bu and came to Yuehu. I thought I could live a peaceful life, but someone still spread those rumors here."

Stella found Liu Zhaohu in the crowd. He didn't meet her eyes, but kept his head lowered, picking at a callus on the palm of his hand from his gun.

"Why do you injure me? Why don't you settle accounts with the Japanese instead?"

She only realized she was shouting when she felt pain in her throat and ears. She heard her voice reverberate off the cistern and the walls.

"Assholes! You're a bunch of assholes!" the commanding officer said. His voice was hoarse, and when he leaned against the staircase railing, he looked as if he had shrunk.

"That's all I have to say. Find something else to wag your tongues about now." Saying that, she swept out of the courtyard.

East American Chinese Herald: In Commemoration of the Seventieth Anniversary of the Victory in the War of Resistance Against Japan

Third Feature Profile: A Story of Righteous Ardor

Ian Ferguson was born to a family of Chicago brewers in 1921. He turned twenty on Sunday, December 7, 1941. After attending church, his family took him to an Italian restaurant to celebrate his birthday. Seventy-four years later, Ferguson still recalls the dark sky that day, which looked as if it might snow at any time. The restaurant was chilly, and the family, seated and still wearing their coats, had just opened their menus when the music on the radio stopped. The announcer's voice came on, low and sorrowful, and it took several moments for Ferguson to understand what he was saying. The US naval base in Pearl Harbor had been bombed by the Japanese, and there had been heavy losses.

The restaurant was crowded that day, but no one spoke. The silence shaped the air into a thin piece of glass that seemed on the verge of shattering. Eventually, someone stood and slowly walked to a stranger in the room, and they embraced. Ferguson heard his mother sobbing softly. That day forever changed Ferguson's destiny. At the time, he was an apprentice at an auto repair shop on Chicago's south side, studying mechanics part time. He was hoping to save enough money to open his own shop after he graduated as a mechanic. Ten years after the war, he realized that dream, moving his family to Detroit in October 1955 and opening an auto repair shop. For over twenty years, he ran a successful business, with three additional branches opening across the city. But on December 7, 1941, he didn't have mechanics on his mind.

That spring, twenty-year-old Ferguson joined Naval Group China. Gunner's Mate Ferguson knew when he enlisted that he would be going to China on a secret mission. But he didn't know how classified his mission truly was until he was pulled from his dorm in the middle of the night, put into a military vehicle covered with black tarp, and whisked away for the intensive training. On a base outside Washington, DC, he spent four months in specialized training for short-range weapons, special explosives, sniping, hand-to-hand combat, cryptography, aircraft identification, evasive tactics behind enemy lines, night navigation, and more. He also had an accelerated course in Chinese language and customs. During her interview with this ninety-four-year-old veteran who assisted China in its War of Resistance Against Japanese Aggression, senior reporter Catherine Yao learned that he still had in his possession the Chinese textbook and the handbook from the training course. The Chinese textbook included the following description of the oratory principles of Mandarin:

> *The first tone is even.*
> *The second tone rises as spoken.*
> *The third tone falls and stops with a hesitation.*
> *The fourth tone is cut off quickly.*

The handbook contained the following rules:

> *Don't call the local people Chinamen.*
> *Don't call local laborers coolies.*
> *Don't comment on the Chinese way of reading from right to left.*
> *Don't comment on Chinese eating habits or call the American diet civilized.*
> *When you are unable to use Chinese to communicate, as much as possible avoid the use of pidgin English.*

After training, he went to a munitions depot in Southern California for a three-month attachment, then traveled by ship from San Francisco to Calcutta, where he waited for the crowded transport line of the Hump to find room for him. When he finally caught a plane to Kunming, then traveled to Chongqing by oxcart, it was already 1943. From Chongqing, he was sent to a series of camps along the Yangtze River to offer special training to Chinese soldiers. In China, he was quickly promoted to gunner's mate first class, in no small part because of his ability with remote-controlled blasting devices. His final posting was in a village called Yuehu, in southern Zhejiang province. This village formed the backdrop for many of his Chinese adventures.

When our reporter met Ferguson in the long-term care unit of the veterans hospital in Detroit, he'd been bedridden for years, but his mind was still agile. In a weak voice, with his nurse's help, he told us about a mission at the Yuehu training camp. Perhaps because of the confidential nature of this work, the US Navy has received less attention for its aid to China than the army and air force. Ferguson's story, as told to Catherine Yao, is a touching example of the US Navy's joint effort with the Chinese military and civilians in the Far East theater.

~

Ian Ferguson had been standing on the hill for some time, silently watching Ghost and Millie play. Ghost and Millie couldn't have been more different. Ghost was a well-trained military dog, while Millie was a little white terrier that had been adopted by a nearby church. Still, they scrunched their bodies together into a ball and rolled down the slope to the bottom of the gully, then stood stock-still for a moment, shook, and licked the dirt that hadn't been dislodged from their fur before joyfully running back up the hill again. Ghost's pace was three to five times greater than Millie's, but Ghost lay down halfway up the slope and waited for her. When she caught up, they'd sprint to the top, again turn into a ball, and roll down the slope. They did this over and over.

When Ghost licked Millie, he was very careful, using only half his tongue and a tenth of his strength, as if Millie were a delicate glass that could shatter at the slightest touch. Millie had to stand up just to reach Ghost's belly. Her tongue was a tiny toothbrush, and his body was a huge carpet. Even if she licked for a lifetime, she might not reach every spot on his body. But they didn't care about energy or efficiency, just the feeling of tongue on fur. Ferguson couldn't bear to interrupt their affections. At that moment, he was feeling a bit sentimental. In the human world, one used words, smiles, flowers, wine, poetry, philosophy, and even money to obtain what in the dog's world required just the use of one's tongue.

The sun was already low, and the clouds had turned a dark tomato red. The days were still long in September, so sunset took some time, but as soon as the sun dipped below the horizon, it grew completely dark in a matter of moments. He didn't have much time. His comrades-in-arms must be ready to start by now. With his fingers in his mouth, he whistled loudly. This was the signal the dog trainer in Chongqing had taught him to indicate for Ghost to "report." Ghost shook his ears, as if he was surprised. He hadn't heard this call for a while. He hesitated for a moment, looked at Millie, then reluctantly tore himself from her and ran to his master.

"Attention!" Ferguson commanded.

Whenever this command was used, the dog knew he was about to be assigned a task. Of course, in dog terms, it's not standing but sitting at attention. Ghost sat straight, his body upright, eyes fixed on Ferguson, but with a look of guilt in his eyes. He knew his recent behavior had disgraced the pedigree he'd inherited from his parents. There was almost no intelligence left in the heat of love and what little remained was only enough to make him aware of his own confusion. He tightened his body, which had been relaxed for too long, preparing to receive a reprimand. He didn't expect his master to take a tin of canned beef from his military bag. It was a gift Ferguson's mother had sent from America. He scooped out two big pieces, put them in his hand, and offered them to Ghost. Ghost hadn't smelled anything like that in a long time, and his stomach growled shamelessly. The last time he had tasted beef had been at the base in Washington, where it had been a reward for completing a difficult task. That was a lifetime ago. Ghost knew his recent behavior didn't merit a reward, so he looked at his master in confusion, not daring to eat. Ferguson patted Ghost's head and said, "Go on, eat. This might be your . . ." Ferguson couldn't finish the thought: *This might be your last bite of beef.*

The master's warm expression delighted Ghost, especially after being reprimanded so much recently. He tried to maintain a respectful manner, slowly eating the beef in small bites, then licking Ferguson's palm for a long time, as if trying to get every trace of meat hidden in every line of his hand. Ferguson waited for Ghost to finish, then put a collar around the dog's neck. This was the signal that they were ready to go. Once the collar was on, Ghost knew all his other identities—pet, clown, lover—no longer existed. From that moment on, he was a military dog, and his only task was to obey orders.

The team set off after dark. It consisted of sixteen Chinese students who'd displayed special talent during their training. Their leader was one of the training camp captains, and Ferguson was their advisor. This was the first time an American instructor participated in field operations alongside Chinese students. The previous smaller-scale operations had been conducted by the Chinese trainees alone. To be allowed to participate, Ferguson had fought a battle with the camp commanding officer that could only be described as fierce. In consideration of their safety, the Chinese commanding officer had strongly resisted allowing American instructors to participate in action. Ferguson's view was that if he couldn't see the effects of his teaching in combat application, he couldn't properly judge the effectiveness of the program. They each had their own view, and neither could convince the other. In the end, they had to refer the matter to headquarters in Chongqing. The one-word telegram from Chongqing arrived just two hours before the start of the mission: *Approved.*

Ferguson wasn't the only American brought along on this operation. He was also allowed to bring his military dog. The practice of sending military dogs into battle as a means of reducing casualties had been researched at length by military scientists, and Ghost's training in America had been rigorous. This operation would be his first actual combat experience, and it would demonstrate whether those scientists were geniuses or madmen. They were going to travel along a mountain road with extremely challenging terrain. It was infested with bandits and had been occupied by a variety of unidentified troops. Ghost would walk in front of the team to detect road conditions and the enemy's position. However, given his recent state, Ferguson worried about his responsiveness.

It was an unusually gloomy night, with thick clouds hiding the moon and stars. Marching under such conditions was both a blessing and a curse. Visibility was extremely low, and most of the area was forest, with a thick humus layer muffling the sound of their footsteps. Unless someone was in close proximity to the marching troops, they would be almost invisible. But the darkness was a double-edged sword. Finding the way in complete darkness was dependent on muscle memory. Most of the Chinese soldiers were from the area and knew the mountain roads intimately, but even so, muscle memory wasn't entirely reliable, so at certain key moments they would rely on Ferguson's glowing compass from his days of covert training in DC.

The darkness made their eyes useless, so their hearing was heightened in response. Ferguson's right ear was trained on Ghost. If the mission had been during the day, Ghost would silently alert Ferguson to danger ahead by raising his hackles. In the dark, at any sign of abnormality, he would stop and sit in the middle of the road, preventing Ferguson from going any farther. Ferguson's left ear, trained on his comrades, noticed one of the soldiers breathing heavier than the others. They'd nicknamed him Snot, since he suffered from severe rhinitis. The captain had given strict orders that there was to be no smoking on the road, no conversation, and no sound. In order to muffle the sound of his runny nose, Snot had plugged his nostrils with rags, so he could only breathe through his mouth, like a fish.

To Ferguson's left was the captain and to his right was the soldier Liu Zhaohu. Liu should have been in the middle, since he was the only one who spoke both English and Chinese. However, in a training session a few days earlier, the small, thin Liu Zhaohu had unexpectedly bested the tall, strong, proud captain. After that, Ferguson noticed they'd been avoiding each other. The captain because he was unwilling to admit defeat, and Liu because he didn't want to gloat. In fact, their mutual avoidance was itself a sort of wrestling. Their stalemate seemed like it would never end, and the sour resentment they exuded sprouted poisonous mushrooms in the night sky. In such a small-scale military operation, with so many complex details, that sort of stalemate could destroy the unspoken understanding within the team. So Ferguson—whether consciously or not—walked between the captain and Liu Zhaohu, trying to keep them from a collision. That's how Ferguson remembered it. Afterward, when he and Liu Zhaohu discussed it, Liu said they placed Ferguson in the middle to keep him safe from traps left by hunters along the mountain paths and irrigation gullies dug by villagers. Liu and the captain were far more familiar with the mountains than Ferguson was, and they knew to take small exploratory steps before putting down their full weight.

From nightfall to dawn the next day, they walked more than a hundred li on mountain paths to a remote wharf. There, the captain's brother, a well-known local pirate, had prepared sampans for them. Several locals who knew the rivers disguised themselves as fishermen and led them through the waterways to their target: a Japanese munitions and supply warehouse near the riverbank. Considering how far it was, the captain had limited what they carried to a rifle, a pistol, dry food for two meals each, and drinking water. The Chinese soldiers' food was parched rice, which they carried in a bag slung over one shoulder and across the body. The munitions were carried in wooden boxes on shoulder poles suspended between two soldiers, with everyone taking turns. Ferguson's load was a bit lighter because his food wasn't parched rice, which was heavy, but compressed crackers that the Chinese soldiers called sawdust. Before departure, the captain suggested Ferguson put his Thompson submachine gun in the wooden box and let the soldiers carry it, but Ferguson resolutely refused.

"You might regret it," the captain said. "Our children can walk a few hundred li when they're only eight, but even your strong men in their early twenties drive for short distances. You're not used to walking our mountain roads." Liu translated, not softening it at all, even mimicking the captain's tone and pauses. Even though there were hundreds of conflicts between Liu and the captain, their views on this were the same.

Ferguson turned bright red, realizing far too late a mistake he'd made. Days before, Ferguson had said that even an eight-year-old American boy could fix a bicycle while a Chinese man in his twenties had never held a screwdriver. At the time, he hadn't noticed that he had wounded their pride, and the captain had waited until just the right time to repay the barb. Ferguson felt the sting, but knew he could only pull this thorn out at the end of the road. He could not believe that an American of such superior size and strength would be outmatched by a scrawny Chinese fellow when it came to endurance.

But it wasn't long after they'd started that he felt the weight of the gun. He had been using it for several months and was familiar with every part. He could disassemble and lay the pieces on a table, then put it back together blindfolded. The gun was like a part of his hands, and he could command it with the flick of a finger. But now, slung over his shoulder, it became a heavy iron knot, and each of his muscles silently rebelled against its oppression. When his right shoulder began to feel sore, he shifted it to his left. But soreness has a long memory, so when his left shoulder began to feel sore, the right still hurt, and that pain was now doubled. Eventually, the weight seemed to spread from his shoulders to his legs. His boots, like the gun, turned to iron and started to feel heavy. He found he could hardly lift his legs, so he dragged his feet along the ground. He wondered what type of footprints these iron clods would leave on the fallen leaves, had there been any light to see them.

He also hadn't expected his mind to be so alert when his body was so tired. He could clearly distinguish the weight of each individual item he carried. The weight of the Thompson was not that of his revolver, just as the revolver was not that of his boots, his boots were not that of his belt, and his belt was not that of his canteen. Even the steel buttons on his plain khakis had their own unique weight that couldn't be mistaken for any other.

He looked back at the two small soldiers carrying the heavy box of munitions. He saw—or, rather, heard—that they were only a couple of steps behind him, the distance neither increasing nor decreasing since the march had begun. They breathed evenly, without straining, not excited or fatigued. He finally understood that the secret of these malnourished people of small stature for walking such long distances was the same as that which had enabled them to endure long-term poverty. They knew how to conserve their resources. They broke their energy into smaller units, using it sparingly, exactly the same way they managed their silver coins. They never used their energy on emotions like anxiety, excitement, depression, or despair. They didn't think about how far they had traveled from their starting point, nor did they consider how far they were from their destination. They just focused on the next step. They calculated precisely how much strength was required for each step, using neither more nor less than required. This skill of conservation wasn't something that could be taught in a course, but was a habit accumulated through repetition, day after day, year after year. Ferguson now knew he wouldn't be able to remove the barb of the captain's insult. That thorn would remain forever in his body, tingling slightly to remind him of his own ignorance. The mechanical skills he had from growing up in America and the walking skills they had gained growing up in China ended in a draw in this seemingly endless march.

Ferguson finally decided to put the Thompson in the munitions box. When the small soldier took it from his hand, he was glad it happened under the cover of darkness so no one could see his face. He was also grateful for the "no talking" order. This sealed the captain's mouth, preventing him from saying, "I told you so." Under the double protection of silence and darkness, he could quietly digest his shame on his own.

After the operation was over, Ferguson wrote a seven-page journal entry detailing the physical and psychological experiences of it. Rereading it later, he was surprised to find feelings there that he hadn't noticed when he was writing. Later, he edited it, removing the more emotional passages, and submitted it to the US military officer to be sent to headquarters in Chongqing as a battlefield report. Below is an excerpt of the original:

> We began marching as soon as it was dark and continued until dawn the next morning, a total of eight and a half hours. About four-fifths of the journey was on mountain paths through the forest, and the rest was through a no-man's-land between two forests.
>
> The weather was conducive to marching. It was late summer, so still burning hot during the day, but cool at night. There was a steady breeze throughout the march, and the sound of the wind and the thick layer of decomposing leaves on the ground all but silenced the sound of our footsteps but also made it difficult for Ghost to detect signs of an ambush in front of us. Ghost was extremely alert throughout the journey.
>
> The first hour and a half, we were in good spirits and confident we'd reach our destination on time. Later, I realized I'd made a mistake that any novice to these mountain paths might make. My strides were too big, and I lifted my feet too high. I was too enthusiastic, and my Chinese colleagues had to adjust their steps to keep my pace. The result was unnecessary physical exertion. A long-distance march is like running a marathon. You need to evenly distribute your strength throughout the journey, rather than exhausting it in the beginning.
>
> As we entered the second half of the second hour, I began to feel some fatigue. The first symptom was that I felt the weight of my weapons and boots. Because we were still quite far from our destination, the resulting feeling of despair outweighed the actual physical fatigue.

In the third and fourth hours, I entered a period of severe fatigue, my mind unable to think clearly, with my hunger growing. As soon as it appeared, the hunger rapidly intensified, forming a sort of thick web from which my mind couldn't escape. I began to think of all sorts of food from back home, wondering if my decision to enlist without my parents' blessing was nothing more than a stupid impulse and fearing what my future would be after the war ended if I were injured during this mission. I even began to wonder if there was any point in war on foreign soil, especially in a country that didn't even border America. The extreme physical fatigue led to a psychological dullness and gave rise to questions I'd never considered before.

At nearly the halfway point in the journey, the captain ordered us to rest for twenty minutes. I loosened Ghost's collar, which for him signaled the rest break. The moment the collar was loose, his body relaxed from its tense state, and he leaned limply against my thigh. I offered him some of my cracker. He sniffed it, but wouldn't eat. I took a few bites myself, then crushed some and forced it into his mouth. Seeming to pity me, he forced himself to take a few swallows, but refused any more. I patted his head and gestured for him to lie down to restore his strength, but he wouldn't close his eyes. Instead, he turned his head and silently licked my hand over and over. Thinking back on it, I think he'd foreseen his own death and didn't want to waste his last few hours with meaningless sleep. He wanted to share all his remaining time with me. His tongue was soft and gentle, as if he were licking not my hand, but my heart. An almost desperate loneliness swept over me, like a beast lurking in the forest, suddenly pouncing and sending me reeling.

If there had been no such place as Pearl Harbor and no such madman as Yamamoto, what would I have been doing then? It was noon in Chicago, so maybe I would be heading out for my lunch break, meeting Emily Wilson at the corner shop for a hot dog or a bowl of chicken soup and laughing about her boss and mine. Or maybe I'd be in the locker room with my colleague Andy, sharing a beer and talking about sports. Or maybe I'd be sitting on the closed lid of the toilet in the bathroom, eyes closed, composing a poem that would never be published.

And Ghost? If there were no war, he'd probably be on a farm in Kentucky, getting up early and fiercely guarding a flock of sheep, then returning home at night to get a sausage as a reward from his master. He wouldn't have met Millie, but he would have met other dogs, and he'd have litter after litter of puppies, each one inheriting his fine pedigree.

I leaned on Ghost and closed my eyes. My body wanted to sleep, but my mind was fighting it tooth and nail. If Ghost and I both survived, I would request that Ghost come home with me when we were demobilized. I would take him back to Chicago, and together the two of us would gradually adapt from wartime to peace.

The Chinese soldiers around me all seemed to be sleeping, aside from the sentry. Some leaned against tree trunks, some lay on the ground, and some leaned against the munitions box, snoring softly. Who were they? Since I had locked their recruitment forms in the drawer in my office, I couldn't recall their names. I couldn't even remember all their numbers. I didn't know anything about their families, or whether they had women they loved, or what they hoped to do in the future. What sort of books did they read? What were their hobbies? If there were no war, I wouldn't know any of them. We ate different foods, spoke different languages, wore different clothes, believed in different gods, and laughed at different jokes. We weren't brought together by one love, but by one hate. Was hate a stronger bond than love, or weaker? When our common hatred no longer existed, would they remember me? Would I remember them?

In the first fifteen minutes after we started up again, I felt more fatigued than before, because using the muscles again after relaxing them took extra energy. After a few minutes, the benefits of the short break became evident, and my body began to experience a strange feeling that's hard to put into words. Almost like numbness.

My brain no longer directed my body, but my feet seemed to move in a spontaneous, mechanical repetition.

In the final hour, I felt the same ease I had at the beginning of the trip, probably because I was more keenly aware that each step brought me closer to a conclusion. I could see a faint glow at the end of the tunnel. This sort of psychological suggestion is a powerful force that cannot be ignored. When we finally arrived at the destination, my body even experienced a sort of illusion, convincing me I still had some energy and could've carried on through a longer journey.

When he rewrote the above journal entry as a report, at the end, Ferguson included several suggestions to headquarters in Chongqing. They read:

1. In the future, when training soldiers for the battlefield in the Far East, it is necessary to strengthen the training in long-distance marches. It is not as simple as physical endurance but also involves complex variables such as lifestyle and mental habits, the distribution of energy, and so forth. Otherwise, it's impossible to explain why Chinese soldiers who are far weaker than American soldiers have such a great advantage over their American counterparts in long-distance marching.

2. When designing military boots for the Chinese battlefield, consider reducing the weight. In a country where there is no real transportation and walking is the basic mode of travel, military boots that are too heavy prove to be a hindrance.

3. Silence will exacerbate the feeling of fatigue during a long march. The Communist army in Yan'an sings while they march. They are leading the world in psychological warfare, so it makes sense to adopt some of their habits. Unless sound renders the mission unsafe, it is advisable to use song or storytelling to shift the attention away from fatigue.

The sampans arrived after dark the next day, and the men disembarked a few hundred yards from their target. The thick clouds had finally dispersed, revealing a faint crescent moon and a scattering of stars. Where the night wind blew, reeds rustled and insects chirped, while the frogs on the beach beat their last round of drums before sleeping. The clear night and the late-summer sounds were coconspirators, providing cover for their footsteps while lighting their way.

Through his telescope, Ferguson had a clear view of the target. It was a temporary single-story structure, with two windows in a long wall covered with shards of broken glass to deter intruders. There was a watchtower at the front, its lights visible from fifty yards away. Two guards with submachine guns stood back to back in the watchtower so that they had an almost three-hundred-and-sixty-degree view. There were tons of supplies in the munitions and supply warehouse, most of which were winter clothes and rain boots. The Japanese planned to transport them to a transfer station, then distribute them to various military camps along the railway line. They were waiting for the truck convoy from Hangzhou, and the five trucks parked at the gate were the earliest arrivals. The intel had come from a cook in one of the Japanese guards' kitchens. According to him, there was also a back gate manned by two soldiers, but no watchtower. The Japanese troops stationed in the warehouse were a small unit, but armed with more than ten machine guns and about twenty submachine guns.

The officers had formulated a plan based on the intelligence they had. The light from the watchtower and the firepower disparity made storming the facility essentially a suicide mission. So the sniper, Liu Zhaohu, would hide beyond the reach of the lights and shoot the sentries at the watchtower. The commotion would provide an opening for Snot to run up and toss explosives over the wall. Snot was the runner because he was lightest on his feet and the strongest jumper. The soft explosives were armed with a delay, giving Snot and his comrades time to retreat to a safe distance before the explosion. The explosives had been packed into the body of a rabbit, and the rabbit's belly was sewn up and covered with mud on the outside, so if anyone found it, they wouldn't know it was an explosive device. Amid the chaos, there was a strong chance the Japanese wouldn't even notice it, and even if it were discovered, it would just be kicked aside. By the time the team had retreated to the water, three sampans would be waiting. The boatmen knew every bend and rock in the river, so they could hug the banks, then shoot away as quick as arrows, fleeing from the searchlights.

But not every factor could be planned for. As they approached the warehouse, the captain noticed a glow about two paces away. It flickered. Someone was smoking. From the hat, he guessed it was a Japanese soldier who, against orders, had snuck out of the warehouse, where smoke and fire were strictly prohibited. Perhaps catching a sound beneath the wind, the soldier turned abruptly, and their eyes met. That split second the Japanese soldier needed to drop his cigarette was just enough to give the captain the chance to leap like a panther and, fast as lightning, clamp a hand over his mouth. He struggled in the captain's arms, like a fish flopping on the shore. The captain glared at Liu Zhaohu and spat out, "Knife!" Liu pulled out his dagger and slammed it into the man's chest. A warm, wet, sticky substance splattered onto Liu's forehead, running down the ridge of his brow into his eyes. He wiped his face with the back of his hand, then rammed the knife into the soldier's chest another six or seven times. He struck with too much force, almost throwing himself off balance. The last stab seemed to strike something hard, making the point slip and get stuck. He jiggled it a few times before managing to remove the knife. The rope binding the man's organs, sinews, and bones broke, and his body went limp, like a noodle.

In the pale light of the first-quarter moon, he saw the face of the man lying on the ground before him. It was very young, with a shadow of mustache on his upper lip and a bunch of purple scars on the sallow face left behind by a summer heat rash. His eyes were open wide, the moonlight pooling in them so clear that one could almost see the mind underneath. He fixed his eyes on Liu Zhaohu, his lips moving slightly. Liu leaned closer, and after a moment, Liu realized he had said, *"Oka-san."*

Snot asked Liu quietly, "What did that devil say before he died?"

Leaning against the tree, Liu sighed heavily and whispered, "He called for his mother."

They fell silent.

Two men went over to strip off the dead man's belt and boots, but Liu brandished the dagger while kneeling in front of the body and said softly, stressing each word, "Who dares?" The blood had congealed on his face, and his eyes stared out from beneath it like two icy flames. Shocked, the men froze, but cast a tentative glance at the captain. The shoes they wore in summer were straw, while their winter shoes were cloth. They'd never had leather shoes and couldn't bear to see a good pair of boots rot on a corpse. They hoped the captain would weigh in. But the captain didn't respond. He just lowered his head silently and wiped the blood from his hands with a leaf. Liu Zhaohu took a stone and placed it beneath the man's head. Removing the blood-soaked military jacket, he laid it over the mutilated body. Only after this did he regain composure.

"We don't have much time. Let's get ready for action," Ferguson whispered, patting Liu's shoulder.

At the edge of the illuminated area, they stopped in the cover of the reeds. Ferguson gestured for Ghost to stand by for orders, and he sat alert beside Ferguson. Liu Zhaohu knelt on one knee, supporting his rifle with the other. His gun was different from the others and had been fitted with a silencer. On such a clear night, shooting at such a distance, the silencer wouldn't muffle the gunshot completely, but it would control the brightness of the flash and change the sound so the person in the watchtower wouldn't know for sure if it was a gunshot or where it came from. While Liu was preparing, Snot picked up the rabbit filled with explosives, ready to go. Liu's first target was the sentry facing them. At the same time, the lighting made the sentry a highly visible target, and Liu could see him easily. Squinting, he aimed between the man's eyebrows, then squeezed the trigger softly. After a sound like beans jumping in a wok, the sentry on the tower shook, like his body was tripped by an invisible rope. He twitched oddly a few times, then fell. The other sentry turned, raised his weapon, and fired a volley of shots into the night sky. This was the alarm. The gun blocked his face, so Liu aimed for his heart. He squeezed lightly, and the man fell against the wall. The arm holding his gun dropped. The man tried to lift his gun again, but his arm no longer obeyed. Liu found his forehead and fired again. His shoulders twitched a few times, then his body slumped to the ground like a sack.

Snot took off toward the warehouse. He didn't stay among the reeds, but ran on the dirt road. There was no cover, and he was exposed in the light, but there was no alternative. The reeds were too tall and would slow him down. He had to get there before others had time to get to the front gate. That's when the second unexpected thing happened. Hearing the gunfire, the five trucks parked in front of the watchtower turned on their headlights, and five gunmen stood up on each vehicle. They were military guards who had been spending the night in their vehicles, waiting for dawn before setting out on their journey. They didn't come all the way out, but balancing their guns on the guardrail of the trucks, they observed the situation around them. In such bright light, the team would be given away by the slightest movement, so they could not provide cover for Snot as planned and had to stay low in the reeds, frozen. The lights in the warehouse came on one by one, and orders were shouted amid noisy footsteps. Soldiers had already climbed the watchtower and were crouching up there. Ferguson couldn't see their bodies, but he saw the fearfully black muzzles of their guns sticking out from the embrasures in the brick wall. Heavy fire broke out. Although it was an unfocused deterrent, Ferguson and his comrades had fallen into a hopeless situation. As soon as a search began, they would be discovered.

Snot had made it to the wall before the hail of bullets began. Leaping lightly, he threw the dead rabbit over the wall. But he didn't retreat according to plan, running instead toward the river. With a loud splash, he leaped into the water behind a big rock, his body creating an arch of waves on the calm water. At the same time, he shot a few rounds from his Thompson into the night sky. He was trying to draw the enemy's attention to cover his comrades' retreat. The guns in the watchtower and trucks did in fact aim at Snot, spraying the river with a volley of bullets. Snot's body sank and a layer of dark red foam appeared on the surface of the water, but he kept his arms in the air, firing the Thompson with one hand and the revolver with the other. He varied the timing of his shots to create the illusion of more people.

The captain ordered a quick retreat. Just then, something slammed to the ground at Ferguson's feet, hissing. It was a hand grenade. They were never sure if it had been thrown at random or if something had tipped off the Japanese, but either way they were lost. In the nick of time, Ghost leaped up and grabbed the grenade in his mouth, then took off running. His mother's speed and his father's intelligence had woke at that moment and formed a powerful alliance. Ghost ran like a puma, feet hardly touching the ground. As he reached the dirt road, he glanced back at Ferguson. That was his final farewell. Ferguson's last impression of Ghost was the gray arc of his body in midair, and his sad eyes as he glanced back. With a bang, Ghost's body was shattered into pieces in the night sky.

Another explosion erupted behind Ghost, and the warehouse was engulfed in flames. Compared to this, the earlier shots had been like a drizzle before a thunderstorm. This sound seemed to come from the center of the earth. The ground continued to tremble, and the branches shook in horror for a long time afterward. Ferguson saw the captain's lips moving, but couldn't hear the words. The unit retreated in the chaos. Liu Zhaohu saw that the captain was limping on one leg and was gradually falling behind. Shrapnel from the grenade explosion had sliced off a chunk of his flesh at the ankle, and his pant leg was soaked in blood.

Liu Zhaohu squatted.

"Get on," he shouted.

The captain hesitated, then realized that Liu meant to carry him.

"You can't carry me!" he said, continuing to drag his leg forward.

"Do you want your comrades to die because of you?" Liu said, his face falling.

The captain relented and climbed onto Liu's back. Liu lurched forward, one knee falling to the ground. Gritting his teeth, he gathered all his strength and let out a low roar. He pushed to his feet shakily and staggered with the first step. But that first step opened the path, and the rest continued from its momentum. With the captain on his back, Liu looked like a skinny horse carrying a mountain, bones creaking under the weight. But he carried the burden, staggering, all the way to the sampan. Liu collapsed in the sampan, panting heavily. A few men came over and took off their jackets to bind the captain's wounds. The captain roared, "Where's the water? I'm damned thirsty."

One of the soldiers handed over a canteen with a little water left at the bottom. The captain was about to drink, but then stopped and handed it to Liu Zhaohu as they rowed away from the shore. Safely on the water, Ferguson drew the cigarette case from his pocket and found that there were two cigarettes left. He lit one and handed it to the boatman, then lit the other, took a drag, and handed it to the soldier beside him. He took a drag and passed it on. By the time it returned to Ferguson, it was only a butt.

No one had spoken. Looking at the fiery red sky behind them, they knew the Japanese would have to march through rain and snow without proper clothes this winter. But they couldn't rejoice. Their eyes were on the empty seat in the sampan. When they had set out, they were sixteen men and a dog. Now they were just fifteen men. They had left their comrade behind forever.

Snot's corpse was returned to camp the following evening.

Ferguson learned later through a long trail of rumors that when the Japanese reached Snot, he dropped the Thompson into the water and put a hole in his temple with the revolver. When the Japanese pulled him to shore, they cut off his head and hung it on the wall as a trophy. Later, the captain's brother made a deal with a Japanese soldier, paying ten silver coins for Snot's body. As Snot's body was carried into the village, the bugler played a long string of low notes, like water running over stones at a river's mouth. The Chinese students and American instructors lined the road two rows deep, saluting their fallen comrade.

Ferguson had seen the bodies of fallen soldiers return to America, their coffins covered with the Stars and Stripes. But this body was just covered with an old straw mat, and the coffin had been borrowed since there had not been time to make one. Snot's neighbor, the cook for the Chinese students, had sent two men to the river early that morning for a few buckets of water to wash Snot's body. When the cook removed the mat, the sight made him collapse to the floor.

"Oh God, what will I tell his mother?" the cook wailed, sitting on the floor.

The captain and Liu Zhaohu took over the task of washing Snot's body. They wiped the bloodstains from his body, neck, and severed head with a towel, then dressed him in a clean uniform. The clothing covered the sieve of his bullet-riddled body, but not the holes in his head, where he'd taken his own life rather than be captured. Snot must have had a strong will to live. So many bullets, but he died by his own hand. The entrance wound was hardly noticeable, but the area around it had caved in, like a wormhole in a melon rind. What was more obvious was the exit wound, a large hole with torn edges and jagged corners. Liu Zhaohu wrapped a towel around Snot's head to hide the wounds.

Finally, the body was washed and properly dressed, but his eyes stayed half-open. Liu tried to close them, but couldn't. Snot's expression wasn't an unwillingness to resign himself to death, but more like mockery. His mouth was turned slightly up at the corner, a kind of smirk at some sinister joke he was waiting impatiently for everyone else to get. Liu asked for old silver coins to place on the eyelids.

The captain sighed and said, "Forget it. He was that way when he was alive. Let him be."

They lifted Snot's body and were about to put it into the coffin when they heard someone at the gate shout, "Wait." Then the whizzing of a bicycle coming to a stop. Without looking, everyone knew it was the American missionary

Pastor Billy, since he was the only one who had a bicycle. A young woman holding a white cloth bag dismounted from behind him. When the captain saw Pastor Billy, he waved and said, "Forget it. Give him a break. He didn't believe in your God while he was alive. Do you expect him to believe now that he's dead?"

Shaking his head, Pastor Billy pointed to the woman, saying, "I'm not here to pray. I brought Stella. She wants to send him off."

She walked over to Snot's body and knelt on the ground. It looked like she might bow, but she sat on her heels, pulled Snot's headless body over, and placed it on her lap. Liu Zhaohu looked panicked. A few days earlier, this girl had accused Snot of attempting to rape her, and he'd been sentenced to death by the commanding officer, spared only to go on the mission at Stella's request.

"What . . . What are you doing?" Liu stammered.

She did not answer or even look up, as if Liu were as invisible as air. As they watched, Stella carefully picked up Snot's head and placed it on her lap. It looked almost like she were holding a delicate porcelain jar. She opened her bag, took out a roll of thick thread and a big needle, and squinted in the failing light as she threaded the needle. Then she aligned Snot's chin with the center of the uniform. She looked him over carefully, then poked the needle into his neck. The crowd of onlookers gasped. She began to sew Snot's head onto his body. Each time she inserted the needle, she hesitated, as if afraid of hurting him. However, each stitch was made decisively, her fingers steady and strong and without any trembling. Snot was thin and small, and his body had shrunk in death. His sleeves and pant legs had to be rolled up to show his hands and feet. On her lap, Snot looked like an oversized child clinging to an adult, refusing to get up from bed. The woman's patient, gentle smile was like that of a mother coaxing a mischievous child to sleep.

After a long sequence of hesitation and resolution, she made the broken body whole again with her needle. Holding the head, now reconnected to the body, she leaned back and examined it, as if admiring a piece of fine embroidery. She took off the scarf tied over her braid and wrapped it around Snot's neck to cover the seam, then placed him gently on the ground.

Ferguson watched her walk out of the courtyard calmly, dust rising from the road with each firm step, her loosened hair shaking softly. This girl made all the women he'd ever known—even his mother, his sister, and his former girlfriend—seem pale and weak.

170

~

That night, the entire village gathered for the long-awaited performance of Xiao Yanqiu's famous theater troupe. Even the American soldiers had been given special permission to attend. The older residents of Yuehu counted on their fingers, then declared that it had been thirty-six years since a theater troupe had last visited the village. They had still been under the rule of the Qing emperor, who held the imperial jade seal in the Forbidden City. News of the troupe coming had been circulating for months, stirring up even the village chickens, whose eggs seemed a little more pink than usual. Tonight's performance was to be *The Butterfly Lovers*, though the older villagers might have preferred something more action-packed, like *Madame White Snake*. But the troupe was performing in exchange for one night's room and board, not even asking to be paid, as a charity to the soldiers, so they would happily listen to whatever the troupe chose to sing. And anyone younger than thirty-six didn't know any operas anyway, so if the actors had just walked around the stage waving their sleeves, that would have been novelty enough.

The stage was small, with a curtain fashioned from six red sheets sewn together. There was no room for the musicians, so they sat among the audience, but no one minded. Crowds surrounded the stage so tightly that if a member of the troupe had wanted to go to the latrine, they would not have been able to squeeze through. The troupe was used to such situations. In fact, whenever Xiao Yanqiu's name was advertised, it was always like this. But this performance was different in one important detail: there was a coffin in the best seat in the front row.

The performance that evening was dedicated to Snot.

Ghost and Millie: A Dialogue

Day 1

Ghost:

Millie, my dearest Millie, you've been here since this morning when they erected the tombstone for me until now, when the mountain has cut off half the sun's face. Almost the whole day, not eating, not moving, not speaking. Your master, the one my master calls Wende, brought your favorite, a bowl of chicken bones, at noon, but you didn't even look at it.

I know you're angry with me for abandoning you for my master. In that moment—a half second or even less—I didn't think of you. I didn't have time to think of anything. In that hair of an instant, I did what any dog would do out of instinct. I protected my master. We aren't cats, or goldfish, or parrots. They can live as pets, enjoying comfort and staying unconcerned about the fate of their humans. But we're dogs. Our fate was decided in our mothers' wombs. We have no choice. The purpose of our lives is to serve our masters.

If I'd been given a choice, I would've chosen to live as a sheep dog, concerned only about the weather and the flock. I could have devoted the rest of my energy to you. We could roll across every inch of grass on the hill and lick every inch of one another's bodies. If I get another life, I don't want to be a military dog again, exhausting my mind and body for a delicious reward. I wouldn't choose to be forced to fly when I hadn't even learned to walk yet. They—those military dog trainers—tried to turn me into a half man, half dog. No, they wanted me to become a superman. They forced me to become an extension of human senses, using me to detect faint smells they couldn't sense, see clues they missed, and hear the birdsong and wind they couldn't hear. They sought to push the limit just a little further, until finally it broke. But I didn't have a choice. A collie-greyhound mix, with gray fur, a roughly one-year-old male. I was perfect for a military dog, so I was put through the meat grinder of war. When I went in, I was a good dog with strong body and mind. When I came out, I was just a bit of minced meat.

Millie, I shouldn't say this. It's both unkind and unfair to my master. You know, he rarely treated me like a military dog. To him, I was neither superman nor half man, half dog or even just a dog. He often treated me simply as a friend he could trust absolutely, because he knew I would keep my mouth shut. Like the day he got the letter from his girlfriend Emily Wilson—no, by the time he received that letter, she was his ex-girlfriend—he read it, but didn't tell anyone. He ran to the top of the hill alone. Well, not truly alone, because he had me. When he was sure no one else was there, he leaned against a tree and sobbed.

"It's my fault. I lost her. I'm the one who lost her," he told me over and over.

He said they'd known each other for several months, but only kissed twice. Once was after seeing a movie, and he walked her home. As they said goodbye, he leaned in and kissed her. The light was on in her apartment, and she feared her aunt, whom she lived with, would see them from the window, so they just touched lips gently, then pulled away. The other time was at his going-away party. He'd invited her. They sat in a dim corner, and he kissed her, his tongue finally finding hers, but then a friend interrupted them, wanting him to make a toast.

Actually, he said there had been other opportunities. One time he was early picking her up for dinner. Her aunt was out, and she went to change while he waited in the living room. She didn't close the bedroom door completely, and he caught a glimpse of her naked back in the mirror in the hallway. The blood rushed to his head, and he felt as if there were a thousand drums pounding in his temples. If he'd taken that moment of madness and slipped through the door, he thinks she wouldn't have refused him. She might've even left the door ajar on purpose. But he didn't want to compromise her chastity before he'd asked her to marry him. But if he had gone in that day, he would've had a piece of her, then when she left him, he wouldn't have been left with nothing. Now, aside from the letter he's read over and over, there is nothing to show there'd ever been an Emily Wilson in his life at all.

When he said all this, I was grateful I was a dog. If I were unlucky enough to be a human, my Millie, there might have been a mountain between us, and I would've had to sing countless love songs for months before I finally dared lick you for the first time.

Fortunately, we're just a pair of dogs. The very day we met, we did all that a pair of dogs can do together, after falling in love. Now, even though I'm gone, I've had you fully, and I left myself fully with you, sweet Millie. So we'll never be apart, really. We'll always have a piece of each other.

All sorrows have an end, but some last longer than others. Millie, have you noticed that my master has a gleam in his eyes again and that he visits Pastor Billy a lot more than he used to?

Of course, it's not really the pastor he's going to see. He often goes when the pastor isn't even there, like on Tuesday nights when Pastor Billy always leads a men's Bible study. Or Friday afternoons, when my master has some free time between classes and dinner and Pastor Billy is usually miles away, visiting an herbalist to learn about traditional medicine. My master went to the church that Friday and invited himself in to sit for a while. Wende made them a cup of tea, and they tried to make conversation while they waited for Pastor Billy's return. He always used us as an excuse. "Ghost has been a little unsettled, and I thought I'd bring him to see Millie," he might say. Or, "Your Millie's been at my place for a while. I thought you might be worried about her, so I brought her back."

Those were beautiful excuses. We didn't mind at all.

Between sips of his tea, he would whistle "Yankee Doodle" for Wende. He would always end with a shrill blast, making Wende laugh. Her laughter was mostly hidden in her eyes, with only the strongest bursts escaping her lips. It was her eyes that captivated my master. He sometimes brought old American magazines to Wende, things his mother had sent from America. She looked often at the photos of Hollywood actresses, whose hair, clothes, and makeup were strange and interesting to Wende. But the only thing she said was, "They're not wearing much."

My master cocked his head and looked into her eyes, asking, "Aren't they pretty?"

She had no choice but to nod. My master laughed and said, "Ugly things need to be covered, but pretty things don't."

Wende was stunned. No one had ever said anything like that to her before.

Sometimes my master would teach Wende a little English. She had her own teacher—Pastor Billy had been teaching her for more than a year. But the English Pastor Billy taught her was all about sickness and souls, while my master taught her silly phrases that might make her simmer with laughter. For instance, he taught her the phrase, "the elevator doesn't go all the way to the top." Wende had never seen an elevator. She had no idea what it meant, so my master used a Chinese metaphor to explain it. He said, "The mind's missing a string for its bow." She understood immediately and even repeated it to you once when you clumsily spilled your food.

Another time, my master asked Wende to guess the meaning of "don't look a gift horse in the mouth." She'd figured out how his mind worked, so after a moment's thought, she said, "If you get something for nothing, don't be too picky about it."

Her intelligence often surprised my master. One time, Pastor Billy was in an especially good mood when he came back from the herbalist's house. He said the herbalist had promised to supply the church herbs at a reasonable price for a long time, so they wouldn't need to go out searching the mountains themselves. Hearing this, Wende said, "Take his words with a grain of salt."

Pastor Billy's jaw dropped.

"Where did you learn that?" he asked.

My master and Wende burst into laughter, almost in unison.

Leaving Pastor Billy's, my master would run excitedly, or really, allow me to pull him, running wildly. At times, I was his master, and he was the dog at the end of my leash. When he got winded, he'd pull me to him and whisper, "Wende is adorable, isn't she? What do you think?"

I wanted to tell him, "Don't make the same mistake you did with Emily Wilson. Just a few love songs are enough. When it's time to act, don't hesitate. Be like a dog."

Unfortunately, though I understood his words, he didn't understand mine. All I could do was lick his hand.

Dear Millie, I've said so much, just so you'll know that my master was a good friend to me. He gave me the best possible gift—you. The trainers knew that a dog's natural urges would affect training, so they suppressed the sex drive in military dogs. Before I left Chongqing, the trainer gave my master detailed instructions on the dosage and frequency of my medicine. He kept it in a wooden box next to his bed, but never once opened it. From his own loneliness, he knew mine. He didn't let that medication become an unbridgeable gap between you and me. He gave me the most precious thing in life, the freedom to love. For that reason alone, he deserved the sacrifice of my life.

Millie, oh, dear Millie. It's dark. Your master Wende has come to take you home. I can hear her footsteps. For my sake, I beg you to go home. Eat a good meal and sleep. Tomorrow, tomorrow when you come again, I want to see the stars in your eyes.

Day 5

Millie:

Ghost, even before your master returned, I knew you were dead. When the grenade exploded in your mouth, I was lying on a little bed of rags my master had made for me. It was like an iron drill pierced my mind, breaking my head into thousands of pieces. I immediately knew something had happened to you.

For the first few days, my sorrow was like dust filling the sky, with no place to settle. I didn't know how to grieve, so I was just angry with you. No, not angry. That's too frivolous a word. I think I hated you. I hated you for abandoning me for the sake of your so-called mission. I hated you for leaving without hesitation, not even looking back at me. But if you had forsaken your mission for me, or if your master had died and you'd returned safely, I wouldn't have hated you. I would've despised you, thinking you no better than a fly or maggot. I would rather riddle you with hate than have a trace of contempt for you. If I have to choose between hate and contempt, then I choose hate.

I've come here to see you every day. I stay from morning until the dim light of night blurs the words on your tombstone. I know it's silly. It's just a hole, with nothing but a clump of fur buried inside from midsummer, when your master cut your fur to keep you from getting fleas. He must've had a feeling you wouldn't be with him much longer, because he picked up a bit of your fur and kept it in a cookie tin. For him, this tuft of fur would be the only evidence that you lived in this world. Unlike your master Ian, I don't need a clump of fur to prove you lived. The little life growing in my belly—maybe one, maybe two, maybe more—that is the ironclad proof of your life.

Ghost:

Millie, you mean you're pregnant? With our pups? One day there will be a few little yous or little mes crawling around—or no, little uses? Then, Millie, I'm not dead. They and their pups and their pups' pups will carry our finite flesh-and-blood existence on to infinity.

Millie:

When you heard your master's call and left me that day, I had wanted to let you sniff at my little belly, which hadn't yet grown round, but you were in a hurry. You didn't even have time to say goodbye. In this, you're no different from humans. The mission is always what's most important. You always said that it was your duty to serve your master, but when you looked at me for the last time, I saw the fire in your eyes. It was the excitement of a dog of superior physical and intellectual ability when he hears the call to do great things. You used your master's commands as an excuse for your own ambition, just like your master used you as an excuse when he visited Pastor Billy. The two of you are the most loyal, reliable cover for each other. Despite all this, I can't help but love you. I even love your ambitions and vanity. I love you completely.

Since you left, I'm always excited when I see Ian. When he stands, I nip at his pant legs. When he sits, I jump on his lap and sniff around restlessly. He's puzzled by my sudden affection for him. Men always are clueless about such things.

"She's searching for Ghost's scent on you," my master Wende said.

She's the only one who understands. I am searching for your scent on him, but I don't know how long the traces you left on his clothes can withstand the ravages of saponin and club in the hands of the laundry woman.

Maybe you noticed I'm later than usual today. I left at the usual time, after Pastor Billy's morning prayers, as soon as Wende opened the courtyard doors. But halfway here, I heard a bugle call and got distracted. Whenever I hear the bugle, my ears tremble involuntarily, like a scared rabbit. That's a habit you've left in me. We hear the bugles every day in Yuehu, but today's was different. Usually, it's a series of short sounds, close and impatient, as if saying, "You're late. You're late." But today's signal was a long, drawn-out high note, as if saying, "Look at me. I'm powerful."

I ran toward it and found the field full of people. As soon as I saw them, I knew something special was happening today, because there was a larger group of guards and a crowd of people outside the camp not allowed to enter. Of course, this didn't apply to dogs. No one would think to guard against a dog, so I squeezed through their legs. The soldiers who'd been wearing straw shoes yesterday were in cloth shoes today. Not only that, but their uniforms were all freshly washed. I could smell the saponin and sunlight from a mile away. And I'd never seen them standing so straight, as if they had rods for spines. Later, I learned that it was their graduation ceremony.

Ghost:

Oh, Millie, I had forgotten! It's their big day. My master and his students talked every day about which big commander would deliver the speech. The higher-ups had kept it a secret.

Millie:

It was a lean old man. They called him Generalissimo. It's a strange word. I've heard of a colonel, brigadier, commander, and a general. But I've never heard of a generalissimo. How high is a generalissimo?

Ghost:

Millie, you're like all the other women in Yuehu. You don't care about these things at all. The generalissimo is their highest officer. Forget the commander—even the chief of staff is below him.

Millie:

No wonder they seemed afraid of him. Usually, the commanding officer walks through the camp like a gust of wind, and his voice is like a cannon fired in the mountains. Today, in front of that man, the commanding officer seemed small, and he couldn't say a single word.

Ghost:

How about the ceremony? Was it interesting?

Millie:

It was very dull. There was no food, no drums, no firecrackers. Everyone just stood still, quietly listening to speeches from one commanding officer after another. Listening to them turned my brain to mush. It's an "autumn tiger" day today, when the sun shines so hot, it's almost painful, as if the summer had returned. The men on and off the stage were quickly soaked, replacing the smell of saponin with sweat. I heard your master Ian whisper to Jack, "It's just a few months' training. Is all this necessary?" Jack's voice was quieter than Ian's, no louder than a mosquito buzzing, and I had to strain to hear it. I only caught two words: "ritual" and "honor."

Of course, there were a few interesting things. When the commander spoke, he thanked the American, Dr. Lewis, saying that under his supervision only one person in camp had gotten malaria, and there were no cases of typhoid fever. As soon as the commander spoke his name, Mr. Lewis fell to the ground, as if the commander had cast a spell on him. He had heat stroke, so two soldiers carried him out. He'd probably never stood in the sun that long in his entire life. You Americans really are useless.

Then, at the end, every graduate was given a gun. I knew from how their eyes lit up that they'd received a treasure. Ghost, you've never seen such a gleam. It was like a poor man finding a piece of silver or a rat smelling sesame oil. The light in their eyes outshone the sun. Then the commander said now that they have their guns, they can set out tomorrow to join the troops.

Ghost:

What about my master, Ian? Is he leaving too?

Millie:

Ian won't be going anywhere. The new students arrive in two days, so Ian will start new classes right away. He's also keeping the one they call 635 around. Since he understands English, Ian wants to keep him on as his assistant.

Day 21

Millie:

I'm sorry, Ghost. I haven't come for two days. Something happened at home. It's a mess, and my master needs me, even though she never said so. My master is a strange woman. She's never said the word "need" to me or anyone else. She guards that word as she guards her life. But I don't need her to say it. I always know exactly when she needs me.

Last winter, I came to Pastor Billy's home. My former masters, a Swedish missionary couple, had to return to their country due to illness. Before they left, they gave me to Pastor Billy, along with several other things they couldn't take. My former master took me out of the bamboo basket—that's how they carried me on their trips—and put me on the floor of Pastor Billy's study, which served as his parlor and operating room as well. They told me, "This is your new home, Millie. Be a good girl."

And just like that, I was left in a room full of strange furniture, books, bottles, and baskets. There was no stove in the room, and the evening sun made a cold white spot on the slate floor. The smell of antiseptic stabbed my nose and eyes. All the colors, lights, and smells were strange, making me feel cold and lonely. Cowering, I hid in a corner, whimpering.

A girl came and picked me up, holding me in the soft nest of her chest and arms. She didn't say anything, just put her face against me. I committed her smell to memory—a mix of earth, plants, and disinfectant. It didn't exactly smell good, but it put me at ease. When I noticed that the arms holding me were shaking too, I realized that we needed each other. I needed the warmth of her arms and breast, even if it came with the smell of disinfectant, and she needed me to fill a hole in her life. From that moment, she was my master. Every time she picked me up and held me to her, I knew she needed my comfort. I understood her, just as she understood me.

I'm not really sure what name I should give my master. Pastor Billy—and he's half master of me too—calls her Stella, which means "star." But your master, Ian, calls her Wende, which means "wind." Because of you, I got used to calling her Wende, so I'll continue doing that, at least when talking to you. But neither Stella nor Wende are her real name. When you examine these names, the selfishness of the people who call her by them becomes clear. Pastor Billy expects her to give him direction during his days of wandering, and Ian longs for her to be a breath of fresh air in his life while he's cut off from the outside world. I can't tell which my master prefers, but I know the name she least likes to be called is Ah Yan. That's the name her mother gave her when she was born. Beneath that name is buried a past that she doesn't want to recall. Her past is a closed and locked door. But a few days ago, I inadvertently discovered a crack in that door.

It had been raining for a while and was starting to get cold. Wende took the bamboo mats off the beds, cleaned them, put them away, and replaced them with quilts. The cook who'd been working in the church for over ten years had suddenly left. Pastor Billy never said why she resigned, but he was looking for someone to replace her. The church was suddenly shorthanded, and the laundry, cooking, and cleaning had all fallen to Wende. It was inevitable that there would be some difficulty.

As Wende changed the mattress on Pastor Billy's bed, she found a book tucked into one corner of the bed. Pastor Billy loves to read, and you might find a book in any corner of the house, even on the lid of the cistern, beneath the washbasin, or beside the toilet. So at first, she thought nothing of it, but then she pulled her hand back as if she'd touched a hot coal. After a moment, she picked it up, knelt on the bed, and looked at the book in the light angling through the window. It seemed to have been read many times. The corners of its cover were worn, and many of its pages were dog-eared, making it loose and thick. Wende wasn't really reading it, but was flipping to the title page as if out of habit, until she saw the name written with a fountain pen. She stared at the name, running her finger over the strokes of the characters slowly. Just then, Pastor Billy opened the door. As soon as she heard the movement, Wende turned around. She tossed the book down, but it was too late. Feeling like a thief caught in the act, she continued wiping the bamboo mats, but she used too much force, as if she wanted to scrape a layer of skin off the mats. Pastor Billy leaned over, picked up the book, and dusted it off.

"I've had this book here for a long time. It should be returned to its previous owner," he said.

Wende stopped, rag in hand, panting with exertion.

"I don't want it. Tear it up. Burn it," she said.

Pastor Billy put the book back on his bed and laughed awkwardly. He said, "Are you speaking from anger? This has nothing to do with me. If you want the book burned, burn it."

She snorted and said, "OK. I'll burn it."

Pastor Billy picked up the teacup he'd come for and walked to the door. He turned and stood for a moment behind Wende. He said haltingly, "He's not as bad as you think. There was just a hurdle he couldn't cross."

Wende didn't answer, but continued dusting the bamboo mat. Her hands were even more forceful than before, and several bitter, forlorn creaks came from the mat.

"He still cares about you. At the dorm when you went to talk to the commanding officer, he stood in front of the gun," Pastor Billy said.

Wende said nothing, but I saw her back heave.

"That gun was loaded," Pastor Billy said cautiously.

Wende turned around forcefully and threw the rag into the bucket, splashing water on the ground.

"If someone stabs you, then rubs a little pain-killing salve on the wound, does that mean they care?" she said.

I had been sitting beside Wende the whole time and was caught off guard by this. Since I'd arrived, I'd never heard my master use this tone with Pastor Billy. She was usually very deferential to him, even if he occasionally said something unpleasant. At most, she would fall silent to express her dissatisfaction. She might display some outward meekness while hiding her internal rebellion as a way of making the old man happy. "Old man." He's not even forty, but in a village where the average life expectancy is short and sixty is ancient, Pastor Billy is seen as an old man by most of the villagers, whether he likes it or not. Anyway, I'd never seen Wende talk back to Pastor Billy before. Pastor Billy's lips twitched a few times. He wasn't angry. It was more like hesitation. He didn't know whether he should pursue the conversation, but in the end, he couldn't help himself.

"Maybe he wasn't the one who spread the rumors. Maybe someone—" he said, then suddenly stopped.

She laughed bitterly. "Aside from you and him, no one else knows I'm from Sishiyi Bu. If it wasn't him, was it you?"

Pastor Billy didn't answer. He just looked at Wende, then walked out quietly. I knew he had more to say. I could hear it rumbling in his belly. Wende took the rag from the bucket and knelt on the bed in a daze. She didn't move, letting water drip from the rag onto the bamboo mat, where it pooled in little dark spots. Only then did I know it was Liu Zhaohu my master kept behind that closed door of hers. I'm sorry, Ghost. I've meandered too far. I haven't visited in two days. So much has happened, and I have so much to tell you.

Three days ago, around midnight, someone knocked on the door. Those who need Pastor Billy don't care what time it is, so I'm used to midnight callers. Pastor Billy opened the door and found a woman lying on a plank. She'd been in labor for two days and had fallen into a semiconscious state. The village midwife was visiting her parents, and the midwife in the neighboring village was forty li away, delivering a child. Not knowing what else to do, the family brought her to the church. Pastor Billy had lived in Yuehu for ten years, but he'd never delivered a baby. People here would never let a man—especially a foreign man—touch their wives' bodies. Though Pastor Billy was a surgeon, he wasn't an obstetrician and had only observed a birth once during his internship. But there was no time for hesitation. He called Wende to boil some water, disinfect the towels and knives, clear the table, spread out a white cloth, and lift the woman onto it. He started to examine the woman, but the two men who had brought her to him—her husband and brother-in-law—stopped him and said, "We want that one."

Pastor Billy didn't understand.

The husband stammered, "The . . . the woman doctor . . ."

They meant Wende.

He said, "No, she's never delivered a baby or even seen one delivered."

The husband said, "So what? The woman doctor's skills are good. When Xu Sancai's wife's shoulder was dislocated, she fixed it. And Liu Mazi's leg bled for half a year, but as soon as she cut it and cleaned it, it never bled again. Having a baby is easier, like a hen laying an egg. Why can't the woman do it?"

Pastor Billy sighed and said, "You ignorant men. Childbirth is like laying an egg? She's been in immense pain for so long, she doesn't have strength for the contractions. It could be an abnormal fetal position or a narrow birth canal. If we delay, she'll . . . she'll . . ." Pastor Billy caught himself. The word he was about to say was taboo. He quickly swallowed it and said, "She'll face very serious consequences." The men looked at Pastor Billy blankly, as if he had just finished reading scripture to them. Aside from the beginning and the end, they didn't understand a word of it.

The pain roused the woman, and her hands grabbed at the air as she called her husband's name. "Tianlin, you son of a bitch! You did this to me! You've killed me!" She sounded like a pig being slaughtered, making my hair stand up.

Pastor Billy glared at the two men, then shouted, "Get out! You two, get out! If you're here, how can the woman doctor go about her business?" They went out helplessly, sat on the steps, and waited for news.

Pastor Billy started to examine her. Though she'd passed out from pain several times, she still felt shame. She pressed her legs closed tightly, not allowing him to look. Seeing this, Wende said softly in her ear, "It's me. We're both women. It's OK. You can relax."

She'd been in pain for so long, she had no strength left. She let Wende remove her pants and disinfect her. Pastor Billy checked and saw that the fetal position was normal and that her cervix was dilated fully, but the fetus was too big for her birth canal. He took a clean towel and told the woman to bite it. He said, "If you can't stand it, then scream, but better save your strength if you can. When I say push, push hard."

He then instructed Wende to get the surgical scissors. When she tried to give them to Pastor Billy, he didn't take them, but held the woman's thighs open with both hands.

"You do it. You've drained an abscess. You can do this."

She hesitated, then understanding what he meant, began to tremble slightly.

"I'm stronger than you, so I'll hold her legs. You make a lateral incision, at a forty-five-degree angle to the left and about an inch and a half in length," he said.

She still hesitated. Pastor Billy leaned over and whispered in her ear, "Forget it's a person. Think of it as the sole of a shoe. Use the skill you always use when you cut a sole. Make the cut, steady and accurate."

She took a deep breath, then cut as Pastor Billy had instructed. The woman's face twisted violently, and a dull squeal escaped around the towel. After a moment, the squeals were overtaken by another sound. It was sharp as an awl, reaching the roof and piercing it. It was a baby's first cry. A boy's cry, to be precise. When the stitches were finished and mother and child cleaned and wrapped, they opened the door and let the men come in. Seeing his child, the father knelt with a crash, touching his head to the ground before Wende, thanking her over and over. Pastor Billy pulled him up and said, "They must stay in the church for two days so we can watch for infection."

The husband refused, saying, "No matter what, I have to take them home before dawn."

Pastor Billy knew he was afraid that people would see his wife in the church and think a man had delivered her baby. He said, "You heard it all yourself. It was the woman doctor who took your child from your wife's belly. Are you so afraid of what others will say that you'll risk their lives?"

Finally, he agreed, and the men were sent away. Pastor Billy looked at the fuzzy little head wrapped in his old cotton jacket, sighed, and said, "Here, with such poor nutrition, where the mother is so small and skinny, she still managed to have this big fellow."

Using old scales, one end lifted very high, Wende found he was nine pounds and six ounces. She scooped water from the vat into a basin to wash her hands. Pastor Billy pointed at my belly with the tip of his cloth shoe, gently hooking his toes under me as I sat at Wende's feet. He said, "Our Millie is the same. A tiny body giving birth to a giant. I hope there won't be complications when the time comes."

He's right. Though I'm not even halfway through my pregnancy, my belly is already so round, it's ready to burst. If I don't tighten my belly when I walk, it almost drags on the ground.

"Congratulations, Stella. You've successfully delivered a child. Your first," Pastor Billy said.

She shook her head, exhausted, and said, "That was just to appease them. I don't have the knowledge. You delivered the baby, not me."

Pastor Billy looked stunned. "You should be proud of yourself. Didn't you hear? They kept calling you the woman doctor. Stella, your greatest strength is that you're fearless in the face of danger. You just need someone to stand behind you and push you from time to time."

She said nothing, silently rubbing her still-shaking hands with soap.

"I'll teach you more gynecology. A few of the midwives in the area here are in their forties. Delivering a baby requires a lot of energy. They won't be able to work much longer, and they don't know Western medicine or how to do simple surgery. In the future, this will be your domain," he said excitedly.

Wende muttered, "I . . . I . . . people . . . ," then stopped again.

Pastor Billy suddenly came to himself. "You're worried people will say you're just a girl who hasn't yet had children of her own, so what would you know about delivering a baby, right?"

He had guessed part of what was on her mind, but not all. What he didn't know was something my master had only shared with me—that her marital status was blurry at best. By fingerprints on documents, she was a married woman. By her maidenhood, she had lost her virginity and thus could not be considered a maiden, yet nobody claimed her as a wife. There was no word under the sun that accurately described her. She was a monster, stuck somewhere between childhood and adulthood, between maiden and wife. She couldn't reconcile such a status with the role of midwife.

Pastor Billy's face tightened. "Stella, gossip is like dust in the wind. After it flies around for a while, it will settle. You can't avoid going outside because of the dust. If you just take the first step, you'll see it isn't as scary as you imagine."

Wende said nothing.

"Here, who can bring a woman a hundred li to a hospital to deliver her baby? No one knows how long the war will go on, but even the war won't stop children from being born. If you become a midwife, you'll never want for food or respect. Even if I were gone, no one would dare harm you then. You would have the whole village to protect you, because their wives' and children's lives would be in your hands. You can't just think about now. You have to consider the future."

That phrase "the future" kept popping up in Pastor Billy's words that day, and without realizing it, he said it more intensely each time, as if afraid it would flutter away. He didn't realize that Wende didn't want the future, just as she didn't want the past. Those sentiments were only shared with me, in one of the rare moments she voiced any complaint. The first time he said it, she was uncertain. She didn't know if she wanted it or resented it. But each repetition was like a stone on her heart. She realized that the future was a heavy thing to carry.

They cleaned themselves up, and Wende told Pastor Billy to go back to sleep. She grabbed a stool and turned down the flame on the lamp, then sat with the woman who had just become a mother and the baby who had just become a son. I jumped up and curled up in her lap. Day was already breaking, and the paper over the windows was turning from black to gray. Mother and child fell asleep, their breathing shallow. The baby was ugly. His thick fetal hair seemed covered with a layer of dirt and the red skin on his face was just a wrinkled mess. It was as if he hadn't fully escaped the horror of the scissors. From time to time, he twitched. I wondered if he was dreaming.

Wende put her face down and gently rubbed my fur with her cheek. "A baby. I delivered a baby," she muttered to herself.

It wasn't joy and contentment in her voice. What I heard was panic, fear, incredulity, and perhaps a trace of doubt. I understood. Wende, my master, was still a child herself. I gently licked her face and hands. For the first time, I felt the incompetence and sorrow of doghood. We understand countless emotions and feelings in humans, but we can only comfort them with our tongues. No, we can do more than that. When I noticed my master was anxious, I hopped onto her knees or sat at her feet, rubbing myself against them, and she gradually relaxed. My contented, rumbling breath could loosen the taut strings in her head like magic. Once I noticed this, I began to try to figure out which scales and rhythms relaxed her most quickly. I'm very good at it now. At that point, I rumbled for a few moments, and her eyes quickly grew sleepy. I thought the day's chaos had finally come to an end.

Wende had dozed off for a moment when someone knocked at the door again. By now, the most diligent roosters in the village were awake, crowing from time to time. The knock wasn't as heart-stopping as the one at midnight, but it was still foreboding. I hopped down from Wende's lap, and when I caught a trace of your scent, I knew it was Ian. Three days earlier, he and Liu Zhaohu had set off with a squad of new students. This was the day they were supposed to return, but they weren't expected at the church, definitely not so damned early.

Pastor Billy and Wende both woke in alarm and ran to open the door. Autumn was in the air, and the wind blew a little chill into the room. The trees were blurred to grayish brown with dew. Ian stood at the door, his face dull and sallow. He was being held up by two Chinese men, both much smaller than him. Wende recognized one of them as Ian's servant, Buffalo. Ian had his full weight on one leg, the other bent with the pant leg rolled up to show a calf covered in dark-purple mud. *Taking Buffalo along had been Ian's idea, he said later. This mission was almost as far away as the one you went on, Ghost. Your last mission.* After that previous long night march, Ian decided to bring Buffalo along to carry his food and weapons. He had learned that pride was trivial compared to exhaustion. Pastor Billy led them into the house and asked what had happened. Buffalo whispered, "It's all my fault." Then, he started to cry.

They were going to a town that had no military significance in itself, but it happened to be on a tributary of a big river. There was actually nothing special about that either, as there were thousands of such waterways in Jiangnan, but this was the birthplace of a man who'd placed second in the imperial examinations during Daoguang's reign. He became an important official in the capital, and when he eventually returned to his village, he used the money he had earned to build a stone bridge. The bridge was built with excellent stone and exceptional handiwork, allowing it to hold not only the weight of ancient mule carts and carriages but also of modern cars. Over the previous month, the Japanese had started using the bridge to transport troops and supplies across the river, after suffering steady losses on the road they'd been using. The mission was to blow up the bridge and force the Japanese back to the original road, then let the regular army deal with them.

They hadn't expected the defenses to be so weak. Things had been quiet for a month, and they'd begun to let down their guard. There were only two sentries, one at either end of the bridge. The one on the far side was leaning against the bridge, asleep. Liu Zhaohu only needed one shot to kill the standing guard. With the silencer and *the branches creaking in the strong wind, the sleeping guard didn't even stir. One of the trainees stuffed the soft lumpy gray explosives into the gaps between two stones on the bridge almost effortlessly. The timing device was set for detonation half an hour later, when Japanese convoys usually crossed the bridge, as they were less likely to be noticed in the middle of the night.*

The mission all went according to plan. By the time the bridge blew into a pile of rocks, they'd retreated to perfect safety down the mountain path. The accident occurred when they were about two li from camp. Buffalo was tired, and he failed to keep an eye on Ian, and Ian slipped and fell into a ditch roughly as deep as a man is tall, with no footholds to climb out. With a great deal of effort, Buffalo and Liu Zhaohu pulled Ian out, but he couldn't walk. At first they thought it was a fracture, but later found it was just a deep, bloody wound. A large, sharp rock had cut a seven-inch-long gash in his leg, scraping away his flesh almost to the bone. It was bleeding badly. Ian was nearly delirious with pain, so Buffalo got a handful of wet mud from the paddy field and plastered it over the wound, saying it was his grandfather's trick to stop bleeding and relieve pain. Ian shouted, "What are you, a fucking witch doctor?" But he immediately felt a slight soothing coolness in the wound, and in moments the pain lessened noticeably, and they were able to get him back to Yuehu. The medical officer in the camp was in Chongqing on some business, so they sent him to Pastor Billy.

Buffalo helped Ian to the guest room, and Wende cleaned him up. The wound was deep, and there was a good deal of mud, dirt, grass, and leaves embedded in it. Wende used gauze, dipping a bit at a time into warm water to wash the wound. With every wipe, he winced. Each time he winced, her brow furrowed. Wende took out the dirty water but didn't return to the room. She couldn't bear watching Pastor Billy's stitches. They had no painkillers or antibiotic, and the church medicine chest was almost empty, with nothing but a few quinine tablets and some sleeping pills left. The Japanese had been especially vigilant guarding the roads recently, and anyone caught smuggling drugs was executed on the spot. The price of black market drugs had risen to where Pastor Billy couldn't afford them with just goodwill, and the camp's medical supply line had been broken, and it was a full three days until the next airdrop was expected.

Pastor Billy told the men to hold Ian's leg, and he started stitching. Howl after howl came from the room, and you could almost follow the needle's pace with its rise and fall. The little newborn woke up and cried in alarm. Wende sat outside the door, covering her ears tightly, but her palms weren't thick enough. The sound seeped in through her fingers, filing her eardrums one scrape at a time. Her body became smaller and smaller, until she looked like a ball with protruding bones and tendons. If you saw her then, you would hardly recognize her as the person who'd sewn the head back on a corpse or the person who'd just delivered a baby. It dawned on me that she had fallen in love with Ian. Love was the only thing that could make someone lose their courage like that, transforming from a powerful warrior to a terrified wretch. I knew my tongue and breath were no use then. Nothing can comfort someone undone by love. I could only hide in a quiet corner, staying out of everyone's way.

When the stitching was finally done, Wende found the courage to go back in. Ian's clothes were soaked in sweat, and his golden curls were plastered on his forehead. Wende wiped his face and changed him into some of Pastor Billy's clothes, then fed him some porridge and helped him lie down. Pastor Billy gave him a sleeping pill and sent the men away. Exhausted, Ian finally fell asleep.

But the baby outside wasn't ready to sleep. He cried until he was hoarse and his throat was raw. He must have been hungry. His mother had not started lactating yet, so Pastor Billy milked their goat, boiled the small bowl of milk, and waited for it to cool before trying to feed it to the baby with a spoon. He'd never fed a baby before, so he was clumsy, dribbling milk everywhere. Wende took over. Putting the child in her lap and holding its head in one arm, she held the bowl in one hand and the spoon in the other. She tested the temperature against her lips, then carefully began to spoon a little onto the baby's lips. The child didn't know how to swallow yet, and gurgling sounds came from his mouth. So Wende wiped her hand on her shirt, dipped her finger into the milk, and then put it into the baby's mouth. He slurped and began sucking. When he'd finished the whole bowl, he fell into a deep sleep.

After feeding the child, Wende told Pastor Billy to sleep for a while, since they'd gotten almost no sleep the night before. She sat beside the bed and kept watch over Ian, just as she had watched over the woman and her son earlier. The vigils looked similar, but they were completely different. The first had been a vigil of the eyes and ears. The second was a vigil of the heart. Ian's skin glistened like a fish, with sweat seeping from every pore. She was afraid that he was losing so much fluid he would turn into a dehydrated skeleton. She wiped the sweat away and dabbed cool water on his lips to moisten his mouth. Still, he only slept for a short while, then the sleeping pill wasn't enough to keep the pain of his wound at bay. He woke not knowing where he was. His lips twitched, and he stammered. Wende tried to understand, but it took her some time to realize he was saying "cold." She heard a rattling and realized it was his teeth chattering. She went to her room and took a quilt, then grabbed her cotton shirts and trousers, which Pastor Billy had bought her when she came to Yuehu. She covered Ian, but he still continued to shiver. After a while, she got a few bricks, heated them in the fire, wrapped them in towels, and put them around him. That finally seemed to help a little.

A while later he started babbling, calling out names. She only recognized the word "mom." Her heart ached, and her mouth twitched involuntarily. Then he started to kick the blanket. One of the bricks fell, nearly crushing her foot. She wiped his forehead, and it was burning with a high fever. Suddenly he opened his eyes wide, looking at her in a way that gave her the creeps. He saw her, but didn't seem to know her. His eyes rotated in their sockets, then suddenly fixed on a corner of the ceiling. His neck arched as if he were desperately trying to see something visible only to him. One hand poked outside the quilt, its fingers curled like hooks. Wende realized he was having convulsions and rushed in a panic to wake Pastor Billy. Poor Pastor Billy had been awakened several times already that night. Sleep oozed from his eyes in a furious current, making him seem like a very old man in that instant. After shuffling into his slippers, he took Ian's temperature: 107 degrees. He shook his head silently, and Wende knew without him saying that there was nothing they could do to help his body cool down, aside from physical cooling. The medicine Ian needed was at least three days away. Ian could only rely on his own ability to bargain with God now.

The cistern was empty, so Wende drew bucket after bucket of water from the well. She wiped Ian's forehead and body with a towel soaked in cool water. After she went through several buckets, he quieted down and stopped twitching. Pastor Billy could not tolerate the fatigue and had gone to sleep again, but Wende wasn't tired. She checked Ian's temperature again. As she held the thermometer up to the light now streaming in through the window, she closed her eyes and whispered something. The mercury was still at 107. She ran to her room again, returning with her sewing basket. She took out two pieces of material left over from making soles, one big and one small, and rolled them into balls. Then she rolled four smaller scraps into cylinders. When she stitched them all together, I saw that they formed a human figure. She took out a piece of chalk and wrote sick ghost *on the little cloth man's belly, then took four needles of varying thickness and poked them into him. She used great force, and once a needle slipped and poked her finger. A purple bead crawled out from her fingertip and turned into a black worm. She quickly sucked the little purple bug, then spat* it onto the ground. At that moment, she looked as delirious as Ian had during his convulsions, and I was a little frightened. She checked again, and Ian's temperature was down to 104. Wende knelt in the corner, palms clasped together and her lips trembling, and whispered:

> The Lord is my shepherd; I shall not want.
> He maketh me to lie down in green pastures;
> he leadeth me beside the still waters.
> He restoreth my soul;
> he leadeth me in the paths of righteousness for his name's sake.
> Yea, though I walk through the valley of the shadow of death,
> I will fear no evil, for thou art with me;
> thy rod and thy staff they comfort me.

I was surprised. I knew "the Lord" was not Wende's bodhisattva—that was Pastor Billy's bodhisattva, and Ian's, and all the Americans. Although Wende went to Pastor Billy's sermons, she'd never worshipped his bodhisattva. But now, for Ian's sake, she threw aside her own bodhisattva.

> Thou preparest a table before me in the presence of mine enemies;
> thou anointest my head with oil; my cup runneth over.
> Surely goodness and mercy shall follow me all the days of my life;
> and I will dwell in the house of the Lord forever.

Wende repeated the prayer over and over, each time swallowing a few words. In the end, there was only "I will fear no evil." She chewed those words, swallowed them, then brought them back up, pushing them from her heart through her throat and out her mouth. They traveled that path so many times that they ground a rut into her tongue.

For the rest of the day, she was in constant motion. Her energy was split among the feverish Ian, the frail mother, the crying baby, and the hungry pastor. Even the goats and weeds wouldn't help, refusing to provide milk and food. Pastor Billy had tried to do the cooking, but the firewood never caught, despite his best efforts with the bellows. Instead, he'd just gotten smoke in his eyes. The boy who helped around the church had chopped plenty of wood before going home, but the woodshed was leaking, so the wood had gotten damp. Pastor Billy realized that God could not be expected to intervene in every disaster, so today he'd have to take care of it himself. He went into the village and found a woman who was breastfeeding and asked her to take the newborn child in for a while. That way, at least one of them was fed.

Pastor Billy's lunch that day was rice crust and leftover radish strips. Wende ate nothing. Under pressure from Pastor Billy, she took a bite of pickled vegetables, but immediately spat it out. There were ulcers in her mouth from worry and sleeplessness, and the salt stung. Both Ian and the new mother needed hot water, so instead of eating, Wende moved the bundles of wood into the yard and spread them out in the sun. It was October, so the sun looked strong, but wasn't. Wende felt the rays of light glaring through the branches and wanted to shield her eyes. The sky suddenly slanted, the light so strong it knocked her over. I rushed to her in a panic and started licking her face, but she didn't wake. I could feel her breathing, so I knew she was alive, just exhausted. She needed sleep, even if it were out in the yard like this. I snuggled beside her quietly, keeping her warm with my body.

Later, she was woken by a strange sound, almost like wind, but weaker and with a twist. She forced her eyes open and looked at the tree. The branches weren't moving, so it wasn't wind. She considered getting up, but her body was too heavy, like someone had nailed her to the ground. She couldn't move. She closed her eyes and listened to the sound like wind that was not wind. Gradually, she recognized a melody. Then she realized it was "Yankee Doodle."

She scrambled up and stumbled toward the house. Her body was weak, and after just a few steps, she felt like she'd been running for hours. She leaned against the door, holding her chest, and only after she caught her breath did she push the door open. She saw Ian, leaning up against the pillow and whistling weakly. At that moment, her mind was a blank, and she couldn't stop herself from running toward Ian and throwing her arms around his neck.

"You . . . you . . . You're oh . . . You're OK . . . Alive," she rambled incoherently.

He smiled a weak, crooked smile.

"You trying to suffocate me?" he said.

She suddenly became aware of herself. She pulled away, a layer of red spreading over her face like dye on rice paper, filling all the ragged wrinkles of exhaustion. The expression on my master's face was a mixture of shock, embarrassment, shyness, *confusion, and maybe some other things. Any one of these emotions would have been expected or maybe even mundane, but all jumbled together, they inexplicably produced a sort of chemical reaction. At that moment, Wende was extraordinarily beautiful. Ian stared at her, then squeezed her hand. "You're shivering. Come, get warm," he said, gently lifting the edge of the quilt. She hesitated, then covered her face and ran out of the room. That night after dinner, Ian asked Pastor Billy for a pen and paper, then wrote a letter to his sister Leah. He wrote the opening a few times, but crossed them all out. He finally ended up with this:*

> *Romain Rolland said misery is like a flint from whence a spark might fly to set the whole soul on fire. We never know what demons may sleep in our hearts . . .*

In the end, he didn't finish the letter. The next morning, Wende found several balls of paper scattered on the floor.

Day 50

Millie:

Ghost, today, everything seems to be a dream, a short, absurd dream. Things happen so fast, and people are unprepared for them. In fact, even dogs are unprepared for them. When it comes, it comes like a thief. In the few moments it took, I didn't even realize what was going on. I felt I suddenly had no legs, no body, no head. But I had eyes, ears, and a nose, because I could still see, hear, and smell. Also, in the human language, the word "crawl" is associated with legs, and I've lost my legs, yet I am somehow crawling on the beams, watching everything happen below me. I see a middle-aged man in a tunic. As he removes the rubber gloves from his hand, he is pacing back and forth, sighing.

"We shouldn't have let them be together. We should have known the size difference would lead to this," the old man says to a girl in the room.

She squats on the floor, looking at a disgusting mess of filth. She may be crying, or maybe not. I can't see her face, only her bowed head. She says, "They were so happy together. Who could stop them?"

She pulls a clean handkerchief from her pocket. I think she is going to wipe her tears, but she crushes it into a ball and gently wipes the blood from the mangled thing. I can see now that it's a dead dog.

"Millie. Millie, how could you leave me like this?" she murmurs.

Hearing my name, I'm shocked. I'm suddenly aware that I'm dead. I died giving birth, and my master Wende is cleaning my corpse. I remember when Wende delivered that woman's baby not long ago, Pastor Billy said something about there being a litter of giants in my little body, and he wondered if I would be able to give birth. He said something else that day, and in his words, I smelled ominous predictions about himself and about Wende's future. Pastor Billy's lips were cursed by the god of destiny, and every name that crossed his lips was likewise cursed.

"Pastor Billy, when dogs die, do they go to heaven?" Wende asked, looking up.

Pastor Billy thought for a while, as if it were a question that required him to consult all his reference books. After a while, he said, "Dogs are also God's creation. He has prepared a place for every soul he created."

The girl's wrinkled brows relaxed almost imperceptibly. She continued to wipe the blood from my body. In my memory, my master's hand seems to repeat that action every day. She wipes oil from the stove, sweat from the bamboo mats, footprints from the floor, blood from between the new mother's legs, sweat from Ian's brow, afterbirth from the baby's body . . . But there are too many bad things in this world. Even if she grows thousands of hands, she can't wipe away all its filth. I want to tell her not to bother. It's done, and that stinking skin sack is not really me. But I can't do that. I've lost my tongue.

"I want to put Millie in a box and bury her next to Ghost," she says.

Ghost, oh, Ghost! I don't have to spend all that time and energy on a meaningless journey to your grave and back. From now on, I'll be with you forever. You may regret that we ended up not leaving any little ones in this world, a little you or a little me, or a little mix of both of us. But really, we don't need them to continue our lives. We're dead, and we won't die again. We have eternal life in death, a life without end.

Ghost, I'm coming. Wait for me.

Pastor Billy and Ian:
Between Goodbye and Farewell

Pastor Billy:

All wars eventually end, just as every night ends, but in war, we don't know when that end will come. Victory, like death, is unpredictable. So when I heard the Japanese emperor's "Jewel Voice Broadcast," my first reaction was suspicion and surprise. Joy came later. This war had been going on for too long. It had been eight years since the Marco Polo Bridge Incident, and counting from the Manchurian Incident, it had been fourteen years. If, on the other hand, we looked all the way back to the First Sino-Japanese War, the Battle of the Yalu River in 1894—and many today see this conflict as a continuation of that one—then this war had been going on for half a century. But even a fifty-year war will eventually come to an end.

I heard of the truce on the radio at the American military camp. I hadn't taken my bike, so, leaving Ian and his comrades, I ran home so fast, I lost a shoe along the way. When I breathlessly delivered the news to Stella, her shoulders twitched. That was her only reaction. She neither cried nor laughed, but was still, as if thinking. After a moment, she walked into the yard, paused under the big tree beside the road, and looked at the sandy yellow road and the livestock prints that covered it. For a long time, she said nothing. She was looking in the direction of her home. More than two years earlier, I had traveled that road and brought her back from Sishiyi Bu. It dawned on me that she was homesick.

I looked at Stella's back and noticed that she'd grown taller. There was a bowl-sized scar on the tree, from some worm or perhaps a stroke of lightning.

When she had first come here, her head just reached that knot. Now, the knot was below her ear. Of course, I couldn't be absolutely sure—perhaps the tree was shrinking. Everyone had lost something in this war, but not everyone had lost everything. She'd lost her father, her mother, her virginity, and her love. After all that, what could possibly be left? All she had was her homeland, even if it was in ruins now. At that moment, I made an important decision. I would go back to America and raise money to build a church in Sishiyi Bu, along with a clinic and a home—a home for Stella and me.

The celebration that day continued until late into the night. Everyone in the village, with the sole exception of Stella, flocked to the training ground, where civilians had always been strictly prohibited. After going through so much, Stella no longer trusted crowds, and she no longer trusted emotions that were too big, such as great sorrow or great joy. At the entrance point of every emotion, she had built a gate. After midnight, the crowd finally began to disperse. Ian was still enthusiastic. He pulled Liu Zhaohu and me aside and said he wanted to have a drink with us at my house. He had two bottles of whisky, and camp rules prohibited him from consuming it on base. He wasn't really concerned about camp rules, but there were only two bottles, not enough to share with everyone. The only way to really enjoy it was to do so privately. Seeing my hesitation, he punched me on the shoulder and said, "Don't tell me your God is like that— aside from killing someone, any sin committed today can be forgiven."

Ian didn't know that I wasn't hesitating for God's sake. On a day like today, there were so many drunks that even God wouldn't be able to keep track of them. I was worried about Stella. She didn't want to see Liu Zhaohu, especially not after what had happened with Snot. Liu Zhaohu also hesitated. Ian thought he was afraid of the commanding officer, so he grabbed his arm and started walking. He said, "Tomorrow, I'll tell him I forced you at knifepoint, or gunpoint, or with a grenade, to drink with me. He can't do anything to me."

Ian had nerves of steel. He couldn't have known that Liu Zhaohu was also hesitant because of Stella. Just as Ian didn't know why we hesitated, we didn't know why Ian was so eager. Standing there between them, I realized that the hesitation and eagerness were tied to the same girl.

We sat in the kitchen and opened a bottle. We held small bowls like old villagers, eating peanuts with grains of salt clinging to them as we drank the liquor. We each had an ear cocked like a rabbit's, listening for a sound from outside the kitchen. Stella's room was dark and quiet, but I was certain she was awake. There was no chance she didn't hear us. But the whole night, she never so much as opened the door. We spoke of our plans after the war. Ian said he had to wait until he acquired enough points before being sent back to America. It might be three months, or five. He hoped it wouldn't be more than half a year. After he got home, he intended to sleep for three whole days, then soak in a bathtub for three more. Then, he would watch all the movies he had missed. After that, he would visit his friends and family—at least, those who hadn't died on the battlefield or of illness, fear, or sadness. "Then," he said, pausing with a chuckle that showed his teeth, all lined up in two neat rows like soldiers in formation, "I'll think about what to do after that." I noticed a yellow stain had formed on Ian's teeth. Perhaps it was the water or maybe his heavy smoking. The war had snapped a section of his youth off, and what he needed to do now was find the broken part and reattach it, like a good mechanic would do.

I asked Liu Zhaohu what he planned to do. He thought for a moment, then said hesitatingly, "I'll see what fate has in store for me."

I dug through his words earnestly, finding no hint of any plans to go home in them. The war had been a wheel of fire, carrying him on a crazed journey, a long escape. He had grown used to the speed, and now that the wheel of fire had stopped turning, he was at a loss. The war had called on him to cast everything aside, and now peace demanded that he pick it all up again. He seemed to have no idea how to deal with peace.

I'd asked about their plans, but neither had asked me about mine. A sudden sadness came over me. I realized that they saw me as an old man. Old men didn't have plans or make changes. Old men stayed in place. At most, they moved in a small circle, then returned to their original spot, waiting for death to come. A little angry, I volunteered my plans. I said I would return to America soon. It had been many years since I'd been there, and I wasn't sure about my parents' health. When I said this, I had no idea that I was serving as a messenger of fate. Each word, whether groundless or absurd, would soon be substantiated, one after another. A month later, I received a letter from my mother saying that my father was in critical condition. I also told them I intended to raise funds in America, a large sum that would allow me to come back and build a church and clinic, maybe even a school. I deliberately left the detail of its location vague. I didn't mention Sishiyi Bu, since I hadn't yet discussed it with Stella. She should be the first to hear.

Liu Zhaohu said, "Pastor Billy, this is good. It's much too hard for people in this region to see a doctor."

Excitedly, Ian patted my arm and said, "If we're lucky, we might be on the same ship home."

That was when Zhaohu said solemnly, "Even if we all never meet again in this world, we should meet here again in the next." The plan we formulated when he said that is finally realized today.

You didn't know that my plan was tied to a girl. Perhaps you thought an old man like me could only give advice about others' romance and not possess love himself. When the bottles of whisky were gone and you finally went home, the sky was growing light. Birds don't know time, only light. They sang a few timid notes, as if testing the sound. When one bird woke, all the birds in the tree followed. Then, the forest was awake, and even the leaves made sound. There was a thin stream of moisture on the dawn breeze, undetectable to the eye, but felt on the face. The air tasted fresh and sweet, like a cool velvet grass gently tickling the throat, making one want to make noise, just to ease the itch.

I didn't feel like sleeping. Though I'd spent the previous day celebrating with the crowd, only now was news of armistice cleared of the entangled mass of emotions to become a calm, true reality. The dust stirred up by the winds of war had finally settled, and the verdant green of life would gradually begin to reemerge. In the end, the chaos had been bound and received the judgment and sentence. This was the order of society and the order of the state. But what about my personal order? What was that? Where was it? Was the plan to build a church, a clinic, and a courtyard my answer? No, they were just the places in which I would establish order. They were the labels, not the substance. My order was Stella, the woman I hoped to make my wife.

Wife. The word shocked me. It was only then that I understood my own mind and stopped avoiding the word that would end ambiguity. In the past, I used ambiguous words like "together" or "share a home" to envisage our future relationship. Wife. In the local dialect, the word suggested she would become a "woman of the house." Yes, I wanted to make her a woman of the house, my house. I had been avoiding this thought mostly because of the age difference. I was thirty-nine, and she was just sixteen. I was old enough to be her father. But what was age? Age was just a number, just as a church was only a building. They were nothing without souls. Stella's experience and courage were remarkable and belied her young years. I'd just been waiting for her body to catch up to her mind. I could easily wait until she was eighteen, then propose to her. I made up my mind. As soon as she woke, I would tell her about my plan to return to America.

I also considered Ian. How could I miss the intention behind his sprinting to the church time after time? Of course, he didn't think I'd noticed. Young people always think their minds are sharp as a knife while older minds have grown confused. I'd seen the sparks in their eyes when they looked at each other, but in my lexicon, a spark is a fleeting thing. Despite being a gunner's mate first class with an innate understanding of weapons, intelligence, and guerrilla warfare, Ian was still unstable emotionally. The war had thrown him into the boring town of Yuehu. The only view in this place was Stella (and she would have been quite a view no matter where she was). I could practically guarantee that once Ian left Yuehu, it would only take a month, a week, or even three days before he forgot Stella. She would, of course, be upset, but I had prepared myself for her sorrow. Whenever she sank, I would be there to catch her, firm and steady. I had done it before, and I would do it for the rest of my life. And she would know that when there was nothing else in this world she could rely on, aside from God, I would be her unchanging constant. Thinking like this, I couldn't wait any longer. Just as I was about to rap my knuckles against her door, reason suddenly woke me, telling me to wait till daytime. It was the longest wait of my life, from dawn until it was fully light outside. It seemed that ninety-nine nights passed in that short time.

When Stella finally woke and opened the door, she saw me sitting on the floor in front of her door, leaning against the wall, and it startled her. She immediately noticed the smell of the alcohol on me.

"My God, Pastor Billy, you . . . you're drunk?" Her voice was ragged with the surprise of it.

She'd never seen me drink so much before. No, she'd never seen me drink at all. The war, this cursed war, had turned a respectable pastor into a spy, a smuggler, a patron of the Green Gang, and now a drunk. I smiled at her.

"I'd prefer you call me Billy," I said. "And I'm not drunk. I've never been as sober as I am today."

She helped me up, and we sat down in the kitchen, where the previous night's unruliness and mess remained scattered across the dining table. I crushed the empty cigarette box Ian had left behind and tossed it into the stove. She took an egg from the bamboo basket, broke it into a bowl, and started to make a steamed egg custard for me.

"Stella, come here. I have something to tell you," I said.

I took her hand and pulled her over to sit beside me. My fingertips were a little sticky, a hint of egg white transferred from her hand to mine.

"I want to talk about your future," I said.

I noticed her eyebrows tense slightly. Almost immediately, they relaxed, as if she was afraid I would notice.

For the first time, I became aware that she probably didn't like the word "future." When I was her age, I didn't like it either. At the time, I felt this word was specifically aimed at my weak points. The word loved to fall on the apex of the heart, and as soon as it touched the heart, the heart was no longer free. When had I unwittingly stepped into my parents' shoes?

"Actually, what I want to discuss is how we should live after the war," I said, trying to ease my tone.

I carefully sliced my plan into pieces and tried to focus practically on each piece, avoiding the grand, lofty vision they formed when connected together. In the end, I couldn't keep myself in check. I spoke of sending her to medical school, then about going back to the countryside to practice after she graduated—going back, of course, with me.

"Two doctors with knowledge of medical theory and rich field experience in a place where there is a lack of medical care can open a medical facility that's more than a clinic, but less than a hospital. That would be a practical goal," I said.

I deliberately omitted the most important part of the plan. I would tell her that on her eighteenth birthday. I should have returned from America by that time. Of course, I couldn't know that my secret would remain with me, to be buried at the bottom of the ocean, alongside my body. She listened without saying anything, not once interrupting or asking any questions. After a long pause, she fell onto her knees in front of me. This wasn't the first time she'd knelt before me. When she bowed to me before, I gave her a stern warning, saying that in the whole world—or at least in my whole world—she could only kneel to express respect before the Lord God. From then on, she hadn't knelt before me again.

200

My heart suddenly tightened. I felt her kneeling was going to bind me into a relationship I didn't want.

She kowtowed deeply.

"You are my second father. I will always stay with you and care for you. When you are old, I will care for you until the end of your days, just as if you were my own father."

I went over each word she said in my head. She didn't mention my plan at all, not one word of it. I felt like a stake had been driven through my heart. I didn't know whether to pull it out or drive it in farther. Either way was equally painful. I had underestimated her emotional maturity. She had already guessed what I was waiting to say on her eighteenth birthday, so she took a step ahead of me and shut the door before I could open it, then locked it shut to me with the word "father." I couldn't keep pace with her. I couldn't catch up with her mind. But I knew that, for her, the real lock barring my entrance was nothing to do with my role in her life. It was Ian. I was disappointed, but not desperate. As long as the lock was Ian, I still had hope. Ian was a lock made of paper, not fit to weather a season of wind and rain. All I needed to do was wait patiently at the door.

"Stella, you have only one father in the world, just as you have only one Father in heaven. I can't be your father. I want to do this, not only to help you but also for myself, because we are partners."

I had said the word "partner" in English. Pulling her up, I used a bit of tea to write the word "partner" on the surface of the table.

"Partner means someone with whom you work toward a common goal," I explained. Of course, I avoided the word's other associations. I was afraid that would scare her.

I told her I planned to travel to Shanghai in autumn, then take a transcontinental ship from Shanghai to America. I would leave enough money for her and would keep the cook and the manual worker to help her. I went over trivial matters related to the daily expenses of the clinic, the chain of medical supplies, and how to get help if there was an emergency. Then, I said solemnly, "I want you to promise me one thing. While I'm away, don't make any major decisions. Wait for me to come back, then we can discuss it."

After a moment's hesitation, she finally nodded.

Several days later, when I was saying my nightly prayers, I suddenly heard a *tok tok* at my bedroom window. Someone was obviously looking for me alone, trying not to disturb anyone else in the house. It was a timid knock, hesitant, and mysterious, even a little strange. I opened the curtain and found Liu Zhaohu standing outside my window. He looked pale in the moonlight. My windowsill was high, so he had to stand on his toes to see in, and a deep wrinkle appeared along his brow. I gestured through the glass toward the door, indicating that I would go open it. He waved violently, stopping me, so I opened the window. Pulling his body up on the sill, he said to me in a voice barely above a whisper, "Pastor Billy, I want you to give a message. To her."

Of course, I knew he meant Stella.

"Tell her yourself. I'll call her," I said.

"She . . . won't see me," he stammered.

"What is it, then? Go on," I said, sighing.

"Tell Ah Yan I've been in touch with my home. My mother is still alive—"

"You mean Stella?" I interrupted rudely. I couldn't stand the name Ah Yan. For me, it brought up filthy things in my mind, abhorrent in color, shape, and smell. Every time I heard this name, my mouth twitched involuntarily. He didn't object, but just continued.

"My mother still lives in the same old place. She said now that the war is over, she wants Ah . . . St-Stella to come home, if she will. She's had the house cleaned for her, ready for her to come home."

I recalled that the day I took Stella from Sishiyi Bu, a woman had cried, "Ah Yan, your aunt is sorry. Please don't blame me." She followed us as we rowed off in the sampan. I had long forgotten her face, but I could recall her voice. That voice had an edge that could gouge out a chunk of flesh. That edge was guilt.

"But has your mother thought this through fully? What status will Stella have if she goes back? Neighbor? Relative? Or friend?" I asked coldly.

Liu Zhaohu seemed to be shocked by my words. He ran his hands down his uniform, as if he were in pain all over his body. The rustling sound in the silent night sounded like a beast in the forest chewing on rotten flesh.

"When you've thought that through, then come back and talk to me." I shut the window firmly.

I heard his footsteps moving away down the dirt path. Each step sounded heavy, as if it would sink halfway into the ground. He didn't come back to see me again.

Before long, the troops in the training camp were ordered to travel to Shanghai, Nantong, and other cities in northern Jiangsu to accept the surrender of Japanese soldiers. The day before his departure, Ian came to see me.

"Pastor Billy, I need to ask your opinion about something," he said.

"What treasure have you bought now?" I asked.

Recently, Ian had been frequenting the market. Each time he bought an interesting item or two, he'd bring them to me for a look. He laughed, revealing two rows of teeth now stained with more yellow.

"It's not that. I want to marry Wende. There's a rumor about some kind of wartime bride act that will let me apply for her to go to America. What do you think of that?"

A huge swarm of bees filled my head in an instant. I'd been a pastor for so many years, I thought I could know someone's intent from their words, measuring the health of their soul through the layer of skin, fat, and skeleton based on just their expression. But I had been way off with Ian.

"Pastor Billy, I haven't discussed this with anyone else. I just want to hear what you think."

His voice punched a small hole through the swarm of bees in my head, coming to me faintly. At that moment, I just wanted to cover my ears and yell, "God, I beg you, take their secrets away! Make it as if I never had ears. Why must I only listen to their secrets? Do I have no secrets of my own? Why? Why?"

"Pastor Billy?" Ian said again.

The bees gradually dispersed, and the buzzing stopped. I came to myself.

"You've . . . talked to Stella about this?" I asked.

I stubbornly called her Stella, just as Ian stubbornly called her Wende. Neither of us were trying to convince the other. We were just recognizing each other's stubbornness, even as we each held to our own ideas.

"No, I thought I'd write her a letter after I'd asked about the application procedures at the wartime affairs office."

I was relieved. As long as Stella remained unaware, the lock was still secure, even if the key had not been completely discarded yet.

"I've heard that the office will only start processing the application thirty days after the documents are submitted." I finally calmed down and told Ian this information I'd gotten from a friend in Shanghai. "Do you know why?" I asked him.

"Because there are a lot of applicants, so you have to wait your turn?" he guessed.

"Yes and no. The wartime commander feels it is necessary to give the soldiers a little time to cool down. There are many men who won't give these poor Chinese women another look once they get back to America."

I looked at him meaningfully. "Do you think you're one of them?" I asked.

At the time, I didn't know that the news I gave Ian was already outdated. In the end, the act wasn't even passed until the end of that year, leaving many lovelorn soldiers without any way to apply to take their wartime brides home to America. I can only assume they didn't want the American government to risk having to invest significant resources in the near future in the annulment of quick marriages. Annulment is much more complicated than issuing a marriage certificate. But despite the inaccuracy of the information, Ian was obviously taken aback. After a moment, he smiled, again his mouth pulling straight apart, like a child who had just woken from a dream.

"I see. Well, that gives me thirty days to think about it," he said.

I relaxed. *Ultimately, I hadn't read him wrong,* I told myself. No matter how outstanding an officer he was, or how well he spoke about sniper tactics, in the end, he was still an immature kid.

"When you get to Shanghai, get your teeth cleaned," I said as he left.

On a bleak autumn evening, the soldiers of the training camp left Yuehu along the sandy road in front of the church. It was the same path I'd walked when bringing Stella to Yuehu years earlier. Their departing footprints passed over those coming in, and in the future, there would be more incoming footprints passing over these. Life is nothing but a series of such overlaps and interminglings.

The sunset was odd that day, like a bronze drum mottled with spots of rust and cracks. The sun shone on the phoenix tree, and the surfaces of its broad leaves looked like they were sprinkled with a thick layer of broken brick. When the troop passed, both sides of the road were lined with villagers bidding them farewell. We could hear firecrackers being set off for several miles. The children were the most excited. They sat on adults' shoulders or climbed trees for a better view. They shouted at the top of their lungs, *"Ding hao!"* This was a Chinese phrase the Americans had taught them meaning "thumbs up." When they said it in the past, they would get a bullet case or perhaps a piece of colorful candy.

But today, no matter how fiercely they shouted, all they received in return was a faint smile. The Americans had given out all the bullet cases and candy, and now they carried other things in their pockets. There was nothing wrong with a smile, but compared to a bullet case or candy, it felt thin and barren, leaving the children a little disappointed.

The long parade finally ended, and the figures at the rear of the unit turned to little more than specks of dust on the road. If not for the scraps of firecrackers fluttering like moths in the breeze, one could hardly be sure they'd ever been in Yuehu at all. The village was caught up in a deep, terrible silence, so quiet one could be startled by the sound of their own breath. It was a silence like the seventh day of creation in the book of Genesis. But no. On that seventh day, it was a virgin silence before anything had happened, before the apple, before the serpent, before Adam pushed the blame for his sin to Eve, and before Eve knew the shame of her nakedness. But it was not so in Yuehu. There had been a training camp here, and Americans, and a war. Yuehu would never return to the tranquility of the seventh day. The war would leave scars, and so would peace. The scars looked coldly at one another, but neither could heal the other.

I didn't see Stella in the crowd, and I didn't look for her. I knew she was nursing her sorrow in solitude. I couldn't intrude on her grief, just as I couldn't let her intrude on my weakness.

Ian:

There's only a whirlwind of impressions left from after the broadcast of the Japanese emperor's "Jewel Voice Broadcast" to the day the training camp cleared out of Yuehu. Drink after drink, with whatever excuse, starting with the USS *Missouri* signing or the ceremony in Nanjing, where the surrender was accepted. Later, when the big excuses had been exhausted, it was someone's new haircut, or the new dish the cook had come up with, or even a giant rat someone caught. Anything could be elevated to an occasion worthy of a toast. At the time, it created the illusion that the world would never stop celebrating.

The Japanese reward on every American's head was no longer in effect. We could finally move around freely. We began to look for gifts to bring home. We bought handwoven fabrics and embroideries, and we searched the pawnshops for gold, silver, or jade jewelry that their owners couldn't redeem. The busiest person in camp was Buffalo. Every day, he took us to shop after shop and engaged in round after round of bargaining as complex as national treaty negotiations, and every round ended in the curtain falling amid the seller's fake look of heartache and the buyer's fake look of helplessness. It seemed like Buffalo was like a high-power pump, drawing the water up from his body and using it to drive this war of words. He even seemed slightly shriveled.

One week before pulling out, our festivities became incandescent. We no longer used celebrations as an excuse, but gratitude instead. We had to thank everyone who'd had any connection to us. We got the cook so drunk his wife had to bring the donkey to get him home. He sat on the donkey, puking over and over, as the donkey would take a few steps, then shake its head, trying to get rid of the vomit hanging from its mane. Pastor Billy saw this and, shaking his head, said, "Why don't you guys save some energy for Shanghai? Wait until you're there, then make trouble."

Jack winked at me and said, "We haven't thanked our spiritual leader yet, have we?"

We all jumped into action and lifted the pastor up, singing "For He's a Jolly Good Fellow" as we carried him in a big circle around the village. Pastor Billy was like a beetle flipped on his back, struggling in vain to get off our shoulders. Finally, we let him down on the side of the road on a pile of firewood.

When we had thanked all the people we could thank, we thanked the fleas who'd bitten us but had not given us typhoid and the rats that didn't give typhoid to the fleas. We expressed our heartfelt thanks to the mosquitoes, which started biting after sunset, but benevolently spared us from malaria. We thanked the chickens, who sacrificed their bodies to our plates, but who we also cursed, saying we'd never eat chicken again. I even thanked the water buffalo who'd chased me and nearly gored me. We thanked them all, drinking to each in turn. Oh, those were happy days! The fear of war had passed, and the responsibilities of peacetime had not yet arrived. We were holding a carnival in the vacuum between war and peace, free even from the law of gravity. Everyone knew there were only a few such days in our lifetimes, so we did what we could to make a lifetime of those days.

One night, for no reason, I woke up suddenly. The moonlight was deep, flattening the branches like ghosts against the glass of my window. I felt that my head, muddled by alcohol, was suddenly very clear. I remembered something crucial. Sitting up, I took my flashlight out from under my pillow, then shone it on every bed until I had awakened everyone, causing a ruckus.

Buffalo sat up from the floor beside my bed with a quick turn, rubbed his eyes, and said, "Sir, urgent meeting?"

Buffalo thought American surnames were hard to say, so he just called all of us "sir." When he needed to refer to one of us specifically, he just pointed.

I slammed my bed with my fist a few times and said, "Urgent meeting my ass. Quick, get the wine and glasses."

"Now? At this time?" Buffalo could barely open his eyes.

"Immediately. Right now. Now," I said.

Buffalo slipped into his shoes and went reluctantly into the kitchen. His footsteps were so heavy, it was like he was dragging a tail behind him.

"We forgot to thank Buffalo," I said to my roommates as soon as he left.

"You couldn't wait till dawn?" Jack mumbled.

"Will my mind hold up until morning? And anyway, the daytime has its own things to toast," I said.

Everyone in the room burst out laughing, all were starting to wake up now. "Yes," they said, "we toasted the fleas and the rats. How could we forget the man who was with us all this time?"

I turned up the kerosene lamp, and everyone got up and sat on the beds, forming a circle. Buffalo brought the last remaining bottle of whisky, along with several bamboo containers that he filled with liquor and passed around. We had learned to drink from these bamboo containers, just like the locals.

"Sir, if you keep drinking like this, it will turn your brain to mush. My great uncle drank till he had no wits left, just like this," he said, pulling on my sleeve hesitantly.

Ignoring him, I took a bamboo tube, filled it, and shoved it into his hand. "Drink. This cup is yours."

He was shocked. He'd never had a drink before. In fact, in many ways, he was still a child.

"This round is for you, to thank you for getting up at four every morning to light the stove, for making sure we woke before the military alarm, and for almost smoking us into yellow weasels when you lit the fire." I found that my Chinese had improved greatly by this time. There were more and more Chinese metaphors mingling with my English phrases.

I held Buffalo's nose and held the cup to his mouth. I let go when he'd swallowed half the cup, and he spat all over the floor, saying, "This is terrible! It tastes like rotten leather shoes."

I grabbed the cup and finished it on Buffalo's behalf.

"If you don't want to drink something that tastes like rotten leather shoes, do you want rotten leather shoes?"

I took my winter boots from under my bed and handed them to Buffalo. They hadn't been worn all summer, and there was still mud on the soles from when I'd stepped in a paddy field the previous year. There could even be a few grains of rice stuck in them, for all I knew. This year's plum rains had also left their mark on the boots. There were a few green spots of mold on the lining, and a small piece of the leather was peeling from the toe of the left boot. They were actually fairly new, sturdy boots, but seemed aged beyond their years.

"Clean 'em up and polish 'em, and they should go for a few dollars at the market," I said.

After the armistice, American goods suddenly flooded the black market—everything from cigarettes to cough syrup to belts to military daggers. Some items even still had warehouse labels on them. But a genuine pair of American military boots was still a rare item. Buffalo stopped coughing and took the boots. He gently caressed the lining at the top of the boots with the tip of his finger. His eyes shone like an oil lamp. He wore grass slippers year-round, only switching to cloth shoes for a few days in the twelfth lunar month, and even those were his brother's hand-me-downs. He'd never had his own pair of shoes.

"No," he said, shaking his head. "I'll wear them myself."

He took off his sandals, brushed the dirt away, and slipped his feet into the boots. His legs were as scrawny as his body, and in the boots, they looked like sticks poking out of two globes.

"They're a little big," he said.

Unable to help themselves, everyone laughed. He pulled his feet out of the boots and carefully placed them in a bamboo basket where he kept his things. He said, "When I go home, I'll ask my mother for some rags to stuff in the front and back. Then I should be able to wear them."

Jack took a paper bag from under his bed and handed it to Buffalo. "I collected these for you," he said. "I almost forgot."

Buffalo opened the paper bag and found it was full of cigarette butts. We'd all seen him pick up the discarded cigarette butts to collect the remaining bits of tobacco and roll it into new cigarettes, which he sent to his family to sell. There were fifteen people across four generations in Buffalo's family, and his income was divided among them. Buffalo smiled as wide as if he'd been given a gold ingot.

"Sir, if you'd give me that too, I can make more rolling the tobacco in colorful papers," he said, pointing at the magazine beside Jack's pillow, an outdated issue of *Time*, covered with three thousand nine hundred fingerprints, coffee stains, flea blood, and who knew what else. I suddenly felt sad. I grabbed my hat and walked around the room.

"Put all the change you have in here," I said.

Everyone retrieved their pants or jacket and emptied their pockets, tossing everything into the hat, making it tremble under the surprising weight. I emptied my pockets too, then took two big notes from my wallet as well.

"Buffalo, listen to me. This money is for when you get married. If you use it to smoke, play mahjong, bet on cockfights, or drink, your children will be born with their assholes sewn shut." I'd learned that curse from Buffalo, so it seemed fitting to return it to the person who'd given it to me.

His mouth opened, and his front teeth looked like two pieces of garlic hanging over his lower lip. I heard a crying sound, but his tears seemed to bypass his eyes and drip straight out of his nose. He wiped it with the back of his hands, but the more he wiped, the more it flowed, until his hands were a sticky mess. I tossed him my handkerchief and said, "Enough already. I hope you're not planning to use those hands to get us coffee in the morning?"

He laughed, snorting so hard a big bubble came out of his nose.

"Who wants a wife?" he muttered. "Even a good woman becomes a tigress once you take her home."

The prolonged farewell lasted nearly a whole week. My goodbye to Wende was thrown in with round after round of celebrations, making it seem almost unremarkable, especially because subconsciously, for me, it was a comma in the middle of a long sentence, not a period bringing it to an end. *It won't be long till we meet again,* I thought. The day before we left, I asked her to meet me at Ghost's—no, I should say at Ghost's and Millie's—graves. We sometimes met there when she came to visit Millie and I came to visit Ghost. Or rather, we each took the visits as an excuse to see each other. That day, Wende arrived before me, and as I approached the tombstones, I saw her sitting on the browning grass with her back to me. The leaves had also begun to change color, and the wind had grown a bite. But it wasn't the grass, or leaves, or even the wind in which I found hints of autumn. It was that view of Wende's back. Perhaps it was the slight rise of her shoulders or the faintly visible shoulder blades, or maybe the long crease on the back of her blouse. I called her name, and when she turned around, I saw autumn in her cheeks, eyes, and lips.

"You didn't sleep well last night?" I asked.

She nodded, then shook her head, negating the nod.

"You've been drinking for so many days. Do you think there's any alcohol left in Yuehu?" she asked.

I could tell it wasn't really a question, but I couldn't tell if it was an accusation or complaint. Both were things unusual from Wende.

I laughed and said, "I can always find alcohol when I want to drink."

I asked if she knew about Pastor Billy going back to America. She said she did, but that no specific date had been set yet. That wasn't what I really wanted to say, but I wasn't sure what was. All the drinking in recent days had worn out not just my stomach but also my lips, and I suddenly felt I needed to say something.

"Wende, I forgot to tell you before. Your English is improving quickly. You'll be more fluent than me next time we meet," I said, finally pulling some words out of my alcohol-soaked mind.

"Next time we meet?" She looked at me blankly.

Next time? I asked myself. *There are many people who won't give these poor Chinese women another look once they get back to America.* I thought of what Pastor Billy had said. *A thirty-day cooling-off period.* Would I even remember Wende after thirty days? I wasn't sure. Thirty days later, I would be in a different world, completely unlike Yuehu. No one could predict what would happen in thirty days. In fact, no one knows what will happen tomorrow. All I could be sure of was today, that very moment. Today, all I could tell myself was that I would remember this woman called Wende. By that, I meant I would recall every detail. I would remember the wind in her hair as she rowed the sampan, and I would remember the sparks that flashed in her eyes when she looked at me, and I would remember the nasal tail that dragged behind my name each time she said it.

"Wende, when I get to Shanghai, wait for me—for my letter, or maybe a telegram . . ."

I nearly poured out my whole plan at that moment, but I quickly held myself back. There were still nearly five hundred miles before I reached Shanghai. I would travel by land and water, every bend potentially leading in a different direction and each gust of wind potentially bringing some unforeseen change. I couldn't tell her something that I hadn't yet done. Just then, I saw Buffalo rushing toward me, panting.

"Sir, the commanding officer's looking for you! It's urgent!"

I stood up and was about to leave when Wende suddenly grabbed my sleeve and murmured, "Ian, I want to tell you something."

Buffalo waved at me vigorously. I touched Wende's cheek and told her I had to go, but that I'd be in touch as soon as possible. That was the last thing I ever said to Wende. And the last thing she started to say to me was still lodged in her throat, unable to escape through her mouth. Many years later, when a strange woman clasping a button in her hand rang the doorbell of my home in Detroit, I suddenly realized how wide the gap between my mind and Wende's was that day.

The next day when we set out, Buffalo wore my old boots, with rags stuffed into the toes and heels, and went to see me off. He insisted on carrying my military pack, which was stuffed so full that it bulged at the seams. Although orders were for us to pack light, we all had small hills sitting on our backs, and we knew that they'd become mountains once we got to Shanghai. When we arrived, all we wanted was to survive. Now that the war was over, survival was no longer enough. We wanted to bring home a slice of meat from the carcass of war. I was a little distracted that day. I was looking for Wende's face in the crowd that lined the path. I didn't find it.

As Buffalo walked alongside us in his boots, he kicked a stone. He suddenly stopped, took off his boots, and scraped the mud from them with a branch. Then, he tied the laces together and slung them around his neck.

"It's not cold. It makes me sweat to wear them," he said.

I knew he couldn't bear to wear them. He couldn't bear to let the rocks scratch the boots. Even after we were out of earshot of the firecrackers, Buffalo walked with me.

"Just for a little farther, sir. Just a few more steps," he said, grinning. My enormous pack made him look like a snail. It wasn't until we reached the sampan that Buffalo finally stopped and returned my pack. He stood on the slope facing the sampan, waving. As the boat drifted farther and farther away, he waved with bigger and bigger gestures. The pair of military boots around his neck swayed like two sparrow hawks jumping about his shoulders. Eventually, he became just a black speck in the mountains. At that time, I didn't know this was farewell. Farewell to these mountains, this bay of water, this row of terrace fields, the strange cattle half-submerged in the water, the malaria, the cholera, and the typhoid we narrowly escaped, and farewell to the people we would have never known if not for the war.

And it was farewell to Wende.

Perhaps I'd guessed it was farewell, but I didn't want to face it. To the person who is leaving, the attraction of what lies ahead is greater than what lies behind. Recollection is something that is left for later.

And just like that, I left Yuehu.

Liu Zhaohu: Chiang Kai-shek's Discarded Old Shoes

Before we came to Yuehu, we each walked our own path and had our own stories. But the war was like a typhoon, blowing us off our own roads and throwing us together. We were wounded by the collision, so your bodies were marked with my blood, and your skin stuck to my wounds. I was part of your story, and you were part of mine.

Compared with our whole lives' experiences, the time we were in one another's lives was actually very short, though it looms disproportionately large in the illusion of my memory. During my life, I used to treat days as units, and I couldn't sift out those overlapping parts, like separating mineral from sand. After I died, I realized those days only measured up to a total of two years—for Pastor Billy and me, only about five percent of our lives. For Ian, who lived to ninety-four, two years is a negligible portion of his time on earth. When we left Yuehu, the fork in the road where we waved goodbye was the end of our story.

I mean our shared story, of course. Our individual stories continued for some time, except for Pastor Billy's. Actually, from the first time I saw Pastor Billy, I had sensed something ominous. Pastor Billy, did you ever take a careful look in the mirror? Your philtrum is very short, creating the illusion that your mouth sits directly beneath your nose. To Chinese people, this indicates that one won't be able to live to old age. You're shaking your head. Your God didn't teach this, so you don't believe it. I didn't believe such things either, but facts proved that seemingly absurd superstitions were actually the accumulation and repetition of experience. I've learned to speak from fact, not emotion.

Ian, I see you yawning. I know you're bored with this. You're waiting for a different topic. I was surprised to learn that even as ghosts, we can still be tired. That night, when we were all drinking in Pastor Billy's kitchen after the news of the truce, I was tired and wanted to go back and sleep. You held my arm and wouldn't let me go. You taught me an English phrase I'd never seen in any textbook: there will be sleeping enough in the grave. I later taught that phrase to my students. Who would've imagined that even now that you're dead, you still don't get enough sleep? I know you're both eager to hear what happened to Ah Yan. But don't worry, my story is closely linked to hers. I can't extract her from my story. Before you hear her story, you must listen to mine, because I'm her cause and also her consequence.

After leaving Yuehu, my army friends and I went to Nantong to accept the surrender of Japanese soldiers. Accepting the surrender was fast, but taking over the enemy's property was complicated and tedious. It was full of all sorts of transactions, both aboveboard and shady, but thankfully I was hardly involved in all that. I was sent to study English for half a year, then assigned to a training school for police officers in Nantong, where I taught English. I met a common acquaintance of ours there: my captain from our camp. He also ended up at the police officer training school—as my direct superior no less. There's a Chinese saying that one can't avoid one's enemy and another that says there's no mutual understanding without a fight. That was the situation between the captain and me. Our countless bumps had smoothed out our edges. We weren't merely colleagues who got along, but friends who had a few drinks and complained to one another when we were lonely. You wouldn't know what it was like at that time, during the last few years of the Nationalist government's rule and their witch hunt for Communists and sympathizers. Everyone grew an extra set of eyes to guard against each other, and the standard for measuring true friends was whether they could drink together and speak the truth without fear. The captain and I were such friends. Continuing the habit developed in camp, I always called him Captain, even though his title at the academy was director.

I had a thousand reasons to leave the school and return to my village. Although I was an instructor and no one expected me to carry a gun into battle, I felt hugely frustrated with the civil wars, which came one after another. I couldn't tell whether peace was the goal or the excuse for fighting. I'd become bored with military uniforms. Also, since my and Ah Yan's fathers had been killed by the Japanese, the Yao family tea garden had been neglected and was in desperate need of someone to restore it. Moreover, my family had been harassed by the Japanese, and my mother was frightened. She'd grown old and sickly and was usually confined to bed. She'd moved to my brother's house, but he was often working in the county seat. My sister-in-law was left alone to care for a sickly elderly person and two mischievous young ones. It was inevitable that she would sometimes struggle. Looking back now, if I'd taken any one of those excuses and left my post to return to Sishiyi Bu, my life and Ah Yan's might have been completely different. But I was always hesitant, never able to make up my mind. I wrote to my mother and told her I had a teaching allowance in addition to a regular military salary. What I earned in Nantong was much more than I could make farming at home. If I stayed, I could better reduce the burden on my brother's family.

Of course, that wasn't the whole truth. My mother and I both knew the real reason I stayed away, and in this we were always complicit. I was afraid that if I went back to Sishiyi Bu, Ah Yan would follow me back. Before leaving Yuehu, I had passed my mother's message to Pastor Billy, inviting Ah Yan to come home. Pastor Billy asked me what role she would occupy if she did so. I didn't answer. I couldn't. My mother inviting her back was a matter of conscience. Conscience was the most vicious mosquito in the world, biting her all the time, day and night, giving her no peace. And when I delivered my mother's message, that too was an act of conscience. Just as the mosquito bit my mother, it bit me too, only much more fiercely. But conscience is such a fragile thing. It couldn't survive the daylight, so I didn't dare say this to Ah Yan's face. I couldn't even escape Pastor Billy's eyes. In fact, I had secretly hoped Ah Yan would refuse me, though this is the first time I've admitted it. I couldn't fail to deliver my mother's offer, just as she couldn't fail to make it. The mosquito would not spare us. But if Ah Yan rejected the offer, the mosquito would have no place to bite, our consciences would be placated, and we would be at peace. My mother and I had never talked openly about it. We didn't need to. At the most crucial time, bonds of blood formed our most reliable alliance.

In Yuehu, I saw Ah Yan's transformation with my own eyes. Her mind grew up, and her original layer of thin, sorrowful skin no longer covered her. She sloughed off the old skin and left it behind, becoming a completely new person. Each time I saw her (and you could count on one hand how many times

I saw her in Yuehu), I could almost smell the youth oozing from her. It was the scent of buds on tree branches and mountain grass growing wild. But that was only against the backdrop of Yuehu. The minute I mentally put her back in the context of Sishiyi Bu, I saw her body crushed beneath Scabby, her legs kicking wildly like a mantis's. The image was carved into my mind, and it would take years before it gradually eroded. Although we hadn't prayed to heaven and earth before the spirit tablets of our ancestral gods or held a wedding banquet before the villagers, I had put my fingerprint on the contract drawn up by Yang Deshun, witnessed by him and the security group head. Even without them, I couldn't lie to myself. As long as Ah Yan and I were in Sishiyi Bu, she was my woman, and I was her man. I couldn't face this reality. In my youth, when my body was strong but my thinking shallow, chastity was a chasm that couldn't be bridged. When my body began to fade and my mind grew stronger, I realized that chastity was just a fragile illusion. Unfortunately, by that time, Ah Yan and I had already taken too many wrong turns.

In fact, even in Yuehu, I realized that Ah Yan had turned the page on me. She looked at me disdainfully, as if I were a pile of shit she had accidentally stepped in. But like most men, I had a bit of ego rooted at the bottom of my heart. That pathetic little bit of ego interacted with the air like yeast, turning "impossible" into "maybe." I was unwilling to let go of the place I had held in her heart, though in reality it was already gone. I was afraid, but I hoped that I was the permanent master of that position. Later, I realized that while I was worried that Ah Yan would follow me back to Sishiyi Bu, she was stuck in Yuehu, waiting for two letters from afar that hadn't come. Of course, they held different places in her heart. One was pure concern, while the other was concern mixed with anticipation. At the time, her heart was full, leaving no place at all for my existence. Looking back now, I see that the years after leaving Yuehu are a series of wrong decisions made at the wrong time in the wrong place. In Chinese, we say, "Yin and yang are in the wrong places." When I should have gone home, I didn't, then when I did go home, it was at the worst possible time. During those years, opportunity was like a mischievous child playing hide-and-seek with me. When I looked for it, it hid in dark corners, outside my field of vision. When I stayed put, it ran ahead of me, tempting me to take a false step.

In the autumn of my third year at the training school, I finally decided to go home. It wasn't an impulsive decision, but the result of the emotional powder keg that had built up over the years and was finally ignited by a few unexpected incidents. It was like a bomb with a long fuse. All anyone saw was the explosion, completely missing the long process of detonation. In fact, it's not even really accurate to put it that way, because the bomb never exploded at all. The fuse was cut just before detonation. That autumn, the civil war opened a crucial, incandescent scene in Liaoning and Shenyang, when the Communist forces began to put real pressure on the Kuomintang forces in northeastern China. In an institution as insignificant as the police training school, we only got information from public sources like newspapers and radio broadcasts, and all the news was of victory, with the same details over and over. If one spent a little effort altering a few things like the time, location, and names of people involved, the same news could be broadcast for any occasion. However, there were always some people at the school who could get another version of the story through other channels. We didn't know who they were, but we knew they were there, maybe stepping on our shadows, because we would find mysterious notes in the pockets of the uniforms we left in the office from time to time. Sometimes when we got up in the morning, there would be several mimeographed newsletters stuck in the crack between our bedroom door and its frame. The content in this poorly printed material, still smelling of ink, was vastly different from the official reports. The two sides need only switch the characters in the events, and it would immediately become the propaganda of the other party. We casually pretended to browse the contents of the papers, then just as casually shredded them and threw them away. We never talked about these reports, but we always read them with a tacit understanding. At that stage, nearly all my acquaintances distrusted the authorities. We had all lost confidence in the current political situation.

But that wasn't the most direct reason for my decision to go home. The dissolution of my hesitation came from a piece of news the captain passed to me at the risk of losing his own head. My name was included on a list of people being secretly investigated by our superiors. I wasn't sure what channels they'd gone through to find out that I had previously conspired to go to Yan'an before applying to the training camp in Yuehu. The investigation found no definitive evidence and was left unconcluded. My former accomplices were at the other end of the Liaoshen Campaign, gaining ground against the Kuomintang, and couldn't serve as the witnesses my superiors needed. Even so, I became untrustworthy in the eyes of my superiors, and my every move was monitored. I was suddenly an inmate in a prison without walls. I decided to leave, citing my mother's illness as a reason.

I had even considered how to deal with the Ah Yan situation. Ah Yan's rape by the Japanese had occurred five years ago, and in the five years since, much had happened. New memories would eventually dilute the old, just as new grass eventually covers old grass. I put my hope in forgetfulness. After I returned home and settled down, I planned to go to Yuehu to get Ah Yan. She was a good woman, and I was a good man. How could two good people be destroyed by a bad thing? We could find a way to kill that horrible demon in my mind, even if in the clumsiest and most time-consuming way. Time would be sandpaper that would slowly smooth away all the scars.

But in the end, I didn't follow through. Just as I was preparing to submit my resignation, I received a letter from my mother saying Ah Yan had returned to Sishiyi Bu with a child who was under two years old. They asked Ah Yan who the child's father was, but Ah Yan just said the child was a gift from God. People in the village began to gossip. They said that the foreign pastor who'd taken Ah Yan in had gone back to America, and before he left, he said he would only be gone for a month or two, but no word had been heard from him since. They said he had left money with Ah Yan, but it had run out, so she slept with anyone, one day getting food from this man, the next day getting a few coins from someone else. By the time her belly grew big, she didn't even know whose child was inside it. Later, when her reputation became totally irreparable, the men would take advantage of her, but would give her nothing in return. When she had no other option, she returned to Sishiyi Bu, because the tea garden was there. Even if it was derelict, it was at least a piece of land she could sell for a little money.

After many years, I realized the rumors circulating in the village were just stories, even if they had real beginnings. But I believed them at the time, because a person's thinking runs in a straight line when they are young, unaware that there may be a curve, a bend, sometimes even a few various branches, in the journey from information heard to conclusion drawn. When I heard a seemingly true starting point, I believed that the conclusion must be true too. The age of the child Ah Yan brought back to the village also seemed to verify the logic of the rumors. The child was less than two, so the affair happened after we left Yuehu. My mother also told me that the first thing Ah Yan did was sell the Yao family's tea garden. These two things convinced me of the truth of these rumors.

So I stupidly—almost obtusely—ignored an obvious flaw in the rumors. Pastor Billy had taught Ah Yan to treat sick people, so she could easily live a much better life than an ordinary village woman in most places. This was especially true in Yuehu, where her abilities were already recognized by the local villagers, and even the cows in the field knew she was the "woman doctor." She didn't need to loosen her waistband in exchange for food, nor did she have to return to Sishiyi Bu to make a living. But a person will always believe what they want to believe. And I didn't understand that a child's age was just a number, and that any number in the world could be changed. The truth of the child's birthday was in the mother's hands. At the time, I never suspected that in order to conceal the child's background, she had deliberately pushed the child's birthday forward by six months. I didn't consider that she'd sold her ancestors' land not because she was desperate, but because she had no hands to maintain it. This chance decision helped her avoid a bigger disaster due to the Agrarian Reform Law after the Communist takeover in 1949. Since she had no land, she was later classified, naturally, as a poor peasant by the new government. But that was later.

I also committed an error in judgment so stupid it was beyond reason. I ignored the fact that homesickness can be the main source of a person's decision to return home. So, upon receiving this letter from my mother, I dismissed the idea of going home. It had taken me so many years to gather enough courage to deal with one beast of the heart before this, and at that moment, I had to face a whole jungle full of them. I couldn't clean the mud smeared on Ah Yan by those rumors, even if I used all the water in the river that flowed below the forty-one steps. I couldn't live with such a woman. I couldn't imagine spending my life in such shame.

So I changed my plan, deciding to spend a few more months at the police officer training school. I could use that time to publish a statement in the newspaper to break off my relationship with Ah Yan, which was the method people living in the city used to disavow a marriage. My disappointment in Ah Yan made me eager to start a family. I would follow the oldest method, using a matchmaker to help me find an honest, modest woman to marry, then take her to Sishiyi Bu, where she would help me take care of my elderly mother, whom I had only seen a few times over the past several years. I was only twenty-three at the time, but I felt like an old bird with broken wings. I just wanted to go back to my nest and live out my declining years. Before I had ever really seen the sky, I'd lost my desire to fly. A few days later, I published a statement in the newspaper in Nantong concerning my relationship with Ah Yan. Fearing no one in Sishiyi Bu would see it, I sent a clipping home to my mother and asked her to give it to Ah Yan. After doing this, I suddenly felt like a large stone that had been weighing on me was finally lifted. Perhaps, subconsciously, I'd been wanting to do this for a long time, but I hadn't found the right opportunity. Now, Ah Yan herself had provided me with the perfect excuse.

But this lightness didn't last long. In the dead of the night, the mosquito that had remained silent for a short while was dispatched again. It bit my conscience—or the thing that was once my conscience and was now just a scrap of lean meat—and kept me from sleeping. There were hundreds of ways I could have ended my relationship with Ah Yan. I could've gone to speak to her in person. I could've written her a gentle letter to explain clearly. I could've entrusted a respected elderly person to pass a message to her. Why should I deliberately choose this method, publicly humiliating this woman who had once been so kind to me? Anger. It was anger.

I was so shocked by this answer that I shot up from the bed. I couldn't lie down again for a long while after that. I'd known Ah Yan since the day she was born. I had seen her mother change her first diaper, and I was the one who taught her her first words. My feelings for her had always just flowed forward, like a river, the scenery changing along the way. Familiarity, pity, affection, concern, sympathy, disgust, surprise, appreciation, jealousy . . . I turned over these complex emotions, but I didn't find a thread of love. Not until I found anger. If I didn't love her, how could I feel such extreme anger? It was only then that I realized that it would be impossible for me to expel this woman from my heart, no matter what sort of statement I issued in any newspaper.

I was plunged into illness for most of that winter, inexplicably running a high fever, which rose and fell for months. Sometimes, my mind was so consumed by its fire, I didn't even know where I was. I was almost grateful for this well-timed illness. My body was conspiring, creating an excuse for me not to go home for the New Year. I couldn't face the woman who carried that clipping in her pocket. My mood during that period was as rotten as a moldy shirt. I needed an excuse for everything—for not getting out of bed, for not going to work, for not going out, for not seeing anyone, for remaining silent, for speaking, for tolerance, or for losing my patience. Heaven still looked after me, providing me the excuse I required when I was most desperate. In the spring, my fever finally subsided. I sat up in bed and found that the oleander tree outside my window was full of pink buds. I sighed, feeling fortunate that I hadn't missed spring. When I took a few shaky steps and knocked on the captain's door, he was shocked.

"My gosh! I couldn't tell when you were lying down, but you're so thin, your pants are barely staying on."

My mood finally settled, and I even allowed the captain to accompany me to the most famous tailor in the city to have a long navy-blue cloth tunic made. I planned to wear it to see the matchmaker and meet my prospective wife. I didn't want to meet the woman who could become my wife in my uniform. As long as I was still alive, I had to actually live, so I planned to shred the past like old rags and get a fresh start. But I never managed to actually make that new start.

In late April, when I had just gotten the tunic, which showed off my skeletal figure, before I even met the woman I was to be introduced to, a big change came to the police officer training school. In the small hours of the night, we were awakened by a sharp whistle calling us to the activity field for an emergency assembly. Under the hurriedly lit gas lamps, I saw that the grounds were full of people. The headmaster's glasses were crooked, and his unkempt hair had peeked out from under his hat, half covering his eyes. It seemed that, like us, he had been surprised. He briefly conveyed the orders from his higher-ups. We had to pack all our things and in half an hour be ready to go on a special mission. I noticed that he emphasized the word "all." Before, when we'd been sent on special assignments, our superiors would tell us to pack light. Regarding our destination, he only said, "I'll notify you later."

We got our things together and set out, only recognizing our destination when we approached. It was a ship terminal. We joined a long line of people waiting to board the ship. There were all kinds of troops, some wearing military uniforms, some in civilian clothes, and some of the higher-ranking officers had their families with them. Without exception, the families were all carrying luggage of various sizes, and every now and then, someone who looked like a servant was carrying a cage of chickens, weaving in and out to make a path through the crowd for his master. It was a little funny.

"Where do you think we're going?" I whispered to the captain, who was beside me.

"Didn't you look at the paper under our door this morning? Nanjing has fallen. We're probably retreating."

His words suddenly caught in his throat. In that instant our eyes met, and we both thought of that little island across the strait, Taiwan. The mimeographed newsletters had been reporting since last year that warships were carrying people and gold there in a continuous stream.

"The police training school is no good for fighting a war. We can only maintain order and prepare for the arrival of large groups of people," the captain whispered.

In a flash the last piece of the puzzle had fallen into place. We'd figured out the truth. By then, we were being pushed up the ramp by the crowd surging behind us.

"I can't just go like this. I've got to at least tell my family," the captain said.

He'd married two years earlier, and his wife now lived in his hometown with their eight-month-old baby. That was the last thing the captain ever said to me.

There was a loud splash, followed by gunshots. Turning, I saw an empty spot where the captain had been. He'd jumped off the ramp, and the lookouts were shooting. The sky was not yet bright, and the water looked like a thick pool of ink. The captain's head was like a basketball tossed into the water, bobbing along on the surface. I couldn't see his face, but the water around him was darker than anywhere else. A riot broke out on the pier. The chickens began to leap wildly in their cages, cackling loudly and sending feathers flying out between the gaps like large pieces of dust. An officer fired his gun into the sky. The gunshot brought me fully awake, heightening my awareness of the present situation. I thought of the words I'd heard frequently during the training at Yuehu. *Be calm. Remember to use your eyes.* I calmed my mind and allowed my senses to open, my ears filtering all the noise around me and clearing a path for my mind. As soon as my mind was quiet, it opened a thousand pairs of eyes, which in turn scanned every object in the opaque morning light and quickly found their target. There was a thick cable on the left side of the ship, dangling all the way down to the water: the anchor line. That side of the ship was backlit, so I couldn't be sure, but below I thought I could see a shadowy patch swaying gently in the wind. If I was right, it was the reed that was most common on banks throughout Jiangnan. They were hollow and could be used to breathe through, making it possible for someone to stay underwater for a long time. My brother and I had often played just such a trick in the river below the forty-one steps when we were children. Sometimes we stayed under the whole morning, and when we got home, our mother gave us a good spanking, saying she thought we'd drowned. *All I need to do now is find a reference point on the ship for where the cable is and remember what it looks like,* I told myself. My eyes climbed up the length of the cable to a row of railings, one of which was covered with white cloth. Those were my coordinates. If I could climb down along that railing, I would find the cable.

"Captain, why couldn't you be less impetuous?" I sighed.

I slowly climbed up the ramp with the flood of people, praying over and over that it would not grow light too fast.

~

"Who are you?"

Panting as I climbed the last of the forty-one steps, I heard the voice as soon as my foot reached level ground. The serious illness I had recently endured had drained my vitality. Along the way, even a leaf brushing against my skin could make me shiver. Perhaps the voice was very soft, but it was magnified by my fear. It sounded thunderous in my ears. I closed my eyes, expecting a gun or dagger to poke at my waist. But nothing happened for a long time. *I'm not on the road anymore. I'm home. I'm safe,* I told myself.

I opened my eyes and saw a child standing in front of me. I couldn't be sure of his age. He looked like he could be a big two-year-old or a small four-year-old, though there was still a milky sound to his voice. His head was shaved, and the back of his head was like a yellowy round stone that had been polished smooth by the weather one season after another. Most of the boys in the village had shaved heads, but they usually left a tuft of bangs at the top. This boy was completely bald.

"Who are you?" I asked the boy, trying to smile.

From the moment I'd escaped the ship, the dangers I had encountered on my entire journey had made smiling an alien thing. I had to relearn to operate the muscles that held the secret to smiling. This boy with the shaved head could be my first practice subject. I'd been away from Sishiyi Bu for over five years, only occasionally coming back to see my mother for a night or two, then leaving again, barely seeing my neighbors at all. I didn't know much about additions to the village in recent years.

"I'm Ah May," the child said, looking up at me, a finger stuck in her mouth.

My God. It was a girl.

Oh God, what sort of eyes were these? The whites were so white, they were almost light blue, and the dark iris had a faint blue tint too, as clear as a sea untouched by sun, moon, or wind. Anything that dropped into such eyes would immediately turn to water, even if it were rock or steel. I couldn't help but pick her up.

"Little girl, why don't you have braids?" I asked.

Ah May wasn't afraid of me. She quite naturally put her face against my shoulder and pulled the wet finger from her mouth, painting a little flower pattern on my clothes with it. It seemed as if she'd known me all her life.

"Mommy says long hair attracts lice," she said.

"Who is your mommy?" I asked.

Ah May thought very seriously for a while, as if it were a difficult question. There were fine ripples in the sea of her eyes. It was a smile. My heart fluttered. I felt I'd seen these eyes somewhere before.

"Mommy is my mommy," she said.

At that moment, I heard the slap of footsteps. A woman flew over like a whirlwind. Seeing the child in my arms, she stopped, clutched her heart, and gasped fiercely.

"You bad child, I took my eyes off you for one moment, and you ran to the ends of the world," she scolded.

"You bad child" was a phrase we often used to scold children in the village. In fact, it wasn't entirely scolding but also carried affection. It was like how northerners called their kids "you little urchin" or the Shanghainese called theirs "you little ghost." Ah May climbed down from my embrace and clasped her mother's leg. The woman wore the clothing typical of Sishiyi Bu, but her body was unlike those of the women in the village. The village women were flat and thin, but this woman was strong and robust, her chest full and her clothes accentuating her figure. Though her body was unfamiliar, her features and voice seemed familiar. I stared at her for a while before it dawned on me who she was.

"Ah Yan," I said.

224

It was obvious she did not recognize me. When I had come ashore, my body was soaked. The police uniform was too noticeable, so I bought a set of old clothes and a straw hat from the fishermen at the jetty with the few copper coins I had in my pocket. The clothing and hat were not a style worn in this village.

Taking off my hat, I said, "I'm Zhaohu."

She was stunned. She looked me up and down, then lowered her voice and said, "You . . . you escaped?"

I was about to ask her how she knew, but she cut me off. She grabbed my straw hat and put it back on my head.

"Come with me. Keep your head down. Don't greet anyone you see," she said.

She squatted and told Ah May to climb on. Carrying her daughter on her back, she started walking. She walked fast, the grass on the path bowing under her feet and her trousers billowing in the wind created by her quick pace. The impressions I had of her from Yuehu were immediately emphasized. I recalled the name Ian had given her: Wende. It was true. She was the wind.

Fortunately, there was no one on the road, and we quickly made our way to Ah Yan's home. It had also been my home, back when the Yao family stayed in the front rooms and my parents and I lived in the back. Of the ten people who had once lived in this courtyard compound, four moved somewhere else, three were dead, and the three who remained had long since transformed beyond recognition. I stared at the small groove that had formed in the threshold from the feet that had crossed it countless times. I felt a lifetime had passed. Ah Yan put Ah May down, then took in a wooden sign hanging on the door. She pushed Ah May and me into the house, then hurriedly closed and locked the door. Written neatly with a brush on a piece of paper affixed to the wooden sign she'd brought in were the words:

YAO'S CLINIC, CHINESE AND WESTERN MEDICINE
TREATMENT OF VARIOUS SYMPTOMS,
COLD OR HEAT, BRUISES AND
SCRAPES, CHILDREN'S MOUTH
SORES, WOMEN'S REPRODUCTIVE
AND POSTPARTUM CONDITIONS.
FAIR PRICES.
NO CHARGE FOR INEFFECTIVE TREATMENT.

"The government army suffered a landslide defeat. They're arresting deserters everywhere. If the village security group head doesn't report you, he'll be jailed. In Liupu Ridge, they found one the day before yesterday, and he wasn't safe even hiding in the cistern. He was executed on the spot, right in front of his own house."

With her foot, Ah Yan pulled over a stool and gestured for me to sit. I wanted to tell her about the captain being killed at the wharf, but I held back. I didn't want to frighten Ah May.

"When it's dark, I'll go to my brother's house," I said.

Ah Yan took a cloth handkerchief from inside her shirt and wiped the sweat from Ah May's face.

"Have you lost your mind? If someone were looking for you, where's the first place they'd go?" she said.

I was startled. I wasn't used to the way Ah Yan spoke. It was the way I used to talk to her. The world had tilted slightly, and we had swapped roles. I was no longer Mr. Professor, and she was no longer my little acolyte.

"I can't implicate you either." I reached out and lifted a small corner of the bamboo curtain on the window. The sun was already setting. It would be dark in a couple of hours.

"It's safer here than at your brother's. No one will think you came here," she said.

"Why?" I said, a little surprised.

She took Ah May and put her on a stool, then took off the girl's shoes and shook the sand from them.

"Who doesn't know that you abandoned me? By right, there's not enough time in the world for me to hate you."

She didn't look at me as she spoke. She put Ah May's shoes together, sole to sole, and slapped a few times. Dust flew in the air. Her tone was exceptionally calm, as if she were speaking of the dust or the shoes. At that moment, I wished there was a hole in the ground for me to crawl into. In the now silent room, I could hear the spiders spinning webs in the corner and the hungry growl of Ah May's belly. I could also hear something steaming from my pores with a rancid smell. It was my humiliation. It seemed like there were splinters on the stool poking through my baggy fisherman's trousers and piercing my flesh. They were too numerous and too thin. I couldn't get them all out unless I peeled my skin off.

"You can hide in the back rooms for a few days. Wait for this to pass, then you can come out," she finally said.

Leaving me, she went to the kitchen, lit a fire, measured the rice, and started to cook. Through the half-open door, I watched her work the bellows. The side of her face turned toward me was gray. I couldn't tell if it was from the ash or the shadows. Ah May picked up the shoes and put them on the wrong feet. She kicked them off and glanced at me. I walked over and squatted, and before I could say anything, she put her foot on my knee.

"Shoes," she said. She kicked her feet mischievously, and the kick landed gently on my heart. At that moment, my heart melted like a bit of lard over a fire, turning into a pool of warm liquid. Ah May and I were meant to be together. From our first glance, we were drawn together, without any preparation or training. Before she was born, heaven had already put me on her path, so that when she had learned to recognize people, she would see my face. I picked her up and carried her into the kitchen. I stood behind Ah Yan, and the fire cast my shadow across her back. She felt my presence, but did not turn.

I cleared my throat and said, "Ah Yan, I just want to tell you—"

"I know what you want to say," she interrupted. "I got the newspaper clipping."

Fortunately, she still didn't turn around. I didn't want her to see my expression.

"I didn't plan to jump from the ship at first. I thought of going, assessing the situation, then seeing if I could think of a way to come back," I mumbled.

It was only many years later that I came to realize how naive I'd been that day. Those who stayed on the boat were forced to say goodbye to their homes forever. A small few who lived long enough eventually got to return to their hometowns—after almost forty years.

"I came back because I wanted to tell you something." The words stuck in my throat, and I was suddenly unable to go on. I coughed several times.

"The rumors about you that Snot heard, they didn't come from me. Really, it wasn't me."

The bellows suddenly stopped. Ah Yan stared at the wall, blackened from the smoke, as if she would bore a hole in it with her eyes.

After a long while, she turned to me and said, "You jumped off that boat just to tell me that?"

~

When Ah Yan took me to the rooms in the back, she locked the door from the outside. She placed a few bundles of firewood in front of the door for extra security. The room hadn't been lived in for a while, and the spiderwebs strung between the corner of the window and the eaves made it seem a good hiding place. Before I went in, she called Ah May and, pointing at me, said, "You know who he is?"

Ah May shook her head.

Ah Yan said, "He's your . . . uncle." Before she said "uncle," she paused, as if sorting through a pile of ugly words for a more pleasant one. Ah May didn't know what "uncle" meant, so she tried rolling it about on her tongue a few times, like a new toy.

"Do you want your uncle to get captured and have his head cut off?" she asked, her face stern as she made a cutting gesture across her neck.

Ah May's features froze, and her mouth turned downward.

"Don't scare the child." I wanted to intercept the tears before they started to roll down Ah May's face. But Ah Yan stuck her arm out, blocking my path like an iron rod.

"If you don't want him to be captured and beheaded, you cannot tell anyone where he is. You can't say a single word about it. Do you understand?"

Ah May nodded in confusion.

"What do you understand? Say it to me," Ah Yan said, her eyes holding her daughter's in an iron grip.

"Don't say anything about Uncle," Ah May stammered.

She suddenly slithered out from under her mother's arm and came to me and hugged my leg. A warm little worm of her tears crept down my leg, intolerably itchy and wet, but I didn't want to move at all.

"Uncle, don't get your head cut off," she said.

As I went into the empty room, I heard the dust groan under my shoes. When the groans quieted down, I met its accomplices in action. The dust that wasn't crushed beneath my feet hovered in the air, with the sadness of suppressed cries. The peace of some souls is built on the displacement of others, if dust could be considered a living soul. With the oil lamp, I located the small wooden bed I used to sleep on. It seemed like that corner of the room had been left undisturbed. Everything was exactly as it had been when I left home. I picked up the dusty blanket and noticed there was still the old pillow stuffed with rice straw lying on the bed, and there was a faint dent in it. I wondered if it was from the last time I had slept there. I lay down. It was a perfect fit. My body was crying for sleep, but my brain refused to switch off. There were all sorts of strange thoughts wandering in and out of my mind, and as my body couldn't fight the mind, it helplessly kept the mind company.

I found myself thinking of Yuehu. Our parting on the sandy road in front of Pastor Billy's house already was three and a half years in the past by this time. It's an awkward place in the cycle of memory, beyond the time of short-term enthusiasm, but not yet distant enough to feel a sense of nostalgia. I rarely thought of Yuehu during this time. But that night I thought of Snot. I couldn't recall his name, since I'd only ever seen it on his tombstone. I thought of him in a series of images—a cloth badge with the number 520 sewn on it, the string of snot that dangled from his nose, a bullet hole slightly larger than a pinworm hole on a melon, a headless neck with the muscles so contracted that it looked like a pink pomegranate.

I also thought of the captain. His real name was Zhao Haifa, which I'd only come to know when we were at the police training school. Similarly, it was only there that he learned I was Liu Zhaohu. Even so, I never called him Mr. Zhao or Captain Zhao, as those titles didn't really refer to him in my mind. He also evoked a string of images in my head—the shock and humiliation in his eyes when I knocked him to the ground, like a leopard that realized it had been bested by a rabbit, and his white forehead desperately refusing to be swallowed by the inky black sea.

He and Snot had died very differently. I would've rather seen the captain die like Snot, in a death that could make a woman who hated him put his head on her lap with an expression as holy as the Virgin Mary's as she made his body whole again.

The captain's wife, home with their infant child, was probably waiting for a letter from him that would never arrive. The only people who knew what had happened to him had taken that ship across the strait, leaving only me behind.

Only I could tell the poor woman the truth, allowing her to mourn and then carry on living. Heaven had let him die before my eyes so that I could take care of his funeral affairs. It would be a funeral without the corpse. The shame was that I wasn't able to attend to it until almost seven years later. Once I had gotten out of prison and managed to find the captain's house after many setbacks, I told his wife about his final moments. She was with their boy, now almost eight. When I told her, she didn't cry. She grinned, showing the few teeth she had left, and said, "It's good he died. If he were still alive, it could only hurt our son." I wanted to say that the captain was trying to return to see her and the child when he jumped, but in the end, I said nothing. She was right. If the captain were alive, he would only harm his family, just like me.

I thought of you that night too, Ian, but differently. I didn't remember numbers, code names, or nicknames, because from the first moment I knew you, your name was Ian Ferguson. Later, when we were closer, you told me to call you Ian, but only in private. In class, I still respectfully called you Mr. Ferguson. You had a confidence that we didn't possess. You walked with the wind under your feet, because you were the only one still called by the name your mother gave you. But more than that, you were a tall, imposing figure, with a physique derived from beef, eggs, butter, and cheese, where our stomachs only knew porridge, radishes, and salted fish all year-round. A wall separated you from the Chinese students, a wall called English. Of course, I was slightly different, since I'd gone to a church-run school that advocated Western education and so taught us English. That English made cracks in the wall between us, and you kept tossing stones over the wall so I could turn those cracks into holes. Eventually, there were only fragments of a wall. I forget how we surmounted that pile of rubble. Maybe you climbed over, or maybe I did—or maybe we both climbed and met somewhere in the middle. Either way, we eventually had a meeting of the minds, without any walls. The unruly English phrases that you taught me, I passed every one of them on to Ah May. By the time she went to college, she didn't hesitate to use these phrases on her pedantic old professors. When she did, they looked at her, as stunned as if she were a madwoman from Mars.

Unable to sleep, I got up, went to the window, and lifted a corner of the bamboo curtain. The moon was not full, but it was very bright. It cast faint shadows, like layered mountains in an ink painting. The insects had already sensed the first hint of summer, timidly trying out their chirps. They chirped intermittently, each new start seeming to make the moon quiver as if it were afraid. This wasn't the first time I'd gazed at the moon, but it was the first time in as long as I could remember that I'd done so in such peace. I had no watch, no calendar, no newspaper, and no radio. I could only keep track of time by counting my meetings with the moon. How many faces of the moon would I see before I met the sun again? I lifted up the string on the curtain and tied a knot. This was my first day in this familiar cage.

And so I settled in that tightly cloistered house, counting the days by tying knots on the string of the bamboo curtain. During the day, there was a constant flow of people in and out of the front rooms. Fearing that Ah May would run to the back and look for me, Ah Yan blocked the passage leading to the rear of the house with a cabinet. Only when the last patients had left at night, the wooden sign was brought in, and the door was locked would Ah Yan move the cabinet.

When Ah Yan came, she would tap three times on the glass at my window, one hard tap followed by two soft ones. That was the secret code we'd set. Only hearing that would I raise the bamboo curtain and open the window. She then passed a pot of food and a bucket of water from the well through my window. She brought me enough food for three meals each day. The well water was not only for washing but also for me to cool the leftover rice in. It was getting hotter by this time, and the leftover food might spoil.

Though I couldn't see what was going on in the front rooms, I could hear the movements. It wasn't just sick people who came to see Ah Yan but also mothers with babies who came to chat. The village was boring, so people came in their idle time to visit with Ah Yan, watch her treat patients, and gossip. After all, it was more interesting than staring at a mother-in-law's face. Mostly the women would talk, and Ah Yan would listen quietly, occasionally inserting a sentence or two. I was surprised that after being away for about six years, Ah Yan had already won the trust of these women. They seemed to have forgotten all the ugly things the Japanese had done to her and even the embarrassing child and the mystery of her father's identity.

My mother had said that when Ah Yan returned to Sishiyi Bu, she hung the doctor's sign outside her door. At first, no one believed her, so the doorway remained empty. Later, a child in the village came down with malarial fever. The parents saw many herbalists and fed the child many tonics, but nothing worked. Seeing that the child was dying, they carried the little one to Ah Yan to let her try. To their surprise, she took a few white things, no bigger than a bean, from a bottle with strange words printed across it and told the child to swallow them, and the fever was suppressed. From then on, the whole village saw her as a miracle-working doctor.

When Pastor Billy left, he'd left behind enough money to support Ah Yan for several years. She put that with money from the sale of the tea garden and found someone to change it on the black market into US dollars. She was far from being in dire circumstances. When she hung out her doctor's sign, it was actually with an ulterior motive. She didn't charge a fixed price for the medical consultation, leaving it to the patients, collecting only the cost of any Western medicine that was required. As a result, all sorts of items started to appear at her door. A bucket of polished rice, a bag of eggs, a basket of freshly harvested melons, or even the offal that was saved after a pig had been slaughtered. She'd used her abilities to win over the hearts of the women of Sishiyi Bu, bit by bit, allowing them to see her goodness and thereby forget the rumors. She only cared about the women, not the men. She knew winning over the men was the women's job. If the women were on her side, their entire families would be too, even the livestock. She quietly won over the hearts of the people so that she could provide Ah May with solid ground to stand on. I'd never imagined that Ah Yan could conquer this ground, nor that it also offered me a lifesaving path. I couldn't help expressing wonder at her great skill, which allowed her such flexibility even in the deepest of mud pits. She told me, "If you catch hold of a patient's illness, you've caught his heel. He can't turn around and kick you then." Of course, I didn't know it then, but the idea had first come from Pastor Billy. Ah Yan built vivid extensions on Pastor Billy's foundation.

When I was in my dark square box of a room, I spent most of the day sleeping. When I had slept enough, evening became my morning. I would wake in the early twilight and stare at the ceiling with eyes wide open, bored, counting my heartbeats and breaths. Humans are strange animals. When it's light, we have only one pair of eyes. When night comes, though, it gives rise to ten thousand eyes. In the darkness, my nose, ears, and every pore of my skin all became eyes. My nose could tell the hour. The scent of the early morning was night dew, which was tinged with the scent of grass, which carried the smell of insects, which in turn smelled of the branches, which were brushed with the scent of the birds perched there. Around four in the morning, these smells remained, and the smell of dogs and chickens starting to stir was added to them. Later, over all the smells was laid the smell of humans. Human smell was strong, masking all the others so then the nose handed the task of keeping watch over to the ear.

The earliest sounds in the front part of the house were swishing noises. That was Ah Yan getting dressed. Then there was a squeak. That was her opening the door. After that was the sound of water being splashed on the slate. That was her emptying the chamber pot. Then there was a clattering sound. That was her dragging the wooden sign to the door. She dragged the sign out very early. I knew she was silently saying to the neighbors, "You can come anytime you'd like. I have nothing to hide." Though she hadn't been trained in espionage, she found the most natural way to seal each telltale hole, even those smaller than the eye of a needle. Then came the sound of the bellows. Ah Yan was lighting the fire to make rice soup. My ears always perked up like rabbits' ears in a breeze around this time, because I knew the sound I was waiting for would soon emerge from the numerous other noises and creep into my ear. That was Ah May's voice. As soon as her voice appeared, all the other sounds immediately fell away. Her voice could stop the turning of the world. It was the sound of heaven, crawling from my ear into the tip of my heart, washing away all the filthy things I had seen, heard, and smelled over the past twenty-three years and making me as pure as a baby just emerged from its mother's womb.

Of course, the sounds didn't always appear in this order. Sometimes the sequence was disrupted, one of the links lost, or something new inserted. One morning after the squeaking of the opening door and the splashing of the night's chamber pot, the sound of the bellows followed, replacing the clatter of the wooden sign being carried out. After the clinking of the pots and pans, I heard the door being locked and the clang of metal against slate, followed by a silence that was rare at this time of day. I knew that Ah Yan had gone out with Ah May, riding the battered bicycle that Pastor Billy had left and that still hadn't fallen apart completely. I guessed she'd gone to get medicine. It'd been almost four years since Pastor Billy had left China, and there had been no news, but his friends remained faithful, and they supplied Ah Yan with medicine for daily use at low prices. Even bandits have codes of conduct, and Pastor Billy's lifesaving grace was something they credited to Ah Yan's account right up until the great upheaval.

Another night, when the air was still thick with the smells of night dew, grass, insects, branches, and birds, and before the sparrows, chickens, and dogs had started their predawn stir, I heard a sharp cry in the front rooms, so loud it felt like it drilled a hole in my eardrums. "Don't cut his head off!" Then, the cries were smothered with a hand and turned into a muffled whimper. I immediately realized I had broken into Ah May's dreams. My heart jerked, feeling the pain of it. I shot up, not bothering to put on my shoes, and jumped out the window. The moonlight in the courtyard was very weak, and a layer of ominous purple washed over the treetops and the eaves. I stubbed my foot on a stone, bringing me to my senses. I couldn't break into Ah Yan's rooms like that.

The next day, Ah Yan knocked on my window at the regular time. She always brought me water and food after Ah May fell asleep. She handed them through the window, gave some simple instructions, then turned to go. I knew the newspaper clipping with my divorce statement still bit into her flesh and refused to let go. But that day, I couldn't help it. I grabbed her sleeve to keep her from leaving.

"What's wrong with Ah May? I heard her crying last night," I said.

"Children forget easily. Don't worry about her. She'll be fine after a couple of days," she said.

A thought rushed up like a burp, and my mind didn't have time to stop it.

"I don't want her to forget," I said.

Even before the burp was out, I realized my abruptness.

"I just . . . I miss Ah May." I explained in a stutter.

Ah Yan didn't respond. There were a thousand hurtful things she could have said, but she didn't. She just told me to hand her the bowl and chopsticks I'd used the night before through the window.

"Can I . . . see Ah May?" I asked hesitatingly.

"No," she said firmly. "She's asked for you several times. Once she even said it in front of someone else. Thankfully that woman is a little slow. She didn't catch it. It would have been terrible if she did."

I didn't reply. I couldn't accept this kindness from Ah Yan and harm her and her child at the same time.

"Do you think you could ask my mother to come here so I can see her?" I said.

This time she was a bit slow to reply, as if choosing her words carefully.

"We haven't spoken in a long time. If she suddenly came here, it would attract too much attention," she said, hesitating.

An inexplicable fire welled up in the depths of my heart. Halfway up, it took a sudden turn and went to my legs. Furiously, I kicked the water bucket. Startled, the water jumped up and splashed onto my shoes.

"I can't do this. I can't do that. Do you want to suffocate me? Let me go. There's no one out at night to see me. And if they do see me, just let me be shot and get it over with. It's better than being imprisoned here!"

Saying nothing, Ah Yan turned and left.

I slapped my forehead, regretting every word I'd said. We're always most hurtful to the ones closest to us. It's convenient, lashing out at them. I replayed all the damned things I'd just said to Ah Yan. I suddenly gained a bit of clarity. It was true that I couldn't stay in that room, waiting for the darkness to drive me crazy and for me in turn to drive those who had rescued me crazy. I'd told Ah Yan the thing that I'd come to say, and now I could go in peace. I knew every corner of this compound intimately. I could wait until the middle of the night, when it was dark and quiet, and escape directly over the backyard wall, avoiding the front door altogether. There was a stool in my room that would be a sufficient substitute for a ladder. With the skills I'd learned in camp about how to move lightly and climb obstacles, I should have no problem landing on this soft ground. As for beyond the courtyard, it was a vast wasteland. There would be no sampan, but I could walk. I wasn't afraid of walking in the dark. I'd traveled through terrain ten times darker than this.

Tonight. It's tonight, I told myself. I used the dagger I always carried with me to cut the rope on the bamboo curtain. That would be the only memento to commemorate my escape. I counted each knot several times. There were ten. I had only stayed in my room for ten days, but it felt like ten years. I couldn't stay any longer. I had to go immediately. As I sat on the bed waiting for the moon to drop closer to the horizon, I heard a soft knock on the window. Knock . . . knock-knock. One hard, two soft. It was Ah Yan.

Surprised, I opened the window, and Ah Yan started handing me something through it.

"Didn't you want to see her? Once she fell asleep, I brought her over."

It was Ah May.

I took Ah May with one hand, and with the other I grabbed Ah Yan's arm. I pulled her up over the windowsill, and in the darkness, led her to the bed.

The bamboo curtain wasn't closed all the way, allowing a pale strip of moonlight to tear a hole in the greasy darkness. The dim light of night became daylight for us. In the darkness, Ah Yan was just a vague shadow. Ah May too was a shadow, but she wasn't vague. It wasn't the faint light that illuminated Ah May, but the thousand eyes that I'd grown that sensed her. Her little bald head leaned back, resting in the crook of my arm, and the roundness of her bottom nestled between my legs. Her tiny hand clasped my clothing, as if she were afraid I would disappear at any moment. She slept soundly, a soft snore escaping from her like bubbles in a boiling broth. Those warm bubbles pierced countless holes in my body. I found that my bones were gone, my flesh was gone, my skin was gone, and all that was left behind was a pool of water.

Later, when I thought about it, I realized what had really made me forget about the shameful circumstances of Ah May's life was not someone else. It was Ah May herself. What really bridged the ravine of grievances between Ah Yan and me was not the kindness we extended or sacrifices we made on one another's behalf. Those things could only generate gratitude or guilt. What closed the gap was this child with eyes as bright as the sea. With her little hand, she had led me. I was not yet a husband, but she'd taught me to be a father.

"She's heavy," I said.

Ah Yan didn't answer. It took a while to realize the reason for her silence. She didn't want to lie to me. Ah May was actually three years old. In fact, the way villagers in Sishiyi Bu would say it, she was riding on the head of four years. She wasn't two, like Ah Yan had told the women in the village.

"Are you planning to leave?" Ah Yan asked suddenly.

I was surprised. She always seemed to see through me and read my mind—often even when my thoughts were still clouded. I couldn't say anything.

"I went to Hawk's place yesterday to get medicine. He said things are pretty chaotic out there. The Communist Party is in secret negotiations with the defense force, but the defense force may not be able to hold," she said.

Hawk was a pirate who operated in the area and an old friend of Pastor Billy's.

Though I had no access to a newspaper or radio and was completely isolated from the outside world, I could still guess what had happened after the fall of Nanjing. I just hadn't expected the Communist force to make it so far south so fast.

"Is the information reliable?" I asked.

"Hawk's men rowed sampans and ferried people from both sides when they met at the Qianyun Temple on Jiangxin Island," she said. "Once the situation clears up, your desertion won't be considered a crime. You may even gain honor. You can wait until then to leave."

I was pleased I hadn't managed to implement my foolish escape plan.

"Do you think you should let Ah May's hair grow? Girls look nice with long hair," I said, just to change the subject.

Ah Yan smiled and said, "I'm too lazy to care for long hair. Wait till she's a little older, and we'll see."

We sat for a while in silence, listening to the insects chirp outside the window and smelling the faint scent of flowers blown in by the breeze. After a while, it struck me that the floral scent wasn't coming from outside, it was beside me. It was the smell of a jasmine flower Ah Yan had pinned on her blouse. I'd seen her like this before, before all the crime, filth, and pain had intruded. The Ah Yan of the past was a pure, clean girl with a pure, clean jasmine flower pinned on her blouse.

"Ah Yan, you must think me such a bastard," I said hoarsely.

She didn't say anything for a while, then sighed softly.

"It doesn't matter. Any man in the same situation would respond just as you did," she said.

There was no reproach in her voice, not at all, but it sounded harsh in my ear. I wanted to jump up and shout, "I'm not just 'any man.'" But I didn't. I knew I was guilty as charged.

Ah May twitched gently in my arms. I didn't know what sort of dreams she was having this time. I pulled her closer, rubbing my unshaven chin gently against her smooth forehead. She didn't wake, but she chuckled and snuggled her head against my heart.

"It'll be light soon. We'll have trouble if she wakes up here. I should take her," Ah Yan said.

"It'll be good if she wakes," I said. "I want to talk to her."

I felt a tingle of pain on my face. It was Ah Yan's gaze.

"You will leave, sooner or later. Don't let her get attached. Save . . ."

I immediately knew what she had been about to say.

"I don't have to leave. There are things I can do in Sishiyi Bu," I said.

Ah Yan stood up very quickly. Her voice growing louder, she said, "Do you know what you're saying? Are you even using your head?"

She wasn't wrong. Much of what I said that night went straight from my heart to my tongue, bypassing not only my brain, but even my throat. Only after traveling some distance did they turn back to slowly find their way to my brain.

Ah Yan took Ah May from my arms. I couldn't stop her, so I helped her out the window. The night had grown thin, and there was a small dent in the dark sky. I smelled fresh chicken droppings. The hens had already begun stirring in the cage.

"I brought you a book. It's on your bed. That should help relieve your boredom. I'll try to get more news from Hawk tomorrow," she said.

In the predawn light, I saw that the book Ah Yan had brought was Yan Fu's translated copy of *Evolution and Ethics*. This book had been a gift from my Chinese teacher, and I'd given it to Ah Yan before leaving for Yan'an. I hadn't expected to see this book again. I flipped through and noticed that there were words written in nearly all the margins on every page in the book. Some were in my handwriting, but many were in Ah Yan's. Mine were my reflections, but Ah Yan's were annotations of new words she had looked up and learned as she read. Most of my thoughts at the time were tragic, sorrowful sentiments. They all seemed superficial to me now, as if it were me in a past life. The present and the past collided, and they stood facing one another, each feeling the other vaguely familiar, though ultimately, they were strangers. This wasn't this book's final destination. Later, it traveled farther, when Ah Yan sent it to me in a package of daily necessities during my days working in the pitch-black coal mines. A few years later, I carried it with me back to Sishiyi Bu. When illness took me by the throat and eventually killed me, the book was one of the two items buried with me. The other was a box containing a lock of Ah May's hair.

The next morning, the order of sounds arranged neatly in my mind in recent days was thrown into confusion. Before I heard the sound of Ah Yan dressing that morning, I suddenly heard a burst of Ah May's cries. It was the frustration of being wakened suddenly. I didn't hear the splash of the chamber pot or the blowing of the bellows. All I heard was the clang of the padlock after the squeak of the opening door, followed by the creak of the old rusty bicycle and the clink of its tires on the mud road. Without eating breakfast, Ah Yan had gone out with Ah May. She was going in search of more news from Hawk. She'd seen through my irritability and was afraid I would do something desperate.

At least half a day was required for the round trip between Sishiyi Bu and Hawk's place, but even before the wobbling clank of the bicycle's wheels had fully faded from my ear, I was already anticipating Ah Yan's return. I was gradually becoming accustomed to waiting. By this time, I'd learned to cut an infinite wait into smaller pieces, like the time between the first crowing of the cock and the first lazy stirring of the dogs, or from the beginning of the spider's spinning on the left side of the bed to the time it climbed along the silk thread to the right end of my bed and to the time it had completed a web for itself, or from the time Ah Yan sang the lullaby "The Moon Shines" to Ah May to the sound of the child's ragged snoring. When I cut the endless wait into smaller pieces, it suddenly had borders, allowing me to finish nibbling on one, then consume another. These tangible borders gave me tiny bits of hope, making me feel that when I reached a certain boundary, I might find an exit there.

I didn't know what sort of news I should expect from Ah Yan. I only hoped that whatever the news was, it would lift the barricade of the bamboo curtain, window, and iron lock, allowing me to say goodbye to the moon and embrace the sun. I even thought about what I would do when I got out. Of course, first I'd go see my mother and tell her with the pleasure of a well-played prank about how I'd been hiding under her nose for so long. Then, I'd run through the open field where the forty-one steps started, spreading my arms and letting the sun wash over my every pore straight into my marrow, until I was burned. I would tell Ah May that the execution blade would never fall on my neck, not even in her dreams. She could call me as loudly as she wanted. And what would I do after all that? I really had no plan beyond that. The future was something only a free person could think about. For someone trapped in a dark cage, to hope for something so distant was absurd. The only viable plan was to become free.

But what if the news Ah Yan brought back wasn't what I was hoping for? My heart suddenly sank at the thought, falling into the core of the earth. I couldn't imagine being a prisoner waiting in an endless line for freedom, then, just as he hears the jangling of the keys, he's told to go to the back of the line and start all over. My patience was already a wrinkled old man. My legs wouldn't hold up for another long wait. Ah Yan was right. I was indeed prepared to make a desperate attempt. Finally, I fell into a drowsy sleep.

Later, I was awakened by a clicking sound. It was a soft sound, quiet enough to elude the ear. It was my nerves that caught it. There were burrs on this sound, each one hooking into my nerves and pulling me awake. By the light streaming in through the bamboo curtain, I saw a black scorpion crawling on the wall a few inches away from my head. It looked strange, like its head was several times larger than its body. All the eyes that my body had grown slammed open, like turning on thousands of searchlights. I realized that there was a huge cockroach between the scorpion's jaws. Most of its body was still free, and what the scorpion had in its jaws was actually just about half its head. The scorpion had clamped the roach's body in its claw. The sound I'd heard was the body of the roach being crushed. The cockroach fought desperately, and the scorpion was almost overcome. Finally growing irritated, the scorpion raised its tail and plunged the poisoned needle into the cockroach's back, once, twice, three times. The cockroach twitched for some time, then gradually, its strength was exhausted. Only its legs continued to move slightly. Then the scorpion began a process like that of a snake swallowing an elephant, chewing the cockroach and slowly savoring the corpse of its opponent. The last long leg of the cockroach remained between the scorpion's jaws for a long time. When only fragments of the cockroach were left, the scorpion waddled unsteadily away.

That was an ill omen, I said to myself with trepidation.

Bored, I fell asleep again. What awakened me next was the sound of the rain hitting the window frame. That year's weather was chaotic, and it had been an uncommonly dry rainy season. This was the first rain I'd heard since coming into this dark room. I wasn't sure if Ah Yan had taken a raincoat with her. If the rain didn't stop, she might not make it back that day. I suddenly realized that it wasn't the sound of the rain that had awakened me, but another sound riding on the rain.

> *Bitter, oh so bitter*
> *A star has fallen from the sky*
> *And someone has left the earth*

It was the sound of mourning. It seemed someone in the village had died. In my memory, every time there was a funeral in Sishiyi Bu, it rained, as if heaven saved its tears for the dead.

Traveling alone, sent off by friends from a hundred homes
You pass on today, to be born again tomorrow

The tail of the voice was raised very high and sharp, almost like a gibbon's howling. It was Scabby's voice.

After I'd given Scabby a good beating all those years earlier, he'd been confined to bed for several days, unable to move. Later, unable to stay in the village, he had no choice but to return to the mountains to live off his mother. When his mother saw him idling all day, she sold a few silver pieces of jewelry and used the money as a bride-price for him to marry a girl blind in one eye, hoping that settling down would keep him at home and out of trouble. He hadn't returned to Sishiyi Bu, so the family of the deceased must have brought him back for the funeral.

The voice like the howl of a gibbon sent a chill up my back. The scorpion put a knot in my heart. This added another one. I predicted that the news Ah Yan brought home would be fatal.

It was dusk when Ah Yan got home. I heard the lock being opened and people coming into the courtyard, followed by that of someone lifting the lid off the cistern to scoop water, which was in turn followed by sounds like a pair of donkeys drinking water, one loud and one soft.

"I'm hungry, Mommy," Ah May said, and I could hear the unswallowed water in her voice.

"I'll start the fire soon," Ah Yan said.

"But I'm hungry now," Ah May said, swallowing the water as her voice became louder.

"Yes, my ancestor, I'll serve you right away, all right?" Ah Yan said.

Ah Yan's footsteps rang back and forth in the kitchen, probably indicating things such as washing rice, adding wood to the fire, and stoking it. The bellows started panting laboriously, and the flames sizzled and licked the sides of the pot.

I wanted to take some clue of the news from the tone of her voice, but her tone was flat, without the faintest wrinkle or ripple. She didn't immediately come to my room. Was that because this was the hour when every house was cooking dinner and she didn't want to attract attention by closing the door? Or was it because she hadn't figured out how to convey bad news to me? I felt that the fire fanned by the bellows wasn't just cooking the rice but also my patience. I was burning with anxiety.

At that moment, the eyes that had sprouted up in my ears weren't working at all. I didn't even notice that someone had walked through Ah Yan's door. Actually, "walked" isn't quite right. I didn't hear footsteps. It was more like a shadow had quietly floated into the room. Judging from the order of the sounds I heard now, he must be standing behind Ah Yan. Or, that is to say, in front of Ah May.

"You're Ah May? The old saying is true. A child without a father is a rare beauty," the person said.

The voice was like peppers hanging high up under the eaves to dry. Compared to a man's voice, it was more like a woman's, but compared to a woman's voice, it was more like a monkey's. I immediately recognized it as belonging to Scabby.

"What are you doing here?" Ah Yan was as shocked as if she'd seen a ghost.

"I brought this for Ah May. A big cricket in a cage. It's rare. You'll only see a purple one like this every eight or ten years. Hang it on the bed. When the moonlight is just right, it will sing for you all night," he said.

Ah May must have reached for it, but her mother shouted to stop her. Scabby's tone turned awkward.

"Ah Yan, dear, actually I just came to explain to you what happened back then." His tone finally dropped from the tenor of funeral music, thudding to the ground. "I'm sorry. I did you wrong. I'd never touched a woman before. I . . . I was in too much of a hurry."

Ah Yan didn't say anything.

"I violated you, but I never actually got to taste the fruit. That damned Liu Zhaohu was too fierce that day. My foot still hurts every time it touches the ground. Let's settle accounts, call it even. Don't resent me anymore," Scabby said.

Ah Yan still didn't answer. I only heard the gasp of the bellows. The rice bubbled, and the smell of cooked rice filled the air. My stomach growled, and I was sure the entire courtyard could hear it.

"Fine. I don't resent you. Now go back to the mountains," she said at last.

"Back to the mountains?" Scabby laughed. "What sort of place is that for a man to live? The dog days of summer can melt lard, and the winter days freeze my balls off. Eventually, I'm coming back to Sishiyi Bu."

The sound of the bellows stopped. I could almost hear the hair rising into needles all over Ah Yan's body.

"You can go wherever you want, but you stay out of my way, and I'll stay out of yours," Ah Yan said coldly.

There was suddenly a clip-clop sound, as if someone was dragging a stool by the leg. When Scabby spoke again, his voice sounded lower. He was probably sitting next to Ah Yan now.

"You still resent me. Your words show it. But in Sishiyi Bu, among all the women and girls, I only had eyes for you. Back then, your family was in a good situation. You were the moon goddess, and I was just a worm in the latrine, so you thought your shit was too good even for my bowl. I'll tell you the truth now, damn it. When I heard that the Japanese had violated you, I was secretly glad. At last, you were at the same level as me. You'd become disgusting leftover goods too, so I didn't need to fear coming to you then."

Ah Yan pulled herself up very quickly, shouting as she overturned the stool beneath her.

"You dare to talk like that in front of a child!" She spat, as if extracting a fly she had accidentally swallowed.

Ah May must have been frightened by her mother. She wailed, on the verge of tears.

"Mommy, I'm . . . I'm hungry!" she whimpered.

"Eat, eat, eat! All you do is eat the bread of idleness! You can't even pick up firewood chips from the floor. If you don't work, who's going to feed you?" Ah Yan shouted.

Ah May had never heard her mother speak like that. She was so shocked, she forgot to cry.

Scabby also fell momentarily silent. Something was stuck in his throat too. He tried several times to clear it before he finally succeeded.

"Honey, don't kick the door while scolding the wall. I know you're talking about me. Aside from laziness, there's nothing wrong with me. And as far as laziness goes, it was my father who spoiled me. From when I was small, he never even let me pick up my own chopsticks. The only person I haven't done right by in this life is my old man. I didn't steal, I didn't rob, I didn't desecrate anyone's grave. I've relied on my mouth, singing for my meals. What right has everyone in the village to dislike me?" he said indignantly.

Then, I heard the bamboo spoon hit the edge of the pot and the bowl. It was probably Ah Yan scooping a bowl of starchy water to satisfy Ah May's belly.

"You should go home and say all this to your wife," Ah Yan said.

"We're having a good talk. Why'd you have to bring her up? It's a mood killer. She's like a stone, and I can't squeeze a word out of her all day."

The soup in the bowl was hot. Ah May blew on it.

"Ah Yan, dear, you know what I mean. You and I are the last rotten vegetables at the bottom of the basket, fit only for pigs and dogs." He let out a long sigh, but it was very thin. You could reach the anxiety underneath it with a gentle touch.

"We're more or less in the same boat. We shouldn't fight."

Those words must have hooked Ah Yan's kind heart. She was silent for a long time before she finally let out a sigh of her own.

"It's dark. Go home now. Your mother and wife are waiting for you." There were still no wrinkles or ripples in her tone, but I could hear a hint of pity.

"Even pigs and dogs have their own way of living. I'll move between the top of the mountain and here in the future. I'll live the life at the top of the mountain when I'm there, but when I'm here, let's get together. I'll learn to be more diligent. You just tell me what you want me to do, and I'll do it. I'll . . ."

Before he had finished, I heard a loud noise. It was the bowl falling to the ground and shattering. It seemed the water had spilled and burned Ah May. She cried like a pig being slaughtered.

"Get out! Get out now, or I'll scream for help," Ah Yan snapped.

Scabby had probably not prepared himself for such a rapid change of mood in Ah Yan. He was stunned for a moment, then chuckled and went over to sweet-talk Ah May.

"All right, no one is hurting you. Uncle wants to be good to you. Your mother is a stupid woman. She doesn't know what's good for her . . ."

There was a series of noises from the front rooms, like pushing and shoving, tearing, a collision, and a soft object struck by a hard one. All these sounds happened almost simultaneously. My senses went into overdrive, and I couldn't discern the order of things.

"No! I don't want you!"

This sound rose above it all, and it was like an awl driven into my eardrum. It was Ah May screaming.

The blood rushed to my head and crashed into my temple like a rock. Unable to bear the pain, I leaped out the window and ran toward the front rooms. I tightened every muscle in my body and curled up like an iron ball, crashing through the cabinet blocking the corridor. The cabinet wasn't as heavy as I'd thought. It gave way instantly, making me lose my balance and fall through the gap. Everything fell silent. The only sound was the frantic chirping of the startled purple cricket in its cage.

Sitting up from the floor, I assessed the scene. Scabby was holding Ah May, and Ah Yan stood less than a foot away from him, holding something in her hand. It was very small, and in the flickering light of the kerosene lamp and stove, it emanated ominous coldness. It was a Browning pistol.

Scabby was like a leech smeared with salt, his whole body going as soft as mud. Ah May broke free from his grip, jumped to the ground, ran toward me, and hugged my leg tightly.

"Uncle, Uncle! Oh, Uncle . . ."

She panted and called me over and over, with every sort of tone and expression—surprise, resentment, shock, grievance . . . I didn't even know what other emotions were contained in the word "uncle." I could only feel that my heart was broken, and a kind of warmth flooded over me. I held her tightly.

"Aren't you a soldier . . . how . . ." Scabby looked at the cabinet I had knocked over. He looked terrified and suspicious.

Ah Yan kicked a stool toward me and motioned for me to sit.

"You don't need to hide anymore. Things have changed in the city, and the world belongs to the Communists now. The Communist Party welcomes deserters like you."

I understood immediately. She was giving me the news from Hawk right there in front of Scabby. Scabby's eyes flinched as he avoided the object in Ah Yan's hands.

"You . . . you put that thing away. It's . . . scary," he stuttered.

"Don't ever let me see you again. My fist won't be restrained," I said to Scabby. I tried to keep my voice soft, not wanting to upset Ah May.

"I just wanted to see how she's doing. I didn't mean anything by it," he said, already halfway out the door.

"Stay there," Ah Yan said to him. "I know your wife is four months pregnant. Right now, I am the only midwife for dozens of li."

Ah Yan slowly lifted the edge of her shirt and rubbed the gun with it. When she finished polishing the gun, she squinted and aimed it at a bird's nest outside her window. Then, she turned back and gave Scabby a sidelong look.

"When your wife is ready to have your baby, you'll need me. When your little one has a fever or boil, you'll need me. When you step on a rock and cut a hole in your foot or fall down the mountain and dislocate your arm, you'll need me too. I hold the lives of your family in my hand. You better behave if you don't want to cut off your family line," she said.

"No . . . no need . . ." Scabby's mouth opened and closed like a fish's, but he couldn't spit the whole sentence out. Scabby stepped on his own shadow as he backed away, not daring to turn around for fear of being shot in the back. It wasn't until he was out of Ah Yan's line of sight that I heard the slap of his feet as he sped away.

It was finally quiet in the house. The fire in the stove gradually dimmed, and the rice sizzled as a crust formed on the bottom of the pot. Ah May had spent the whole day bumping on the back of Ah Yan's bicycle, and then suffered a shock when she got home. Weary, she fell asleep in my arms, but the hunger continued to gnaw at her belly.

"Where'd that thing come from?" I asked, nodding at the Browning where it lay on the table.

"Pastor Billy left it with me," Ah Yan said.

"Be careful with it, especially when there's a child around," I said.

"I carry it when I go out. When I'm at home, I keep it somewhere that even a ghost couldn't find," she said.

"You haven't had any news from Pastor Billy?" I asked cautiously.

"He's dead."

I was surprised. "How did you hear that?"

"I didn't need anyone to tell me. If he were alive, he would've contacted me. My mother and father might leave me, but he never would have done so."

Her tone was light, but there was a conviction on her face, as if sure that the sun would always stop the rain, no matter how long it took, and daylight would always end the night. In her tone, I heard a single word: trust. It was the feeling that allowed her to jump from any precipice, because she believed there was someone to catch her at the bottom of the long fall. I felt a sting in my heart, like a wasp. In the past, Ah Yan had trusted me in that same way. Then, when I watched her fall from the highest point, I let her fall, crushing every bone in her body.

"Uncle," Ah May called softly.

Thinking she was waking, I looked down, but she was still asleep. The space between her eyebrows was knitted into a soft line, and one hand was balled into a fist, holding the corner of an imagined garment. I opened her fist and put my finger in her palm.

"Everything has changed. There's peace now. I don't need to hide. I can stay in Sishiyi Bu," I said.

Ah Yan didn't reply. She pulled three sets of chopsticks from the bamboo holder and set them on the stove.

"I can set up a school here and teach the children to read. There aren't any schools here. It's a dozen li just to reach the missionary school. If the adults can't get there, their children never learn to read."

Ah Yan's bamboo spoon quivered, and rice spilled onto the stove.

"I won't charge tuition. I just need each family to feed me," I said.

Ah Yan picked up the spilled rice with her fingers, popping each grain into her mouth.

"You should be discussing this with your mother, not me," she said, spacing her words.

"I don't intend to discuss it with anyone. I'm just telling you," I said. "And when our Ah May is older, I'll teach her to read."

As soon as the words were out, I realized I had used a word that surprised even myself: "our."

~

Scabby didn't return to Sishiyi Bu for a very long time. Even when his wife was ready to have the baby, it was his mother and another woman who brought her to Ah Yan to deliver it. Scabby's mother said he'd gone to the county seat after someone had come and invited him for singing lessons. She never said whether he was teaching someone to sing or learning to sing. Scabby's wife had a boy weighing 4.72 jin. Scabby had left instructions saying that if it was a boy, he would be named Jianguo, and if a girl, she would be Jianhua, meaning "building the Chinese people." It was a popular name at the time, with the new government in place. So the baby was named Yang Jianguo, meaning "nation building."

When Yang Jianguo was born, the umbilical cord cut and his body cleaned up, the first person he saw wasn't his mother. The poor woman was so exhausted, she'd passed out. It also wasn't his grandmother. She was busy in the kitchen making brown sugar water. Rather, it was Ah May, who was drawn into the room by his cries. She saw that wrinkly face, no bigger than a rice cake, looking like he wanted to smile, or maybe cry. In fact, Yang Jianguo wanted to have a good cry, but he didn't have the strength. He only half opened his mouth and made a squeaking sound, like a rat whose back leg has been caught. Ah May stuck one of her fingers into his mouth, and Yang Jianguo sucked on that muddy, sticky finger, which perhaps even smelled a little sour, and suddenly calmed down.

Many years later, when Ah Yan spoke of the day when Yang Jianguo was born, Ah May didn't remember any of it. But Yang Jianguo claimed, with a mischievous smile, to remember every detail clearly. He said that the minute he opened his eyes, he fell in love with the girl standing in front of him. When he said this, Yang Jianguo was a twenty-nine-year-old research student at the China Central Academy of Fine Arts. He was desperately studying English, in hopes of going to the US to continue his education.

Scabby's mother, an honest woman, didn't know how to express her thanks in words, but as a gift of gratitude to Ah Yan, she left a stack of cloth shoes of different sizes, tied together in a bundle with a straw string. Until she started middle school, Ah May always wore shoes made by Scabby's mother.

I next saw—no, actually, heard—Scabby on the second day of the first lunar month the following year. It had snowed the previous day in Sishiyi Bu, and a heavy wind followed close on its heels, lasting throughout the night, covering the snow in a layer of ice so thin even a mouse couldn't run on it without it creaking. That day, even the chickens refused to go out looking for food, but early that morning, a group of people in gray uniforms carrying bedrolls came into the village. The dogs didn't know them, so they poked their heads out and barked. Then, a sharp whistle sounded, as if pulling everyone from their beds, and someone began to sing. The song was unfamiliar, both the tune and lyrics. It didn't sound like a funeral or wedding, but a little like a song welcoming the spring.

> *Hey-oh!*
> *The land reform comrades are here*
> *On both sides of the mountain*
> *The plum blossoms open*
> *And the peasants rejoice*
> *Welcoming their loved ones*

The dogs quieted down. They recognized the voice. It was singing a new song Scabby had learned.

Over the next few months, some earth-shattering things happened in Sishiyi Bu. Please don't take the cliché "earth-shattering" as merely a rhetorical device or figure of speech. Understand it in its most direct, most literal sense here, because these things were in fact connected to the division of the land. To explain simply, people who didn't own land, such as the families of Scabby and Ah Yan, suddenly acquired land. Those who owned land found that, while they slept, their land had been given to others.

My family was assigned a scrawny plot of land of a few acres, but I wasn't really involved, because my mind was completely occupied with plans for the school. After much discussion with several highly respected villager elders, I got permission to open up a school in the front courtyard and hall of the unused temple of the bodhisattva, at the end of the village. Several younger villagers and I moved the clay statues of the bodhisattva to the back courtyard, then cleaned and painted the front hall, turning it into a classroom. I compiled the textbooks myself, using the local method of carving into wax tablets to print material like the leaflets we'd gotten at the police academy. My biggest problem was students. The villagers were all tea farmers, not very cultured or educated. No matter our gender, from the time we could walk, we all worked on the tea plantations. No one wanted their children spending their time learning to write. In their view, there was already a literate person in the village, just as there was a butcher, a fortune-teller, a tailor, and a barber. Since we already had Yang Deshun, it was not only a waste of time to write but also practically stealing his livelihood.

I went to every household in the village, asking them to send their children. Sometimes I felt as if I were asking for a virgin to be offered to the Dragon King. When my little school finally opened, I had five boys between six and ten years old, and I knew that when it was time to harvest the Qingming tea, this group would shrink further. But I wasn't discouraged. I knew that words were like magic. As long as the first seed was sown, it would sprout, and more seeds would be generated, eventually growing into a whole forest. All I had to do was plant that first seed. At the time, I didn't know that the initial flame of "bringing words to the door" that my Chinese teacher had stoked in my heart would burn throughout my life, and even on my deathbed, I'd still be clutching a piece of chalk.

I was looking forward to the day a girl's voice would mingle with those from my group of unruly boys. I hoped she would learn to read and write as well as any man and take charge of the family finances when she grew up to be a woman. I also had a private wish that I couldn't tell anyone then, but I will tell you in a while. In hopes of recruiting my first female student, I brought Ah May to my classroom. I hoped she would be like those magical words and draw other girls into my school with her presence. She was younger than the boys, not at an age when she could sit still and study, so I let her bring a rag doll Ah Yan had made for her and a butterfly cage I'd given to her, then told her to sit in the corner and play. I was, however, in for a big surprise. I found that from the moment I started teaching, she put her toys aside, and her eyes grew as round and deep as bottomless pits. There was a whirlwind in the depths of those pits, greedily sucking into it everything I said. By the end of the lesson, she was the only child who wasn't distracted. Her expression called to mind Ah Yan when she was a child.

To reward her, I bought her a gridded notebook and a box of crayons. When I got to class the next day, I found that a child's name was written across the front of the pink notebook in blue: Yao Enmei. It was Ah Yan's handwriting. In my mind, she'd always been Ah May, and I never thought to ask her full name. Whether consciously or not, I was probably avoiding the labyrinth her full name might reveal. When I inadvertently learned her full name that day, I guessed that the word "en," meaning "grace," was a reflection of Ah Yan's love for Pastor Billy. I'd known a few Christians in Nantong, and they often had this character in their names. Ah May's full name meant "beautiful grace." It was still several years before I came to know the full meaning of her name.

When I taught the children to read, I didn't begin with books of ancient poetry, but with general terms, such as sun, moon, water, fire, mountain, rock, field, and soil. From there, I went on to words related to names, numbers, units, crops, and other practical knowledge. I knew it was unlikely that my students would go to middle school. In fact, only a few would even finish the two years of primary school. I didn't expect them to become scholars, though there was a slim possibility their children or their children's children might. I just hoped these students would be able to read contracts, write simple letters, and know how to calculate their daily shopping without being cheated. I had to roll up my sleeves and fight against time, desperately scattering my seeds in the narrow space between one tea season and the next. But I was wrong. One of the seeds I dropped ultimately grew into a huge tree in my own lifetime. That was Ah May. More than a decade later, she became the first person to leave Sishiyi Bu to study at the university.

After the busy Qingming tea harvest season, the students who had been diverted from my already slim group actually returned, bringing the numbers back to what they had been before. One day, I walked into the classroom to find that I had seven students, and one of the new students was a girl. The girl, seven years old, was the great-granddaughter of the old village scribe, Yang Deshun. He was the only man in Sishiyi Bu who understood the importance of literacy, aside from my poor father. When I first started the school, he'd been a bit nervous, fearing my students might snatch the rice bowl from his family's hands someday. Over the years, he'd quietly taught his oldest grandson his special skill, reluctant to let the task of writing letters and contracts flow into someone else's hands. When he saw that my students were returning, he realized it was useless to oppose it. Instead of allowing the children of other families to soak up all the light, then, he decided to send his own family's little ones to learn to read, so he sent his own great-grandson and great-granddaughter to my school to learn from me. When I pushed the door open and caught sight of the girl in a floral blouse that day, I was almost dizzy with delight. *The sign has finally come,* I said to myself.

When I started the school the previous year, I had planned to remarry Ah Yan. Using the word "remarry" not only lacks rigor, but is a bit absurd.

According to the contract to which we had affixed our fingerprints, she was my wife. According to the announcement in the Nantong newspaper, she was my ex-wife. In truth, she had never been my wife, much less my ex-wife. Now, though the woman I wanted to marry had never been truly my wife or my ex-wife, the only word I could think of to describe what I hoped to do was "remarriage." Even if I had skin as tough as sandpaper, I wouldn't be able to look Ah Yan in the eyes and say the word "marriage" to her, so I prayed that heaven would grant me courage. Before I started the school, I'd burned incense and prayed to my ancestors and secretly asked for a sign from heaven. If heaven would send a female student to my school, I would speak to Ah Yan about marriage. For this marriage, I wanted to do something grand, in front of all Sishiyi Bu, to wash away the shame of the newspaper declaration. As for the ill will in my mother's heart, it would only take one word to defuse it: I would tell her Ah May was my daughter.

That day when I walked into my humble classroom, I felt there was no shadow that could hide the sun, no worms infecting the trees, no burr in my throat, and no crooked tendon in my ankle. I felt as refreshed as a newly born child who'd never experienced any filth or pain. I was so happy that I decided on the spot not to teach from the textbook, but to teach my students a song. I taught them "Picking Tea Leaves and Catching Butterflies," a song that everyone in the village learned to sing at an early age, but only in the local dialect. That day, I wrote the lyrics on the shabby blackboard, and I taught them the proper Mandarin pronunciation for each word.

The stream is clear and long
With beautiful scenery on both banks

Even with a song so familiar one could sing it in their sleep, when the lyrics were rendered into the official language, it was a little funny. The children couldn't help but turn into a giggling bundle as they sang, rubbing their bellies. As we laughed, two strange faces appeared at the window. I first noticed the two noses looked like white water chestnuts pressed against the glass, then the blue uniforms. Finally, I saw Mauser pistols on their belts. I thought a new task force had arrived at the village. I didn't realize that their arrival had anything to do with me until they burst into the room and shouted my name.

"Spy trained by American imperialists, evil remnant of the Kuomintang . . ."

They read out my crimes one by one. There were many. A fleet of planes flew through my brain, until finally all I heard was the gale bursting from their wings.

They handed me a piece of paper, words crawling across it like hundreds of ants. I gave my temple a hard pinch to try to knead the scattered fragments of my brain into a whole. I saw then that it was the registration list from the training camp in Yuehu. I found my name on it, with my number beside it, embraced in parentheses, 635. In a blank space on top of the paper was an oval stamp, washed dark red over time. The seal read "Top Secret." As I was pushed out of the classroom in handcuffs by those two men, Ah May suddenly roused from the shock. Like a leopard, she leaped up and hung herself from my arm with both hands. Her fingers almost embedded themselves in my flesh. Nobody could have peeled her from my body without an ax or a knife. She hung on to me, dragging along the ground for some distance. Eventually, the police officers had no choice but to release me and let me persuade Ah May to let go.

I picked her up, sat her on my knee, and said softly in her ear, "By the time you go home and finish learning the words in the textbook, I'll be back." But I couldn't keep that promise. When I saw her again, it was five years later. She'd finished the primary school textbook I'd made and was using it to teach Yang Jianguo, who was almost four years younger than her.

I was thrust into a beat-up military jeep, and, as I was driven to the entrance of the village, I suddenly heard a sharp cry from Ah May. The shattering cry broke the sun into a million pieces, turning it into a gong full of cracks.

"Daddy!" she cried.

Sitting in the car, I felt pain where she had hung on to my arm. The farther away I moved from Sishiyi Bu, the sharper the pain became. I started to convulse, and yellow beads of sweat appeared on my forehead. This pain followed me for the rest of my life. The malignant tumor that later hollowed my body into an empty shell may have taken its first bite into me at that moment.

That place where Ah May dragged her feet—will the grass ever grow there again? I asked myself.

Pastor Billy: An Apology Seventy Years Overdue

I'm sorry, Liu Zhaohu. I have to interrupt you. The feet of the little girl in your story, Ah May, are not being dragged through the dirt of Sishiyi Bu. They're being dragged through my heart, leaving a trail of blood behind them. It really hurts me. It's strange, but the spirit still feels pain. I always thought that the spirit was the smoke that rises from life's ashes, a gust of wind that sees the whole absurdity of life, but has escaped the fetters of life's trivial emotions. I never imagined I could still be hurt.

The last time I felt pain was autumn seventy years ago, when I lay dying in the third-class cabin of the *Jefferson*. When I drifted awake from my high fever, I was surprised to see the Angel of Death. What I mean is, I saw his wings. No one can see the face of the Angel of Death, except God or the devil. His wings fluttered silently, and his huge black shadow fell on the wall. The wind from his wings made my skin freeze. The ship's doctor must have seen the Angel of Death too, not on the wall, but in my eyes. I heard him whisper to his assistant to find a priest to take my last confession. My remaining strength was just sufficient for me to shake my head weakly but firmly. They'd probably forgotten that I wasn't Catholic. Besides, I was a pastor, and I'd held the hands of countless people on the road between heaven and hell. I was familiar with that road, and I could walk it alone.

"Do you have anything to say?" the doctor whispered in my ear.

I knew it was euphemistic. He was asking if I had anything to confess before my soul was handed over to God. The ritual was like an examination. Once it was handed in, there was no turning back.

No, I said to myself. *I've already said what should be said to God long ago.* I knew the impermanence of life better than anyone. I didn't leave any words until the last moment, because the last moment comes like a thief, and it can't be foreseen.

Suddenly, I felt a sharp pain, not in my finger, which was swollen big as a wooden club, but in my heart. I could see Stella's expression before me as she sat on the steps in front of the church in Yuehu, waiting for a letter that would never come. Now I know she was already pregnant when I left. All three of us—Liu Zhaohu, Ian, and me—we all abandoned her in the midst of loneliness, helplessness, panic, and fear at the same time, leaving her to fend for herself like a weed in the cold wind.

If I'd known I was making my final journey when I set out from Yuehu, I would have let go of the secret I'd held on to so tightly. If I had done that, maybe Liu Zhaohu wouldn't have needed to jump overboard, risking his life to tell her the truth. Maybe he wouldn't have even been on that ship at all. Maybe everything would have been completely different for both of them. The secret was that there was still a crack left open for Liu Zhaohu in Stella's heart until the incident with Snot occurred. Stella could understand his distress about her virginity—that was a flaw common to most Chinese men. She could accept a universal flaw, but she couldn't forgive a unique evil. The unique evil, in Stella's mind, was that someone had circulated rumors about her at the training camp, even after she'd paid the price of abandoning her home to escape those rumors. She'd concluded that the person was Liu Zhaohu. Her suspicion wasn't unreasonable, since the only people who knew about her past were Liu and me.

But I knew Liu was innocent. The real gossip was my cook. She'd helped me nurse Stella twice, and she knew all the details. She solemnly swore to keep her mouth shut, and she did, mostly. But unfortunately, she failed to keep the secret in the privacy of her bedroom. She just couldn't help but tell her husband, who was the cook for the Chinese students at the training camp and from the same village as Snot. In this way, the rumor went from one mouth to the next, each mouth hoping the next would be a clamshell and the rumor would form a pearl inside. Everyone who tells a secret hopes the listener will keep it. But sadly, no one's mouth is a clamshell, and rumors leak everywhere. My cook, that poor, godly woman, knew that her failure to keep her promise had caused a great disaster. She felt she couldn't face God, nor could she face Stella or me, so she resigned and left. Before leaving, she begged me not to tell her secret, so I never told anyone the reason for her departure.

I knew this incident was the final nail for Stella. From that time, she truly closed the door on Liu Zhaohu. At first, I concealed the truth because of my promise to the cook. Later, it was for my own selfish motives. I had fallen utterly in love with Stella. My selfish reason expanded, eventually completely overwhelming the original motivations for my silence. I knew Stella didn't love me in that way, but I didn't care. The war was a meat grinder and also a roller. It ground all life into meat and loam. It squeezed love into sympathy, attachment into trust, and carnal lust into a need to stay together for warmth. I firmly believed that sympathy, trust, and the need to stay together for warmth were stronger than love. In the ruins the hurricane of war had swept her through, the only person Stella could rely on was me, even after Liu Zhaohu and even after Ian. The only thing I hadn't anticipated was that the Angel of Death would tower abruptly between Stella and me. If I had worn the prophet's mantle, I would have long ago helped untie the knot in Stella's heart and handed her over to Liu Zhaohu. Everything would have been different then.

Of course, even without me, the knot in Stella's heart, like every knot, would eventually loosen, through some inexplicable karma or just the corrosive power of time. Resentment, misunderstandings, and alienation bred during the long waiting process, when this time could have been used to harvest love, happiness, and children.

So, Liu Zhaohu, I owe you a solemn apology, even now, seventy years later.

Liu Zhaohu: Secret Curls

Over the next several years, I had the same dream over and over. In the dream, a crimson ball of fire appeared in the sky and scorched my eyes, plunging me into darkness. It wasn't an ordinary darkness, but a red darkness, like a patch of dark earth covered with crushed tomatoes. In that red darkness, there was no shape, no texture, and no layers. Unlike black darkness, no light could penetrate it. It went on forever, without limit or boundary, without beginning or end, creating the illusion that my eyes were always open. In my dream, I raised my arm, as heavy as a rock, to rub my closed eyelids, which were just as heavy. I was horrified to find that even when I closed my eyes, the red darkness was still there. It never got weary, and it never rested. I woke up in a sweat and was almost pleased to find that my surroundings were shrouded in a black darkness. Later, I came to realize that my recurring nightmare arose from my longing for daylight. My thirst for sunlight strayed when it entered my dreams and turned into the red darkness by mistake.

I'd been sentenced to fifteen years of imprisonment, during which I was to work in a coal mine in a neighboring province. Every day when I got out of bed, changed into work clothes that fastened with straw strings in front, and crawled into the cage to be lowered down the shaft, the sun hadn't yet shown its face. When I finished work and returned to the mouth of the shaft in the cage, the sun had already gone down. At night, while the stalemate between fatigue and insomnia raged, the neurons in my brain were unusually active. I calculated that fifteen years amounted to approximately 782 weeks, or 5,475 days, or 131,400 hours, or 7,884,000 minutes. Of course, these were just rough calculations, but they drove home a cruel fact. I would miss out on 10,950 opportunities to see the sun, a total of 5,475 sunrises and 5,475 sunsets.

Of course, I would miss more than sunrises and sunsets. I would miss the spring, the fields, the grass, the crickets, my chalk, and Ah May's childhood. If I survived the 5,475 days, Ah May would be a grown woman. She would never again clasp my leg or hang on my arms, experimenting over and over again with various tones and expressions that could go with the title "Uncle"—but no: "Daddy."

At six every morning, the loudspeaker would sound. After "The East Is Red"—the popular folk song praising Mao Zedong—there would be a series of long and short beeps, then a broadcaster with a firm, simple voice would accurately announce the date and time. I didn't need to use knots in a rope to count the days like I did while hiding in that dark room, but I couldn't fully trust the metallic voice, so I still stubbornly tied knots in the rope in my head. These knots were letters from Ah Yan. She wrote to me twice a month without fail. Each letter was a knot. I kept track of the days if I kept track of the letters. One letter was two weeks, two letters was one month, and six letters was one season. When I received the twenty-fourth letter, I knew I had been there an entire year.

Ah Yan's letters were neither long nor short. They always kept to around two pages, always relating simple facts. For instance, the harvest was good, and the tomatoes had to be eaten that season, though the cucumbers and beans would keep for a whole year if they were pickled. Or, the village committee had been established based on the Chinese Peasants' Association. The director was Yang Bashu's son, Yang Baojiu. I noted that Ah Yan used this strangely formal, almost scientific, name instead of the nickname everyone knew him by, Scabby. She wrote about how the primary school in the temple had been reopened after a three-month closure, and a new teacher was sent from the county. This new teacher was an outsider, and he spoke formal Mandarin with poor articulation, so Ah May didn't understand him. She wrote that my middle school classmate Chen Kaiyi had been appointed minister of the county-level party committee, and that her small medical clinic had changed its name and moved into the village committee compound to become semipublic, and that Yang Jianguo had gotten diphtheria but had been fortunate enough to obtain a costly box of penicillin that both saved him and prevented the illness from spreading to others (though Ah Yan didn't mention who paid for it). She wrote that Ah May was still learning from my textbook and always asking about new words and giving her headaches, and on and on. She never advised me with words like "reform well" and didn't ask me about my situation. Her letters were regular domestic trivia, but nothing that was overly cautious, deliberate, faltering, or insincere.

Ah Yan's letters were simply dry facts. She never added emotion or offered any sort of interpretation or exposition. Her letters were so pure that even the most sensitive hound couldn't find a suspicious scent, but they were so rich that I could practically smell her fragrance and hear her voice. I read each one over and over, stretching out my antennae like an insect, carefully examining any clue that might exist between these seemingly isolated facts. I came to several conclusions that I thought were solid. First, Scabby had gained power, but Ah Yan still held his heel. Second, things were smooth for Ah Yan and Ah May. And third, Ah May had not forgotten me and was waiting for my return.

Ah Yan's letters rarely mentioned my mother. I thought the rift that had developed between them over the years must still be there. Later, though, I learned my mother had died of a heart attack three months after my arrest. Something else that made me feel strange was that Ah Yan always addressed the letters to "Yao Zhaohu" instead of "Liu Zhaohu," and she wrote it in a striking size, larger than appropriate for a name on an envelope. It took some time for me to understand Ah Yan's outstanding self-taught espionage skills. She'd dissected a huge rescue plan into small parts, scattering them over seemingly unrelated details, waiting for me to figure it out. I was slow and remained so fascinated with the superficial details, I let the most important information pass by right under my nose.

The letters I wrote in reply to Ah Yan were shorter. I didn't want to tell her that I'd learned to crawl through the narrow coal mine like a snake. My belly button, nostrils, every strand of hair, and every pore were coated black. If I shook my bedroll, a patch of glittering black dust rose in the room. The phlegm I spat out from my mouth was like mud. This was my daily life. What was there to tell Ah Yan after I'd decided not to mention any of that? All I could do was copy the erroneous character strokes or misused terms from her letter and add corrections or comments as if I were still the fashionable student returning to the village from the county seat, peddling insights I'd gained in the city and classroom with great excitement. When I received the forty-sixth letter from Ah Yan, I found a few awkward, childish strokes at the end of her letter: *I finished the book. You didn't keep your word.* Black tears streaked down my cheek.

From then on, every time I received a letter from Ah Yan, I first looked at the end of it. I was eager to find a line of handwriting different from Ah Yan's, but I didn't hear the small voice hidden in that strange handwriting again until three years later. It was the one hundred nineteenth letter Ah Yan had written me. At the end of the letter, I found an unfamiliar handwriting. It was still immature writing, but one could see that the foundation had formed. It read, *Yao Zhaohu, Yao Zhaohu, you are Yao Zhaohu.* Ah Yan had crossed that pencil text out with a fountain pen and written beside it, *Ah May is practicing her writing. Examine it closely and let me know what you think. Has she improved?* A week later, just after I had descended into the shaft, I was called back up and told someone was there to see me. I was taken to the manager's office. There were two police officers with the mine manager and secretary in the office. This time, there were no guns on their belts.

"The comrades at the top need to verify some details of your situation," the mine manager said to me, his tone almost warm.

"Do you recognize this paper?" One of the police officers took from his briefcase a piece of paper that had been folded many times and was full of creases. When he spread it out on the desk, I finally saw that it was the marriage contract that I'd signed with the Yao family to help me escape recruitment.

I nodded.

"Is this your fingerprint?" he asked.

I nodded again.

He took out a piece of white paper and an ink pad, asked me to make a new fingerprint, blew it dry, then carefully put the paper away. After that, the two officers left without saying another word. A week later, I was released. They told me that I'd been wrongly taken when I was mistaken for a criminal who had a similar name. Three people had written in with evidence that I wasn't the same person as the Liu Zhaohu listed on the roster of the Sino-American Cooperative Organization, because my official legal name had already been changed to Yao Zhaohu in the spring of 1943. The witnesses were Yao Guiyan, the other party to my contract; Yang Baojiu, the party secretary of Sishiyi Bu; and the writer and witness to the contract, Yang Deshun, the village scribe. The testimony was the last document Yang Deshun produced. Two days later, while eating dinner, he fell from his stool and never got up again.

A letter from the minister for the county party organization, Chen Kaiyi, my former classmate, played an important role in this rescue plan. He provided evidence that I was arrested and imprisoned as a student activist while attending school in the county seat. He confirmed that I'd planned to travel to Yan'an with him, but I was unable to catch up with him because of a change in my family situation.

It wasn't until after I'd left the coal mine, carrying a bedroll so greasy it shone, that I realized the meaning hidden in the words Ah May had tagged on to the letter.

~

I couldn't have imagined that after more than 3,600 missed chances to see the sun, I would finally see it again in such a perfect setting. As soon as I entered Sishiyi Bu, I saw an unfamiliar sunflower forest. My feet said that the land beneath them should be the tea forest that had been blown up when the six planes bearing the emblem of miniature suns had flown to the village more than a decade ago. That was not the sun I had missed. Those six suns were from hell, with a fishy, foul blood oozing from their every pore. I would rather face a million years of depravity in the darkness than ever see those suns again.

At some point in time while I was gone, the abandoned tea fields had been replaced by a sunflower forest. The land had long forgotten the tea trees that had been rooted in its flesh for generations. It embraced the new species with fresh enthusiasm. The new roots roped themselves around the old tangled root system, quickly finding a place to settle. However, on such a beautiful sunny day, who could blame the land for its disloyalty? Even I didn't miss the tea trees.

The sunflowers were full and solid, each golden face looking like a woman who knows how to flirt, free of bashfulness, turned to look at the sky. Everything was golden that day—the rows of finely scattered clouds on the horizon, the bees buzzing on the open flowers, the butterflies flitting through the forest, and the dew clinging to each leaf. I closed my eyes, imprinting the golden memory on my mind as I breathed in the golden breeze. When I opened my eyes again, I suddenly noticed a figure wearing a golden straw hat in the heart of the sunflower forest. She opened her golden arms and flew toward me. A breathless sound passed through her golden lips, piercing a soft, golden hole in my eardrum.

"Daddy!"

I dropped my rolled-up quilt to the ground, scattering golden dust. I wanted to embrace this golden girl, but I found I couldn't lift her.

~

I slowly walked back toward the heart of Sishiyi Bu, then stopped in front of the remains of a wall no higher than my ankle. This wall had once been high and covered with slate-gray tiles. The tiles were now built into chicken coops, firewood sheds, and canopies on various other families' land. What had happened to the door? Though my memory wasn't as strong as before, I hadn't lost it completely. I remembered the wooden door, its black paint peeling off in some spots and its threshold worn by the feet of the seven people who constantly crossed it. Those seven people were my father, mother, brother, sister-in-law, two nephews, and me. Where the stove, dining table, and bed had been, there were now new occupants—branched horsetail, dandelion, green bristlegrass, purple amaranth, and affine cudweed. It is a common mistake to think that humans are the only occupants of this world. Actually, there are thousands of varieties of silent, contending species all around us. They can't wait for us to vacate our homes. They will move in to occupy the spaces once taken by human bodies as soon as the former masters move out. At this time, it had only been four years and three months since my brother's family had left home for distant lands.

"Daddy, let's go home," I faintly heard a golden voice say in my ear.

"Home?" I asked, confused.

Saying nothing, she took my hand. I realized how weak I was then. I needed a nine-year-old child to lead the way home.

That night, I slept in a strange bed smelling of saponin and sunshine. I didn't dare to exhale, afraid the soot in my lungs would blacken the bed with each breath. In the middle of the night, a soft body climbed into my bed. With her lips, her hands, and her body, she took this thirty-year-old virgin and transformed him into a man.

"Nothing. I have nothing."

I was like a child, clinging to that body and weeping. She didn't try to comfort me. She just let me weep a whole life of tears between her breasts until my tear ducts finally dried up. When I'd finished, she patted me on the back, like she might comfort a child.

"You still . . . have me," she said.

When I woke up in the morning, I didn't know where I was. I pulled the bamboo curtain open, and the sun came in with the might of a hundred mad bulls, nearly smashing the walls into a patch of white ruins. I thought about my long-awaited reunion with the sun in the sunflower forest the previous day, but I couldn't remember if it was real or a dream. I wasn't used to the sun. In fact, I wasn't used to the sun or to cleanliness, order, quiet, sleeping sprawled out, or resting. There were two quiet voices outside, as soft as the stirring of bees' wings. I had to strain to pick up a few words.

"Softly . . ."

"Exhaustion . . ."

"Don't worry about food . . . enough sleep first . . ."

I crept out of the bed and put on my shoes. My soles felt strange without coal dust or cinder beneath them. I snuck to the entrance of the kitchen and saw the backs of two people in the room. The fire in the stove had gone out, but the porridge continued to bubble over the embers, and one stirred the pot while the other sat reading in the sunlight. The reader wore a scarf over her head, which rustled with every breeze in a green flutter. The reader's posture was strange, shoulders high and head bent low, as if sniffing each word for its smell. That's how I'd always sat when I was young. I didn't know how she'd stolen my posture, like a miniature me sitting on the threshold. I felt something soft and warm like rubber enfold my body, almost making me itch. I didn't dare move, afraid the slightest touch would break it.

That was when I saw the drawings. They were pictures drawn directly on the wall in crayon, covering all four walls and in some places reaching almost to the ceiling. I could tell the drawings were put together piecemeal, and at each seam, I could see a shift in the colors and drawing style. Those seams only marked divisions of time, though. The scene itself was continuous. I couldn't see where it ended or began. It was a drawing of the village but also a market, with houses, trees, streets, and people. The people were varied—women crouching to wash clothes, small children playing beside the road with chickens and dogs running behind them, old men leaning against doorways smoking, old women carrying bamboo poles on the road. There were even a few young people around a tub selling salted fish. I could tell immediately these were child's drawings. The figures were built from a few geometric shapes, and the details were still in the gestation process. The colors were extremely strange. The sun was green, the fish yellow and blue, and the leaves red, with a few black lines. The smoke from the chimney was half-purple and half-yellow. I looked at the pictures again. In the strange combination of color and light, the figures on the wall suddenly started to bulge and move. I grew a little dizzy. I didn't know if the wall was moving or I was, but I let out a little cry of astonishment.

The person in front of the stove turned around. As soon as she saw me, she asked, blushing slightly, "Are you hungry?"

I nodded. Pointing at the pictures, I asked, "Did Ah May draw this?"

The person sitting on the threshold turned back and snorted. She said, "That's baby stuff. I don't do that anymore."

Ah Yan laughed and said, "Yang Jianguo drew them."

I said, "Aren't there walls in his house? Why does he draw here? Aren't they living in the landlord Yang's main house now?"

Ah Yan turned to the stove, sighed, and said, "Remember his mother, the one with one eye? Last year during the Spring Festival, the village kids played a prank on her, putting a firecracker in her arms, and it scared her out of her wits. She can't care for her son anymore. Yang Jianguo comes here every day to play with Ah May. He draws here. I can't bear to clean it off. I like it."

Ah May snorted again and said, "I didn't want to play with that little kid. I was teaching him to read."

"Who would've thought Scabby would have such a son. Maybe he'll get his big break one day," I said.

I had a strangely accurate view on this matter. Yang Jianguo did in fact become a famous painter later. But no, by his time, painters weren't called painters anymore. They were called artists. Two of his paintings were placed at the Metropolitan Museum of Art in New York, where they were visited by people from all over the world. Of course, that was a long time later, long after I already lay in a grave on that hillside.

Ah Yan glanced at me and said, "Don't call him Scabby in front of the others. Everybody calls him Party Secretary now."

I snorted. "When he grows hair on that bald, scabby head, I'll stop calling him Scabby."

The reader burst out laughing and said, "Even if he grows hair, he'll still have scabs."

Ah Yan glared at her and said, "Don't get me into trouble. You only got out of trouble this time because of his seal on that paper. If something happens again, how could I save you?"

I knew she said that for my benefit.

There was something I wanted to ask. It bubbled in my belly, but I couldn't get it out. At least, I couldn't say it while someone sat on the threshold, listening.

That something was, "What did you have to do to save me this time?"

~

The shoes were Liberation brand sport shoes, but he was certainly not the first owner. The shoes were two sizes too big, and I could almost see his toes dancing in the empty space in front. It's hard to explain his pants. The fabric may have been gray when they were new, but other colors had gotten mixed in during the washing process. Now, they were some combination of gray, green, and blue. They weren't the style of baggy trousers with a long waist and narrow cuffs normally worn by the villagers, but were the same width all the way down, with a pleat on the front. If the pants were his, they certainly weren't from the village tailor. He would've had to travel at least as far as the county seat to find a tailor familiar with this fashion. I didn't recognize his shirt either. It couldn't have been made by a tailor, so it must've been a uniform given out by the state. It had a stiff collar that stood straight up and four pockets. The pocket on the left had a flap that, when lifted, revealed a slot with a fountain pen in it. His hat matched the shirt, the color faded to almost exactly the same degree. It was obvious they used to belong to the same owner and had been washed in the same basin by the same hands.

When he stood in the doorway of my house—if I can call Ah Yan's house my house—he hesitated, as if unsure which foot to lift over the threshold first. In that moment of hesitation, I had already inspected him from head to toe—no, actually, from toe to head. Anyway, whichever direction, I had sized him up carefully. In the end, he decided to cross the threshold with his left foot.

When his right foot followed suit, he shouted his question toward the house, as if announcing himself.

"Yang Jianguo, you rotten child, is your butt a millstone? Once you're here, you sit all day. Don't you ever come home?"

The boy sitting at the table writing dropped his pencil and slid down like a loach, avoiding the hand reaching for his ear. The air stirred up by the arrival quickly grew still. With her eyes, Ah Yan urged me to pull a stool out for the guest.

"Just talking about coming to thank you, after getting a little rest," she said to the guest.

I knew the subject omitted from her sentence was me.

He sat and took off his hat. His face hadn't changed much, but his head had. He had even less hair, and the spots that had earned him the nickname Scabby now unscrupulously occupied the area vacated by his hair. His eyes kept pecking at me here and there, like a bug striking against a window.

"You didn't get beaten, did you? You look all right," he said, dragging out the question. I saw his toes wiggle with excitement in his shoes.

"I survived," I said.

He searched through his pockets, left to right, top to bottom, and finally found a box of Labor brand cigarettes. He then began another search, this time from right to left and bottom to top, but he didn't find what he was looking for. Ah Yan tore a bit from a page of Ah May's old workbook and twisted it into a thin roll. She reached into the dying fire in the stove, lit it, and passed it to him. The cigarette flared up, then dimmed, then brightened again before it lit properly. A flattened circle of smoke slowly squeezed out from his lips as he sucked hard on the cigarette.

"You're lucky. You muddled through. Still, your secret is like a fire bug hidden in a paper lantern. Just a gentle jab will expose the light," he said.

My eyelids twitched. Ah Yan gave me a sidelong glance, a meaningful and heavy glance, sealing my lips shut before I could open them.

"If somebody jabbed at the lantern, no one would be spared. You stamped the seal. You'd be doubly guilty. Just for the seal, they'd kill you twice," Ah Yan said.

Ah Yan spoke in the calm, familiar tone, no ripple or wrinkle of emotion. His toes trembled, then stopped dancing.

"Doesn't matter who gets shot. We'll all be in trouble, so it's best not to make trouble." He finished his cigarette, then tossed the butt to the ground. He snuffed it out with his foot, then rose halfway from his chair, as if unsure whether or not to go.

Ah Yan nudged Ah May, who sat at the table, writing. "Go pack up Yang Jianguo's schoolbag so his dad can take it home with him," she said.

He had to get up then.

"I need a stamp," Ah Yan said. "I'm going to the pharmacy in town to buy tetracycline. The clinic is out of medicine."

He cleared his throat and said, "May as well leave the stamp in your pocket. You use it most." Then, he lumbered out the door.

Ah Yan hurried after him. Standing in the doorway, she called to him, "Can you let the leaders know my husband Zhaohu needs to go back to the school and teach. There are many children, so it's good to have two teachers. And anyway, it was his position."

The fellow stopped and called back, "I'm not in charge of that. It's up to the leaders."

Ah Yan laughed coldly and said, "Who are you kidding? Your boy Jianguo's been eating at my house for years. Have I asked you for a bucket of rice? Or a bundle of sticks? Do you want me to break down all the expenses?"

He didn't answer, his Liberation shoes grinding the stones on the road as he lumbered into the distance.

Ah Yan came back to the house and sat on the threshold. She didn't say anything. She knew anything she said might start a fight. She waited for me to find an outlet for the anger boiling up inside me.

"Son of a bitch," I suddenly spat out.

Ah Yan was startled. It took a while for her to recognize that it was English. She hadn't heard anyone speak English in ten years.

"Baldy," she replied after a while, also in English.

As if we had planned it, we both leaned on our knees, overcome with laughter. Ah May looked at us in surprise and asked, "What devilish language is that?"

I wanted to explain, but neither my mouth nor my body would do what I told it to. Whenever my eyes met Ah Yan's, we laughed as if we were crazy.

That was when the idea of teaching Ah May English was born. At first, I just wanted a secret language for the three of us. Then, we wouldn't need to be afraid of cracks in the walls, window frames, and ceilings, or ears that sprouted tongues and eyes that sprouted teeth. But eventually, I found that Ah May was drawn to the language, and what was first a tool became the finished product, and the path became the goal. At a time when everyone was crazy to learn Russian, Ah May quietly studied English under the pretense of learning Russian. By the time she entered middle school, she no longer needed the Russian cover. The situation had changed, and Russian was banished into the ice fortress. In the newly established English class, she was immediately chosen as class head, because while her peers were still torturing their brains to memorize the twenty-six letters of the alphabet, she could already carry on a short conversation with her teacher.

bird

tree

grass

flower

I used these simple words to lead Ah May into the world of English. But that wasn't enough for her. She wanted to know "this bird in this tree," or "the grass beside the stone." So we added some more specific terms to our conversation— sparrow, swallow, eagle, tea tree, willow, reed, dandelion, sunflower, rose. She soon grew bored with these, wanting to give these things hands and feet—or wings. These things began to walk, fly, run, touch, and float. When she was used to the activities of these objects, she generated new ideas, and she hoped I would give them expression. I had to think hard to remember the vocabulary I hadn't used in many years, and finally I found a few adjectives.

happy

sad

lonely

excited

beautiful

Gradually, each of these words extended to the periphery, trying to form relationships with adjacent words. It was a course filled with explorations and risks, so some absurd sentences, full of flaws, came out of her mouth.

This rock fly lonely.

This sparrow sad touch.

My sunflowers happy float.

This tireless little sprite, who practically oozed curiosity from every pore, wore on my patience, greedily demanding new knowledge from me, tightening up the neurons I'd let grow slack in recent years. There were thirty-two students in my class, but the energy I expended on those students combined wasn't sufficient to keep up with this one little mind. She drove me with an invisible whip, allowing no laziness, no rest, and no aging.

Every day after class, we went into the forest and expanded the realm of our private language inch by inch. At first, there was just enough space to stand up, but gradually we found room there to stretch our arms, legs, and bodies. Eventually, we were able to stumble around in our tiny world. One day, suddenly, with an earth-shattering burst, the solid walls encircling our little kingdom toppled. New walls grew on top of the ruins. We pressed against these walls and found them as pliable as rubber, flexible enough to accommodate our infinite thoughts and feelings. So we moved the world to the woods. When we departed from the forest, everything we said there turned to stone.

The initial motivation for Ah May and me to develop this private language was simply to allow us to avoid those ears with tongues and eyes with teeth. Eventually, this mode of communication became a habit. In that resilient realm with blurring boundaries, Ah May and I could express our endearment, fondness, or concern in a way that, if we'd used the language that flowed in our blood, we would've felt embarrassed and pretentious. It was as my poor mother had often said when she was alive, that it's always easier to use someone else's things. And one day, I learned that this foreign language that I thought of as "someone else's thing," was actually in Ah May's blood. Or, I should say, half her blood.

It was her father's language.

One day, as we continued to find our words, it began to rain heavily without warning. Ah May's straw hat was blown off by the wind. She held her hands over her head, as if it were a bomb that might detonate if she released it.

"I don't want to become a scabby baldy!" she said in horror. She looked like she'd not lost her hat, but her heart or her liver.

I'd never seen her so panicked before. I laughed as I comforted her, telling her that if one could get a scabby bald head just by getting wet in the rain, I would have had one long ago.

"It's different for you," she shouted at me, sounding like she was close to tears. "Mommy said I had scabies when I was little, and if my head is exposed to sun or rain, it will turn out like Yang Jianguo's father's."

I realized I'd never seen Ah May not wearing a hat. She wore a straw hat all summer and a wool cap all winter. She even wore a cloth hat when she slept. Ah Yan said it served as protection against the summer heat or winter cold and to keep dirt from seeping into the pillow.

I laughed and said, "Is that what your mother told you? And she's a doctor? Scabies don't just grow on your head. Your head is like your body, it needs sun and rain. I don't understand how you can go around with your head covered up every day and not catch cold."

Ah May peeked at me dubiously from under her fingers, then suddenly opened her mouth and sneezed. I took off my half-damp jacket and put it over her head. As she loosened her grip, my hand suddenly turned to stone. I saw a row of wet waves in her hair, even though it had been clamped down by numerous hairpins. Ah May's eyes, as deep and bright as the ocean suddenly flashed and rippled. Her eyes and hair were like siblings separated for many years, now unexpectedly reunited. They cheered, leaped, and embraced, all language superfluous. Anyone would know in an instant that they were related by blood. Ah May suddenly became another person. Behind the Ah May I knew there hid an Ah May I seemed to both know and not know. All the pieces of puzzle fell into place with the rain, spelling out the whole truth for me. Of course, heaven had already given me all the clues. I was just slow and needed the rain to help me put them together. I finally knew who Ah May's father was.

That day, when I returned home with Ah May, her hair hanging loose and drenched, Ah Yan rushed out of the house and stood, stunned, at the door. I looked at her. It was a pointed look, and she understood immediately. Her lips twitched, but she made no sound. Ah May went into the house, dried her hair, and changed her clothes. I sat by the stove, rolled a cigarette, and let the rain water drip from me, forming turbid yellow puddles on the ground. I'd learned to smoke back at the training camp, but now, I went at it with a new ferocity. A silent wall separated Ah Yan and me. It was made of granite and would blunt even the hardest blade in the world.

"There's a natural phenomenon called atavism," I finally said, after a long silence. "In some organisms, some traits of one's ancestors reappear after several generations."

Ah Yan didn't dare take up the conversation. She still wasn't sure which way I'd go.

"My great-grandfather lived in Ürümqi, and my family has Uighur blood. Their descendants, of course, sometimes have the hair of those ancestors," I said.

Ah Yan didn't say anything, but her silence built a defensive alliance with me stronger than any words, writing, thumbprints, or red seal. My family were outsiders to Sishiyi Bu. My parents were dead, and my brother was far away. I was the only witness to my family's history. My words were our history.

I heard Ah May's footsteps as she came out of the room after changing her clothes.

"Please tell Ah May she never had scabies, and she won't get a scabby bald head if she goes without a hat," I said to Ah Yan.

~

Ah May skipped one level in her primary schooling and one in her secondary schooling, and at the age of sixteen, she was admitted to the English department of the provincial normal school. With her results, she was eligible to choose a better school, but she chose a normal school because it came with a living stipend. Ah Yan's clinic had been turned into a public health clinic, and a graduate from a vocational health school had been sent from the county seat to run it. Ah Yan was now just a medical assistant and, like me, received a meager monthly wage that was barely enough to survive on.

In the autumn, when Ah May left home, the pain in my arm suddenly intensified. This was the old wound from when Ah May had hung her whole body from my arm as the officers were dragging me out of the classroom in handcuffs. It was a memory embedded in my bones. The memory of the bones is different from that of the flesh or the brain. The memory of flesh and brain is soft, worthless, and unreliable. A beloved face, a comforting word, or even warmth or a cool breeze can change its shape anytime. But the memory of the bone doesn't know the season or the direction of the wind. It only has one stubborn tendon. The memory of the bone reaches all the way to the grave. So the memory Ah May had left on my arm when she was six, which had been hurting me for ten years, would continue to hurt until the day I died.

That year, the pain in my arm spread to my whole body. It drew all the bones in my body into an alliance, not even letting the smallest bones in my toes escape. After successfully conquering the skeleton, it recruited my throat. When the pain in my bones broke out, my throat roared with dark pleasure, as if eager to pull out my lungs and put them on display. Showing loyalty to the bones, my throat sometimes went a step further than my bones had dared, so that once my bones had tortured themselves to exhaustion and entered a brief cease-fire, my throat was still relentless.

I could tell from my students that my condition was getting worse. At first, the children would exchange one or two mischievous glances when I coughed, passing notes and making small jabs at one another while I recovered. Later, the time it took me to recover allowed them time to finish a joke about their mothers, fathers, or livestock. Eventually, they took my coughing fits as an opportunity to catch a short nap, and by the time they woke, they found that I was still coughing and spitting some grim substance into my wrinkled handkerchief.

The pestilence had probably been lurking in my body for some time, whether from the time Ah May had clung to my arm or from the time I spent crawling in the mines. Maybe even earlier. I couldn't see it, but it could see me, and it watched my every move. When Ah May was at my side, she pulled me forward with never-ending curiosity. I was strapped to a perpetual motion machine, and I couldn't stop to get sick. Now that Ah May was gone, the clockwork that ran my nerves was loosened, and my body began to unwind. The disease was the first to know, even one step before I did. It seemed to take it a single second to switch from latency to full force. In the blink of an eye, it was all over my body.

It started with a stubborn cold and with the arthritis that developed in the cold, damp coal tunnel. That was Ah Yan's initial diagnosis. After giving me baskets of a variety of traditional Chinese and Western medicines to relieve rheumatic pain, nurse a cold, and stop inflammation and cough, she finally realized that the superficial medical knowledge passed on from Pastor Billy was enough for emergencies, but not to deal with this sort of chronic illness. She started wading through mountain streams, traveling hundreds of li away to seek some secret ancestral remedy. That autumn, every pot in the house was stained with the smell of traditional Chinese medicine. Even the crow of the roosters gave off the offensive smell of herbs. But these remedies were nothing more than bowl after bowl of expensive black water that was hard to swallow. They couldn't reason with my bones or make peace in the battle between my throat and lungs.

One evening, I sat on the threshold soaking up the sun, and my throat made a fierce attack on my lungs. I noticed that the sun had changed color, becoming a huge taupe coal cake. After a moment, I realized gray dust from my throat had blackened the sun. I had a long dream that night in which I dragged the sun down the forty-one steps of the village and soaked it in the water to wash it, but even when the whole river turned black, I still couldn't clean the sun back to its original color.

When I woke the next morning, I found that the sun was finally clean. It lay round, bright red, and wet on my pillow. It was the first little sun I spat out from my lungs, but in the not-too-distant future, it would have many companions. I quickly tossed the pillowcase in the water bucket, but I was too late. It didn't escape Ah Yan's eyes. Her face changed, looking like a piece of coal. Leaving no room for negotiation, she carted me off to the county hospital. I lay on a narrow, cold bed that day and let the doctor turn my scrawny body over more times than I could count, leaving countless fingerprints all over my flesh. I watched as the nurse extracted enough blood from my veins to paint nine suns. She stripped my clothes off and put me behind an X-ray machine, revealing the lily-white, scimitar-shaped ribs inside me and the two black lobes of my lungs. I felt almost guilty for the thoroughness of the check-up that day, because I wore out the doctor, the nurse, and that poor machine all at once. When it was over, the doctor didn't say anything to me. He just glanced at me with tired, sympathetic eyes, then called Ah Yan into the office and closed the door.

It was a long time before Ah Yan came out. I knew the doctor wouldn't have much to say. It was only plain facts from his mouth. Facts are always simple, and the harsher the facts, the simpler things are, requiring just a few words to lay it all out. Ah Yan only stayed in the room so long to erase all evidence of tears from her face, just as I had tried to erase evidence of the sun from my pillow.

"There's an infection in your lungs and bones. You'll need nutritional supplements to enhance resistance, then you'll be fine," Ah Yan said.

Her tone was its usual calm, but her skin belied that, flushing from nose to forehead, saying something that undermined the words from her mouth.

"You've got late-stage lung cancer, and it's spread to your bones. Go home, eat well, and wait for death," her skin told me.

I immediately understood. In fact, this was written not only on Ah Yan's skin but also elsewhere. I saw it in the newly formed fine line at the corner of each eye, in the new vertical groove between her eyebrows, in her hurried footsteps, and in the two bottles in her hand with my name written on them. One of the bottles held painkillers, and the other cough syrup. I knew my body had been hollowed out by black pestilence like dense ants, and I heard it devouring my internal organs. The poor doctor was helpless to fix that.

Over the next few months, it was no longer the bitter Chinese medicines simmering on the stove. First it was chicken and egg drop soup. I didn't expect the chickens to go so fast, though. Before long, all the cages were empty, which also meant no eggs. The extinction of our chickens and eggs did not mean the stove remained idle. Next, the smell of carp escaped from beneath the lid of the pot. This fish was like leeks, infinitely available because it was sold every day at the market, if you were willing to spend some money. I used the skills I'd developed teaching math to figure out our household income and expenses and found that my calculations always put us in the red. But faced with my questions about our financial situation, Ah Yan always answered simply, "We're fine." She put different things in the soup each day, sometimes tofu, sometimes radish, sometimes dried shrimp, sometimes yam or lotus root. As I ate bowl after bowl of Ah Yan's fish soup, I felt like a woman who needed to produce milk. One day, my stomach finally complained about the feelings my mouth had already been having. When I saw a layer of milky white gelatin on the surface of the soup, I couldn't help but spit up a few mouthfuls of yellowy green bile.

After that, the contents of the pot changed again. Ah Yan told me she got some pig liver when one of the villagers slaughtered a pig. Over the years, Ah Yan had delivered babies for every family in the village. More than half the children in the village called her Qin Niang, "godmother" in the local southern Zhejiang dialect. It was reasonable for her to ask for a bit of pig liver. At least, that's what I thought at first, but after I was served several pig livers in a row, I became suspicious. The villagers usually slaughtered livestock only in the twelfth lunar month, when they could dry the meat to preserve it, so it could last all winter and even into early spring. It was counterintuitive that people were slaughtering pig after pig when it was not the twelfth lunar month. One day I saw Ah Yan with her sleeves rolled up as she washed, and I noticed a series of bluish-purple needle marks on her arms. I realized then that it was not gifts of pig liver that had graced my plate, but liver purchased with Ah Yan's own blood.

At dinner that night, when Ah Yan put down the plate of shiny fried pork liver, I took a bite, then spat it out. This was a performance put on by my throat, tongue, and teeth, but my stomach didn't participate. Saying nothing, Ah Yan sighed, picked up the pig liver I'd spat out, and ate it.

"I'll make something else tomorrow," she said.

Next she tried mudfish. She couldn't remember who had told her it was nourishing and provided energy. Mudfish were as common as earthworms where we lived. Without lies, without needles, and even without money, one would never face a shortage of mudfish. So I ate with a clear conscience all sorts of mudfish—deep-fried, stewed, stir-fried with minced meat bits . . . I add the word "bits" to "minced," though it sounds off, the way someone talks when they're confused, because I want to emphasize not only how small the pieces were but also how scarce. On the plate, they seemed smaller than ants.

The days of the famine had passed, and bran was once again chicken feed, but meat was still rare. So my brain, the only territory in my body unoccupied by the pestilence inside me, took a dictatorial command over my stomach, eyes, tongue, and teeth, insisting that they eat every bite of the mudfish and all its accompanying items, with no hint of revulsion. In executing these orders, the various parts of my body conspired to feign cooperation, consuming what they could when Ah Yan was looking but spitting out what they had taken in when she was distracted.

Though I was dragged to the gate of death with all kinds of pain, I still felt lucky. If I had fallen ill earlier, I would've dragged Ah Yan into an even darker abyss. The great famine was over by this time. A year or two earlier, the pots had forgotten even the fragrance of rice, the stoves didn't remember how they warmed oil, and people were eating chicken feed while the chickens' guts were filled with pebbles. If I'd fallen ill then, the only thing Ah Yan could have fed me was her own flesh.

One day, she told me with great excitement that the livestock in the commune could supply us with a small quantity of fresh milk. All we needed was a certificate from the team leader. At noon that day, Ah Yan ran to Yang Jianguo's house, but she returned depressed. She said nothing, and I knew she'd failed to get the necessary red stamp on the paper. The following morning, she went out early, and by the time she came home, the sky was dark. When she came in, she was carrying a thermos in a bamboo casing. She took a cup and poured the contents of the thermos into it, then put it on the table beside my bed.

"Drink," she said softly, "it's still warm."

It was milk. Her expression was as flat as a piece of paper, neither happy nor dejected. It was as if she'd handed me nothing more than an ordinary cup of boiled water.

When she turned around, I saw a corner of the back of her shirt stuck in her waistband. In an instant, my brain generated a strange line of thought. I saw the pig livers, the bits of meat mixed in with the mudfish, and the oil blossoms floating in the carp soup all suddenly turning into waistbands. When was the first time Ah Yan's waistband had been loosened? When she asked for a red stamp on my identification paper? Or when the veins on her arms had become so hard, she couldn't poke through them? Or when I spat out the fried pork liver? The first time, it might have been difficult, but easier the second time. By the third time, it was habit. Perhaps now she didn't even need a waistband anymore.

The cup of milk placed before me was white and pure, with a layer of fat so smooth a fly could slip on it. It suddenly brought back all the memories from the last time I had seen milk. It stretched out thousands of hooks and caught my nose, and my nose extended the hooks into my stomach with the same force. My brain split in two. One half screamed, *Dump out the whole cup!* But it was no use. My hand didn't listen, nor did my stomach. Even the other half of my brain didn't hear. Desire shamelessly beat its drums in my temple, and my hand reached out tremblingly toward the cup. I watched as it raised the cup and poured the contents into my mouth, all of Ah Yan's blood and lies and her waistband too. I drank every last drop of it. My stomach buzzed with satisfaction. The air around me seemed embarrassed and turned from me in shame. Even the bedding was covered with goose bumps.

There are so many ways people can become animals. The quickest route was to lose our sense of shame. I knew that what finally crushed my will was not the pestilence that hollowed my body out, but my shame. From that day on, I stopped eating. I built a Great Wall of my teeth, stubbornly resisting any food that Ah Yan shoved toward me with a spoon. I quickly approached death. Seeing that I was determined to go, she sent a telegram to Ah May, who still didn't know about my situation, telling her to come home.

When Ah May saw my skeletal form, she burst into tears. With the same hands she'd used to hang from my arm when she was four, causing me a wound from which I never recovered, she hugged my neck tightly.

"Daddy, Daddy. How can you be so heartless?" she said.

She was like a broken record player, repeating the same song over and over.

I wanted to say, *Ah May, I wish you could go back into your mother's belly and be born all over again, so I could spend your whole childhood with you this time.* But I had no strength, so these words remained somewhere between my heart and my lips, never seeing the light of day.

There was another thing stuck in the same space, this one for Ah Yan: *I wanted to give you a child, but I couldn't.*

Learning to fight at the training camp, I had been injured so badly, I became permanently infertile. I'd known from the beginning, but didn't tell Ah Yan. This regret was too heavy, and I was afraid Ah Yan couldn't bear it.

I took my last breath in the arms of Ah Yan and Ah May. It had been eighteen years since Pastor Billy died on the *Jefferson*. Five years later, Scabby was killed during a stupid fight, and his crazed wife disappeared. Twenty-four years later, Ah May followed Yang Jianguo to the States for his studies. And fifty-two years later, Ian died in the veterans hospital on the outskirts of Detroit.

In the end, that was how I abandoned Ah Yan.

It wasn't just me who abandoned her, but you too, Pastor Billy and Ian Ferguson. We entered her life at different stages and all led her to the summit of hope, then left her in our own unique ways, letting her fall into the valley of despair to face life's storms and clean up the aftermath on her own. After I became a ghost, I was secretly glad I didn't have to live through the greater humiliation Ah Yan suffered during the Cultural Revolution. My selfishness goes on and on.

From the time of her birth to my death, we knew each other for thirty-four years. She signed her life away on a piece of paper without hesitation to help me escape conscription. I delayed my journey to Yan'an for her, changing the course of my entire life. I jumped off the boat of an uncertain future for her and was ultimately imprisoned. She sacrificed to hide me and rescue me from prison, risking her own life over and over. I poured my whole heart out for her and Ah

May, and she poured her heart out for me. No, she poured out more than her heart. She also poured out her blood, her reputation, and her chastity for me. Perhaps all there was between us was sympathy, compassion, pity, loyalty, and mutual aid in difficult times. I don't know if the sum of all those things is love, but I know love is eclipsed in their presence.

Looking back now, I see that Ah Yan and I never talked about the war that completely rewrote our lives. It was taboo to both of us. We were separated by that taboo and so forever missed out on sharing our full hearts.

Ian Ferguson: The Tale of a Button

In the first few years after I went home, memories of the war were so fresh, it was almost like I was still there, but they were eventually buried beneath the monotony of everyday life, only awakened at reunions with my old comrades (and I didn't always attend the reunions), after which they'd go back to sleep until the next one. It was only in old age when the dust of life settled that those memories fully returned, retaking the space those trivial things had pushed them out of, like grass returning to a vacant lot or a spider returning to a neglected corner to spin its web again.

The memory of war isn't the same as the war itself. Memory overlays a mosaic on a bloody scene and alters the original colors and textures of an event. For instance, when I thought of Snot, I forgot how his head had been tanned from exposure to the sun and only recall the rising and falling cadence of his sniffing in the classroom. Memory not only modifies the image but also distorts the sounds, giving them a layer of glaze more palatable to the ear and eye, causing them to produce a false phonology and poetry.

In 1988, I took my wife to China, but I didn't visit our old stomping grounds, because Yuehu wasn't open to the outside world then. I made it to Hangzhou, capital of the jurisdictional region that included Yuehu, but that was the closest I could get to Yuehu. I found a little river and a group of ducks on the outskirts of Hangzhou, and we sat by the water, my nose twitching like that of a dog scenting a rabbit. I wanted to see if the river smelled like the lake at Yuehu. The water was clean, and so were the ducks. They floated on a surface as smooth as a mirror, and the reflection made each duck look like conjoined twins.

"No, Yuehu's ducks aren't like that," I said aloud.

I told my wife about Yuehu. I told her how a farmer herded a group of ducks with a bamboo pole into a field where the crops had just been harvested. The ducks didn't move as individuals, but in a neat row guided by the pole, like a disciplined squad of feathery soldiers. The farmer drove the ducks to the field, then left them there searching for whatever rice remained on the ground. When it was about to get dark, the farmer drove the full-bellied ducks back to the river with his pole, while his wife and children picked up the eggs the ducks had laid, eggs as round and white as pebbles washed by the rain.

It wasn't the first time I spoke of Yuehu to Emily. She looked at me, smiled, and said warmly, "Yes, of course, Ian," like she was indulging a whimsical, mischievous child.

Emily. That's right. Emily Wilson, later Emily Robinson, had as her final name, the name on her death certificate, Emily Ferguson. The woman I was planning to propose to when I went off to war. While I was serving in China, she went and married that Robinson fellow. God was merciful, though, because she not only crushed my heart but also played a part in shaping the fate of a Chinese woman named Wende.

Under the points system, I made my way through the long line to return to America between the spring and summer of 1946. That Christmas, I ran into Emily in a café in Chicago. Her husband had died five months earlier in a car accident. Fate is full of mockery. She'd left me in an attempt to escape life's impermanence, marrying a man she might not have really loved. She couldn't have known that she'd run headlong into the very thing she'd been trying to escape. On the other hand, I, who she'd thought was much closer to death, returned safely from the war and lived well beyond the natural span of life to become an obnoxious old man, from both a physical and a spiritual perspective. We quickly rekindled our romance. War had been a reasonable cause for all betrayal and separation. It created and also healed all emotional wounds.

The next Easter, Emily and I got married. The life that had been cut off by the war gradually fell back onto its original track. I completed the mechanics course I'd dropped out of, passed the licensing test, and after a few years working as a mechanic in Chicago, we moved to Detroit, and I opened my first auto shop, just like I'd always dreamed. In the decades that followed, I expanded it into a chain of auto shops. Emily worked as a secretary and bookkeeper in my company, but later decided to stay home full time, after we had three kids.

Compared to Liu Zhaohu's turbulent life, mine was calm for decades after the war. The days were monotonous and repetitive. I did the same thing every day. I went to work, and I came home, working hard so I could pay the mortgage on a house in the suburbs, tuition for private school, and of course piano and ballet lessons. I called the teachers to find out how the kids were doing at school and made pediatrician and dentist appointments. I took the family to the park for a picnic on weekends (weather permitting), and we drove back to Chicago for Thanksgiving and Christmas to visit my parents, just like our kids came to visit us when we were old. It seems those days were all spat out like pages from a copier, each copy just like the original. If you've seen one, you've seen them all.

The first bolt of lightning in my tranquil life came in 1992. I was seventy-one, recently retired, and adapting to the new rhythm of doing nothing. The storm seemed to come abruptly, but it had been brewing for a long time. It was the product of the war. Like a hurricane hidden in the darkness, gathering in the distance, waiting for the right conditions, it finally swept across the ocean. When the first wave landed at my door, it had more than forty years of momentum behind it. The tempest threw open the doors to my emotional world and revealed the demons deep inside, demons I didn't even know were there. The waves of that storm continued to crash in until the last moments of my life.

It was a winter morning, and it was cold, but the sun was bright, and the pigeons cooing in the distance were peaceful. I'd just had breakfast and was drinking coffee and reading the morning paper. My eyelid suddenly started twitching violently, as if an invisible rope was being pulled by an invisible hand. I suddenly recalled Buffalo, who'd served me so faithfully in Yuehu, and what he'd told me. *When the left eye twitches, it's good luck, and when the right eye twitches, it's bad.* Or maybe it was *When the right eye twitches, it's good luck, and when the left eye twitches, it's bad.* Anyway, it was my left eye that twitched, so the odds were fifty-fifty.

Just then, the doorbell rang. It was a short buzz first, followed by two more, with a gap of a second or two between them. The third ring may have been my imagination, but even if there was no actual sound, there was an echo of the second. I could almost hear the anxiety of the person ringing the bell. I opened the door to a middle-aged woman, seemingly Asian. I say "seemingly" because it was difficult to pin down her ethnic makeup. The parts of her face that seemed Asian were immediately obvious, but it took a little time to figure out which features were different. Perhaps it was the slightly deeper set of her eyes, or the vague blue-gray in her irises, or the partly visible waves in her bangs. She wore a coat that was obviously out of fashion and had been washed so many times the stitches showed. She wrapped her arms around herself, as if cold. When she spoke, I found her English to be quite fluent, with a slight accent.

"Sorry to bother you. Are you Mr. Ian Ferguson?" she asked.

I nodded.

"Your middle name is Lawrence?"

I nodded again.

"During World War II, you were stationed as gunner's mate first class in Yuehu in southern China?"

The detailed nature of the woman's questioning made me suspicious. After so long, the only person who remembered my rank and location that precisely would be the US Navy archivist. Or maybe an FBI agent.

"Who are you?" I asked warily.

She didn't answer, but pulled a two-inch-square wooden box from her pocket. It was covered with a layer of black lacquer. New, it had had a ring of gold flowers on it, but both the black paint and gold flowers were faded by time. I knew it was a woman's small jewelry box from southern China. She opened the box and pulled something wrapped in tissue paper out and handed it to me. The tissue was also old, marred with years of wrinkles and worries, looking like it might disintegrate at the slightest touch. I carefully unfolded the tissue and found a button inside. Its surface might have been plated with gold or silver, but it had eroded over the years, leaving only a piece of dark metal. Even in its ruined state, you could see its former brilliance.

"Do you recognize this?" she asked.

I shook my head blankly.

"The button is yours," she said, emphasizing the word "yours." She went on: "In the fall of 1945, before you left Yuehu, you pulled this button off your uniform and gave it to a Chinese girl."

Memories that had been buried deep inside me began to emerge. I felt them crawling through the gullies in my head. The face of a girl gradually emerged, bit by bit, like a puzzle. First eyes, then eyebrows, then the tip of her nose, then the fine line of soft, colorless hair above her lip. Then there was her hair, the hem of a garment . . . wind united all these into one, the kind of wind that comes from a conch shell or the hole of a tree.

"You said you'd go back," the woman said.

The woman's tone carried neither blame nor empathy.

"I'm your . . . daughter. Biologically speaking, anyway." She hesitated on the word "daughter," as if it had a sharp corner that had caught in her throat.

A bolt of lightning struck me with terrifying force, catching me off guard, rendering me blind and deaf. I fumbled in the dark, silent chaos for quite some time, feeling the weight of the sky pressing down on me. My body bent to the ground. I should have known at first glance. The blue flash in her eyes, the firm and almost haughty arc of her eyebrows, the trace of a smirk on her slightly upturned lips . . . it was my face refracted in an old mirror, blurred, distorted, and losing its proportions.

"My wife is sick," I said, irrelevantly.

She laughed coldly and said, "Don't worry. I'm not going to disrupt your life. I'm not looking for a father. I had a father. Anyone else would pale in comparison. I just wanted to have a look at the person who contributed half of my genes, to see what kind of person he is."

What kind of person I was? When I had inadvertently given her life, I didn't know who I was. And now, more than forty years later, I still didn't know.

"She's sick. My wife. Cancer. She can't take any . . . stress," I heard myself stammering helplessly.

She glanced at me from the corner of her eye, as if I were too small a thing to fill the whole of it.

"I'm not here for money either. My husband teaches at a university. He has a salary."

As she got emotional, her accent floated to the surface, and thorns poked through the outermost layer of her English.

"Who are you talking to, dear?" Emily called from upstairs, sticking her head out the window.

I hesitated, then looked up and said, "Someone asking about donations for the Boy Scouts."

When I blurted the words out, I sounded very calm. The sense of dread came later, and my heart started beating like a drum.

"Tell her we already sent a check to the Boy Scouts headquarters," Emily said.

I could tell that a layer of armor had hardened over the woman's skin. She'd become a steel plate, with no holes or cracks. She turned and walked down the street, her old-fashioned, freshly washed jacket billowing behind her like a cape. Her shoes against the asphalt sounded as harsh as a steel bar striking granite.

"What's your name?" I caught up to her and stopped her.

She didn't look at me and just stared at my feet, as if my eyes were inside my shoes.

"Does it matter? My name—does it matter to you?" she asked.

I wanted to say it mattered, mattered very much, but my lips were trembling too violently, and I couldn't speak. She continued walking. After a few steps, she turned back and said a name. It was a Chinese name. The first was Yao, her family name. The final word sounded like the English word "May," but I didn't catch the middle word. I wanted to ask her to repeat it, but she was already too far away.

That was the only clue my daughter, if I could call her that, left me about her identity. For twenty-three years after, I never stopped looking for her. I discovered that looking for someone whose name you don't know in a place as huge as America was like looking for a needle in a haystack. Later, she found me again. This time, she was a reporter. Perhaps, unconsciously, I was waiting for her to find me before I could leave that world for this one. Three days after we met a second time, I died in my sleep.

Pastor Billy: What We Took Away and What We Left Behind

Wikipedia describes a stroke solely in terms of poor blood flow to the brain resulting in cell death. I don't entirely agree with it, though I was once a doctor. There are many possible descriptions of your condition. For instance, from the perspective of meteorology, the symptoms of stroke are the ruins left by a hurricane sweeping through a complex domain with densely distributed waterways and ravines. From a psychological point of view, a stroke is the process by which a person enduring difficulties blocks a memory he doesn't want to face, like stemming a flood with sandbags. There can be theological, philosophical, and even biological explanations, but I won't go into all that. The three of us, me, Liu Zhaohu, Ian—or rather, our ghosts—have rushed from Yuehu to this municipal hospital to see you, so I must use our time sparingly.

I'm sorry. I don't want to give you the impression—if you can even have impressions—that we took a long journey, traveling day and night by land and river, like trainees at the camp walking endlessly on an overnight mission. In fact, for ghosts, a difficult journey is only in our minds. We are no longer affected by our soles, shoes, rusty bicycle wheels, lofty mountains, high ranges, rivers, marshes, or the merciless rain, sun, or snow. Wherever we wish to go, we are there. So when I say we rushed here, it is only to indicate our eagerness to see you, so many decades later.

The private room you're in is the most spacious and brightest suite in the hospital, with air-conditioning and an attached bath. You can stay here safely as long as you want, not only because your grandson is head of this hospital but also because your son-in-law, Yang Jianguo, is paying your medical expenses. His paintings are now sold by the foot, just like the silk in the old Yuehu market. Of course, the prices are quite different. According to Liu Zhaohu, at the Christie's auction last fall, his ink and wash painting *Mother* sold for $1.3 million, and the breastfeeding woman in the painting looks a bit like you. The rice you spared him from your own bowl back then didn't turn him into an ungrateful, selfish person.

Stella. Oh, my Stella. Today, after the first sight of you, it took me a long time to look again. I can't bear it. In my memory, you're the little star who could brighten others even with her tears. How can I reconcile that with this old woman's body that looks like an empty sack?

Who emptied this sack?

It was the war.

How much I wish I could go on saying that. Unfortunately, there is no truly innocent person in the world. War is a black cloth that blocks heaven's light, preventing it from shining on the earth, and under its cover, no one can see their own conscience. The war put the first evil hand into your full and fruitful bag of life, and we followed behind it and stretched out our hands too. This "we" includes not just me, Ian, and Liu Zhaohu but also Ah May, Yang Jianguo, Scabby, Snot, the cook who spread rumors on her pillow, and the sentry who pointed a gun at you in front of the camp. "We" includes everyone who ever passed through your life. Each of us has guilt on our hands. Each of us reached into your heart and stole something from you.

My sinner.

I hear God calling me.

Tell me, please, what have you taken from this poor woman? he asks.

Not much, I answer. *A little trust, patience, comfort, courage, goodwill, and at the most, you might add a good set of teeth, a bright forehead, and two full breasts.*

Then what did you leave with her? God asks.

Quite a lot, Lord, like a worn-out bicycle, a dirty metal button, a disintegrating copy of Evolution and Ethics, *and some humiliation that was not recorded on bamboo slips, silk rolls, ink on paper, or within any national law, town management law, marriage law, family law, or even law of public security, but which walked around on tongues and in whispers for centuries.*

We took so little, and we left so much. Really, I say to God.

Stella, on the wall above your bed, there's a newspaper clipping from the *East American Chinese Herald*. There are three columns, beneath an old black-and-white photo with blurred edges. In the photo are two people, Ian and Liu Zhaohu. Of course, at the time, Liu Zhaohu had no name, but was just 635. They probably just returned from training. There's sweat on their foreheads and shoulders. The military dog Ghost stands between them, his front paws on Ian's arm. From the photo, I can even hear his ecstatic bark when he sees his master. From three thousand miles away, he can smell Ian's sweat.

That was a cruel time, but also so simple and innocent. Ian didn't know Liu Zhaohu's past. Liu Zhaohu didn't know Ian's past. Neither of them knew my past. And no one knew Ghost's past. The war erased everyone's history, and we only spoke in the present tense, which required no modifications.

There is a basket of flowers on your bedside table, large white lilies mixed with large pink ones. They're a few days old, and the petals are somewhat wilted. The signature on the red ribbon, in Chinese, is The Anti-Japanese War Veterans Volunteer Service Team.

Who dug six feet underground and discovered Liu Zhaohu, dead now for so many years? Who leaked a seventy-year-old secret? Was it the registration list, left behind somewhere again? Was it a key to a filing cabinet that was misplaced? Someone with loose lips? They—I mean the media and the wallets behind the media—found Ian and Liu Zhaohu after all. If they found these two men, did they follow the vine to the melon and discover the secrets between three men and a woman?

If there'd been no war, I probably would never have met you. You probably would've been Liu Zhaohu's Ah Yan forever, never my Stella or Ian's Wende. You make things difficult for me. I don't know if I can say I'd rather I had never known you than to have gone through the war or if I should instead say that I'd happily endure the war just for the sake of knowing you. You were a source of warmth and light put on my path by God, my whole little universe. Having you meant I had the world. So, if I can face myself with complete honesty (which presumably only a spirit can do), I would rather have known you, even if it means the earth crumbles and the map is torn to pieces by war.

War? My sinner, whose war was it? I hear God ask.

Yes, whose war? I ask myself. *The emperor's? Tōjō Hideki's? Yasuji Okamura's? Roosevelt's? Chongqing's? Yan'an's?*

All of these, and none of these. It was your war, God says.

It's true. It was my war, when I tucked my tunic into my waistband and rode my worn-out bicycle back and forth to camp with covert intel obtained from the black market.

It was also Liu Zhaohu's war, when he took the recruitment announcement from the tree trunk and wore through a pair of cloth shoes as he hurried to Yuehu.

It was Ian's too, when, on his twentieth birthday, he walked out of the Italian restaurant into the cold Chicago street in winter and decided to enlist.

And in fact, didn't it become your war, Stella? When you rowed the sampan carrying Ian to the commissariat to get the mail or when you sewed Snot's head, stitch by stitch, onto his body?

It was our war. If we dissected the immense body of that war, we'd find each of us holds a small part in our hands, and that is how it becomes a personal war.

It was our choice, and each of us must pay our dues for the small piece of it that we hold in our hands.

Ha ha.

I hear laughter.

My Lord, why are you laughing? Could it be that you have a prophecy for your servant?

Prophecy? I only give prophecies to a very few. Perhaps a parable, like the parables recorded in the Gospels, God says.

There was once a huge ocean liner, bigger than the Titanic, *that sank in the frozen sea. It set out from Boston and sailed slowly toward Manchester. There were ten restaurants on board, each of which could accommodate a thousand guests. There were five ballrooms with professional bands, each of which could support the weight of three thousand pairs of dance shoes. There were four theaters, simultaneously staging the most fashionable plays, the most amazing magic shows, the most famous concerts, and the newest Hollywood blockbusters. Aside from the cabins, all public spaces on the ship were open and accessible twenty-four hours a day. There were twenty-five floors in total. Visiting each one, top to bottom, enjoying every salon, bar, café, pool, wave pool, casino, fitness center, and entertainment venue would take two full days. Every guest thinks they can go wherever they want and do whatever they please. But they forget that, no matter how many decks and no matter how much entertainment there is to choose from, the ship will always arrive at Manchester in the end.*

Do you understand, my servant?

I remain silent for a long time.

"I understand, my God," I finally say. "No matter how big a chessboard you give us, in the end, we are always just pieces in your hand. You have long ago set out a circle of action for us. My Lord, you also drew out such a circle for the war, and the war was just a chess piece in your hand."

~

"Grandma, please have a bite."

Stella, I see your grandson, the neurosurgeon who used the earnings from his father's—your son-in-law's—paintings to finish his studies at Johns Hopkins University School of Medicine. He's feeding you a liquid diet now, of purees and protein shakes. Those eyes looking at you glitter with light like crystals. They haven't yet tasted the bitterness we have tasted.

You mumble something. After the blood vessels hardened, your tongue lost its elasticity, becoming more like a wooden board than a rubber band. He doesn't understand, but I do. There's one other possible explanation for a stroke, a strange pathological change that destroys the original sensory system and breaks down the barrier between the worlds of the living and the dead.

I know that you are saying, "Wind. Wind."

It's the sound of our ghosts passing by your window. Your grandson can't hear it, but you can.

Your eyes turn to the window, and they suddenly change.

You see us.

Epilogue

Shanghai Urban News Online

Headline: A Letter Lost in the Dust of the Centuries

While renovating his house in Jing'an District, a Shanghai homeowner found a letter hidden under the floorboards seventy years ago. The building served as a post office during the Republican era in China. The letter is stamped and postmarked, but was apparently never mailed. Perhaps a post office employee forgot it, and it was never found. The envelope was damaged by moisture, so the writing is partially illegible. The name of the sender is Ian Ferguson, and the address is Broadway Mansions (today a hotel by the same name). The name and address of the addressee are obscured. The postmark year is 1946, but the month and day are smudged. The letter itself was also damaged in many places, though it is still partly legible. Ferguson was apparently an American soldier sent to support the Chinese effort, and he was writing to a Chinese woman named Wende. The stationery is the rice paper common at that time, and the words are written in Mandarin with a brush, likely by a hired scribe. The letter is short, like a telegram. It reads:

> *Dear Wende,*
> *If you are willing, when you receive this letter, please meet me at*
> *XX the address on this letter. I intend to apply for a XX license at*
> *the XXX Office. Recently, XXXXXX XX has increased dramatically,*

and the waiting period is XXXXX months. I'll tell you specific details in person. Please quickly XX.

Yours,

Ian

The *X*'s mark the places where the text is illegible. The old letter, sealed for seventy years in the dust of history, is undoubtedly of interest to researchers of the anti-Japanese war. Our column hopes to locate the "Wende" and "Ian" mentioned in the letter. We ask anyone with information to please contact us immediately. Your help may allow us to restore a forgotten story to its owners.

ABOUT THE AUTHOR

Photo © 2018 Li Zhou

Zhang Ling is the award-winning author of nine novels and numerous collections of novellas and short stories. Born in China, she moved to Canada in 1986. In the mid-1990s, she began to write and publish fiction in Chinese while working as a clinical audiologist. Since then she has won the Chinese Media Literature Award for Author of the Year, the Grand Prize of Overseas Chinese Literary Award, and Taiwan's Open Book Award. Among Zhang Ling's work are *Gold Mountain Blues* and *Aftershock*, adapted into China's first IMAX movie with unprecedented box-office success.

ABOUT THE TRANSLATOR

Photo © 2016 Susie Gordon

Shelly Bryant divides her year between Shanghai and Singapore, working as a poet, writer, and translator. She is the author of eleven volumes of poetry, a pair of travel guides for the cities of Suzhou and Shanghai, a book on classical Chinese gardens, and a short story collection. She has translated Chinese text for publishers such as Penguin Books and various organizations, including the National Library Board in Singapore and the Human Sciences Research Council. Her translation of Sheng Keyi's *Northern Girls* was long-listed for the Man Asian Literary Prize in 2012, and her translation of You Jin's *In Time, Out of Place* was short-listed for the Singapore Literature Prize in 2016. Shelly received a Distinguished Alumni award from Oklahoma Christian University in 2017.